LET THE EMPEROR SPEAK

LET
THE EMPEROR
SPEAK

A NOVEL OF CAESAR AUGUSTUS

Allan Massie

DOUBLEDAY & COMPANY, INC.
Garden City, New York
1987

For Alison

The extract from
POETS IN A LANDSCAPE by Gilbert Highet
©1957 is quoted by kind permission
of Curtis Brown Ltd.

Library of Congress Cataloging in Publication Data
ISBN 0-385-24156 9
Library of Congress Catalogue Card Number

First published in Great Britain in 1986 as AUGUSTUS
by the Bodley Head Ltd
30 Bedford Square, London W C I B 3RP

List of principal characters

AUGUSTUS : born Gaius Octavius Thurinus, later
Gaius Julius Caesar Octavianus, later
Augustus

His family and their relation to him

Julius CAESAR	: uncle and adoptive father
PHILIPPUS	: stepfather
CLAUDIA	: first wife
SCRIBONIA	: second wife
LIVIA	: third wife
OCTAVIA	: sister
MARCELLUS	: nephew, later son-in-law, Octavia's son by her marriage to Gaius Marcellus
JULIA	: daughter.
TIBERIUS	: stepson, later adopted son
DRUSUS	: stepson, Tiberius' brother
GAIUS	: grandsons whom he adopted; Julia's
LUCIUS	: children by her marriage to
	: Agrippa (q.v.)
AGRIPPA POSTUMUS	: grandson, brother to Gaius and : Lucius
ANTONIA	: niece, daughter of Mark Antony (q.v.) and Octavia, married to Drusus
GERMANICUS	: step-grandchildren, also great-
CLAUDIUS	: nephews, sons of Drusus and
	: Antonia

His friends

Marcus Vipsanius AGRIPPA	: his greatest general, later married to Julia, and therefore his son-in-law

v

Gaius Cilnius MAECENAS	: his closest adviser
Publius Virgilius Maro (VIRGIL)	: poet and mentor
Quintus Horatius Flaccus (HORACE)	: poet

His rivals

Marcus Tullius CICERO	: orator and statesman
Marcus Antonius (MARK ANTONY)	: fellow triumvir, later enemy in Civil War
Marcus Aemilius LEPIDUS	: fellow triumvir, later rival
Marcus Junius BRUTUS	: Caesar's assassin
Gaius Longinus CASSIUS	: Caesar's assassin
Sextus Pompeianus (POMPEY)	: son of Pompey the Great, obstinate Republican
CLEOPATRA	: Queen of Egypt

Miscellaneous

MACO	: a Centurion
SEPTIMUS	: a soldier
TIMOTHEUS	: a catamite and secret agent
ANTONIUS MUSA	: a doctor
Terentius Varro MURENA	: a consul
Gnaeus Calpurnius PISO	: a consul
LUCIUS Antonius	: a general, brother to Mark Antony

FULVIA	:	a terrible woman, wife to Mark Antony
TERENTIA	:	wife to Maecenas and sister to Murena
VIPSANIA	:	Agrippa's daughter, wife to Tiberius

Chronology

BC

63 : Birth of Augustus.
44 : Murder of Caesar (March).
43 : Augustus consul (August).
    Triumvirate established (November). Proscriptions.
42 : Battle of Philippi.
41 : Siege of Perusia (Perugia)
39 : Mark Antony marries Octavia.
38 : Augustus marries Livia.
36 : Defeat and death of Pompey
    Demotion of Lepidus.
31 : Battle of Actium.
30 : Deaths of Antony and Cleopatra.
29 : Augustus celebrates his Triumph.
27 : Constitutional settlement, receives name of Augustus.
    Augustus.
23 : Murena's Conspiracy. Constitutional settlement
    revised.
    Death of Marcellus.
20 : War in Armenia, Treaty with Parthian Empire.
19 : Death of Virgil.
17 : *Ludi Saeculares* (Secular Games) celebrated.
12 : Death of Agrippa. Tiberius compelled to divorce
    Vipsania and marry Julia.
8 : Death of Maecenas.
5 : Tiberius retires to Rhodes.
2 : Augustus named '*Pater Patriae*' ('Father of his
    Country') by the Senate.
    Julia scandal breaks, Julia disgraced.

AD

2 : Death of Lucius. Tiberius allowed to return to Rome.
4 : Death of Gaius. Augustus adopts Tiberius.
6/7/8: Pannonian Revolt, suppressed by Tiberius.

ix

BOOK ONE

Preface

Nothing in recent years has aroused more intense speculation and interest than the discovery of the lost Autobiography of the Emperor Augustus in the Macedonian monastery of St Cyril Methodius in 1984, for this book, mentioned by Suetonius and other ancient writers, had been believed irretrievably lost for all eternity. The copy, found during restoration work being performed in the monastery, appears to have been made in the early thirteenth century, possibly for a Frankish lord during the brief and shameful Latin Empire which was established after the Fourth Crusade of 1204. Certainly the circumstances of its discovery substantiate this theory for the copy exists in the original Latin, not in the Greek into which one might have expected it to have been translated; moreover it was found in what has been construed as a prison cell, or even execution chamber (for there was also discovered there the skeleton of a man in early middle age) bricked up from the outer world. It has been suggested that the copy was made then to justify the Latin/Frankish occupation, and that there was a malign humour, of the type we recognize as Byzantine, in the Greek decision to incarcerate, indeed immure, it with the lord who had procured it. All this cannot however be more than speculation such as is irrelevant both to my present purpose and to the content of the manuscript.*

First, however, it was necessary to substantiate its authenticity. This was done by a team of international scholars with, remarkably, no dissentient voice. The British representative was the distinguished historian who is Master of Michaelhouse College, Cambridge. His assurance was categorical: 'Even the briefest examination of the photocopy of the manuscript must remove any doubts of its authenticity. It

---

* For a thorough examination of the provenance and significance of the manuscript, see A. Fraser-Graham: 'Augustus: An Essay in Late Byzantine Detection' in *Journal of the Institute of Classical Strategies* Vol. VII.

is assuredly the work of the Emperor Augustus and, as such, a unique contribution to our knowledge of the Ancient World.' The Master's international reputation is such that no one can dispute his authority. The reader may therefore rest assured. These are indeed the authentic memoirs of Augustus, now translated into English at the request of the Editorial Committee by the novelist and historian Allan Massie, author of a deft, if derivative, study of *The Caesars* (Secker & Warburg, 1983).

Some questioned the choice of a novelist as translator, and with reason that fell only just short of cogency. The decision was however based on the nature of the Memoirs themselves which are full of dialogue, dramatic scenes and dramatic presentation of the characters. Some may also feel that Mr Massie's version is indeed, in the event, too racy, too full of contemporary slang (or perhaps the slang of two or three decades ago), and that it suffers from the novelistic determination to make the Emperor's language consistently lively. I am bound to confess that I am sympathetic to these strictures; in our translator's defence I can only say that Augustus's Latin is itself full of expressions never previously encountered in classical prose, and that the style of the Memoirs veers from the extremes of colloquiality to a serene and formal beauty.

Those wishing for a more sober, scholarly and (I fear) accurate rendering must abide the completion of the great annotated edition now being prepared, also under my direction, by the scholars of thirteen American universities, or the even more ambitious quadri-lingual edition (with annotations in the same four languages: Latin, Greek, German and English) being undertaken by the team under the direction of Professor Otto Friedrichstrasse, both of which editions, crowning peaks of contemporary scholarship, have been ambitiously and courageously scheduled for publication before the end of the century. Meanwhile the English-speaking reader unable to read Latin (and, alas, how few can do so in these degenerate days!) must content himself with Mr Massie's version, whatever its deficiencies.

That the Memoirs are of uncommon interest goes without saying. My purpose here is merely to guide the reader ignorant of the labyrinth of Roman History, or whose knowledge of it is derived only from inadequate and frequently ridiculous representations of the Grandeur that was Rome offered by the Kinema and the BBC.

The Memoirs exist in two Books written at different periods of Augustus's life. Together they offer a reasonably coherent chronology, inasmuch as Book II takes up approximately at the point where Book I terminated. Their mood however, it is fair to warn the reader, is different. Book I is self-confident, exhilarating, a story of triumph, Book II much darker. It can hardly be denied that Book I offers livelier entertainment, for it is full of colour and excitement. Yet I must confess that, for me, it is the second part of the Memoirs where the Emperor broods reflectively over the course of his his life, seeks out its meaning and attempts to marshal his philosophy, which offers the more intense attraction. We know from Suetonius that on his deathbed Augustus asked 'How have I played my part in this comedy of life?' We can see now that this was no final whim, but that the same question tormented his last years, and it must be a solemn warning to us all that this greatest of Romans felt himself to be in so many respects unfulfilled, even a failure. All who are interested in the meaning and effect of power on character will read these subtle and disillusioned pages avidly!

The First Book is addressed to the Emperor's grandsons Gaius and Lucius, children of his daughter Julia and the great marshal M. Vipsanius Agrippa. These boys he himself adopted and created *Principes Iuventutis* ('Princes of the Youth Movement'); he intended they should succeed him. The Book is therefore tailored to this choice audience. It cannot be exactly dated, but it seems reasonable to suppose, from tone and content, that it was written (in fact, dictated to slaves or perhaps freedmen) around 7 or 6 BC: Gaius, the elder of the boys by three years, would have been thirteen in that earlier year. It does however include a few pages—those dealing with his reception of the news of the murder of Julius Caesar—which appear to have been written at an earlier date. It is known too—and he confirms this in the text—that Augustus composed a fragment of autobiography while campaigning in Spain in 24 BC, and parts of this earlier book seem to have been incorporated in the text of the later memoirs written for his grandsons. Certainly there are passages where he seems less conscious that they constitute his audience. It seems unlikely too that either part of his Memoirs was fully revised by Augustus himself. The form in which we possess them doubtless owes something to his secretaries or literary executors.

Book I begins with Caesar's murder and ends with the deaths of Antony and Cleopatra fourteen years later. It tells the story therefore of the rise of the boy Gaius Octavius Thurinus (as he was still called in 44) to the position of supreme authority in the Roman world. It is a story of glittering achievement. Even two millennia later it remains astonishing, for at the time of his uncle's murder he was only nineteen, Rome was torn by faction and civil war, and no one could predict, none indeed predicted, that this slim youth could imprint his personality on the Republic, and succeed where Caesar, Pompey, Sulla and Marius had failed in restoring peace and order to a distracted world. That he did so is still remarkable, and his own account is gripping and, within the limits of political language, surprisingly honest: he does not shrink from confessing the cruelties and deceits unavoidable in his rise to power: in particular, his accounts of the Proscriptions of 43 and of the manner in which he wrested Antony's Will from the safe-keeping of the Vestal Virgins in order to publish it to his own political advantage are amazingly candid. His delight in his own intelligence, political skill and success is infectious; one cannot help wondering if the grandsons in whom he so delighted ever in fact experienced the pleasure of reading this book written for their edification.

Perhaps not, for it breaks off abruptly, though there was no good reason for ending Book I with the defeat of Antony. It would indeed have seemed more suitable to end it with the celebration of his Triumph in 29, but that awaits description till the second chapter of Book II. One surmises therefore that it was discontinued on account of the onslaught of the family disasters which befell Augustus from 5 BC and which are movingly chronicled in the final chapters of Book II. It seems therefore appropriate to limit my observations here, and resume them with an editorial preface to that second Book when the reader has had the chance to enjoy the happy buoy-ancy of the Emperor's letter to his beloved grandsons; for Book I essentially offers us just that: the chance of hearing Augustus address these two boys; accordingly it offers also an invitation to intimacy rare, well-nigh unique, in our reading of the Ancient World.

One final note: dates are given, in this introduction and in the text, according to our modern system of dating. This is unscholarly. Augustus of course dated events a.u.c. (*Ab urbe condita*: from the foundation of the City). Mr Massie however urged that we should employ the system BC and AD, on the frivolous grounds that 'everyone understands it and it seems less remote'. I protested at the absurdity, but reluctantly gave way when the publisher added his pleas to the translator's.

Meanwhile: *Princeps ipse loquatur!*: Let the Emperor himself speak!

A. F-G

I

I AM AFRAID MY FATHER'S ACCOUNT OF HIS GALLIC WARS IS AMONG THE DULLEST books ever written. I remember, Gaius, how your tutor once expressed indignation when you complained of its tedium. But you were quite right though it seemed to me then inexpedient to admit as much, and I only suggested to your tutor that he make due allowance for the ardour of youth. One reason why it is unsatisfactory is Caesar's pompous tone, and this owes much to his unfortunate decision to write of himself in the third person: 'Caesar did this, Caesar did that, Caesar acted to save the situation . . .'; it grows more wearisome and seems even more self-admiring than the perpetual 'I' of autobiographers.

Then that much-praised first sentence: 'All Gaul is divided into three parts', has really only the single virtue of lucidity. It is far from accurate, for the divisions of Gaul are more numerous and much deeper than he suggests.

In fact the book is fundamentally untruthful. Not surprising; it was written for an immediate political purpose—when did a manifesto ever speak the truth? The Triumvirate formed by Caesar, Pompey and Crassus had broken up. Caesar's enemies in Rome were baying for his blood and demanding his recall. He appealed to public opinion with this vainglorious account of his Gallic conquests: he would show them what he had done for Rome. It worked. Even the dullness of which you complained was deliberate; many had thought Caesar flashy; now they should be soothed by the impressive sobriety of his prose.

So, my dear Gaius, and Lucius, too, (for I cannot imagine your tender imagination responded to Caesar's prose, though you would be too mild and mannerly to complain) your early criticism was justified. 'On the spot', as you would say yourself. It has always seemed to me an example of how not to write your memoirs. There is no personal voice. What you hear is an actor. Of course it's also true that Julius Caesar was always acting: the real Caesar, if he existed by the time I knew him, was buried deep beneath layers of artifice. Still, most of the parts he chose to play were livelier and wittier than the role he wrote for himself in his 'Gallic War'.

All the same, now that I bring myself to write this account of my own life, for you—for your instruction and, I hope, pleasure—I confess that the pompous tone is hard to avoid. Autobiography sets out to recapture experience, but the business of writing it requires the author to abstract himself from the self that lived these experiences, and to construct a figure that can hardly fail to be, as it were, theatrical. To put it another way: the self you write is never quite the self that lived. (I hope you don't find that concept too difficult. It's a modern idea of course which you certainly won't find in the authors you have studied and I am only too sadly aware of the inadequacy of my attempts at philosophical exposition.) I was anyway struck with this when I wrote a first sketch of my life about twenty years ago when I was stuck in a small town in the Pyrenees recovering from an illness. I found it heavy going, I assure you. It began, if I recall, with a genealogical chapter. Everyone is interested in his ancestry of course, but I could not bring mine to life. It was profoundly unsatisfactory.

So, engaging on this book for you, my boys, I propose to imitate Homer or follow his advice at least. He recommends you start in the middle of action.

Therefore: here we are: Greece, late March, blustery and cold, snow on the mountains, in my nineteenth year.

* * *

As we lay in the rest-room after our baths Maecenas ran his hand over my thigh.

'You see, my dear, I was quite right. Red-hot walnut shells are absolutely it. You have such pretty legs, ducky, it's a shame to spoil them with fuzz.'

And then, with his hand still stroking me just above the knee, and Agrippa snorting something about bloody effeminate dirt from the next couch—then—it is a scene I hold clear as a vase-painting—the curtain was thrown aside, and a slave burst in, with no ceremony at all.

'Which of you is Gaius Octavius Thurinus?' he cried.

'This one is,' Maecenas said, not moving his hand. But I sat up, shaking him off. When slaves forget their manners, all the more reason to behave decently. The man thrust a letter into my outstretched hand, and disappeared without waiting for a reward. (I know why he did that; he was aware he was the bearer of bad news—slaves always know what their missives contain, I suppose they check with the secretaries and it is passed down the line—but in this case of course he could hardly have failed to know what the whole world would ring of—and he had all the Greek superstitious fear of the fate that waits the bringer of evil tidings.)

I turned it over. 'It's from my mother,' I said.

'Oh God,' Maecenas said, 'mothers.'

'That's no way to talk,' Agrippa said.

'Well, who's little Miss Good Citizen now?'

Their bickering is memory's sour accompaniment to the solo of my mother's letter. It was short enough for something that shook the world:

My son, your uncle Julius was this day murdered in the Senate House by his enemies. I write that bluntly because there is no way to prepare such news. And I say merely 'his enemies' because all here is uncertainty. No one knows what may happen, whether this is the beginning of new wars or not. Therefore, my child, be careful. Nevertheless the time has come when you must play the man, decide and act, for no one knows or can tell what things may now come forth.

I let the letter drop. (One of the others picked it up and what they read silenced them.) I let my fingers play over my smooth legs and bare chin, and wondered if I was going to cry. I have always cried easily, but I had no tears for Julius either then or later.

Very soon there was a clamour without. We dressed hurriedly in some apprehension. One does in such circumstances. No one likes to be caught naked when there is danger of sword-play. My mind was full of all that I had heard and read of the proscriptions in the struggle between Sulla and Marius; how Julius himself had nearly lost his life then, for, said Sulla, 'in that young man there are many Mariuses.' I could not be certain that the slave who had brought the message was not the precursor of those who had constituted themselves my enemies as well as Julius's. I was his next-of-kin; it would make sense to dispose of me. I was indeed prudent to have such fears, for my death would have been an act of prudence on their part.

They should have killed me. I wonder when they realized that themselves. It is known that they regretted not putting Antony to death at the same time as my uncle. Cassius, wise man, wished to do so. The ostentatiously virtuous Marcus Brutus over-ruled him. The truth is, there was never so thoughtless a conspiracy. They imagined, these self-styled Liberators, these besotted idealists, these disgruntled fools, that if they killed Julius, the Republic would resume its old stability of its own accord. They were futile men, without foresight.

That night in Illyria Agrippa organized a guard for me, alert to our peril. I had gone out before the crowd and stilled their tumult. To express grief for Julius, I tore my clothes (Maecenas having first thoughtfully run a knife along the seam). I begged the crowd, whose grief I knew to be as great as mine—they liked that assurance—to go home and leave me to mourn. To my surprise it worked. They were a poor lot and even more confused than I was myself.

'Well,' I said to Maecenas when we were alone.

He stopped plucking his eyebrows, a task he would normally have left to a slave.

'Well,' I said, 'I am head of the family. Julius had no other heir. I am almost his adopted son.'

'You are only eighteen,' he said. 'There are other leaders of the Popular Party. Mark Antony and his brother Lucius.'

'They may have killed Antony too,' I said. 'Why shouldn't they? It's five days since Julius was murdered. Anything could have happened. My mother tells me to act the man. But how?'

'We must go to Italy,' he said. 'You are in no more danger

there than here. And whatever you do, nobody will believe you plan to do nothing. So you might as well act with decision. The Gods,' his tongue flickered on his lips, 'have thrown the dice for you. You must pick them up, and roll again. Tell Agrippa to see to a ship, employ his vast administrative talent. As for me, well, Nikos tells me he has a new consignment from Asia. He has promised me a Phrygian boy with a bottom like a peach. It would be a shame not to pluck it before we sail. Nothing, my dear, is sadder than the remembrance of lost fucks.'

*　　*　　*

You will wonder, I am sure, why I tolerated Maecenas; he is hardly the type you would find around me now, is he? Of course I have grown staid and respectable with years, but even then your natural father Agrippa could not understand it. He often rebuked me for this friendship and inveighed against Maecenas, of whom he was intensely jealous, and whom he would call 'a pansy whoremaster'. You will wonder too why I record the light nonsense of Maecenas' lascivious conversation, that quip about my legs for instance. To tell the truth, I am surprised to find myself doing so. I can only say that nothing brings back those last moments of boyish irresponsibility so keenly to me as the echo in my memory of that affected drawl.

And to answer the first question: no one in my life ever gave me more consistently good advice.

Agrippa couldn't stand that knowledge either.

*　　*　　*

Certainly not my mother's husband Philippus.

We had arrived in Brindisi in an April dawn. The sun was just touching the mountains of Basilicata. Even this early though, the port was in a ferment. It swarmed with disbanded or disorganized legionaries—we were told that a ship bringing back some of the last remnants of Pompey's men had docked the day before, and the streets round the fishmarket were thronged with these veterans who had no idea what to do with themselves. Ours seemed an unpropitious arrival.

Then, so quickly does news get about, a century of legionaries in good marching order wheeled round the corner of the harbour offices, the crowd falling back. Their centurion halted them on the quayside, as if they constituted a guard of honour; or possibly, as I remarked to Maecenas, a prisoner's escort.

The centurion boarded the ship, followed by a couple of his men. He called out in a loud voice:

'I have information that Gaius Octavius Thurinus is on board.'

I saw the captain of the vessel hesitate. I drew back the cloak with which I was covering my face, and stepped forward.

'I am he.'

The centurion saluted with a great flourish.

'Publius Clodius Maco, centurion of the fifth cohort of the twelfth legion, served in Gaul, fought at Pharsalus and Munda, wounded and decorated in the latter battle, at your service, sir. I have brought my century as your escort, sir.'

I advanced towards him.

'Welcome, friend. I am happy to see you.' Then I raised my voice so that I could be heard by the troops drawn up on the quay. 'You are all Caesar's soldiers and colleagues. I am Caesar's adopted son. You wish to avenge your general, I seek to avenge my father. You offer me your protection on the road to Rome. I offer you my name and my father's name as a talisman, and I grant you my protection in all you do. Caesar living brought us first together. Caesar's blood, shed in most foul murder, has united us to death or victory . . .'

They gave a great cheer, without breaking ranks, a good sign. The two soldiers who had boarded the ship behind Maco hoisted me to their shoulders and bore me to the quay. I bade them set me down, and, taking a risk, announced that I would inspect the guard, my first command. It was a risk worth taking. If they had shrunk from that assertion of my authority, they would have been useless for my purpose. But they didn't. They drew themselves up, set their shoulders back. I was relieved and impressed. They were serious men, and their leather was polished, their brass and weapons shining. Maco was a good centurion to have seen to it that his men were in such fine condition in a world that was crumbling into uncertainty.

'Where now?' asked Agrippa.

'To the magistrates,' I said. 'It is important that they realize why we are here.'

'What's all this about being Caesar's adopted son?'— Agrippa was full of naive questions when we were young— 'First I've heard of it.'

'It must be in the will. If I'm not that, we're sunk.'

* * *

'My dear boy, nobody admires your spirit more than I do.' My stepfather leant back in his arbour overlooking the Campagna and toyed with a mug of his own yellow wine; the fingers of his left hand played little drumming tunes on his swollen paunch; the mug almost vanished in the fat of his face. 'Nobody, not even your dear mother, who dotes on you and who has been in tears, floods, I assure you, since it happened. But, dear boy, consider the facts. Look at yourself. You're scarcely more than a child. I don't want to be rude, but there simply are times when a chap must tell the truth. How old are you? Sixteen?'

'Eighteen,' I said.

'Well, eighteen, eighteen, and you want to set yourself up against chaps like Gaius Cassius. To say nothing of Mark Antony. Oh I know he's meant to be a Caesarean, but Caesar's dead, my dear. And I know you think I'm an old fogey, but still even you must admit that old fogeys have seen a thing or two. And I know Antony, know him well. He has beardless boys for breakfast. And, take my word for it, what Antony is now is an Antonian, nothing less ... no,' he sighed deeply before resuming his wearying unwearied flow of counsel, 'take the money old Jules left you. Take that like a shot naturally, but waive the political inheritance. Just say you're too young and inexperienced. Let them look elsewhere. They'll be relieved as like as not. I don't expect either Cassius or Antony really wants to cut your throat.'

'There's that danger,' I said, 'I'm not too inexperienced to recognize that. There was a cohort sent south to arrest me, you know. I turned them round and they're on my side now, but it shows...'

'Only,' he sighed, 'because you will insist on drawing attention to yourself. Once announce that all you want is a quiet life, and no one will trouble you. Chaps don't come trying to clap irons on me, you know... Besides, you must admit, the whole Julian connection is fortuitous. A bit thin, what? I mean, if your mother's father hadn't married his sister Julia, what would you be? Nothing. Nothing significant. Decent folk of course, but small town worthies. That's all. Your own dad was the first of your family to enter the Senate, you know, and only because of the connection. What do you think all the really top families make of that? You know they sneer at Cicero as a parvenu, and he's a man of genius. You're only a boy, and your grandfather was a moneylender.'

'Let's say banker.' I kept a smile in my voice. 'Do you think my banking blood should be potent enough to persuade me to take the money and do nothing else? Do you think anyone would believe I was satisfied with that? What do you think my own soldiers would say?'

'Your own soldiers?' He sighed and poured himself wine. 'It's a fantasy, child, a boy's game, but it will end in blood, your blood, I fear. Well, your mother can't say I didn't try to dissuade you.'

* * *

It is hard to make you, my beloved boys, who have been brought up in peace and order, understand the mood of a crumbling state, of an incipient revolution. If I talk of fear and uncertainty, what can these be but words to you children of sunshine? In the same way, you know me as a man on the verge of old age; you can hardly remember your natural father Agrippa. You, Gaius, were only eight when he died; you, my dear Lucius, an infant of five. I myself could never imagine Julius young, and yet I saw him in dangerous action. And you have been brought up in the Republic which I restored; how can you imagine a world that was falling apart, where no man knew his friend?

I trusted Agrippa and Maecenas of course. Apart from affection, they had nowhere else to go. But I trusted no other

16

man above the rank of centurion, and not always them either. Even Maco said to me, 'You know, sir, my brother's with Antony. I could get him to let us know the feeling in his camp . . .' I assented of course, but how could I be sure of the honesty of any answer? And it wasn't really true either that Agrippa and Maecenas were bound to me; traitors are always welcome, for a time at least. Yet I had to act as if their affection, of which I was sure, could continue to determine their interest; which was more doubtful.

There were at least five parties or factions in the State, including my own.

Antony had inherited part of Caesar's following. He was consul which assured him direct command of at least five legions, and, even more important, gave him legitimate authority.

The chief of the self-styled Liberators, Marcus Brutus and Gaius Cassius, still posing as true friends of the Republic, had withdrawn in panic from the city which had vociferously rejected their gift of blood. Though they had only been assigned in the previous elections the unimportant provinces of Crete and Cyrene respectively, within a few weeks it was known that Brutus had gone to Macedonia, Cassius to Syria, where they were raising rebellious armies in the name of Liberty and Republican virtue.

Lurking in Sicily was Sextus Pompey, unworthy son of an over-rated father. Pompey the Great had cleared the sea of pirates; Sextus was little better than a pirate himself. Yet he had attracted to him the most irreconcilable remnants of the old Optimate party, those who, unlike the Liberators, had never made their peace with Caesar.

In Rome itself you could find the constitutionalists; their chief was Cicero. He was at least a voice, a marvellous and fecund organ.

And then, myself. I had got the nucleus of an army. It burned to revenge Caesar, and would continue to burn as long as I could pay it.

'Money,' Maecenas said, 'money is how it is done.'

Agrippa snorted, but I knew Maecenas was right. To this extent anyway; without money it couldn't be done.

★ ★ ★

Mark Antony had grown. That was the first surprise. I have since seen other men contract in office, as if the possession of authority revealed their deficiencies to them. His manner too had changed. He had treated me before like a younger brother. I had disliked his assumption of intimacy; he had had a habit of putting his arm round my shoulders and hugging me towards him which I found particularly offensive. Now he lay back on a couch, with two greyhounds resting beside him, and, having dismissed the slaves, looked me straight in the face.

'You're making trouble,' he said. He spoke as if I was a defaulter, and didn't ask me to sit down. Nevertheless I took the other couch. (Perhaps he regretted not having had it removed.) In the silence the babble of the morning forum rose up to us.

'I grant you,' he said—and I felt I had won the first round by compelling him to make the running in the conversation—'that you have secured the south. I even grant it was well done. But the stories you permit to be circulated can only serve our enemies.'

'Our enemies?'

'Yes,' he said. 'I want those soldiers you have. How many is it? A legion? Half a legion? You realize of course that as consul I have the right to command them, and that you as a private citizen are acting illegally. You have no official position, and at your age you can't have one. You can't command an army anyway, you've no experience, and I need the troops. Decimus Brutus is loose in Cisalpine Gaul, the other buggers are raising armies the other side of the Adriatic. I need those troops.'

'And what will you offer me?' I asked.

'A place on my staff. A consulship years before you're qualified. Safety. After all, boy, if I fail, you're done for.'

He may even have been frank. Certainly, for Antony was the sort of optimist who believes that the expression of a desire is miraculously translated into its achievement, he seemed to think that my silence betokened consent. At any rate, he now called on a slave to bring us wine, drank off a cup himself, and began to give me a survey of the strategical situation; Julius had once told me not to underestimate Antony: for all his flamboyance he was a good staff officer, with a grasp of detail you don't often find in drunkards.

'There's another thing,' I said. 'My inheritance. Caesar's will...'

He closed up, walked over to the window; and I knew at that moment I would have to fight him to be anything. Antony was a chronic debtor. Having a treasure like Caesar's at his disposal was a new and exhilarating experience. Even if he had not needed the money, which Caesar had left me, to pay his troops and buy popularity, he couldn't have brought himself to relinquish something so novel and delightful.

'You are right,' I said to Maecenas that evening. 'Money is how it's going to be done. I'll have to pay my soldiers from my own resources. See what you can do about it. And meanwhile make me an appointment to see Balbus. He financed my father; let him finance me too.'

Agrippa said: 'I don't know that you were wise to turn down his offer. After all we're all Caesareans. We've got common enemies. We can sort things out between us when we've dealt with them. And Antony is consul. He has got a right to command.'

I said: 'You don't understand. There are no Caesareans. It's a meaningless term since the Ides of March.'

I couldn't blame Agrippa. He wasn't alone in his failure to understand. Yet in that general failure, in the confused incomprehension of how things actually were, lay the strength of my position; it was that which gave me freedom to manoeuvre. I despatched Agrippa into Campania to raise more troops—he had a genius for recruiting, and I knew they would come in in orderly fashion. Meanwhile, I had Maecenas, with all the considerable ostentation of which he was capable, pay Caesar's legacies from my own fortune and credit (people laugh at a banking background, but it's invaluable when you have to raise money in a hurry). And I resolved to woo Cicero.

★ ★ ★

Cicero is at most a name to you, my sons, because I have

19

never permitted you to study his writings. You may, in the course of this narrative, come to understand why. Yet, if you are to make sense of my account of the next few months, I must tell you something about this man of the greatest genius—for another time and another city.

Marcus Tullius Cicero was the cleverest man I have ever known; yet I outwitted him at every turn. He was born in the municipality of Aroinum in the year 106 BC, so that he was by now an old man. The events of this terrible year show however that, if he was failing, it was in judgement, not energy of mind or body. I had sympathy and respect for Cicero, even affection. We were both after all from the same sort of background, and he too had risen by his own genius. He was consul in 63, the year that saw the conspiracy of Catiline, which he suppressed with vigour and, it must be said, a fine disregard for the legality he spent the rest of his life claiming to uphold. For this exploit he was granted the title 'Father of his Country', which, as you know, the Conscript Fathers have thought fit to bestow on me also. Yet he never learned the lesson of his own consulship: that power makes its own rules. Nobody was more aware than Cicero of the decrepitude of the Republic, nobody analysed it more acutely. He saw that the extraordinary commands entrusted to the Republic's generals enabled them to create armies loyal to themselves but not to the Republic; yet he never saw how this had come about. His proposed cure was preposterous: he believed that if all the 'good men' would come together and cooperate, they could restore the old virtues of the Republic as in the day of Scipio—if not that stout old peasant Cincinnatus. He did not see that the structure itself was rotten. Yet he had proved it in his own life: to combat Caesar he had been forced to propose that Pompey receive one of those extraordinary commands that were destroying what Cicero loved; crazy.

I envied him his love for the idea of the Republic; he was infatuated with virtue. (But, my sons, you know the root of that verb 'to infatuate', don't you? You realize I have chosen it with the utmost precision to describe its effect on this man of genius.) He had beautiful manners too. Having discussed the matter with Maecenas, I went to visit Cicero taking with me humble and homely presents—a pot of honey from the Alban hills, a caciocavallo cheese, the first (very early, for it was a marvellous benign spring) wood strawberries from Nemi. He received me with a dignity that did honour to us both.

He began by speaking of Caesar. 'You must not think I did not respect him,' he said, 'even love him. Who could fail to admire his abilities? What a power of reasoning, what a memory, what lucidity, what literary skill, what accuracy, profundity of thought and energy! His conquest of Gaul! Even though, as you will understand, I cannot think of it in its consequences as other than disastrous for the Republic, nevertheless, what an achievement! His genius was great, well-nigh unparalleled of its type; yet, my boy, and I say this with tears in my eyes, consider the consequence of his illustrious career: he brought this free city, which we both love— do we not?—to a habit of slavery. That is why I opposed him. That is why I welcomed his death. It is painful for me to say this; it is painful for you to hear it. Yet I must be honest if we are to work together, as I hope we may.'

'It is my hope too, sir,' I said.

'These gifts you have brought me, so aptly and significantly chosen, they give me assurance that that hope may not be vain. There is measure and restraint in your choice; a just severity of judgement.'

I said: 'They are nothing. I merely hoped they might be pleasing to the Father of our Country, who saved Rome from the mad wolf Catiline.'

His manner, which had been public, ornate, rhetorical and insincere, changed.

'Ah,' he said, 'you know about that. I can never believe they teach any history now. My own sons and my nephew would have known nothing if I had not instructed them myself. And indeed you see truly what Catiline was... But what else is Antony?'

I was amazed at his audacity, for I had been accustomed to hear men mock his timidity. I had not known before how some men become bolder as their future shortens.

'Do you know what Rome is?' he said. 'Ah, how could you, child? But come.'

He took me by the sleeve and led me over to where we could look down on the city. The sky was of the most intense blue; the temples on the Capitol glittered. Below the hill rose the hum of the city, a constant movement, a coming and going, a jostling animation; law courts were babbling, baths teeming, libraries attended, cook-shops and taverns sizzling. We withdrew into the cool of the atrium.

'It is a city of free men,' Cicero said, 'with liberty of discussion and debate, where none legally wears arms or armour; a city of noble equals; and that mad dog, whom I shall not dignify with Catiline's name of wolf, that drunken pirate, threatens to stop our mouths with the swords of his legionaries.'

'I have legions too, sir.'

The first smile lit up his face; he chuckled.

'Of course you have, dear boy. That's why you are here, child. The question is, what will you do with them?'

'My legions are at the service of the Republic,' I said.

He let a long silence of sceptical memories fill the air.

'But,' I continued, 'what are the intentions of the Republic towards me?'

'I am not sure,' he said, 'that just at the moment the Republic can be said to have any intentions. It is as bereft of will as it is of legions. That, dear boy, is the crux of the matter.'

*　*　*

When Antony promised me safety if I delivered my legions to him, there was mockery in his voice. There was an even harsher note: contempt. He believed I would indeed be ready to buy safety. 'You, boy,' he would say, 'with your banker's blood, who owe everything to a name . . .' Such an assumption on his part hardly caused me to respect his intelligence: did he truly fail to realize that I too had let the dice fly high when I chose to accept Julius' legacy and acknowledged Maco's salute at Brindisi?

Cicero praised me in the Senate. His words would have overwhelmed me if my vanity had approached his own. Agrippa was hugely impressed. He repeated over and over again that we had really arrived: 'I don't see that they can now deny you legitimate authority. Not after such advocacy.'

Maecenas I saw smirking. 'You don't agree, do you?' I said. 'Oh,' he said, 'who am I to speak? Remember I am not a true Roman. I don't understand your Senates and Assemblies. My ancestors were Kings in Etruria. So it is hard for me to estimate the effect of oratory on a body like the Senate. But we have a saying in my family: beware the man who speaks well of you. Besides, haven't you heard the story that's going about? Someone said to Cicero, "Why on earth do you praise that young man?" The old boy looked over his shoulder to see who might overhear, and replied, "The young man must be praised." "Must be?" asks his chum. "Must be," says Cicero, "he must be praised, decorated and ... disposed of..." What we mustn't forget, my dears, is that Cicero was cheating serpents before our daddies were weaned.' I looked at Maecenas. 'We must never let Cicero suspect that we guess what he has in mind. He is our dearest friend and essential ally.'

* * *

It was a spring of the utmost delicacy. The wild weather of the March of Julius' murder was scattered by a sun that promised more than we could find time to enjoy. I had got myself an army, but hesitated whether to use it or disband it for the moment. Antony returned to Rome about 20 May, bringing with him a bodyguard of thugs ready to control any vote in the popular assembly. With money that was rightfully mine he bought the alliance of Cicero's son-in-law Dolabella. At the beginning of June he staged a plebiscite to prolong his own provincial command for three years.

We met again in a house that had once belonged to Pompey; whether he or Antony was responsible for its vulgarity, I could not tell. But I had time enough to study it, for Antony had the insolence to keep me waiting. No doubt he thought to disturb me. When he at last granted me an interview his insolence continued. He again absolutely refused to disgorge Julius' money.

I accepted his insolence in silence. Do not, my children, ever underestimate the value of silence. It disconcerts bluster and distorts judgement.

When I left his presence I let it be known that I would pay all Julius' legacies; 'If it costs me my last penny,' I asserted.

I wrote to my friends in the legions in Macedonia complaining that Antony was refusing to avenge Caesar.

This was not strictly true, for by midsummer Antony was actually besieging Decimus Brutus in Mutina. This disturbed Agrippa. 'It seems to me wrong that we're not working with Antony,' he kept saying. 'I tell you our centurions don't understand what you're up to. They don't like it. They joined us to avenge Caesar and here you are fucking about with the Senate and that old woman Cicero.'

'Run away and practise your sword-play, ducky,' Maecenas said. 'We do have heads on our shoulders. We're not just blundering about.'

'Well,' Agrippa glowered at me, 'that's what it fucking well looks like. If you've got a plan, perhaps you'd be kind enough to tell me what it is?'

I thought about that.

'There you go again,' he said. 'You just sit there like a little owl, and let him make fun of me. You don't tell me anything, but it's me as has to go out and find you soldiers, and then try to keep 'em happy. But they're not happy, they're bleeding not. So what's your flaming plan?'

'I don't have one,' I said, 'not the sort of plan you could write down.'

And this was true. I have talked to you about this, Gaius and Lucius, but I have never put it in writing for you. The value of planning diminishes in accordance with the complexity of the state of affairs. Believe me: this is true. It may seem paradoxical. You may think that the more complicated a situation is, the more necessary a plan to deal with it. I shall grant you the theory. But practice is different. No plan can be equal to the complexities and casualties of political life. Hence, adherence to a plan deprives you of the flexibility which you need if you are to ride the course of events; for a moment's reflection should enable you to see that it is impossible (even with the help of the wisest soothsayers and mathematicians) to predict what will happen; and it is folly to pretend that you can control the actions of other men with any certainty. Therefore a plan is only suitable for the simple operations of life; you can plan a journey to your country house, but you cannot plan a battle or a political campaign in any detail. You must have a goal, my sons, but to achieve it, nothing is more important than that you retain fluidity of thought. Improvisation is the secret of success in politics, for most political action is in fact and of necessity reaction.

So I said now to Agrippa, 'I have no plan but I have purposes. I intend to avenge Caesar and to restore the Republic. And first I intend to safeguard our position. All my manoeuvring is directed towards these aims. You ask about Antony? You call for a reunion of the Caesareans. Well, so do I. But does Antony? As far as he is concerned, Caesar is dead and Antony is his successor. He must be persuaded that it is not so, and that he, Antony, is less than half our party.'

*   *   *

Meanwhile, as Maecenas was quick to tell me, Antony was doing all he could to destroy my reputation. He spread many rumours about me. I shall set them down, because I am not ashamed to have been slandered.

He let it be known that I had played the role of catamite to Caesar to encourage him to adopt me. He added that, subsequently, I had submitted to the lusts of Aulus Hirtius, Procurator of Spain, in return for 3000 gold pieces: 'The boy lends out his body at interest,' he said, 'it's his banker's blood, no doubt.' He accused me of effeminacy and sent agents among my troops to ask why they let themselves be commanded by a boy-whore.

The accusations were false of course; it was ridiculous to suppose that Caesar would so reward a boy who behaved in such a disgusting way. As for Aulus Hirtius, he was so repulsive that one of his slave-boys hanged himself rather than endure his embraces. (The boy was a Gaul too, and everyone knows that Gallic boys think it no shame to sleep with mature men; the Druid religion encourages youths to prostitute themselves to the priests, and Gallic warriors are accustomed to choose the boys who look after their war-horses for their good looks.) Besides, it was absurd to suppose that 3000 gold pieces would attract a young man of my fortune.

Curiously these allegations did me no harm with the troops. They didn't believe them. Even if they had, Antony should have known that soldiers take pleasure in the vices of their commanders. Caesar's legionaries had delighted in the story of their general's seduction by King Nicomedes. They had even sung a dirty song about it, which I shall not repeat to you.

Agrippa of course was furious. He told me I was bound to have such stories made up about me as long as I associated with a pansy like Maecenas. He said that even if my men chose not to believe them, the senators whose support I was seeking would hardly like it to be thought that they were associating with a tart.

'Don't be so silly,' I said, 'there's nothing to worry about. Everyone knows Antony is a liar.'

All the same I was displeased myself, though my displeasure was mixed with the satisfaction that the circulation of such absurd and malicious rumours showed that Antony was taking my rivalry seriously. Nevertheless, I thought it as well to do what I could to disprove the lies. I stopped shaving my legs for one thing, and grew a beard too; and I took care to let pretty slave-girls be seen round my quarters. Maecenas introduced me to one Toranius, a dealer who was able to supply me with the most delectable fruits of the market.

I tell you these things, my sons, not for any pleasure I feel in the memory—to speak the truth I look back on them with a mixture of amusement and distaste—but for two reasons: first, that you may learn from my own lips what manner of man I have been, and so be able to discount the malicious and disreputable rumours with which I am sure you will be fed; and, second, because you may learn in this way how much prudence, self-control and decision are necessary to manipulate public opinion. I was careful to arrange that Maco should see a Circassian girl slip shiftless from my tent as he awaited an interview. I knew he would go back and say, 'He's a right boy, our general, you should have seen the bit of fluff he had last night . . .'

Antony was fighting only for himself; but I had a vision of Rome. No one knows how ideas are formed, what influences operate on the mind, to what extent a man creates a world-view for himself. These are deep matters which I have discussed with philosophers, and, as the poet says, 'evermore came out, by that same door wherein I went'; and with

Virgil, who was something more profound than a philosopher, a true poet. Here let me say a word on the subject of poets. Most of them are no more than versifiers. Any gentleman should of course be able to turn a verse; you, Lucius, have written elegiacs that please me. Beyond that, when it becomes a profession, there is too often something despicable in the craft. It encourages conceit and extravagant behaviour, monkey-tricks. True poetry has a moral value, most verse none; some is frankly immoral. Occasionally however you find a poet who offers more even than that. He is a man possessed of insight, a man through whom the Gods have chosen to speak. (By the way, I am glad that I have never heard you mock the Gods; only those with no rudder, men who trust complacently to their own natural buoyancy, do that. I fear the man who does not fear the Gods, for he lacks proportion.) I am fortunate to have known one such poet, Virgil. The spirit of Rome inhabited him; he saw what was hidden from other men. There is no man I have more deeply revered. I am sometimes tempted to believe that the core of my political thought derives from Virgil. And yet this is false. I was moving in that direction before I ever talked with him. Is it possible that ideas can exist, as it were, in the air?

Caesar was naturally an inspiration. Yet, speaking under my breath to you, my sons, let me confess I never cared for Julius. There was something meretricious in him, something rotten. He revealed the full decadence of the Republic; when he led his legions across the Rubicon in that winter dawn, it was as if he tore a veil away from a shrine and discovered to all that the God had abandoned it. He was a great general; his conquest of Gaul and defeat of Pompey were imperishable feats. But what did he do then? He was tempted by monarchy—I have it on good authority that when Antony three times presented him with a kingly crown on the occasion of the Feast of the Lupercal, both Caesar and Antony expected that the crowd would hail him as king, and thus allow him to accept the crown. Inept politicians! Not to have arranged that the wind would blow that way! There was a vanity to him; he wore the high red boots of the old kings of Alba Longa; can you imagine me behaving so absurdly? But there was room for such vanity—it filled a vacancy at the heart of his imagination. Having achieved supreme power, he did not see that he was only at the beginning of his labours.

I often talked of Julius with Cicero that long summer ago. When he sensed—oh he had the sharp intuition of the great cross-examiner he was—that I too had my doubts about my father, Cicero let slip the cloak of discretion which he always wore as if it chafed him. He ran his hand through his grey hair, leaned forward and thrust his scraggy neck towards me:

'The truth is,' he said, 'he was an adventurer, a gambler. He had no purpose beyond the immediate. He had no sense of history, no sense of the relationship that must exist between the past, the present and the future. He had never analysed the causes of his own elevation because he believed it had been achieved by fortune and his own merit; his genius in short. Such nonsense!'

'Do you think,' I said—I made a habit of seeking Cicero's opinion even when I had no need of it—'do you think that there was any deep purpose behind his admission of Gauls to the Senate?'

Cicero flushed: 'There was certainly a purpose, but it was simply to insult the senators by making us associate with barbarians. Can you imagine anything more contemptuous?'

'No, sir,' I said, shaking my head and keeping my face straight, 'but tell me how in your view, garnered from your life's distinguished harvest, the Free State can be restored.'

Cicero sighed: 'I had almost come to believe it impossible. Perhaps, my dear boy, you have been sent by the gods to make it possible. What is needed is resolution, and the agreement of all good men throughout society to work together, and obey the laws. There is no fault in our laws. The fault, Octavius, lies in our own natures. Let me give you two examples. Have you ever heard of Verres?'

'Who, thanks to your sublime oratory, has not heard of Verres?'

'Well, yes, my prosecution made some stir in its time. I am glad it is still read. You remember what I said? Let me at any rate refresh your memory. I dislike quoting myself, but I know no other way to make my present point . . .'

And he did; it lasted half an hour (all from memory of course) and he was (as I guessed) hardly half-way through

when he was suddenly taken by old man's weakness and had
to leave me to empty his bladder. I shan't weary you with his
speech: suffice to say that Verres was a dishonest and extor-
tionate Governor of Sicily, whom Cicero had very properly
prosecuted (nowadays of course a modern Verres would not
be able to commit even a quarter of the offences of the original, and we have more efficient ways of dealing with such
malpractice than by public trial).

I had thought the interruption might spare me the rest of
the speech. Not a bit of it; he was in full flow before he was
properly back in the room, doubtless lest I should change the
subject.

Eventually he paused a moment. 'My peroration,' he said,
'has been called sublime.' And he gave it to me elaborate and
fortissimo. (I would never advise anyone to copy his mag-
niloquent and excessively mannered style of oratory. It was, I
suppose, superb or sublime, if you like; but prolix and too
carefully prepared to convince. All right in its time I daresay,
but terribly dated and disgustingly florid in my view. However, I applauded as was only polite.)

Then he said: 'Now look on the other side. I myself have
been a Governor too. In Cilicia, a province lamentably looted
by my predecessors. I refused to follow their example. No
expense was imposed on the wretched provincials during my
government, and when I say no expense, I do not speak
hyperbolically. I mean, none, not a farthing. Imagine that. I
refused to billet my troops on them. I made the soldiers sleep
under canvas. I refused all bribes. My dear boy, the natives regarded my conduct with speechless admiration and astonishment. I tell you it was all I could do to prevent them from
erecting temples in my honour. Innumerable babies were
named Marcus, I could hardly object to that. When I took
slaves in my campaigns I deposited in the Treasury the 12 million sesterces I received for their sale. That's how to govern;
that's the way it should be done. Not like Verres, not like
Marcus Brutus.' He broke off to giggle. 'Do you know, dear
boy, what interest he charged the wretched Cypriots under
his care. No? You won't believe it. Forty-eight per cent.
That's right, it's true. Forty-eight per cent. Imagine. But,
dear boy, you see what I mean? There is nothing wrong with

the Republic that a change of heart and a return to the stern morality of our ancestors will not put right. Meanwhile though, we have this wild beast Antony to account for. The stories he has spread about you! It's shameful. An old man like myself can stand slander; it must always hurt the young.'

Such optimism, such naivety, in one who had seen so much!

II

By late summer Antony had hardly advanced in his aim to dominate the State. In August Cicero returned from the seaside, invigorated by the benign climate and other delights of the Bay of Naples, and attacked Antony in the Senate. I did not of course hear the speech. My brother-in-law Gaius Marcellus told me it had been 'the usual thing, wind, wind, wind'. For all that, it goaded Antony. He had been thinking himself into the role of proconsul; it irritated him to have the old man remind everyone of his patchy history and moral insufficiency. The Senate may indeed have emptied during Cicero's speech ('the younger men call him the dinner-gong, you know,' Marcellus said), but the speech was copied out and went round the forum. It made an impression. People saw Antony could not be trusted. They sought a man they could rely on. Cicero was too old, the consuls Pansa and Hirtius too obscure, the self-styled Liberators could never hope to overcome the antipathy of Caesar's legions: the way was opening before me.

Antony blundered. Early in September Agrippa came to me, sweating with agitation.

'We're done for,' he said. 'We'd better pack our bags.'

'What is it?' I said.

I sat down and called on Agrippa to do likewise. This is invariably the wisest and most effective response to signs of incipient panic. Either sit down yourself, or tell others to do so, or both. Why, I once quelled a mutinous cohort by snapping out the order to sit down. You can have no idea till you see it how effective such a command can be. A crowd on its feet feels its corporate strength. Make them sit down and you restore their sense of being individuals. You make them conscious of themselves.

'Antony has sent a letter to the Pontifex Maximus.'

'Much good may that do him. Lepidus is nothing but a bag of wind.'

'You don't understand. He's published the letter, and he accuses you of plotting his murder. He requests your arrest and immediate trial.'

I rang the bell for a slave.

'Find Maecenas and ask him to come here. And bring some wine. You look as if you could do with a drink, Grippa,' I said.

'Well,' I said to Maecenas when he appeared. 'Have we planned many murders lately?'

'Not many.'

'Not even the consul's?'

'Not that I know of. I hope you didn't disturb me from a very interesting couch just to play the fool. What is this?'

'Tell him, Grippa.'

'No,' Agrippa said, afraid now of being laughed at, 'you tell him.'

'But this is wonderful,' Maecenas said. 'I don't regret my postponed couch at all. It's the first point he's really lost to us.'

'Precisely. How do we exploit it?'

'Laughter.'

'My own opinion, but it shows he is taking us seriously.'

I went to my desk and wrote for a few minutes.

'How about this?' I said, and read the following to them:

'Friends, Romans, Countrymen: you will all remember that less than six months ago, the Consul Mark Antony prefaced his eulogy of my murdered father with these very words. In that noble and moving speech which his secretaries provided for him, he praised my father's noble generosity and with a nice irony exposed the dishonour of his murderers. Well and good, my friends; my gratitude for that speech is still warm. Irony, however, is a corrupting habit, not unlike wine in its operation. Drunkards begin by drink-

31

ing with the same discrimination as the ordinary man who likes a glass of wine. But, whereas the ordinary man is moderately enlivened and improved with wine, which he has prudently mixed with water, drunkards are enflamed by it, and their judgement quite destroyed. So with the habit of irony. It can possess a man. I can only assume that this has happened to our noble and honourable consul. (It must be irony, for it could not be wine, could it?)

'Why do I say this, you ask? Well, there has come to my knowledge a story said to be related by the consul. It appears that he is accusing me of plotting his own murder.

'The charge is so preposterous that I do not intend to offer a defence. I shall not insult the consul's momentary aberration by pretending to take it seriously. Had such a charge been offered by any other man, I would have supposed him drunk. The consul of course cannot have been in his cups. No man, guiding the affairs of the Republic in this terrible year, would be so rash and irresponsible as to fall into intoxication. We all know the consul's devotion to duty and the sobriety of his judgement. I can therefore only assume that he has fallen victim to the habit of irony, and that the accusation is an elaborate private joke. My only complaint is that it is an unfriendly one. Not everyone will see it, for not everyone shares the consul's delicious sense of fun.

'And I deny it only because I should not like it to be thought by my father's friends that my feelings towards one of his lieutenants were anything but warm. Of course I don't blame the consul, especially as it occurs to me that he may have taken seriously a jest propounded by his wife Fulvia. And we all know who her first husband was, what standards of public spirit and private honour he always displayed, with what delighted wit Fulvia and he concocted similar accusations, what a practised hand she is, and how wisely and firmly she guides the consul.

'That,' I said, 'ought to do for him.'

'Beautiful.' Maecenas leapt up and embraced me. 'You've caught him hip and thigh. They'll laugh at this all over Italy. The only thing is, my dear, you may have over-estimated the intelligence of the public. You can go broke doing that, as any theatre manager will tell you. Let me just tinker with the last bit ... da–da–da–di ... how about this now? Start from where you bring in Fulvia, and go on: "and we all know that Fulvia used to be married to the ex-noble Clodius, whose religious zeal was such that he even dressed up as a woman to attend the sacred Festival of the Good Goddess; whose devotion to truth caused him to testify in a thousand law-courts; whose love of the Republic was so strong that he became a plebeian in order to qualify for election as a tribune; and whose sense of the ridiculous was so acute that he caused himself to be adopted by a man young enough to be his own son. No wonder therefore that Fulvia is a practised hand"—I like that expression, your own is it? Never heard it before—"at concocting such accusations. Of course, not being the consul and so not having perfect knowledge of matters of which I am completely ignorant, I cannot say definitely that this accusation is Fulvia's work. And I am alas too young to have any personal memory of her first husband. But from what I have heard of him, there is a whiff of Clodius here. A whiff of petticoats too. And anyway we all know how wisely and firmly Fulvia guides—I shall not say, governs—and advises the honourable consul." You've got to spell it out, lay it on the line, my dear. But I reckon that'll laugh 'em out of court.'

'Lovely,' I said, 'just one more refinement. I think this might be the occasion for one of my diplomatic stutters. So: "We all know Fulvia used to be married to the ignoble—I am so sorry, I mean ex-noble—Clodius". What about that?'

'Oh you're both very clever,' Agrippa said. 'It's a pity you can't ever be serious.'

'There's nothing,' I said, 'more serious than the right sort of joke in politics.'

'Well, I may be very thick, but I don't understand.'

He was very thick of course, but I soothed him. I couldn't let my Agrippa go off in that bear-mood.

He was in good company. Cicero didn't understand either. He had believed Antony's accusation and only regretted that I had 'lacked the confidence or capacity to execute such a worthy intention'. He was baffled by my response. I suppose it was too modern for him. He found the levity inappropriate. All the same, he couldn't resist chuckling over our broadside at Fulvia. There was no one he had hated more than

33

Clodius, and he extended his hatred to Fulvia: 'a terrible woman, a harpy, a Stymphalian bird, mad for power'. His judgement was sound enough there.

As for me, I suddenly needed Cicero more than ever. Antony's credit was pricked by my riposte, which also stung him into action. He began to collect soldiers fast. At Suessa that autumn he purged his own army, then marched to Brindisium and secured three legions, the II, the IV and the Martian, which were returning from the East; his speed forestalled my own agents. On the way back north he picked up Julius' favourite legion, the Lark. He was ready now to march determinedly against Decimus Brutus in Mutina with a formidable force. Despite what I had achieved he was very close to being master of Italy, all in a few weeks. I needed to build up my credit with the traditional Republicans who feared and loathed Antony. So I wrote, passionately, to Cicero, and begged him to advise me, and to save the Republic as he had done in his youth.

How far did I fool him? We were in a sense bound together. I needed Cicero who alone could reconcile the traditionalists to me; but he needed my sword and the command I had over Julius' veterans. There are marriages like our relationship, things founded on common interest and reciprocated distrust. I could not forget his gibe: that I must be made much of, decorated and destroyed. Letters he wrote to his friend Atticus—letters which I was to read when I impounded his private papers—show how wise I was to be wary: I was a mere boy, he said; yes, he was sure of my opposition to Antony, but not of my intentions to the Republic; he saw war-clouds gathering over the Apennines. He longed for Brutus and Cassius, whose purpose was reliable.

Yes, I was right to distrust him, but he was mistaken in his judgement. I revered the Republic too, as my subsequent action in restoring it and resigning my power have proved. But I had a different sense of what was practical. I knew even then that things would have to change if we wanted them to stay the same; that Rome could only be preserved from despotism if its nobility would accept government.

★ ★ ★

That November the fog was as thick in Rome as you find it under the Alps. I arrived back at the beginning of the month and stationed three thousand men outside the city in the hilltown of Alba Longa. We held a council in my stepfather's house on the Aventine. Marcellus spoke first, then my stepfather. Both argued that we had made no real advance since the spring while Antony grew stronger.

'You are in danger,' Marcellus said, 'of falling between two stools.' 'I have always said,' Philippus insisted, 'that you can't run with the hare and hunt with the hounds. It's beyond nature.' He spoke with the authority of the man whose backside is pinned to the fence. 'You have only two real choices,' he said. 'Either throw in your lot with Antony and take whatever he is willing to grant you, or do as I've always advised: give up the whole game and retire to your vineyards and beanfields. I know which course would please your mother.'

The Council achieved nothing. Maecenas yawned through it, Agrippa glowered. He had reconciled himself to our opposition to Antony, having been shocked by the murder accusation and angered by a gibe about 'the boy supported by the plumber's mate and the pansy'. He urged me now to call a public meeting and explain my case to the People. 'It's the Roman course,' he kept saying.

It made sense to me. Accordingly we arranged a meeting in the Temple of Castor for 10 November. The crowd's mood was uncertain. A tribune, Titus Cannutius, spoke first, attacking Antony and receiving excited applause. On the spur of the moment I jettisoned my prepared speech. I had been up all night writing it and had a fever coming on. This may have impaired my judgement. At any rate I was hardly launched before I knew I had not caught the mood. The art of public speaking consists first in sensing the audience's mood, in achieving a tacit empathy, so that you say what the crowd most deeply and unconsciously wants to hear. I failed. I attacked Antony of course, but I was too light, too mocking. I had not caught the intensity of the people's fear. They sniffed war and proscriptions on the chill tramontana that blew from Antony's northern camp. My mockery did nothing to dispel their apprehension. It made them rather distrust

35

me: I seemed to lack the gravity and steadfastness of purpose that were needed to avert catastrophe. Even as I spoke I knew this. I suffered like an actor who finds himself in the wrong part. What had gone wrong? Later I decided I had been addressing myself to Maecenas instead of Agrippa. It was a lesson I was never to forget again. Meanwhile I plunged deeper. I heard myself launched on praise of Julius. That failed to restore the situation, for, instead of contenting myself with a recital of what he had achieved for Rome and a reminder of his generosity to the People, I heard my tongue declare my own intention 'to attain the honours of my father'. The words emerged from the fog and hung, nakedly ambitious, in the air. I sought to retrieve matters by dwelling on the indignities I had suffered from Antony. 'He has spread libels about me, he has accused me of shameful vices, he has even alleged that I was plotting his murder.' It was no good; it came over shrill. I felt my stature shrink in the imagination of those who heard me. The audience was even beginning to trickle away. I stopped in mid-sentence. Agrippa pulled me down and stood up himself.

'See here,' he said, 'it's simple. You all know what Antony is. I'm an ordinary man myself. I know you can't trust Antony. He'd make off with his granny's last sow. You know that fine. There's not one of you will feel safe if he wins. That's what this meeting's about. Now I know Octavian here better than any of you. You may think he's a bit on the young side. Well, just ask yourselves what sort of mess his elders have got us all in to. I tell you a pig in shit would find it stinking. What sort of future will they give you and your children? Maybe it's time they turned over and gave youth a chance. At least we don't have criminal records. We're not drunkards and we haven't murdered our benefactors. Octavian here's a good lad. All right, he's young, but he offers you all the chance of a decent future. You just think about that. If you've got any nerve at all, or anything but sawdust in your top storey, you'll back us. To the bloody hilt, if you've got your wits about you.'

Maybe it didn't quite convince them, but it saved the day. The colour crept back into Maecenas' cheeks. He had really been afraid. Being what he was, he never trusted a crowd. It was his constant fear that one false word and they'd tear us apart.

I learned a lot that day. Cicero's reaction was characteristic: 'What a speech', he wrote to Atticus. 'Have I over-rated the boy's capacity, and underestimated his inheritance from Julius?'

The tenth of November left me much to retrieve.

Fortunately, when you let yourself down, you often find that your enemies make mistakes which allow you time to recover.

We scurried out of the city that night, in a welter of baggage, recrimination, confusion and panic. Philippus, trembling like a man with fever, received us in his Sabine villa.

'You've blundered terribly,' he said. 'What were you thinking of? Were you mad enough to attempt a coup? You've put yourself outside the pale, outside the law. No respectable man will dare work with you now. Even Publius Servilius Isauricus, who's been your best friend among the consulars, has got cold feet.'

'He lent us Titus Cannutius,' I said. 'The tribune is his man, and it was with Publius Servilius' agreement that he led the attack on Antony.'

'Quite, absolutely, but it failed. And Publius Servilius wants no more of you. Look, here's a letter to that effect. Why, he even urges me, for my own safety, to deny you my house. What will your mother say? Why, oh why, didn't you listen to me? This is the price you are paying for disregarding my advice...'

I looked at his ignoble middle-aged terror, and turned to Agrippa.

'You were wise,' I said, 'in what you told the crowd. We have stumbled, no more. Stepfather, believe me, the game is not lost. But what I must know is where Balbus can be found.'

'He won't help you now either.'

'I think he will,' I said, 'and we need money. Money. If Balbus will raise me another half-million we shall come through.'

*   *   *

37

I have hardly mentioned Balbus. Perhaps I hoped, with that vanity that never absolutely deserts us, to tell you my story without reference to him. Yet, if I wish to instruct you (and tell the truth), I cannot avoid doing so.

Balbus was a phenomenon, a citizen of Gades in Spain, whom Julius had got to know in his first campaign in the country. His wealth, based on silver mines, great latifundia, and banking was enormous; it early became self-perpetuating. You will hardly understand that, my sons; indeed, despite my own banking blood, I do not know how it happens. There is, it seems, a law of the God Moneta: those who devote themselves to his service discover the secret of perpetual fertility. Beyond an indeterminate point money breeds money. Balbus early reached the stage when he could not consume the interest on his investments; before long he could not consume the interest on the interest which he laid out at interest. As long as he avoided injudicious investment, it seemed that his god had granted him a licence to coin his own money.

When I arrived at Brindisi at the end of March, I had found a note from him: 'Draw on me for whatever you need from Anaxogoras the Greek at the sign of the Fish in this city,' it said. I had my friend Publius Salvidienus Rufus take the note thither for verification of the seal. Then, by night, accompanied by Rufus and Agrippa, cloaked and hooded, we slipped through the darkened town on slimy cobbles to the Greek's house. He had received his own instructions. It was then I first sensed what no born gentleman realizes: the occult expedition of money. There were chests waiting for us, loaded with gold pieces. Where they had come from, I do not know. It is a religious mystery. All I had to do was sign for the gold. I dispatched Agrippa to fetch Maco and his legionaries with carts. It was that gold which financed my first march on Rome.

Now, in extremity, I said to Philippus: 'I am for Aretrium in Etruria. If Balbus will produce another half-million, we shall come through. Don't be afraid.'

I named the sum at random. I had no idea what we would need. Balbus later said to me, 'I backed you the way I corner wheat when my agents get the first rumours of a bad harvest.'

That is how money works, like all mysteries, through its initiates.

★   ★   ★

But not only Balbus saved me in this crisis, producing magic credit which enabled Agrippa to raise more troops, enabled me also to send out scores of agents into Antony's camp; Antony himself misplayed his hand.

He was in Rome a fortnight after I left the city. He left most of his troops at Tibur, but his bodyguard was still strong enough to overawe and frighten the disaffected. His temper was high, he arrived in liquor and stayed half-drunk for four days. He called a meeting of the Senate for the twenty-fourth, but failed to attend himself. Cicero (and others) let it be known that the consul was too drunk to be seen in public. As if that ever stopped Antony! I had better reason to know what prevented him. On the same day as he entered Rome my agents distributed leaflets among the men of the Martian legion; not only leaflets, as you may imagine. Maco himself had approached their camp and sought out old comrades among Antony's centurions. He dealt out gold and golden promises. Would they fight against Caesar's son? he asked those veterans of the Gallic War. Could they live with themselves if they destroyed their master's heir? He touched their hearts; he fed their appetites. The Martian legion declared for me and shut themselves up in Alba Fucens. With one stroke, while Antony dined in Rome, I had retrieved what seemed lost less than two weeks before.

My position was still dangerous. All that year I diced with death and dishonour—which was worse. (Remember, my sons, that your actions must always be such as will permit you to live with self-approbation.) Antony let everyone know—he shouted it to the rooftops—that I had been guilty of what he chose to call illegality. I was innocent, for legality was nowhere to be found that year. Legality rests on the point of the sword; when swords are raised against each other, legality floats into the heavens to await the decision of the Gods. If no one can enforce the laws, all strong men assume the right to do so. It is inevitable. Antony however played

39

high; I admired him for that. On the twenty-eighth the Senate at last met. His creature, Q. Rufius Calenus, was ready to bring in a bill denouncing me as a public enemy. Caesar himself had been so denounced—and had scattered his accusers before him. Conscious of the rediscovered loyalty of the Martian legion, of the success Agrippa was meeting in recruitment, I could afford to regard the threat with equanimity.

Then Antony's nerve failed him. He dared not press the charge against me. That was prudent, for my agents were doing their work among his legions. They played on their natural reluctance to take up arms against me. Caesar, Caesar, Caesar . . . the magic word ran round the camp till Antony pressed his fingers in his ears against it. Yet he too was caught; he too aspired to share Caesar's legacy; he himself depended on my father's glory. We were linked in a dance to a ghostly tune.

He marched against Decimus Brutus, determined to dislodge him from Cisalpine Gaul. I sighed in relief; he had turned to his true work. Meanwhile the IVth legion followed the example of the Martian and crossed to my side. I had got myself the most formidable army in Italy: five legions, two of Campanian veterans and one recruited in Etruria by Agrippa, as well as the IVth and the Martian. Now, with deliberation, hoping to avoid battle, ready to make a show of it, I marched northward, in Antony's wake.

It was blue-cold in the mountains, a biting north wind. For a few days I felt I had no control over this force which I had called into being, and which was growing every day. (Two more legions were on their way to join me from Macedonia.) I caught a chill, fell into fever, was carried two days in a litter over the mountains, lay sweating and shivering in a mountain hut, while my disordered mind replayed the events of the last half-year. Yet, even so deranged by wild fancies and feverish dreams, I never doubted my future. The star I had seen rise over the mountains of Illyria beckoned me on. No man can hope to triumph unless he is willing to be the instrument of the divine powers that shape this world. Julius appeared to me in delirium, in a bloody and torn toga. He urged me on, applauded what I had achieved, and commended my decision (which Agrippa had so fiercely opposed) to acquiesce in the election of his vilest assassin, Casca, to the tribunate. 'Revenge is a meal to be eaten cold.' Casca's hour would strike when he felt more secure.

★   ★   ★

In Rome, as one year passed into another, Cicero addressed the Senate, unwearied. The body of his speech was devoted to my praise. The honey with which I had coated his vanity was well worth what it cost me.

'I know intimately the young man's every feeling,' he said, lying. 'Nothing is dearer to him than the Free State, nothing has more weight with him than your influence, nothing is more desired by him than the good opinion of virtuous men, nothing more delightful to him than true glory ... I will venture even to pledge my word that Gaius Caesar will always be as loyal a citizen as he is to-day, and as our most fervent wishes and prayers desire.'

In the midst of his self-deception he spoke truth. I have always been a loyal citizen.

Cicero had lost all the discretion with which he had guarded his person for the last fifty years. He upbraided Antony in language that only victory could justify. He spoke warmly of me, but his praise was as insincere as his invective was heart-felt. My own heart responded less than it would now—youth is more impervious to approbation, which it takes as its due, than old age is—and my mind stood detached. But what Cicero said worked. The Senate clamoured to be permitted to honour me. They babbled in echo of Cicero: 'What godlike youth has come to save the Republic!' Maecenas said to me: 'There's not a man there would not slit your throat with a smile on his face.' I played my hand on his. They voted me a senator. (It is therefore, my sons, now forty years that I have been a member of the Conscript Fathers, the most noble assembly in the history of the world, even if its conduct and collective wisdom sometimes fall short of what they should be; never neglect to honour the Senate.) They associated me with the consuls Hirtius and Pansa in command of the army against Antony; they granted me the imperium of a pro-praetor.

'So far, so good,' Maecenas said. 'We are no longer adventurers, my dear.' He poured me a cup of wine—I added water. 'Let us drink to what we have been.'

'Let us drink rather to where we have arrived,' I said.

Agrippa raised his goblet: 'The future'.

('Oh dear,' Maecenas sighed, 'crowsfeet, the failure of performance before the death of desire, yes, ducky, the future.')

'To our glorious leader', said P Salvidienus Rufus. Is it hindsight that lets me believe I cast him a look pregnant with scepticism and irony?

★   ★   ★

Antony sent me a letter:

Octavius: what fool's game are you playing? I don't know whether to be more amazed by your rash folly or by your ability to persuade these deluded half-witted soldiers to follow you. I don't ask for gratitude, but I must point out to you that you have chosen to associate yourself with those who murdered Julius (whom you now call your father) in the vilest way imaginable, against me, who served Julius loyally and serve his memory and his cause still. Don't you realize, you poor boy, that your new chums are as twisted as a dragon's tail? They approached Caesar pretending to be friends; I have held his bloodstained toga in my hand. Some of them owed everything, including their lives, to Caesar. Yet they did for him. They owe nothing to you. What sort of fate do you imagine they are cooking up? Haven't you heard what the old verbal balloon Cicero is crowing? The kid must be flattered, decorated . . . and bumped off? And I hear you address that old goat as Father too, you must be out of your mind. If you don't get yourself out of that galley bloody well straightaway, I'll think you a half-wit yourself and will offer thanks to Mars and Bacchus that I had sense enough to have nothing to do with you. But if you do get shot of them and bring your legions back to me, I'll see you're all right. As it is, laddie, you're in the minestrone, and it's beginning to bubble.

'In character,' I said, 'spluttering, bombastic and on edge.'

'What'll you say to him?'
'Oh, I shan't reply.'

★　★　★

War engages the full faculties of man, but in memory only
odd discordant moments emerge. Of that sharp scrambling
campaign to which historians give the name Mutina, I
remember very little. Decimus Brutus was shut up in the
town. He sent us news, by carrier-pigeon, that his garrison
was near exhaustion . . . it behoved us therefore to force the
passes to relieve him. Hirtius and Pansa met me to dictate the
strategy; I listened, impressed by neither. I had only one fear
and generals could not alleviate it. I therefore called Maco to
my tent. I gave him wine, to set him at ease and persuade him
to speak the truth, not what he thought I might wish to hear.
'We have come a long way,' I said, 'in a short time, and I
don't suppose either of us thought it would come to this.'
'No sir, can't say as I did, sir.'
'This army, these allies, they must seem an odd mixture to
a veteran like yourself. You can't have bargained for it.'
'Well, no, sir.'
I drew my fur cloak about me. The candle sputtered in a
gust of wind. A screech-owl cried out, hunting in the valley.
'That cloak, sir,' Maco said, 'pardon my asking, was it
his . . .?'
'Yes,' I said.
He put out his hand and touched it. 'Do you mind, sir? I
remember him wearing it, that dawn we crossed the river
into Italy. You've heard tell of that morning, I'm sure, sir,
how we were drawn down to the river bank by this figure
that was piping. Some said it was the God Pan, sir. I wouldn't
know. I just know we felt—well—obliged somehow. Sir.'
His hand rested on the cloak. 'Sit down,' I said, 'and have
some wine . . . tell me, Maco, how do the men feel about our
friends . . . and enemy?'
'Some of them trust you, sir. We're none of us that happy,
but that's not exactly because of just who they each are. Fact
is, sir, we none of us like fighting fellow-citizens. Well, you
never know which old mates may be marking you in the
other side's line-up. Mind you, if it was my brother-in-law I

43

wouldn't mind taking a swing at him. Proper little bugger he is, sir, if you don't mind me saying so, excuse my language. But in general, sir, it's awkward and makes the men uneasy. Himself understood that, sir. He knew it wasn't like lining us up against Gauls. The more of those painted buggers you can bump off, the better, but fellow-citizens, that's a different kettle of fish.'

'And when my father's legions are on either side?'

'Well, sir, we don't like it. But then you know, there's the other side of the coin. The obverse, they call it, don't they? Antony's boys are going to feel the same way. They're not going to be clapping their tiny hands with glee to be lined up against us. And don't forget, sir, they know who you are, they know you're Himself's son.'

'I hadn't thought of that,' I said. 'So what would you recommend?'

'Well, discretion, sir, but not despair, and be bloody sure to let the other chaps know who we are. Let them bump off your allies, right lot of treacherous and degenerate sods, if you don't mind my saying so. What we want, sir, is a cushy billet and the fruits of victory.'

And that is just what I contrived to get us. I was therefore able to bear with absolute equanimity the reports spread by many old Pompeians that I had shown the white feather during the battles. My men knew just what colour of feather we had sported. Maco told me they were saying they'd got a proper card running things now, chip off the old marble block, sir. Even Agrippa admitted I'd made a good impression on the troops. Antony was driven over the Alps. I was master of Italy, for the Gods willed that both Hirtius and Pansa should be killed. Neither had been of much account, but their departure certainly cleared the air and opened an avenue to power.

*   *   *

I wrote formally to the Senate requesting that they appoint me consul in the place of Hirtius or Pansa. I informed them of what I had achieved for the Republic. I scrupled to point out that I commanded the only army south of the Alps.

They did not reply directly. But their measures indicated

their changing yet ever-treacherous temper. They voted Decimus Brutus a Triumph. 'Ye Gods,' said Agrippa, 'he's done nothing but sit on his arse and pray we'd arrive in time to save his bacon...' They summoned the sea-thief Sextus Pompeius to command the navy of the Republic. They confirmed the Caesaricides, vain Brutus and false Cassius, in command of the provinces which they had illegally seized. With insolence bred of folly and prejudice, they commanded me to hand over to Decimus Brutus Pansa's legions which had flocked enthusiastically to my standard; and they even had the audacity to demand that I surrender the IVth and the Martian to him also. I was not mentioned in the vote of thanks to the army. I was not placed on the commission appointed to revise Antony's decrees. I was refused a triumph and an ovation.

It was clear that Cicero's epigram was being enacted; they had concluded it was now safe to discard me.

*　*　*

I summoned a council: Maecenas and Agrippa of course; my brother-in-law Marcellus; P. Salvidienus Rufus, quick-tempered, vain, touchy and acute; my stepfather Philippus. As is my wont on such occasions I said little myself. I asked each of them for his assessment of the situation.

Philippus moaned that we were lost and wrung his hands: 'You have overplayed it,' he sobbed, 'Fortuna is offended and the Gods are drawing their skirts away from you.'

'What would you advise, stepfather?' My voice had all the honey of the Alban Hills.

'You must do as they wish. You must show yourself humble and respectful. You must inform them that you have no other purpose, no other desire, but to do the will of the Senate. You must appear there and speak politely and submissively. All may not yet be lost. You have still the rank of propraetor, and you must confess yourself sensible of the extraordinary honours the Senate has been gracious to confer on one so young. In this way you may yet salvage something.'

'In other words,' Maecenas said, 'you must eat dirt, and say you like it, while throwing up the game which is hardly half-played.'

'Marcellus,' I said, 'you know how I respect your experience and capacity.'

'What Philippus advises is absurd. The Senate would receive you with contempt. Worse, the soldiers who have trusted you would never do so again. Certainly, you would be in no danger. You would be in no danger because you would be of no account. You would have surrendered your position as Caesar's heir and you would take your place in the Senate as Philippus' stepson.'

He had risen as he spoke, and, when he talked of the soldiers, he threw open the flap of the tent. We could see tents stretching into the evening distance, smoke rising from the camp-fires to lose itself in the river mist. We could see the obscure night closing around us.

P. Salvidienus Rufus rose also and placed his hand on Marcellus' shoulder.

'What Marcellus says is absolutely correct. I associate myself with him all the way. You won't be surprised to know that we have discussed the state of affairs. And we are agreed. You hold the line here, and meanwhile send an embassy to Antony—I am ready to go myself as your ambassador. Propose an alliance which he will now be willing to accept on your terms, or as near your terms as dammit. Then the pair of you march on Rome. That's what you must do. You've got yourself mounted on the wrong horse. I've always said so. It's time to change horses.'

'Thank you, my friend,' I said. 'As ever your advice is to the point—and all but cogent. However, let us hear our other friends. Maecenas?' I said, though I could see that Agrippa was fretting to give his opinion.

'What can I say? Marcellus and Rufus have analysed the situation with their customary acuity, and they are adept in Roman politics as I shall never be. I cannot, I regret'—he bowed to Philippus—'find myself in accord with you, sir. Your counsel is, in my humble opinion, the delicious and tender fruit of your paternal care and affection for Octavius, but, it seems to me, that you are attempting to separate the private person who is your cherished stepson from the political force he has become. And such surgery appears, in my humble opinion, to be impossible. It is what he is—Caesar's heir—which makes him of consequence; and it is the political skill he has displayed in this last year, guided of course by the wisdom of his friends and fructified by his own willingness to hearken to their advice, which have made him ... formidable. Such qualities, such achievement cannot be resigned; if I know that, half-foreign aesthete that I am, mere dabbler in the murky waters of politics, how much more certainly do our friendly foes! So, I must bow rather to the judicious advice tendered by Marcellus and Rufus. Yet may I suggest—tentatively of course—that their masterly analysis leaves two factors out of account. In the first place, Octavius now has power, but no real authority. He requires that if he is to treat with Antony. Second, there are armies in Narbonnese Gaul and Celtic Gaul and Spain commanded—pray correct me if I am mistaken—by Lepidus, Plancus and Pollio respectively. I don't know how many legions they have of course—I'm sure Agrippa can enlighten us—but I do know the real question: whose side are they on? Don't you think we should discover how they stand? My own uninformed guess is that they will drift, willy-nilly, to Antony ... and, if they do, he will surely outnumber us. Moreover while we should make conditions, they won't. Can you imagine poor Lepidus making conditions stick? Now if I can guess this—so can Antony. Therefore the fruit that represents the alliance with Antony, which must—I agree of course—eventually come, is not ripe for plucking. We must have more to offer than we do now.'

I nodded gravely. Maecenas had delivered with persuasive perfection the speech we had rehearsed in the small hours of the previous night.

Agrippa stood up. 'Too many bloody words,' he said. 'Too much damned subtlety from the lot of you. Look at the boys out there. I may not know much about fine bloody politics, but I know them. They'll have your guts for garters if you follow Philippus' course. That's sure to begin with. And it'll bloody well serve you right. As for Antony, let's twist his tail a bit tighter first...'

★ ★ ★

We marched on Rome. I stayed with the army, though I sent

Maecenas and Marcellus posting ahead. Naturally I was tempted to go with them, for there was work to be done, there were arms to be twisted and ears to be soothed with honey; but I had listened to the undercurrent of Agrippa's words. I stayed therefore with the legions as we swung down the great road to Rome, through olive groves and vineyards, past grazing cattle and flocks of sheep, by heavy-flanked oxen bearing sweet-smelling hay on lumbering wains. There was a surge and exhilaration to that march. Italy's maidens emerged from doorways to deck us with roses. The elders of each community presented me with an address. It held us up dreadfully, to Agrippa's irritation, but I told him to open his eyes: Italy, I said, was acclaiming us, pledging her loyalty, acknowledging that we alone could restore peace and fruitfulness to the land. 'The moral effect of the reports of our reception which the Senate will receive compensates for any delay; besides,' I said, 'it boosts the morale of our troops. Soldiers, good ones anyway, like to be loved; it's only the degenerates who are pleased to inspire fear.'

Then I sent Agrippa on ahead. 'There are three legions,' I said, 'two from Africa blocking the Flaminian Way. We do not want a battle. To fight within earshot of the walls of Rome would change everything. I would arrive as a conqueror to a scene of terror.'

Agrippa galloped into the dawn. Two days later a messenger returned. Agrippa would meet me at the cross-roads ten miles north of Tivoli. I was to bring only a handful as escort. Philippus, twittering into my tent with another letter in his hand, picked up Agrippa's. I suppose he turned pale. At any rate when he spoke he twittered worse. I was being tricked, he said; Agrippa had defected; he had been bribed; how could I have thought it safe to trust a man of neither birth nor breeding; I was going to walk into a trap; much more in the same womanish vein. (No, that is unjust, my sons; one should not talk so of women; Livia has never given me weak advice in our many years of marriage.)

I said to Philippus: 'Stepfather, I understand of course that you are afraid of my mother, and that you have promised her to see that no harm will come to me, and I realize also that as an old Pompeian you are a snob who doesn't understand democratic politics; but have you no nose that functions? Can't you feel the direction of the wind? I don't ask you to share my opinion of Agrippa, which is (by the way) that he is the most trustworthy man I know, but I do ask you to realize that he is a chap of some intelligence, even if his vowel-sounds are long and provincial. So, even if I agreed with you concerning his character, I would still tell you your fears were groundless. I mean, have you ever heard of a rat leaving a ship in full sail? What's that you have in your hand now?'

'This? Oh this is another worry, which may destroy that complacency you now show. Listen to what my correspondent tells me. Cicero has been in touch with Lepidus. He has offered him the dictatorship. What do you say to that?'

'How generous of him to offer what he has no means of delivering.'

★ ★ ★

I took Maco and half a dozen men and we rode into the sun. We rode some two hours and saw no soldiers, nothing but quiet villages and farmers working in their fields. Then Maco touched my sleeve: 'There's a glint of metal in that oak grove there. Shall I ride on to check?'

'No,' I said, 'it will be Agrippa.'

'Can't be sure.'

'It will be Agrippa. Have no fear, Maco. I'm not being rash, you know. There's no chance in the business to-day. The dice have fallen. All we have to do is pick up our winnings.'

(How much of this, you ask, was acting? How much conviction? Such a question would have been almost meaningless even then. I had to behave as I did. My men must know that I never questioned my destiny; nor, on this occasion, did I. I don't say that it was always so, for I have known nights of doubt when the blankets seem to shroud me, as I am denied restoring sleep; nights when I felt that the Gods had abandoned me and when I walked in empty wind-swept passages. But on this occasion I had all the certainty of the great artist who finds a long-projected and much brooded-on work slowly assuming the perfect, hardly-understood, shape before his eyes; a moment of magic, as Virgil once described it to me, 'When everything you have ever known or dreamed assumes an unknown and undreamed-of reality and rightness.' So it was with me in those August days.)

Agrippa was drinking wine and eating pecorino cheese and apples in the midst of some dozen men. They had tied their horses under the oak trees, in the shade. 'You see,' I had said to Maco as we drew near, 'no sentries even. That's a measure of our victory, our self-confidence and relaxation.' 'Nevertheless', he said, and proceeded straightaway to do what Agrippa had thought unnecessary. That 'nevertheless' was why Maco was such a fine sergeant-major—he never took things at face value; and why he stayed a sergeant-major—there are times when face value is true value.

'Well?' I said.

'Well. Have you eaten?'

'No, I don't think so.'

'Well, you bloody should. I've told you that often. You'll wear yourself out, shrimp, if you don't eat. You'll get ulcers. Told you that too bloody often, you don't bloody listen, do you? You feed your horse, don't you? Wouldn't let him go without food, eh? Well, then, don't be such a bloody fool. This is good cheese. Here, you!' he called, 'Bring the general bread and cheese and wine. Look sharp about it.'

'All right, all right,' I said, 'you don't need to go on. I've nothing against food, you know.'

'I should hope not. It's only the bloody rich can afford to despise food.'

'Well, I'm rich,' I said. 'Bloody rich, if you like. So what's the news?'

Agrippa began to laugh.

'All right,' I said, 'I concede. You've forced me to ask this time.'

I picked up a piece of bread. 'Look,' I said, 'I'm eating. So what's the news?'

'They'll all desert, bar a few of the stuffier officers. But on one condition. You yourself must advance to them, ahead of your army, with no bigger escort than you have here. They want to make it seem spontaneous, not as if they've been coerced.'

He paused, gave me a crooked smile. 'Do you buy that?' he said.

'Why not? It's not that proposal I'm buying, it's your judgement. And I bought that a long time ago, and see no reason to go back on the deal. You obviously think it's fine, or you wouldn't be eating this bread—which is on the stale side by the way, and the wine's sour—sitting here on your backside. You would have been posting back to camp, fairly sharply I should say.'

'Too bloody right I would,' he said. 'It's OK, they're yours. There are no hostile troops between here and Rome.'

★ ★ ★

It was very hot the next few days. Agrippa drank great draughts of beer and sweated it out almost as fast as he engulfed them. As for me I contented myself with sucking at lemons and pomegranates and sipping white wine in which a block of snow brought down by mule train from the high Apennines had been allowed to dissolve. We were lucky, they said, to get snow to cool our wine so late in the year.

There was a constant coming and going of secretaries. Letters were flooding in from the municipalities, from the priestly colleges, from individual senators, from the trade guilds and the equestrian corporations. 'If we'd realized you were this loved, my dear, we wouldn't have delayed all these dreary months,' Maecenas said. 'I can't wait to be in the city. To visit the baths and the theatre. I've heard there's a sensational new dancer from Spain, a real yum-yum, only sixteen and not an ounce of puppy fat, hard as a camp-bed (to coin a phrase). Give me another glass of that muck, ducky, I can hardly wait...'

'What the hell are we waiting for anyway?' Agrippa said.

'Things must be done properly,' Marcellus said. 'We are not entering the city as conquerors. We must arrange the right sort of reception. It takes time.'

I experienced a curious peace as I listened to them, a peace such as I had indeed not known before. It was as if we had rolled the whole last year of struggle into one ball, which was now hanging on the lip of the hole as in a game of marbles. For the moment there was no need of decision, no further struggle. I have known the same feeling since; it comes when

51

the flood of events has taken direction of one's life out of one's hands. No doubt despair can affect one similarly. I have never known despair.

Now all I said was: 'Besides I must first go to see that all is well with my mother and sister.'

★　★　★

Octavia was confused.

'You look the same,' she said, 'when I look at you properly, but I would hardly have recognized you. Why haven't you brought Marcellus?'

'Staff duties,' I said.

'Pig.'

'Besides,' I said, 'if you think I've changed, well, it seems to me that marriage has changed you. I don't really feel you are my sister when I see you playing his wife. That's really why I found him staff duties to-day, I'm jealous. How's Mother?'

'Preparing the banquet.'

'You should have stopped her. I can't eat banquet food. You know that. Anyway I haven't time.'

'Just you try stopping her. How's our stepfather?'

'Prosy, apprehensive and a damned bore. This time to-morrow I'll be consul. You know that, don't you? But he's still afraid we'll get our throats cut. It's incredible. Still, he's been very useful, that's got to be said.'

'Him useful? I make a rude gesture to that.'

'It's true, sis. You see he's invaluable in council. Nobody wants to be associated with him, so I've only to invite him to speak first, which I invariably do of course out of my respect for our relationship and his grey hairs...'

'And his fat belly.'

'Yes of course, and his fat belly—how could I forget the famous belly—well, I've only to do that to make quite certain that everyone else proposes more or less what I want, since that's bound to be the exact opposite of what old Flutter-fingers has advocated. Oh yes, I'll be able to tell Mamma her man has been invaluable.'

'She won't care, she'll know you're mocking him and pulling her leg, but she won't care. She's really proud, you know.

She keeps saying you've proved you're a true Julian.'

I looked out into the summer sky where a hawk hovered, then dropped sheer on its prey.

'No,' I said, 'she's wrong there. I shall never be a real Julian.'

I couldn't avoid the banquet, though I managed to excuse myself from eating the lake fish on the grounds that it would make me bilious in the hot weather. Before I left my mother said to me: 'Remember, Brutus and Cassius live.'

*   *   *

Cicero met me at the gates of the city. There had come first a crowd of senators few of whom I knew even by sight. Most of them tried to smile; sullenness and fear showed through however. I used Philippus and Marcellus to mingle among them. 'Be affable,' I said. I plucked Salvidienus by the sleeve. 'There are some of your family here, aren't there?' 'My two brothers'; he flushed as if my question indicated distrust of his absolute loyalty. 'Do pray introduce me,' I said. He complied with an ill grace, and his brothers looked sheepish as men do who have backed the defeated side. I urged them to regard me as their friend, but I could see they were enviously counting the years between us.

A hush fell on the assembly, broken only by a high-pitched giggle—Maecenas of course. I looked round for explanation. An ornate purple-canopied litter was emerging from the shadow of a narrow street into the full sun of the piazza. It was carried by half a dozen slaves, mountaineers from Anatolia by the look of them. It halted before the dais on which I was standing. The curtains were withdrawn to reveal Cicero.

I have been much criticized—both at the time and later—for what happened next. I can only say it seemed the most natural thing in the world to me. I leapt from the dais and advanced towards the litter. For a moment I thought the old man was going to lie there, even extend his hand to me as if I had been a client or supplicant. I am sure the thought crossed his mind. He must however have calculated that the satisfaction to be obtained from such a gesture would be no more than momentary, for, with a visible effort and an arthritic groan he stuck out his scrawny neck, heaved his legs round, and disembarked from the litter. I resumed my advance and embraced him (he smelled of old yellow papyrus) with the words: 'Ah, the last of all my friends.' I am not ashamed of the words, which were well and deliberately chosen. If he had been more prominent and constant in friendship, this point would never have been reached. All the same, as I spoke, I felt him stiffen. He kissed my cheek, and held me a moment in a grip like a vulture's talons.

* * *

The next day I was elected consul. I chose as my colleague an obscure cousin, Quintus Pedius, recommended by my mother as a man who would hinder me in nothing. (Unfortunately she exaggerated his amiability; he was a damned nuisance.) I paused in the act of taking the auspices for the first time, and directed my gaze to the heavens. Naturally the crowd did the same, and there was a moment of awed silence before they broke out in loud huzzas at the sight of a dozen vultures winging in the direction of the Janiculum. Of course I had known what to expect; Marcellus had reminded us that a similar flight had greeted Romulus when he first performed that ceremony, and Maecenas had undertaken to obtain the birds through his theatrical connections ('I don't suppose buzzards would do? So much cheaper'). But I was impressed by his staff-work which had seen to it that a sufficient number of the crowd were aware of the precedent. Such manipulation of the emotions of the public may seem cynical to you, and I can indeed hardly deny the imputation. Nevertheless there are times when such manipulation is necessary. It was poetically right that vultures should make an appearance to link me to Romulus, first Father of Our Country, but the workings of nature are inclined to be capricious. Besides, vultures are much rarer in Italy now than they were in his day—'I daresay they were common as crows then', as Maecenas said; it is permissible to give fate a nudge from time to time. I must tell you however that the occasional fabrication of omens in no way invalidates those that appear spontaneously. I was not of course impressed by the birds, but the crowd were. That was the great thing: they accepted the flight as confirmation of my authority. There was only one uncomfortable moment. A

54

pair of the birds suddenly lost height; for a ghastly moment it looked as if they were about to plummet into the Tiber. I held my breath, wondering if we had been too clever by half. However—and here is substantial evidence of how hard it is to disentangle the human from the divine—they recovered more abruptly than they had fallen, and were soon lost in the pine trees of Janiculum. The crowd had been silenced by the fall and Maecenas seized the chance to improve the situation: 'See how the Gods favour the consul,' he cried, 'if he stumbles Jupiter himself lifts him to safe triumph.' The crowd broke out in renewed cheers. Later he said to me: 'Bloody birds, I could have died, my dear. I'll have that bird-seller flayed. He swore to me he had given them all a good trial flight in the Campagna.' 'Oh,' I said, 'let him alone. Your intervention improved things, don't you think?'

The next day I had the court clear my adoption as Julius' heir. Henceforth I was Caesar: Gaius Julius Octavianus Caesar. This done, I paid my troops, which had taken the first steps to restore order and the rule of law in the Republic, their promised bounties, from the public treasury. I ordered the law which had granted an amnesty to Caesar's killers to be rescinded on the high moral grounds that the murder of the head of the Republic, perpetual dictator and pontifex maximus, could never be legally condoned. I set up a special court to outlaw the murderers who had styled themselves Liberators.

Two days later Cicero left Rome. He wrote to me asking permission. His health was poor, he explained; he required sea air. He thanked me—for what I was never certain. He asked forgiveness for the Past and indulgence for the Future. I replied that I had nothing to forgive, and that I would ever value his counsel as I had always valued it, that he stood where he had always stood in my esteem and gratitude, and that I hoped the sea air would correct his disorders. I never saw him again. He was the saddest of men, one who had seen greatness beckon and failed to grasp the God's proffered hand. He failed because he disdained the true source and nature of power, and thought cleverness a substitute for vision; in the end he had no faith in his own destiny.

III

Agrippa never knew a day's illness (till he died). In contrast, as he told it, I spent my youth sneezing and expectorating, coughing, wheezing like a pair of holed bellows, shivering with ague, sweating with fever, stricken by migraine, oppressed by bile, frequently unable to sit a horse or carry on a conversation that wasn't interrupted by nose-blowing, nose-bleeds or nausea. He exaggerated; he wasn't far wrong. I spent my first three weeks as consul and Caesar with a tortured throat, a runny nose, spots before the eyes and a high temperature. I was working eighteen hours a day. It is hard to concentrate when your shoulders are heavy with lassitude and your whole body trembles. But it was work I could not leave to my secretaries.

We advanced by slow stages north. Most of the march I had to be carried in a litter, and that experience taught me something about my relationship with the legions that I have never forgotten. Had I been Julius, or even Antony, they would have chanted ribald songs about my condition and mode of transport. As it was, they marched past the litter in respectful silence. I knew they trusted me, admired me even, were amused by what they regarded as my cunning — 'He's a smart bugger, our general,' they would say — but they did not love me. There was hardly a man except those I kept round my person at Headquarters who would die for me. The magnetism of my personality does not operate at any distance, as Julius' did. I mention this because success in great endeavours depends so much on a just appreciation of one's assets and defects. Neither of you, my dear boys, suffers in this way. But you have other peculiar problems and weaknesses; are you aware of them? 'Know thyself' is the wisest of philosophical advice.

Yet — there is always a 'yet', a 'nevertheless' — such self-knowledge can be inhibitory. The man who has never examined his own mind and spirit acts with a spontaneity denied me.

(On the other hand Maecenas used to say that I was able to deceive others because I had first deceived myself. I don't think he was right. I record his view merely as evidence of that diversity of interpretation that makes judgement of our fellows so difficult.)

We halted in a plain on the south bank of the Po. The men, grumbling, pitched camp in the discomfort of a thin rain driving down from the mountains. With night the wind dropped and the river mist seeped through the camp. I sat wrapped in furs and sipped hot wine, aromatic with nutmeg, and still shivered. A slave read Homer to me till I sent him away. All round me the cold bustle of the camp made my tent's silence more acute.

I called Maco to me. 'Are there lights across the river?'

'Too foggy to see, sir.'

'What's the men's mood?'

'Not good, sir. Puzzled like and apprehensive. They're afraid, that's what, sir, afraid of a battle, afraid of it all starting over again.'

'There will be no battle by my will.'

'Ah, sir, will ... many a battle starts by accident ... you should go to bed, sir, you really should ...'

'I can't sleep ...'

Waiting is always the worst. It was cockcrow when a cry came that a punt was edging across the river, and by then there were few voices in the camp, only the occasional challenge of a sentry or the cry of a man whose sleep was disturbed by fear. There came the swish of boots in the wet grass, the tent flap was thrown back and Agrippa and Marcellus came in.

'Lord,' said Agrippa, 'I'm tired, and I'll have a head tomorrow. It's all right though. The meeting's on. We held out for the island as the venue. The only point we gave way: he insists on Lepidus being there, wouldn't take no.'

'I see. He can control Lepidus, and the pair of them will always outvote me. Nevertheless, we accept. When is it fixed for?'

'The day after tomorrow. Well, that's tomorrow by this time. At breakfast. That was a facer for Antony, breakfast, but he rallied.'

57

'As for Lepidus,' Marcellus said, 'your interpretation's obviously right. But there's one other factor, Antony doesn't fancy being alone with you. You ought to think of that, brother-in-law.'

'Thanks,' I said, 'I already had. You have done well, both of you. Now we can sleep.'

* * *

I almost called the meeting off. I had after all been denied sleep and my fever was worse. The doctor gave me a draught of some herbal concoction, which brought on immediate nausea, but then to my surprise calmed my pulse and dulled my headache. I still felt weak as a sick kitten, as my old nurse used to describe it. 'A half-drowned weak rat' she would also call me.

At first light Maco presented himself at my tent to find me still in my dressing-gown. He urged me to eat some bread, but one of the slaves brought me a sort of gruel, thin corn porridge mixed with honey, and I found that sufficiently reviving to dress.

The punt was poled out by a couple of Gallic mountaineers who didn't seem to mind being half-naked in the raw morning. In midstream it was still thick mist and the bow had almost touched the bank of the island before I was aware of land. Maco and the half-dozen guards we had agreed should make up the escort disembarked first. I followed with Agrippa, Maecenas, Marcellus and Rufus; we had left Philippus behind. My stepfather had served his purpose. There was no place for him in a conference of the leaders of Caesar's party.

Antony had not yet arrived—'such a surprise' sighed Maecenas—but Lepidus was already waiting in the tent that would serve as reception centre and ante-chamber to the smaller one where we three principals would bargain. I had never met Lepidus before, as it happens, but I recognized him easily. He was quite remarkably handsome, with smooth utterly regular features and dark hair hardly touched with grey, that curled on his temples as if arranged for a sculptor to copy. He greeted us with ceremonious affability.

'So this,' he said to Marcellus whom he knew well, 'is the wondrous boy who has surprised us all.'

His voice was light, trilling and ingratiating; I disliked it intensely, and not merely for its note of patronage. I recalled that Cicero had described him to me as the most sordid and base of fellows: 'He takes hold of your elbow and mutters dishonourable filth in your ear.' I could well believe it and was glad to observe that the blandness he strove to display incompletely marked a lack of true ease. He couldn't stop talking and his hands fluttered from man to man, a press here, a squeeze there, a light deprecating touch on the next shoulder.

'We can't expect our great Antony on time, that's for sure,' he said. 'I wonder whom he tumbled last night . . . not Fulvia, that's for sure . . . though he's scared stiff of her, I have that on the very best authority . . . and how did you leave Rome, my dear Caesar . . . do you know it's over two years since I saw the city . . . I pine for it, that's for sure . . . but I'll tell you something, old boy,' he leaned over me, disgorging an unattractive scent of musk, 'not half as much as Markie Brutus must. You see, old boy, I know I'll feast on the Palatine again. He must be beginning to fear he never will, and serve him right, the poor sod.'

Yes, you see, my sons, he was a horrible man, and I am ashamed to have associated with him for so many years.

I was on edge myself, wondering, as I had during the night, how Antony would greet me. Would he be embarrassed (as I was) by certain memories of Spain and by the insults we had traded for the last year? He had of course shown no sign of embarrassment in Rome? still it was different now. Would he resume the elder-brother tone he had first adopted when I joined Caesar's staff? Would he aim at being cold and statesmanlike?

He arrived in a swirl of purple and no apologies for his lateness. He embraced Lepidus and turned to me: 'You look ill,' he said, 'and not the pretty boy I knew in Spain. Well, we've put the last year's nonsense behind us and we'll soon put the roses back in your cheeks. You've done remarkably . . . I hadn't thought you had it in you.'

He was intending to throw me off balance. I smiled and

59

acceded to his proposal that we should cut the preliminaries short and get down to business. There was, as I said, a small tent set aside for the three of us. We would converse first in private and then summon slaves to whom we would dictate a statement. Though an agenda had been prepared by our aides, both Antony and I had been firm that the negotiations should be restricted to the three principals, and be kept as informal as possible. My ready agreement to this had surprised him.

So many versions of our island discussions have been given that the whole negotiation has been enveloped in a cloud of exaggeration, misrepresentation, party animus, private revenge and the sheer human tendency to prefer the more lurid of any two stories offered. I have never till now put on record what was said, and I never discussed the course of the conference with anyone but Livia, years later. Of course my friends and I analysed the decisions, particularly after the first day's talk, lest I should be committing myself to anything which might turn to my disadvantage. But that is all. Lepidus of course chattered. Antony later gave his version, or rather (for I wish to be fair) the intolerable Fulvia published an account which she claimed to be Antony's. In these versions I stand out as the one who was coldest and most implacable, most bent on revenge. This is patently absurd. I had no private revenge to seek. The law which I had had passed in Rome satisfied my legitimate desire that my father's murderers be punished. Otherwise no private impetus drove me. My political career had been too short to let me accumulate a host of scores to settle. Let me make that quite clear. In our decisions on that river island I was impersonal, driven only by that pure motive which I have called 'reason of state'.

By common consent Antony acted as chairman. (I am not afraid to confess that; it would have been presumptuous in me to have assumed the role.) He had a natural authority; for all his many faults of character I can no more deny that, than I can remember him without affection, despite his treachery, selfishness and untrustworthiness. And, when he bent his mind to business, he revealed a brilliant lucidity and mastery of the structure of politics and strategy of war. I would never wish to take that away from his memory.

He began by summing up the situation—a sparkling *tour*

d'horizon. He showed a generous appreciation of my own achievements. 'You made things tough for me, kid,' he said, 'and there were several moments when I thought your own rope-dance would end in disaster for you. But you brought it off—there's nothing after all that succeeds like success. So here you is—no longer Kid but Caesar, even if to me'—he got up and walked round the table and squeezed my shoulder—'you'll always be, in some part, just Kid. Still, it's quite something—no longer Kid but Caesar. Do you remember when they called out to Him, that he was planning to make himself King, and he snapped back, "My name ain't King, it's Caesar"?'

I thought to myself: before I have finished Caesar will be more than a name. An odd discordant thought: perhaps it will be more than King?

'Anyway,' he said, 'to sum up: the West is ours. I don't say there's no disaffection left, especially in Italy, but it's at a level that we can control. The high-minded skunks are on the run. They're our next problem . . .'

'Pompey?' I suggested.

'Pompey can wait. It's what Pompeys are good at doing, the indecisive so-and-sos. Our job is to clean up Marcus Brutus.'

'My information is,' Lepidus stuck in, 'that Brutus and Cassius have raised more than forty legions and plan to land at Brindisi in the spring.'

'They won't,' Antony said.

'If they ally themselves to Pompey, they would have a fleet.'

'They won't move that fast. They're a committee.'

'They moved quite quickly on the Ides of March,' I said.

'Murder's a short sprint,' Antony said. 'You need staying power for war.'

He leaned back; his face had become deeply lined in the last year, and that made it look stronger. He had lost the playboy look. The big mouth turned down at the corners now, and his eyes were a little bloodshot. He had been through it; I felt a shaft of affection. His deep voice warmed the room.

'You've just come from the city, kid,' he said, giving a mighty and possibly calculated stretch and yawn. 'What's the state of the Treasury?'

61

'I paid my troops out of it,' I said, and looked him in the eye. 'As consul,' I said; his eye did not drop, but wavered towards Lepidus.

'Perfectly correct,' that worthy yelped. He had been left out and was fidgeting to intervene. 'Perfectly correct ... I wonder if you would sanction a payment to...'

Antony interrupted: 'Nobody, kid, questions your correctness. I wasn't either trying to needle you. Look, by my calculations—supplied in part, I don't mind telling you, by my agents in your camps—don't look like a grey gander, Lepidus, if you don't have any agents in my camp, you bloody well should have—Caesar here has squads of 'em, don't you, kid?—so, as I was saying before being interrupted by our chum here having the dry heaves—talking of which, it's a hell of a long time between drinks, as one proconsul said to the other—Lepidus, before I resume, would you mind tinkling that dong so that we can get ourselves a snifter? Ah boy, a flask of white for the generals.'

He paused. Lepidus puffed and blew and wheezed and drummed his fingers, till the boy returned with the wine.

'Just pour it out, will you, and then be off with you, and don't try listening. It's deep politics we're talking, way beyond you, child. Right, where was we? Yup. I reckon we have forty-three legions between us. I suppose yours like mine are a bit under-strength, so let's say a total force of about 200,000 men. Well, those boys may love us, but they'll want pay too. So again I ask, how's the Treasury, kid?'

'It won't support that force for more than a few months. What's more,' I said, 'we'll get no tax revenues from Asia while our enemies hold Greece and the seas...'

'That Egyptian bint of Himself's ain't going to disgorge either. I'd a note from her the other day, saying, much as she would like to fulfil her obligations, blah-bloody-blah, she couldn't entrust tax money to the sea while Pompey held it. A bloody good excuse of course. Did you ever meet her, kid?'

'Only just.'

'Himself was crazy about her. Usually it was the other way round, but he was silly on her. The boys thought she'd bewitched him. Maybe she had. I wouldn't say it was beyond the bint. He nearly got our throats cut in Alexandria while she teased his cock.'

These were precisely Antony's words the first time I heard him speak of Cleopatra. Like all my father's friends he had deplored and feared the influence she might exercise over him.

'So,' he said, 'money's going to be a bit of a problem. Like I say, my boys dote on me, but they won't fight for love.'

He was fishing for an answer I was loth to provide. Let him supply it himself, I thought, and then felt ashamed. I had after all to be ready to take responsibility for the actions that were going to be forced on us.

'Others have been in the same case,' I said.

'Such as who?'

'Sulla for instance.'

The name fell into the conversation like a stone thrown into a pool. I knew it would have that effect. Since I have hitherto advised your tutors that your historical studies should be confined principally to the heroic age of Republican virtue, you may not know why Sulla was so disturbing a name.

L. Cornelius Sulla, a man of most respectable family, was yet the first Roman to seize the city by force of arms. He did so, I hasten to add, with the laudable intention of freeing it from the tyrannical chaos that had been imposed on it by Cinna and the Popular Party. Having occupied Rome, he had the Senate name him dictator. Though not short of money, for he had just returned from an Asiatic war, he proceeded to confiscate the property of his opponents, some of whom were put to death. He did this partly to discourage the others from holding on to what they had imagined to be their rightful possessions. Sulla even went to the length of having lists of those whom he had decided to proscribe posted in the Forum. This made it easier for men to acquire merit by aiding the dictator. Not surprisingly many families hold the name of Sulla in especial horror. As a matter of fact my own family was among such. Indeed Julius himself found his name on the death list. The dictator was only persuaded, very reluctantly, to remove the name and spare the boy, by the intercession of one of our aunts. It is rum to think that had she failed I should probably have passed my life as a small-town banker.

Nevertheless I am not ashamed to admit that I introduced Sulla's name to our conference. It had to be done.

Antony's smile rewarded me. Lepidus of course twittered. True, his father, also M. Aemilius Lepidus, had opposed Sulla; he should however have been man enough to know that there is no point in maintaining feuds beyond the grave. Sulla's memory was a thing of value.

Antony said, 'Julius always swore he would never imitate Sulla, that Sulla's conduct had been hated and deplored by everybody, and that in a civil war clemency to the defeated was essential.'

'And the words do him credit,' Lepidus chirped—really, the discrepancy between appearance and voice was remarkable and disturbing—'I remember him saying that often. We shouldn't forget, now, should we?'

Antony looked at me: 'Well, kid?'

I said: 'Sulla died in his bed. You yourself picked up Caesar's bloody toga.'

Antony shouted for a member of his staff.

'I've got a list,' he said, 'a list of the thirty richest senators and the hundred and fifty wealthiest equestrians who have declared friendship for Brutus. Fetch that list.'

'We do not wish to campaign in Italy,' I said. 'We cannot risk leaving disaffection behind.'

'We understand each other, kid,' Antony said.

I hope this makes it clear that I accept my full responsibility for the proscriptions; reason of state made them imperative. Duty can be a harsh task-mistress.

*   *   *

The second day we started naming names.

*   *   *

We were delayed first by a procedural point raised by Lepidus. I don't know which of his advisers had put him up to it. Some of them were quite clever.

'One thing worries me,' he said. 'It is unclear in what capacity we are proposing to act. Of course our dear Octavian is consul, but only till the end of the year—another couple of months. We both have proconsular commands, but they give us no imperium outside our provinces. And that is all. Is it enough to let us act with authority?'

'We have more than forty legions,' Antony said. 'Only an old woman would seek further authority.'

I could not agree. The legions gave power, not authority. There was meat in Lepidus' argument. It is frequently necessary in politics to depart from the book, but it is rash to seem contemptuous of formalities, precedent and legality.

'Unfortunately,' I said, 'Antony has abolished the office of dictator. Otherwise I would suggest he took that title, like my father and Sulla.'

'You would?' Antony said. 'I believe you, sure. Thousands wouldn't.' A smile broke through his mask of settled scepticism such as I have seen slide over the faces of practical men as they listened to philosophers debate.

'But of course,' I said.

'Formalities!' Antony said. 'I'm old enough to remember how Himself and Pompey and that great eunuch Marcus Crassus carved up the State at Lucca. Is that not precedent enough?'

'But that was condemned by all good men as sheer gangsterism.'

'Sure it was! So what?'

'A moment,' I said. 'I think it provides us with a model but one that we should refine further. Let us indeed institute a triumvirate, a Second Triumvirate, but let us do so by legal process. Let us get a tribune to introduce a law in the Assembly empowering the three of us, for a period of, say, five years, to order the Republic. He can spout a lot of high-minded stuff to let people vote with a good conscience for what they may not like but yet see is necessary. Such a law would grant us full imperium; it would mean that the legality of our measures could not be subsequently questioned, and it would let us control all elections; we could simply nominate sole candidates, for years in advance. Wouldn't some such scheme serve?'

(I knew it would. Marcellus, Maecenas and myself had hammered it out over beer and sandwiches the night before. Maecenas had then had himself ferried across to Antony's

65

camp to discuss it with Antony's chief of staff Asinius Pollio. I was therefore hardly risking much in making this proposal, even though it seemed that Pollo had had no time to brief his general, or perhaps had not found him in briefable condition.)

Before Antony could reply, I added, 'Though it may prove at some time expedient for one of us to hold a consulship during the period of our ... rule, I don't think it's a good idea that one of us should do so at the start. I therefore propose to resign my consulship as soon as we have ratified our agreement.'

It was later put about that Antony had compelled me to give up my office; I am happy to take this opportunity of denying that and giving the true account.

My proposal lightened the atmosphere. We all now felt comfortably ensconced in legality, for we had of course no doubt that such a measure would be put through the Assembly. So we were able to turn our attention to those whom we were about to proscribe.

At first it was easy. Our several staffs had provided us with lists of those senators known to be inclined towards the 'liberators' and of similarly disaffected (and rich) equestrians. Many names were to be found on all three lists. We pricked them with equanimity. These were men who had chosen their side and knew what they risked losing. Our humanity was not affected, for most of them had already fled Italy, many more would do so on learning of their inclusion in our list. We were after their property; few had such personal significance as to make their deaths desirable.

Yet, as the listing continued, distrust and rivalry entered our hearts. We were each putting ourselves in a position in which we would appear to ill advantage; our proscriptions would arouse hatred as well as fear. Each death would breed vendetta. It was expedient therefore that all should be seen to be equally involved.

Antony drank more and more wine as the debate continued. I despised him for that. It was my first reminder of that weakness of character which would in time destroy him; he shrank from the reality of his actions, and grew boisterous and over-stretched.

'Lepidus,' he cried, 'your brother Paullus must go.'

'Paullus! My brother?'

'Look at his wealth, look at his record! Himself spared him. Himself bought him, didn't he. Did he get the support he paid for? Prick him down, kid.'

'You consent, Lepidus?'

He shrugged his shoulders, 'I have done what I can. Very well. On condition Antony sacrifices his mother's brother, L. Julius Caesar. He's a connection of both of you, and a Pompeian. You must be joined equally in blood guilt with me.'

Antony hid his mouth in his wine-glass. The man was old, blameless (I believed); he had opposed Cicero's demand that the Senate name Antony a public enemy. The glass was lowered.

'Very well. He has not long to live in any case. And he has, as you say, a history as an undeviating Republican. Prick him down ... to sacrifice a Julian and a Caesar ...' he broke off and took a swig from his wine.

'Will convince any doubters,' I said, 'that we have bound ourselves to the wheel. From proscriptions there can be no retreat.'

'Atticus,' Lepidus said, with a snake-flick of his tongue. 'No one will spill more gold than that fat banker.'

He was warming to his work. I learned then that a weak man's thirst for blood is fiercer than a strong man's. In drawing up this list Lepidus was repaying the world for his own sense that he was less than his name.

Antony gave me no lead. He had recently received conspicuous kindness from Atticus, acts which had been reprobated by the Senate's grandees. Now he was silent. His generosity of spirit stopped short of paying debts. I made a note of that, and myself said:

'There are many reasons for including Atticus on the list as our colleague suggests. His wealth for a start; the protection he has extended to Brutus' mother; the effect such a pricking would have on others. Yet I think we should consider the matter more closely. We may be about to embark on a long war. It is not only Brutus and Cassius whom we must confront. There's Sextus Pompey too. Who knows how many years it may take us? Now, proscriptions on this scale cannot be repeated. They must be regarded as a once-for-all capital levy. But when we have exhausted its proceeds, we shall still need money, often in a hurry. Who knows how to raise funds or advance credit better than Atticus or his fellow banker Balbus? They are men we shall need in the future. The wise course now is to bind them to us by manifest obligation. Therefore I move we omit their names from our list. We shall get more in the long run that way . . .'

I pitched my argument low, to convince Lepidus. All the same his lips pushed forward in a discontented pout; he felt disregard again envelope him like a bad smell.

Antony, shifting his pen, muttered: 'I agree. Carried, two to one. Atticus lives.'

'And Balbus.'

'Oh yes, Balbus too.'

The lamp went out. We sat in a thin twilight and felt cold. I drew my sheepskins round me, and still shivered. The brazier which alone heated the tent was low.

Antony spoke. We had waited for his words: 'Cicero must die.'

Neither responded.

'His attacks on me have been past, past anything. Himself spared him—oh, old Cicero is an ornament of our culture, he said—and less than a month after his murder, that ornamental mouth spouted forth: "Is there anyone except Antony and those who were glad to have Caesar reign over us, who did not wish for his death, or who disapproved of what was done? All were responsible, for all good men joined in killing Caesar. Some were ignorant of the plot, some lacked courage, some opportunity. None lacked the will." Those were his very words, they are engraved in my memory. Some ornament, some culture. These words alone should be enough to condemn this most insidious of our enemies. We have the opportunity; surely we do not lack the will?'

Antony's hands trembled on the table. I thought of the old man flattering me, digging his teeth into a fig, interrupting his declamation of his speech against Catiline to heed a call of nature and then resuming it at the exact point at which he had broken off; I felt his old crooked arthritic hands press against my shoulder.

I said, 'As you wish it, Antony.'

He turned a face, moonlike with wonder, on me. Lepidus emitted a little hiss of excitement. I repeated:

'As you wish it, Antony. "The boy," I quoted, "must be flattered, decorated, and got rid of." Cicero has had flattery enough for a lifetime; he will receive honour from generations that have forgotten us. Let that be sufficient epitaph. Let him depart.'

I do not propose to defend my decision now in other words than I employed then. That evening Marcellus urged me to send a messenger to warn the old man of the fate decreed. I replied that the publication of the proscription lists would give him ample warning. As all the world knows, he delayed to act, moved either by vanity or indecision. The manner of his death, which did credit to his virtue, is too well known to repeat here.

IV

Cassius died at Philippi, in the first battle, falling on his sword in imitation of Cato. Brutus, three days later, fled to the mountains; he hesitated to kill himself and besought the freedman who was his last companion to perform the work. These battles were Antony's triumph, not mine. My health was poor throughout the campaign, but that was not the only reason. Civil war is a horrible business; I could never forget that the legions which opposed us were themselves made up of our countrymen. Yet, after the battle, when the defeated were led before us, they hailed Antony as 'imperator'; they reviled me. I stood on the dais, sick at heart and in my belly, while they cursed. The body of Brutus had been brought down from the high mountains to the forum; in an actor's gesture Antony covered it with his own purple cloak. Stony-faced, I accepted the verdict of the defeated; it recognized that it had been my determination to avenge my father which had created the army that destroyed them.

That night Antony grew maudlin. He spoke lovingly of

Brutus, of their friendship in youth. 'He was the noblest of us,' he said over and over again. 'The others envied Caesar. He alone acted out of true public spirit, honest and true to his conception of the Republic. He had principles; he died for them. Whatever else you say of him, he was a Man.'

I kept my argument to myself, and spoke soothingly. Antony was sunk in the guilt of victory. I did not then recognize it as such. It took his own death more than ten years later to let me feel it; a battle won in a civil war can be crueller and more bitter than a battle lost. Right can never be concentrated altogether on one side. The dead bodies of citizens reproach the living. Pray, my sons, you never have such experiences.

I am glad I soothed him. Yet my true feelings were quite other. I had no tender memories of Brutus. For me he was a dishonest rhetorician. I saw the man Caesar had spared and honoured with his love, who had then drawn the dagger against him. Is there anything in literature or history more terrible than that moment in my father's agony when he looked on the face of Brutus among his assassins, and clearly said: 'You too, my son?'; then covered his face and abandoned all resistance? Only a man of the most abnormal self-conceit could live with such a memory; Brutus managed to do so. He was inflated, like the frog in Æsop, with self-importance; carried through treachery, dishonesty and crime by his consciousness of his own virtue. I am glad I had his head sent back to Rome to be thrown at the feet of Caesar's statue.

Brutus' self-righteousness was shared by his colleagues: one of the other murderers, Quintus Ligarius, had the insolence to look me in the eye, and demand that he be given honourable burial. 'That is a matter for the carrion-crows and vultures,' I replied. My flash of temper was unworthy; I hope you do not think it uncalled for. On the other hand the story that I told a father and son who pleaded that one at least should be spared, that they should themselves decide which by casting lots or throwing dice, is a calumny. (You will note that when this story is related, no names are mentioned; always distrust the anecdote with anonymous subjects.) It was this rumour however which caused Marcus Pavenius to abuse me with filthy epithets which I recall with horror even now. To receive such insults from a man who is about to die is like the touch of an icy finger; what reports will he carry to the Immortals?

Antony and I had come close together after our meeting on the island. It was like our first days in Spain again, before shadows fell between us. I warmed to his Sun, to his spontaneous affection. Antony had a great need to be loved; this made him lovable wherever he let his radiance light. So I had been happy to seal our bond by agreeing to marry his stepdaughter Claudia; the pleasure this gave Antony and the legions over-rode my natural distaste for any connection with the girl's mother Fulvia. But now, after Philippi, I sensed that Antony, ever a ready victim of rumour (as gossips generally are) was drawing away from me. My inability fully to share his boozy sentimentality about Brutus distressed him; he was perturbed by what he saw as my coldness of heart. Almost overnight he stopped calling me 'kid', and it was only once or twice in later years that he resumed the habit. He was still able for a long time to be affectionate at a distance, his letters to me were lively and loving, but my presence froze him; it was as if the carrion-crows and vultures settled on the table between us.

★　★　★

I sailed back to Italy, sea-sick as usual, to arrange for the demobilization of 100,000 men. Antony meanwhile turned to the rising sun to undertake my father's long-meditated war against the Parthian Empire. Agrippa grumbled all the way back across the Adriatic that Antony had pinched the glory and left us the dross; but then, Agrippa, unlike me, was a soldier at heart, even though I knew that his true genius lay in administration. (But that, let me remind you, dear boys, is the necessary foundation of all military success; that general triumphs best who best organizes supply. Look at the history of Alexander's campaigns for proof of this adage.)

'Besides,' I told Agrippa, 'Antony is moving to the frontier, where anything can happen. Think of Crassus.' (The fat booby Marcus Crassus allowed his army to be surrounded in the desert sands. That was the end of Crassus. They threw his head before the Parthian king as he sat watching some Greek tragedy. According to some versions of the story, it was actually carried on to the stage.)

'We, on the other hand,' I said, 'are given the chance of establishing ourselves at the seat of power.'

'Oh sure,' Agrippa said, 'you mean we're going to get our throats cut, left and right. We'll never get enough land, or good enough land, to satisfy the veterans; yet every municipality and every landowner we dispossess will be an enemy for life.'

'We shall pay whenever possible.'

'Sure again. The campaign's emptied the Treasury. And don't think we'll get any help from Fulvia or Antony's brother Lucius, who is—let me remind you—booked in as next year's consul.'

I needed no such reminder, for I saw trouble there. Nevertheless I persevered in my appointed task. Most of the business of government is a matter of long hours and assiduous attention to detail; its only satisfaction is the consciousness of work well done. That has been the main part of my life. There is hardly any story in it; yet, without such work, without such scrupulous devotion to the minutiae of administration and justice, this great Empire of Rome would crumble. I am not sure that you realize this; your mother's husband, my stepson Tiberius, for all his faults of character and ungracious demeanour, appreciates it as I do, and as your natural father Agrippa did. You could do worse than look to Tiberius as a model.

Very occasionally the drudgery of administration is lightened by the chance to perform some conspicuous benevolence. One such opportunity was given me this arduous year. Maecenas called one morning with a petition. There was—to cut through what I used to call his 'myrrh-distilling ringlets of speech'—a young protégé of his, a poet called Virgil, of whom I certainly would not have heard, whose family farm, near Mantua, was on the list of those to be confiscated. Wouldn't I, to oblige Maecenas, stretch a point and reprieve the farm to which the young poet was devoted? Now such agricultural enthusiasm was not typical of Maecenas' protégés, and my curiosity was aroused. 'Is he a good poet?' I asked. 'I doubt if there is a more promising one in Italy,' Maecenas said, surprising me with the unaffected simplicity of his language. 'Very well,' I said, 'a reprieve will be granted, providing you promise to introduce the poet to me.'

*　*　*

There was nothing poetical about the young man who was ushered in; I already knew enough about poets to find that pleasing and impressive. He was slim, dark-haired, with a tender mouth and blue-grey eyes. Though he was only a few years older than I, the dark hair was already streaked with touches of grey around the temples; long hours of study had grooved his forehead and drawn lines down to the corners of his mouth. When he spoke he did so without hesitation, but slowly, with broad vowels and a heavily rolled r. His speech had no affectation, though the soft voice had something of the Gallic lilt in it. He first thanked me for granting him an audience. I told him how highly Maecenas spoke of his poetry and he answered that he was too kind; 'I have accomplished little yet.'

I brought the matter quickly to the point, for I already divined that for me the occasion of our meeting was no more than excuse. I cannot say what made me sense his quality so quickly; only that from the first instance I discerned in Virgil an authority such as I have known in no other man. It was not the authority that emanates from one accustomed to command; naturally my father had such authority; men jumped to do his bidding; they would die at his word. I knew such authority; I possessed it myself. Virgil's was quite different; his authority derived from the mastery of secret truths, from his penetration to the innermost heart of things. I have never subscribed to Plato's philosophy. It seems a wild, indeed poetical, exaggeration to interpret this world as a mere shadow of reality. The theory of Forms flies in the face of that knowledge we acquire from experience; to deny the reality of the material world is mere word-spinning. And yet, note, my sons, that I talk only of an 'exaggeration' not an absurdity. Though I have been initiated into the Eleusian Mysteries, I am too much a practical man (as I have had to be) to fancy myself a mystic, or indeed to give much credence to any of

73

the innumerable mysteries and mysticisms which have clamoured for my attention. Nevertheless I cannot rest content with the material world; it is indeed, metaphorically, the shadow of a deeper truth; perhaps, to get away from the Platonic language, I should say it is to the real truth as our skin is to our hearts. (Heaven knows, skin is real enough, quick enough, delightful enough; and yet...) There is, lost in the mists of unconsciousness, something we must call 'soul'; and there is a soul in things as well as in men. Our fathers recognized this when they honoured the spirits of groves and streams and laid out offerings to tutelary deities. Such truths are easily obscured by the bustle of existence and the inevitable cynicism engendered by public life; Virgil brought them to my attention. All his work, of which I am proud to have been patron, speaks with a murmurous authority of subliminal joys and sorrows.

That day we quickly concluded the business on which he had come. He asked that not only his family farm but all the lands pertaining to Mantua should be reprieved from confiscation; Mantua, he said, is alas too near to poor Cremona, which had been selected by me as a town obstinately adhering to the defeated party and so ripe for spoliation. In Mantua, he said, there were only farmers, with no interest in politics. Would I not be so gracious as to exempt Mantua?

I immediately resolved that I would, but, first, in order to let him understand the value of my concession, I expatiated on the problems that faced me.

'My task,' I said, 'is to restore peace and order to a land that has known neither for almost a hundred years. In that time small farmers have been deprived of their holdings and driven out to form an urban proletariate, while great estates have been created and worked by slave labour. You know the misery and unrest this has provoked. Meanwhile,' I said, 'to fight these accursed civil wars, armies of unprecedented size have been called into being. They cannot and must not be maintained in arms. You will of course see that. Therefore the veterans must be found land. Such a provision serves a double purpose; it satisfies their natural ambition, and it brings new life to the countryside. I hope my measures will lead to the revival of agriculture in Italy and to a desirable reversion to old patterns of landholding. Unfortunately, in a reform of land tenure on such a scale, some innocent parties must suffer.'

'Oh, I see that,' Virgil said. 'You can't make an omelette without breaking eggs.' He observed my puzzled expression: 'A Mantovan proverb', he said. 'An omelette is a savoury egg dish we country people enjoy, it's extremely good, you should try it, Caesar, next time you're in the North.'

I promised to do so (he was quite right by the way; omelettes are delicious, whatever Livia says), and then questioned him about farming. His answers were both informative and deeply-felt; he spoke with reverence of the partnership with nature that is the farmer's lot; of how he must strive for both domination and sympathy; of how these were not, as the vulgar or ignorant might suppose, opposites; 'They are in truth yoked together, like oxen; nature must be dominated, and yet the aim is harmony; it is like training a dog or breaking a horse,' he said. 'Real mastery is impossible without the understanding which derives from profound sympathy.'

What is that but a definition of government?

Now I recognize what he said to me that morning as the essence of his Georgics. He developed my theme of Italy, 'earthly paradise, mother of crops and mother of men,' as he would call our country in one of his noblest passages. I heard in his speech my profound affinity with him. He thought of Italy and of Rome's mission as I did; I was born to make his words flesh. Later, in the great epic of Rome which I urged him to write, he told of how the Gods promised Aeneas 'limitless empire', even as he fled from burning Troy. And I have already reminded you of his interpretation of my work as being 'to bring back an age of gold to fields where Saturn used to reign'.

* * *

My work was interrupted by vice, folly and jealousy. Antony had vanished into the Arabian sands. His wife Fulvia and brother Lucius set themselves up as guardians of his interest, and accused me of favouring my veterans at the expense of his. Absurd charge, mere excuse for trouble-making. Lucius hoped to break the triumvirate and force himself on his brother as an equal partner in greatness. The vile Fulvia knew that Antony had wearied of her virago-rages (as he had told me often enough in Greece; she was eager to impress him with her indispensability).

The situation was aggravated by a corn shortage. Sextus Pompey was operating a blockade with more ability than I had credited him with possessing. For a few weeks it seemed that my achievements were slipping away. Philippus again flapped round my quarters like an over-fed Cassandra. Even Marcellus spoke of compromise with the remnants of the old Senatorial party who were using the corn shortage as an occasion to stir up animosity among the common people—and of course to obstruct my reforms. The mob rioted in Rome, and with the self-destructive madness typical of mob violence, burned the granaries where the last of the previous harvest was stored. I ordered Agrippa to discover the agents who had provoked these disturbances and bring them to summary trial.

Meanwhile I naturally sought to appease Lucius and even Fulvia. ('Waste of time, ducky,' Maecenas said. 'Chuck a bucket of ice water over her—that's the only remedy for a bitch on heat.') I say 'naturally' for I had no wish to quarrel with my colleague's connections, and was dismayed by the prospect of a new outbreak of war in Italy, which I was working so hard to settle. I could not be unaware also of my own men's apprehensions. So I assured Lucius and Fulvia that I was completely loyal to Antony, that his interest was mine (and mine his); I even offered to submit any matter of controversy to the judgement of the Senate or independent arbitration.

Fulvia's reply was to gird on a sword, assume the guise of a general and occupy Praeneste. I invited them to meet me at Gabbii; they declined; they would not come, they said, 'to any Senate in uniform'. What could I do? They were determined on a test of arms. I sent a legion to Brindisi to guard against Pompey or his lieutenants, with whom I feared they were in correspondence. I left Lepidus two legions with which to guard Rome. I despatched Agrippa with another two legions after Lucius. By the autumn the rebels had thrown themselves into Perusia. Agrippa invested the town and threw up siegeworks. My heart was bitter.

Perusia is a natural stronghold perched on the rim of the Apennines. Winter brought deep snow, hard night frosts, biting and lip-chafing winds. In the town Fulvia—so my agents told me—announced herself Rome's new she-wolf, the men her litter. She did not hesitate to bite more savagely than any wolf; one of my agents, an ex-centurion of the Martian legion, was discovered. They bound him with chains, and Fulvia herself commenced to torture him. The brave man kept silence and died the death of a thousand cuts. She who had delivered the first then ordered him to be eviscerated, plunged her own hands in the reeking entrails, and cried that she read my doom there. Her own legions shrank back, appalled, and spat on the ground covered by her departing shadow.

The siege endured all winter, till, with the first melting snows, we were able to identify and block up the springs that fed the town's wells. Then the hardships afflicting troops and citizens doubled. They begged Fulvia to surrender; she hanged the two leaders of the embassy. Lucius, who feared his terrible sister-in-law as much as any slave did, sent a messenger secretly to Agrippa. Realizing the end was near, he summoned me to take the surrender.

Even then Fulvia's lust was not slaked. She had her slaves set the municipal buildings on fire. From the siege camp we watched the flames leap to the moonless sky and assume ghastly shapes against the higher mountains; we listened to the shrieks of the women and the wild cries of looting soldiers—some managed to make their way into the hills in that night's confusion; others tried to cut a path through our camp and died in the attempt.

In the grey morning, buffeted by March winds—we were, with the unrelenting irony of Fate, one day short of the Ides of March, the grim anniversary of my father's murder—I rode through the dismantled defences into an air still swirling with ash and heavy with the stench of burning, blood, spilt wine and death.

Lucius, assembling the shreds of the soldier he had been, had collected the remnants of his legions to make a formal surrender. His breath too stank of wine; his tunic was stained with blood, sweat and smoke-grime; he had always been less than Antony; now he looked like his brother's ghost, a spectre from whom all nobility, all presence, had departed; a man abandoned by the Gods of War.

Agrippa urged me to put both Lucius and Fulvia to death. 'They have made war against the Triumvirate,' he said, with absolute truth. Lepidus sent the same message, all the more eagerly. I do not deny I was tempted. Their actions could not be forgiven; they had tried to disrupt my settlement and destroy me. Fulvia too had revived the mean and baseless scandals about my private life.

Yet of course I could not dispose of them. They were still Antony's kin. I knew he cherished Lucius. I knew that, though he might be weary of Fulvia, he could not stomach the insult of her death at my hands. My position was absurd, acutely uncomfortable. I could mete out death to those Senatorial diehards, old Pompeians, connections of the 'Liberators', whose irreconcilable nature had been fully demonstrated, and who had long ago exhaused their ration of pardons. I could seize their estates for distribution to my veterans (if they had not already been taken during the proscriptions); all this with perfect justice and equanimity. But I could not touch those they had chosen to follow.

Those whom you cannot punish you must appease. I came to terms with Lucius. I summoned him to my presence, alone. He entered, humbled and still battle-stained, for I had given instructions that he be permitted neither to bathe nor change. I could keep him at that disadvantage at least, a couple of weeks in a cell dug out of the rock on which Perusia is built. I could make him fully sensible of the clemency he was about to be granted.

The interview was disagreeable. He abased himself before me. He blamed everything on Fulvia—'that terrible woman'—and begged me to spare his life. It was all offensive; I preferred the insolence with which I had been greeted after Philippi. Lucius promised future loyalty. Defeat had scattered his wits. His promises were worthless and he should have realized how impossible it was for me to treat him as he deserved. Instead I raised him up, embraced him, ordered a slave to make a bath ready for him and lay out clean raiment, promised him we would dine together and then talk. It was all a charade; it restored his spirits.

That evening I offered him the post of Governor of Further Spain with command of two legions. My pleasure in this magnanimity was increased by the knowledge of how it would fret Lepidus.

As for Fulvia, I refused to see her. It would have appealed to an element in my nature I have learned to distrust to have granted her an interview. I sent her a letter commanding her to be ready to journey to Rome under escort, where she must take up residence in the Temple of Vesta, till I had fully acquainted her husband with the record of her crimes. 'It is for Antony to punish you,' I wrote. 'It is not seemly for me to be your prosecutor and judge.' 'That should make the bitch sweat,' I said. Meanwhile I wrote to Antony and told him of what I had done for his brother; I advised him to rid himself of Fulvia. 'She is an insurmountable obstacle to our common labours,' I said. I suppose I was doing him a service.

I took the opportunity to divorce Claudia. The conclusion of the so-called War of Perusia was therefore happy.

V

I have been married three times. That with Claudia was hardly a marriage, for it was never consummated—I could not look on her without being reminded of Fulvia; this chilled the desire her kittenish charm aroused; I knew the wildcat she would become. (I was wrong, poor thing; she eventually fell into melancholy-madness, which Greek doctors call 'depression' and drowned herself in a fish-pond.)

Soon after the end of the War of Perusia I married, to Maecenas' amusement, your grandmother Scribonia. His amusement was justified. She was twenty years older than I, and had been married twice. Both her previous husbands had been consuls, though men of no personal note. I married her because her daughter was Sextus Pompey's wife; it seemed a prudent and potentially valuable connection. Even so, I would hardly have committed myself to the marriage, which was arranged by my stepfather, if I had met the lady first.

I never cease to be baffled by the tricks of heredity. How, I wonder, could that gap-toothed, big-breasted scold be the mother of my adored and beautiful Julia? Scribonia herself felt the absurdity of our position—for one thing I was several inches shorter, as well as being younger than her daughter. Nevertheless the marriage fed her ambition. On our wedding night she said to me:

'You're very lucky, my lad, to be marrying a woman of my experience, and I expect to be treated with respect. I know that you now call yourself Julius' son and that you have made him into a God. Well, there is sense in that. It shows me you have a head on your shoulders. But it's a young head, my lad. What's more, I'll point out to you that I knew your real father, and very common he was. I'm told his grandfather had been a ropemaker. It doesn't surprise me. Of course old Philippus is a gentleman, but he's no blood-relation of yours. Well then, you must see that I am demeaning myself by this marriage. We have seven consuls in my family, one of them fought beside Coriolanus. Both my previous husbands were consuls too, so that makes this a remarkably good marriage for you. Now, there's something else I must say. I don't like your associates. Marcellus is all right of course, but the rest of them are ill-bred or degenerate or both. Nobody, I must tell you, can afford such associations unless his own family is above reproach. Real aristocrats can mix with riff-raff without losing face, but, when someone of your background does, then it is merely evidence of vulgar tastes. I can see I'll have to educate you. Meanwhile you will despatch those friends of yours to some suitably distant employment. There's another thing too. I've heard stories about you that do you no credit. Everyone knows just what your relations were with your uncle Julius. Well, you're a pretty boy of course, and Julius was well . . . Julius. I don't blame you for that. He had terrific charm and personality. I'm a moral woman myself, but, if Julius had asked me, well, I'd have had to say yes. But I'm told you prostituted yourself to that awful Aulus Hirtius. And I've heard about those walnut shells— that surprises you, eh? Now I won't have that sort of thing.

My first husband used to say that boys who went in for that sort of thing were no better than Greeks. Or Asiatics. Syrians even. I like a man to take pride in his appearance, but I can't stand effeminacy. So, if I catch you at that sort of trick, you jolly well watch out for squalls, my lad. I'm a plain woman . . .' (my God, she was) 'and blunt-spoken. What I admire is the old Roman virtue. As for sex, that's important in a marriage but it must be on my terms. With your reputation and experience you won't know what pleases a woman. Well, I'll be frank. If you can't satisfy me in our marriage bed, I'll let the world know about it. I won't stay married to any molly-coddle or nancy-boy. I know fine you have married me for political reasons and it's in my interest to further your political career. I'll see that my precious son-in-law Pompey toes the line—if, that is, you keep me happy in bed. I'm a strong woman in the prime of life and I need it three times a week. I can't speak plainer than that. Mind you, I expect to be treated with respect in bed too. You needn't hope to see me naked' (I shuddered). 'I daresay we'll do all right when you've learned what I want.'

I have condensed her discourse of course. She went on like that and like that for three hours. Then she dismissed me with instructions to return in half an hour. Agrippa was waiting for me with a jug of wine. 'I reckon you are going to need this, boy,' he said. He was, as so often, quite right. When I returned, fortified, she was sitting up in bed with a night-cap on. 'I've told my women we are on no account to be disturbed,' she said, and blew the candle out. She seized me vigorously, like one who has waited too long. I set myself to other imaginings. Not even images of twining tawny slave-girls' limbs helped me much.

She was a horrible woman, but she gave me Julia. I suppose, on reflection, she may have been congenitally unhappy. Certainly I never knew her other than discontented. When I came to divorce her I explained that I did so because I could not bear the way she nagged at me.

★　★　★

Of all the noble families of Rome, none is more remarkable than the Claudians. According to a popular song the Claudian family tree is like an apple tree which bears two kinds of fruit: sweet apples, that are delightful to eat and of great culinary value, and crab apples that are sour and distasteful. Certainly popular history divides them into good and bad Claudians. People still delight to tell of that Claudius Pulcher who took the auspices before a naval battle and found that the sacred chickens would not eat. 'If they will not eat,' he cried, 'then let them drink,' and threw them into the sea where they drowned. (The subsequent battle was, not surprisingly, lost.) Publius Clodius, the gangster who had been Fulvia's first husband, was another wild one; you know of some of his outrageous acts. He burned one of his mistresses in her bed too. Fulvia's half-insane violence was, I always felt, a reflection of his. There was also Appius Claudius Superbus who, in the early days of Rome, tried to enslave a free-born girl called Virginia whom he had already raped. On the other hand there were great servants of the State like Claudius Claudex, who expelled the Carthaginians from Sicily, and that Claudius Nero (I am told that 'Nero' means 'strong' in the old Sabine dialect, though some say it means 'black') who defeated Hasdrubal. The Claudian women are reputed equally to be of the same two types.

No family has been more important to me, but I think that the man who pretends to understand a Claudian is a fool. One reason why my love for Livia has never diminished, but has grown steadily deeper and more powerfully pervasive through the long years of our marriage, rests in her unfathomable Claudian nature. The man who fully understands his wife soon reaches the end of his marriage.

Nothing is harder to understand than the condition of marriage. Politics, that deep mystery, is child's play in comparison. We enter on marriage lightly; it becomes the deepest thing in life. That is a paradox perhaps; there is a sense in which my memoirs will be a sustained commentary on it.

I say 'lightly', for we usually marry for political or family reasons. The woman herself is the least important element; we choose her because she will cement our political connections, or simply because she brings us some desirable property. Most marriages then start thus. Many never advance beyond this point. They remain a convenience. Even you,

82

my dear boys, must have observed how few husbands and wives live in and for each other. Self-styled wits indeed regard marriage as a joke, the marriage-bond simply as providing spice for adultery. I find this shocking, yet easy to understand. Most marriages are empty affairs. Yet there are some, among which I count myself blessed of the Gods to number my own, which nourish both husband and wife, which provide unfailing delight, and which enable both man and woman to grow in sympathy and understanding. Marriage is first a legal contract, but some few are fortunate enough to find in wedlock a profound communion which, to revert to Platonic theories again, seems to offer the substance rather than the shadow of some ultimate God-given reality. We mock the uxorious man; yet only he whose marriage is profound and true can know the deepest happiness of which human beings are capable. Inasmuch as the philosophical concept of divided souls has any significance, its resolution can only be found in marriage. Nevertheless this deep understanding is based on a residual mystery. One's beloved wife is at the heart of existence, the union is complete, and yet one cannot ever fully know her, or escape consciousness of her other and separate being.

Livia herself is descended from that Appius Claudius Pulcher who advised the Senate not to ally the Republic with King Pyrrhus of Epirus, and so gained a reputation for wisdom. She was, when I first knew her, married to a cousin, Tiberius Claudius Nero; and they were my enemies. Her husband, who knew nothing of her nature, was a shiftless fellow, who had gone through the Civil Wars like a man playing dice. He had supported my father, then abandoned him. He had urged the Senate to honour Caesar's murderers, and then drifted to Antony's camp. At Bononia we had named him praetor for 42. He had adhered to Lucius and Fulvia, and had survived the terrible siege of Perusia during which your stepfather Tiberius was an infant. He then fled to Sicily and made terms with Sextus Pompey, that indiscriminate man. In 39 we concluded peace with Pompey at Misenum, and, after a brief skirmish in Campania, Tiberius Claudius Nero presented himself in my camp.

This irresolute man, consistent only in failure, was still

haughty. Why? He was a Claudian. That being so, all was permitted him. Claudians survive any disgrace: they are not only better born; in their own estimation they are born better. His young wife was no different. She approached me as a great lady might a client, not as the partner of a vanquished and discredited man.

She approached, and stopped my heart. She is, as you know, the same height as I, or perhaps an inch taller. She wore a white gown fringed with pink, and no jewels; she has always disdained any jewels but her eyes. I said to myself: so Helen must have looked when Paris saw her in Menelaus' house. And then I saw that she was angry. Those liquid eyes, which in my fond imaginings—by distant camp-fires, on cold unfriendly shores—are ever tender, were hard and scornful. Was the scorn for me, or for her husband? I could not tell, but I felt, all at once, guilty. She has never lost the power to make me feel guilty, to make me ashamed.

She would not speak. She stood a little aside in an attitude which, simply because it was not at all provocative, aroused in me a most terrible lust, such as I had never experienced before. I say simply, but there has never been anything about Livia properly called simple. I believe that if she had even for a moment given me some sign of desire, if she had played the coquette even that instant, my lust would have abated, and I would have been able to listen to what her husband said. That might have freed me into anger, for he too, though I knew his feebleness, assumed a superiority to which nothing but his Claudian-consciousness entitled him. But I could not attend; Livia's restraint conquered me.

VI

My sister Octavia was a pearl among women: chaste, intelligent, devout, loving, faithful; grey-eyed, modest and comely as apple-blossom. I sacrificed her happiness to the needs of the Republic (for Marcellus had opportunely died, and though Octavia grieved, I could not regret the opportunity thus given . . .)

★   ★   ★

Fulvia died, snarling. Even with her last breath she hissed poison in Antony's ear; I had cast him, she said, as Pompey to my Caesar.

'Antony won't have listened,' Salvidienus Rufus assured me. 'He has other interests.'

'Other interests?'

'Cleopatra.'

'Politics,' I said. 'The co-operation of the Queen of Egypt is necessary if he is to make a successful invasion of Parthia. As you know, I am against that. I think the first rule of Roman generalship should be: don't invade Parthia.' (Make a note of that, my sons. I believe it even more firmly now than I did then.) 'But Antony is wedded to the policy. I can't dissuade him. And he needs Egypt's help. He needs Egypt's subsidy. Politics.'

'This sounds like politics?' Rufus said. 'Antony was waiting for her as she voyaged up the Cydnus. She travelled in a barge the like of which you've never seen. It was quite indescribable, all purple and gold and with scented sails. She reclined on a throne with a single circle of gold on her head and a single golden chain round her neck and no other jewellery but her eyes. Her cheeks were touched the palest of pink rose and her mouth—have you heard of her mouth?—it's beyond compare, it is the dream-kiss of all eternity. And her eyes were violet and slightly damp. Flute music sounded lulling and languid airs and four Cupids, beautiful half-caste boys, half-Greek half-Syrian, wafted fans over her. Antony

85

saw this vision swan towards him and Fulvia was forgotten. He loves Cleopatra and lived with her all winter, and you say politics. How young you are, Octavian, to know nothing of love!'

That was last winter, before I met Livia. My mind darts over those months like a swallow, forward and back.

Antony objected to my confiscation of Gaul. He wrote to me in angry terms. I suppose the letter exists somewhere, but I cannot be troubled to unearth it. The sequel however was dangerous.

He acted with his usual impetuosity and lack of scruple. Instead of waiting for my reply, he patched up an agreement with Sextus Pompey and Ahenobarbus (one of Caesar's killers who had a pirate fleet), and the three of them sailed to Italy. Naturally I commanded my garrison at Brindisi to forbid them the harbour. His response was to blockade the port and land his legions at Sipontum a few miles up the coast. I hastened south, heavy-hearted at the thought that Antony's folly should once again expose Italy to war.

Maco said to me, 'The men don't like it. Their hearts won't be in any battle.'

'Nor will mine. I don't like it either.'

That night I wandered through the camp. There was a straw summer moon and the mountains of Apulia loomed over us like jagged and angry bears. I had pulled a rough woollen cloak round me and half over my head and when I crouched down beside a group of legionaries (keeping in the shadows, just out of the firelight), none recognized me. Their mood was sullen and nervous.

One said, 'You, Gaius, like all the rest of old Caesar's soldiers, can't think of anything but the next bloody battle. You're hooked on it, you're drugged by war...'

'That's what you think,' was the reply, 'you don't know a thing. Old sweats like me like war least of all. It's one thing bashing up Gauls, there's some sense and satisfaction in that, but I've been a soldier now twenty years, I've been decorated ten times, I've fought in more than fifty battles and skirmishes and I've wounds to show for it, and I never knew any good come from fighting other Romans.'

'Why do we do it then? Why do we let the bosses muck us

about? Why don't we bloody tell them to get on with it hand-to-hand, if they're so effing keen?'

That raised a laugh.

'Can you see our wee general get in the arena with Antony?'

'It would be. . .' the speaker left the outcome open and shut in one sentence.

'He's too fly for that, is our wee Caesar.'

I said, 'Well, what do you think he wants? Nothing but power and blood, would you say?'

'Friend,' said the veteran called Gaius, 'I don't know who you effing are but you know eff all about the world.'

'Come off it,' I said, 'these politicians are all the same. They don't care what happens to their men as long as it helps them to power. And, if you ask me, young Octavian's the worst.'

'Friend,' Gaius said, 'would you like a taste of my sword for an early breakfast?'

'Just saying what I think,' I said: 'You tell me why I'm wrong.'

'In the first place,' Gaius said, 'have you any idea how much land he has aready handed out to the boys?'

'Oh, that,' I said, 'that don't signify anything to me. That's just a politician building up a group of clients, if you ask me.'

'Nobody's asking you. You're too effing ignorant to ask. I'm telling you,' Gaius said.

'If you're so clever,' I said, 'tell me why you think we're here. Tell me why we're lined up to fight Antony, when just a few months ago we were all bosom chums engaged in common butchery. Tell me that, you grey-bearded know-all.'

'Listen, shithead,' he said, 'we don't want to fight Antony.'

'Too bloody right we don't,' said another.

'Hear, hear, I've got two brothers with Antony.'

'I only like to fight when I'm sure of winning,' said a fourth, 'and I'd never back our boy against Antony.'

'Oh, generalship,' I said, 'generals don't matter that much. All this talk of generalship is horse-piss. It's how us men feel that counts. What they call morale.'

'I don't know who the hell you effing are,' Gaius said, 'and indeed I'm beginning to wonder if you're a spy sent in to our camp by Antony, in which case I'll hand you over to the senior centurion and volunteer to nail you to a cross myself...'

'Thought you said old sweats never volunteered...'

'This time it would be a pleasure. Still, what you say is true enough, up to a point. It's what men feel that decides battles, decides whether they stand their ground or run away. But you see, one of the things that decides which they do, is what they feel about their general. Not just about their general but about the legion and the whole army. If they don't trust them, they run away. It's that simple, it's why Julius won all his battles ... we would always stand our ground for him ...'

'And what about the cause?' I said.

His voice had grown gentler in the last speech, as he began to think. I have often noticed how the crudity of the spontaneous and regular speech of soldiers gives way to something more admirable when they begin to reflect.

'You always say it doesn't matter,' he said. 'That you fight for pay, because you're told to, because the centurion will flay you if you don't, and because you're afraid not to, and it is all true. And yet, underneath it all, there is something more. Men fight better when they are fighting for what they believe in. I'm old enough to remember Vercingetorix at Alesia. That was a battle of battles because the Gauls were fighting for everything that was theirs that we were going to take from them and change.'

His voice dropped. Someone threw a branch on the fire and flame spurted up, illuminating his set, scarred face. A flask was passed round. I was included in the circle as if the altered tenor of the conversation, the sense that we were all being made free of everything Gaius had come to know in his life of soldiering, dissipated the suspicion with which I had been viewed and made me part of the group.

Gaius waved the wine aside. He said, 'Our boy's cause is right. He stands for Italy and homes and farmlands and public order.'

'But this time,' another said, 'what is there to fight Antony about ...?'

88

'Maybe nothing,' Gaius said, 'except that he's here. And it's got to be finished. If Antony insists, we have to stand our ground.'

I threw the hood back off my head and stepped forward so that they might see who I was.

'You are quite right, Gaius,' I said... 'No,' I smiled, seeing his consternation, 'don't apologize for having threatened to nail me to a cross. I have no wish for this battle, but, if it has to be, it has to be. You know what my father said after Pharsalus when he looked on the faces of the dead Pompeians. "They wanted it this way", those were his words. And you are quite right too in saying what I stand for. I stand for the Republic, for farms for my soldiers, for decency and peace. We have come a long way and cannot hide from our destiny...'

'That's all right, General,' said one man, a thin-faced boy with a cauliflower ear, 'but destiny's a big word for us boys. I reckon destiny belongs to the likes of you.'

'What is your name?' I said, and sat down beside him.

'Septimus,' he said, 'being the seventh son, you understand.'

'Well, Septimus,' I said, 'if a seventh son doesn't understand destiny, who can? But you're wrong, you know, we all have a fate to work out. And let me tell you, I know, whether we have to fight Antony now or later or not at all, that my star is fixed. I shall achieve for you and all Italians just what Gaius has said I'm aiming at. Trust me in that. We're here, not just for ourselves, but for our children.'

'Don't have any,' said Septimus.

'You will have.'

'Not him, Caesar,' cried another, 'he's not up to it,' and the wine-flask flew faster amid ribaldry and good-humour...

But I was still awake as dawn crept to us out of Asia, over the still grey Ionian, across the inland sea and the still silent marshes. Then the first birds called, sea birds and curlews and redshanks, and then, very slowly, the camp began to wake, horses shifted their feet, rattled their chains and snorted, voices were heard, cooks called to breakfast, and I woke a slave and sent him to fetch Maecenas.

89

It took him a long time to come and he was still rubbing sleep from his eyes. He wore a dressing-gown of gorgeous taffeta, yellow and deeper gold, adorned with red dragons. A slave attended him bearing a tray of breakfast meats, smoked peacock breast, scampi in a sauce of lemon and saffron, cold boiled lobster and a jug of iced wine.

'I know, Caesar,' Maecenas drawled, 'that you breakfast in too Spartan a manner for me. Very affected I call it, my dear, to eat soldiers' food.'

He yawned: 'What is it, ducky, that could not wait till a more gentlemanly hour?'

'It is,' I said, 'this absurdity.'

'Absurdity? You're naive,' he said. 'You have this strange fancy that Antony is a serious man in the same way we are. Antony is a bar-room type. He wants power and esteem. They make him feel good. It's no use talking to Antony of ideals, ducky. He don't know what you mean. Still, I agree in one respect. It's too soon to fight him. I'll see what I can do. . .'

I fretted all day while Maecenas debated with Antony's envoy, Asinius Pollio. There is nothing more irksome than the position of a principal while his agents negotiate. It was very hot; I had my slaves three times prepare a bath for me, and on each occasion found some other little matter to distract me. I had made up my mind what must be done, and I felt guilty. I knew Antony too well to feel other than guilty, and I prepared myself to face my mother's reproaches.

Later too, Livia said to me, 'You claim to love your sister. She is perhaps the only woman of whom I could feel jealous. And yet you subjected her to this marriage. Why?'

'Not for myself,' I replied. 'For Rome. For the whole world.'

When Antony met me to sign what came to be called the Treaty of Brindisi, he laughed. He stretched forward his hand to pinch my cheek in the old manner, hesitated a moment, and then nipped quite hard. 'Marry your sister, kid,' he crowed. 'Well, that is coming full circle.'

I drew back. I said, 'There is one other thing. This marriage is expedient, but I love my sister.'

'She's a beauty,' he said, 'and they tell me, Caesar, as virtuous as she is beautiful, unlike some I could mention, eh, and
wise enough to be Caesar's sister too. So what's this other
thing?'

'Cleopatra,' I said.

'Oh, the Queen? What of her?'

'Rumour has it that you and she are lovers.'

'One up to rumour,' Antony said. 'But she's an awful
woman all the same. Sees herself as she-who-must-be-
obeyed. I'll be very glad to have a good Roman wife to protect me against the Queen. But you must realize our
relationship's primarily political. I need Egypt.'

'Rome needs Egypt,' I said. 'Does Rome need Cleopatra. . . ?'

Antony beamed.

'You're a deep one, Caesar,' he said. 'The same thought
had occurred to me.'

That conversation cleared my conscience, or could have
done, if my conscience allowed itself to be deceived by
words. But I knew I was doing wrong, and yet it was what
had to be done.

I explained this to Octavia herself. I told her that Antony
and I must hold together and that this was only possible if she
agreed to act as the bond.

Octavia said, 'He must promise he will not see the Queen
of Egypt alone.'

Antony gave that promise. There are those who talk of
Antony and Cleopatra as great lovers. I have noticed this tendency among some of your mother's aristocratic friends.
They should know that he gave that promise. There was no
deep love between them, believe me.

Octavia also said, 'Caesar married his daughter to Pompey
to cement their alliance, and it lasted while she lived. I know
what duty demands of me, brother.'

Octavia has a pale face, a priestess's face, and it was very
still and lovely, like a priestess before the altar, as she said
this. She said one other thing: 'After all, I have known love
with Marcellus. That is more than many women can say. But
I have one request, brother. I do not wish my son, the young
Marcellus, to grow to manhood in Antony's household. I do

not wish to surrender him, but I shall leave him with my mother and ask you to make yourself responsible for his virtue, well-being and education.'

I said, 'I shall love him as a son or younger brother.'

So the marriage went ahead, though my mother was indeed furious and never ceased to reproach me for having, as she put it, 'sacrificed' my sister. She was right, but the sacrifice was necessary. The Treaty of Brindisi confirmed me in possession of Gaul; it left me a free hand to deal with Sextus Pompey, whom Antony abandoned with a readiness that should have chilled the blood of any of his friends (and which I did not fail to remark myself). In return Antony now took control of the whole Empire of Rome from the Ionian Sea to the Euphrates; I promised him five legions from Gaul for the Parthian War on which his mind was fixed.

'Well, this all seems satisfactory. Have we forgotten anything?'

'I don't think so.'

Maecenas tapped me on the shoulder and leaned forward. 'Lepidus,' he said.

'Oh Lepidus,' I said.

'By Jupiter, yes,' Antony said, 'our noble colleague, our fellow triumvir. How could we come to forget him? What about the noble donkey?'

'Let him keep Africa,' I said.

'Why not?' Antony said, and the conference ended on a fit of giggles.

★　★　★

There are in Germany dark and trackless forests. Huge trees join their branches to deny the sun to the ground below. The undergrowth is thick, tangled and full of briars which lacerate the traveller's legs, and even reach above the protective leggings of ox-hide such as Ulysses wore when he drove his plough in Ithaca. These forests are numinous, spirit-haunted by the demons of delusion. In the absence of paths, the traveller must trace his journey by notching the trees with his knife. The forests afflict the nerves; no Roman who spends any time there comes out unimpaired, but rather prey to nervous disorders, stomach troubles, strange shudderings. He sighs for the lucidity of the Mediterranean world, for the stark truthful landscape of rock and sky and water; he longs for the certainties of these harsh realities.

For five years after Caesar's murder I lived in a world like that German forest. Though in retrospect I can discern a pattern, at the time I moved from restless day through sleepless and wary night. I had a sense of my general direction, but I moved without precise knowledge, apprehensive, circumspect and often fearful.

Livia brought me into the sunshine, as if I emerged from the forest to find a fruitful plain spread below me. I fell in love with her at first sight; yet for three weeks she refused to see me. She regarded me as an enemy; I was the young disturber of the social order, the champion of those without property and family—her lovely head was full of the stuffiest aristocratic notions, and her gull-witted husband resentfully encouraged them. I sent her letters, flowers, gifts of fruit and shellfish—to no avail—though I had at least the sense not to send her my verses. Then I invited the pair of them to a dinner-party, and sent Maecenas to warn the egregious Tiberius Nero that the invitation was in reality a command. She arrived in a white gown with no jewellery, and her face expressed disdain. I set myself to be charming and failed to charm. Of course I had next to no experience with young girls of good birth, and clearly neither of my marriages had prepared me. I tried to talk nonsense, not realizing that Livia had no taste for it; later she told me she had thought me a disappointing buffoon.

Conversation was sticky; no doubt about that. I knew Maecenas was laughing at me, and should have realized that his was just the sort of presence to revolt Livia. What, I wondered, itching with impatience and almost stammering with nervousness, would the girl like to talk about? War and politics were out; we would only disagree. I tried poetry; she said she never read it. I asked her about her family:

'I loved my father,' she said, 'he was an honourable man. He was killed at Philippi. I have been told he was killed after the battle.'

Her chin tilted upwards and she looked me full in the eyes with no flicker of understanding, but only challenge.

93

I said to myself: she is going to despise me if I knuckle under and don't meet her defiance.

I leaned across the table and poured wine into her cup.

'It was an ugly business, Philippi,' I said, 'and it followed on an uglier—the murder of my father. But I am sorry to hear of your father, believe me. There can never be anything but pain and grief in shedding the blood of a fellow-citizen.'

'That is easy to say, Caesar.'

'And difficult to prove?'

'Impossible, I should say.'

Her eyes held mine.

'You are right,' I said. 'It is impossible. I can only ask you to believe me, and to remember this: had Philippi gone differently I would be in my grave myself, and I do not think it would be honoured. War between Romans is foul, wicked and wrong. If I have one aim in life, it is to bring an end to these civil wars, which have disfigured and deformed the Republic since the days of Sulla and Marius. But to bring them to an end it is not sufficient to conquer; the social causes of civil strife must be treated, for the body politic is diseased. The true mission of any Roman of conscience today is that of healer, but to cure disease requires first the surgeon's knife. . .'

A smile, like the first shaft of dawn sunlight striking a cold wall, touched the corner of her mouth.

'I am glad you are no longer talking to me as if I were just a pretty girl,' she said. 'I am glad you can be serious with me, Caesar.'

She rose from her couch, and, either catching her foot in the hem of her gown or slipping on the marble, tumbled abruptly to the floor. I was at her side in a moment.

'My ankle,' she said.

I glanced down the table. Tiberius Nero was blearily deep in the wine-flask, paying no heed to his wife. I picked her up.

'We'll have it seen to,' I said.

'Ouch,' she said, 'you're stronger than you look, though.'

'It's very difficult,' I said, laying her on a couch in the antechamber and feeling the ankle, which was already swelling, 'to forget that you are a lovely girl.'

'Why do you wear that disgusting beard?' she murmured.

'To please you, I'll remove it.'

The ankle was badly sprained. I ordered the surgeon to instruct that she should be moved as little as possible, and so invited her and Tiberius Nero to be my guests. And that was how it began.

'Tell me about yourself?'

'What do you want to know?'

'Everything.'

'You can't know everything.'

'But I must.'

'Must, Caesar?'

'Must. If we are going to pass our life together.'

'Oh, are we?'

'I'm working on it.' I took her hand and placed it against my cheek. 'Feel,' I said, 'I've sacrificed my beard. For you. It's the end of one period in my life. I stopped shaving on the day I heard of my father's murder. Now I'm shaving again. You've changed the pattern.'

'I wish you wouldn't call that man your father. You had a real father, I suppose. What was he like?'

'An average man. Nothing remarkable. He liked fishing in mountain streams.'

'Very informative, that tells me a lot.'

She had a quick abrupt way of speaking, a slightly metallic voice. There was some nervousness behind it, some sense of insufficiency. It was quick and decisive and yet it suggested, even from those first days, when just to look at her lying back on the pillows, her pale face with its translucent skin and huge blue-grey eyes framed by the tresses of hair the colour of beech-leaves in autumn forests, sent my blood coursing, pricked me with sharp and anguished desire (and the fear that I might never have her, that she might always in the end deny herself, retain a mysterious and secret part). Her voice, I say, suggested even then a limitation of sympathy, a narrowness of understanding; it was perhaps this that made her so complete, and so completely desirable. She was so certain and yet at the same time so vulnerable because the world was more complicated than she found it to be, and somewhere in the recesses of her spirit she apprehended this, and, for all her courage, feared the knowledge.

'And the Dictator,' she said, 'what was he really like. . . ?'

I looked away, out of the window. The sun shone on the heights of distant Aspromonte; in the nearer foothills the woods of chestnut glowed with a deep refulgent green; a rose-bush thrust pink flowers in through the window; purple wisteria spread itself over the terrace wall; a lizard basked on the broken masonry.

I said, 'He had charm. I was afraid of him. I owe everything to him. I didn't like him.'

She pressed her hand against mine. 'Oh,' she said, 'I am so glad to hear you say that.'

Her hand was strong, as big as mine (which as you know is rather small); her grip firm and dry.

I said, 'He was an egoist. He used people shamelessly. There was something cruel and self-regarding in his clemency.'

(As I spoke, I thought: Am I describing myself?)

Livia said, 'How can you love me? In my condition?'

'It's what my mother's friends genteelly call "an interesting condition".'

'I'm six months in pig,' she said.

'Oh Livia, as if that mattered. . .'

I leant forward. I put my arm round her and raised her head. I kissed her on the lips. It was like burying one's face in rose-petals. There was a faint smell of musk. She leant back, receiving the kiss.

She breathed: 'You're not one of these boys who just likes pregnant ladies, are you?'

'Will you marry me?' I said.

'Is that a polite command, Caesar?'

'No, Livia, I shall never command you'; and I never have.

'You have a wife, I have a husband.'

'Let's divorce them. They can marry each other. . .'

'No,' she said, 'not that. Still, you did shave your beard. . .'

I kissed her again. This time she responded. Her arms folded round my neck. We lay some minutes in joy, basking in love and desire, like the lizard in sunlight.

I divorced Scribonia as soon as possible. The timing was unfortunate for the divorce was ratified on the day that your mother, Julia, was born. However, I made it clear from the start that she was my responsibility, not Scribonia's. Tiberius Nero made no difficulties. In fact he said, 'Frankly Caesar, you'll find she has a mind of her own. And quite a temper. I can't say I'm sorry you're taking her off my hands. You'll look after the boy won't you, and whatever's on the way. I'll expect, mind you, that you put a few things in my way yourself.'

Livia's second son, poor Drusus, was born three days after our wedding. I know some people say I was his father, but this is not true.

VII

The rain, blowing on a squally horizontal, reached us even in the shallow cave. Septimus, the thin-faced boy with the cauliflower ear, whom I had taken into my personal service, tried to shield a spluttering fire with his cloak. I drew my own about me and shivered. The gash in my thigh throbbed. I rested my hand on the bandage and it came away damp and sticky. My stomach heaved and my head ached. I laid my helmet aside; there was a dent that ran from the crown down to my left temple. I hadn't realized the Nubian had hit me so hard; no wonder I had a headache.

There were just six of us crowded in the cave which was really little more than a depression in the rock-face. The wind blew hard out in the bay. The ship that might have taken us off swayed like a drunken man on the jagged rock which it had struck. I watched it toss for a long time in the gathering gloom of the October afternoon. The last push of the year, I thought to myself, and it has come to this. It was a long time since the last desperate boat, launched from the ship, had disappeared from sight. Another had been carried round the point; it was possible it might be swept to land. But for a long passage we had gazed at the heads bobbing in the water. They were no more than sixty or seventy paces out to sea. We could hear their cries clearly; even, over the wind, identify the Gods whose aid they implored and who were deaf to them. And then there had been no voices, only the cry of gulls.

The light began to die. The sea still growled against the rocks away to the right, but below us, as the beach darkened, it was hard to tell where water stopped and sand began. A pall of grey-black enveloped everything. Then Septimus conjured his fire into being. The flames danced on the men's streaked and stricken faces. Eyes glinted red. Nobody spoke. All huddled as close to the fire as they could.

I could not give any orders. It was Septimus who took charge, sending a couple of the men back to the camp we had been forced to abandon. They were to seek out food and wine. They demurred, afraid; surely Pompey's men would have occupied it? 'Surely we'll starve if you don't,' Septimus said. They sat a long time in silence. Septimus crossed and whispered to them. I caught dark glances directed at me; my stomach quivered, my head throbbed and my mouth felt dry and sour. There was nothing to stop them seeking glory and riches by asking for Sextus Pompey himself. For a moment I was near commanding Septimus to keep us all together.

Then the two got to their feet, without talking, and slipped out of the cave. Septimus crossed over to me:

'It's all right, General,' he said. 'They'll do well enough. The camp will be full of looters. There's no one will know they're your men.'

'Are they?' I said.

He whistled a few bars of a tune, shrugged his shoulders, looked out to the invisible sea.

'What about your wound, General?' he said.

'It's in the heart,' I replied.

'I could do with a glass of wine,' he said. 'Do you want me to have a look at your thigh?'

I shook my head.

'We were betrayed,' I said. 'The scouts. . . .'

'Maybe so,' he said, 'we walked into it anyway. . .'

Night closed impenetrably about us, in a profound silence but for the sea's swell.

'Reckon they've scarpered,' said one of the two remaining unknown soldiers.

'Or had their throats cut,' his companion said. Through the firelight they fixed their eyes on me, and I had nothing to say.

Time passed. I longed to sleep. I drew my cloak tighter about me, but the ache in my head did not diminish, my thigh still throbbed, and I felt a new dull but persistent pain in my heart. My mouth was dry and my tongue touched salt-caked and broken lips. At such moments, men say, the mind flies to happier places. Broken soldiers are reputed to dream of home. But I had no thought of Livia, no longing for her. I felt emptiness. My attention was held by the dying flames, but there were no patterns in them. When I moved my leg it was like trying to lift the hoof of an unwilling horse.

One of the soldiers started to snore. He had stretched out like a dog and gave no more thought to the future than a dog gives. His companion slipped his hand under his tunic and began to masturbate. My gaze was held by the pumping movement, and I felt envy of the pair of them, then shivered. The screech of a hunting owl broke the night. I crawled to the entrance of the cave. The rain had stopped at last. The moon, emerging through breaking clouds, laid a pale yellow hand on the still sea. Behind us, somewhere on the island, Pompey's troops slumbered.

I felt a hand on my shoulder.

'Can you walk, General?' Septimus said.

I shook my head doubtfully. He flicked a glance back into the cave. Both our companions now seemed still. The first still snored deeply. The other now lay, with his hand still under his tunic, and his legs curled up, but his head now rested on his comrade's chest. Septimus crossed light-footed and shook him gently. The only response was a deep and incomprehensible muttering.

'Reckon that's all right,' Septimus said. 'But I don't trust these two no more. I didn't like the way they put their heads together a while back when you were dozed out. We'd best get out of here, General. Can you slide down the rock to the beach, if I go first and get ready to hold you at the bottom?'

Septimus unbuckled his sword and threw it down on the sand. Then he went back into the cave and collected mine, and a shield and the knapsack which, alone among us, he had retained in flight. These followed the sword. He slipped down to the sand himself. The fall was perhaps the height of three men, and I hesitated before lowering my body. My foot searched for a toehold. My nails dug into the loose earth. I felt myself giving way. For a moment my left heel found a hold. I shifted my hand to grab a scrubby bush that grew out of the rock-face. I lowered myself a little. Then, with my right arm at full stretch, the bush began to tear itself out of the rock. My foot slipped off its hold. For an instant I dangled in the air. Then the bush ripped away and I tumbled to the beach. I fell awkwardly and knew at once that my thigh-wound had opened again and was bleeding.

Septimus helped me to my feet and hooked my arm round his neck. We began to hobble along the beach. Every step was painful. We had hardly gone more than fifty paces before I felt faint. He turned towards me, his face swimming in my eyes.

'This'll never do,' he said. 'I maun get you on my back.'

He crouched down before me and got his arms round my legs. My own flopped round his neck, and he straightened his legs, and, at first waveringly, like a drunken man, started to march along the beach. Gradually he found his rhythm, I hung there, helpless and dependent, like old Anchises when Aeneas brought him out of burning Troy.

I do not know for how long he carried me, or how far, nor whether he paused to rest, for I fainted, and was therefore borne, a mere sack of flesh and bone and guts, through the night and even into the morning. The dawn was up when I recovered consciousness, and I lay under a thorn-bush, with dew glistening, and Septimus lying at my feet, as a dog might sleep. He awoke as abruptly as a dog, on sensing that I was stirring.

'I didn't like to leave you, General,' he said, 'for fear that you'd wake and think I'd deserted you. But if we're to get out of this I've got to find something for us to eat and drink. I think you're safe here for the moment.'

He laid his hand on my shoulder and let it rest there a moment, even giving me a squeeze, as to a comrade. There was a wind blowing and I watched the sea-grasses slap his ankles as he marched off. He turned once and waved to me. I remained in wonder, pain and bemusement.

I do not know how long he was gone, for despite my danger and my determination to watch lest I be surprised by the enemy, I drifted into unconsciousness again. I had no dreams, though my sleep must have been fitful for I found on waking that I had torn up and shredded a plant growing by my side and I had no awareness of having done so.

I lay for some time. The clear weather promised by the moon had disappeared and the sky was low, grey and heavy. A sour wind blew through the scrub and rushes of a world empty but for a few sea birds. There was no sound or sign of man. It was as if the legions which had met yesterday had been swallowed up. It had been a sad helter-skelter affair after our ships had been driven to shore and Pompey's men, a legion of cut-throats and troops of Numidian cavalry, had swept down on us before we had time to recover our organization. It had hardly been a battle; no more than a mêlée; and I had received my wounds in a vain attempt to rally a group of fugitives.

Away to the left, on the edge of a promontory I could now discern the columns of a temple. I could not believe the Gods inhabited it. Then below the temple two figures descended a winding track: a man and a horse. They moved very slowly as if the going was rough, or as if they were old or tired. When they reached the bottom of the track, they turned towards me. I eased my hand round my sword hilt, and waited, my eyes fixed on the black shapes moving across the grey sands. Then I relaxed; the horse was only a donkey; and then I saw that it was Septimus who led it.

He said, 'Things are looking up, General. I've found a farm up in the hills. They've run away from it, whoever's it is, but I found some wine and a sort of biscuit and some olives. Here,' he began pulling them out of a bag strung round his neck. 'Have a bite and a drink. Not too much now on an empty stomach.' He crouched down beside me. 'I haven't seen a soul,' he said. He picked up the goatskin and handed it to me. The wine was thin and sour, but I forced down two mouthfuls. He rubbed his palm over the lip of the goatskin and swallowed deeply himself. 'We're going to be all right, General,' he said, 'just you see.'

The donkey was a bony ride, with an awkward gait. We hadn't gone far before I grew dizzy and Septimus had to place his hand against me to hold me steady on its back. 'This'll never do, General,' he said, 'you're as weak as a kitten.'

And I was; but Septimus, this peasant from the Sabine Hills, with his ungrammatical Latin and long vowel sounds, was not only strong; he knew what to do in a crisis where I found myself lost. Of course, even at the time, I could excuse myself on account of my wound, of my battered head and the little fever that afflicted me. Yet the old saying is true: whoever makes excuses for himself, accuses himself. The fact was: our disaster—the wreck of the ships, the scattering of my legions by a numerically inferior enemy—had for the moment at least annihilated my faculties. I was incapable of thought, decision, action. I was reduced to a state of utter dependency on this nineteen-year-old farmboy.

He got me to the farm and dressed my wound and I slept while he kept watch. I woke again in the dark night and he was sitting on a barrel by the doorway gazing into the rustling vacancy of the *macchia*.

'Have you slept?' I said, and he shook his head, abruptly, even angrily, as if I had been accusing him of dereliction of duty. I placed my hand on his shoulder.

'Where have they all gone?' I said. 'We might be alone.'

'We're not alone. There have been rustlings and sounds of distant movement, and before the light failed, I saw a troop of horse ride out of the next valley and turn to the coast. But we're safe enough for the moment.'

'Safe?' I said. 'There are no stars,' and by that, I meant that my own star was invisible; for the first time since Caesar died.

He said, 'I would it would rain. You were bleeding the last few miles. They could follow us by the blood.'

He fell silent, and fell asleep. Poor boy. The donkey shifted in the room behind me. The boy's words echoed in my ears: 'They could follow us by the blood.' So might anyone tracing my career work, following me by the blood shed. Yet none was shed for joy of killing; only for necessity. But, I thought in that night which seemed already Stygian, as I imagined

Pompey's cavalry ranging the valleys in search of me, if I died now, if it ended here, then all that blood was shed to no purpose. The Proscriptions, Philippi, Mutina, would have served Rome not at all, and my soul would descend bloodstained and worthless to the world below. I had believed myself a man of destiny—I had told that group of soldiers among whom I first encountered Septimus, as they huddled round a camp-fire, fearful of battle, that I knew my destined work for Rome—and here I was, wounded and dizzy with defeat, hiding in an abandoned farm on a Sicilian hillside, with my fleet scattered and my only companions a thin boy with a fighter's ear and a lame donkey. 'We have to pray to the Gods Agrippa comes,' the boy had said, but my messenger might never have reached Agrippa.

Towards morning the wind dropped. Cocks crew from higher up the valley, alarming me lest the evidence of life there might attract Pompey's soldiers. I hobbled back into the room and took a swig of wine from the goatskin. Septimus muttered and shifted in his sleep. I thought, for the first time since the disaster, longingly, of Livia. Was I failing her as well as Rome?

All my life I have lived much in my own mind. Yet at the same time I have little experience of solitude. We are a social people, our households tumbling over with slaves and family; our business taking us to the forum, the law-courts, the Senate House and the camp. Thoughts are pursued in the midst of chattering distraction; Cicero hated to be alone. His mind worked at its most agile in the press of men. Caesar too detested solitude; he used to say that one should never trust the lonely man; who knows what he is brooding? Only Virgil of all my acquaintances knows how to hearken to the long silences of lonely places; his senses vibrate in tune with the numinous. I now found the stillness of that Sicilian hillside oppressive, and—for I have vowed to myself that I shall tell the truth and conceal nothing however shaming in these confessions—fearful. I longed to wake Septimus merely to hear his rough and homely tongue. Some pride restrained me; let the lad have his necessary sleep, I told myself. But my hands shook, and little needles of fear or apprehension darted up my arms.

We rested in that cottage for two days. On the second morning the intermittent bleeding of my thigh-wound ceased. Gradually my headache dulled. The feeling of nausea never quite left me, though Septimus found more wine with which we calmed our stomachs. I could not but admire his composure, as I still was disturbed by the little tremors in my hands and arms. It was easy to tell myself that he had nothing but life to lose, nothing but death to fear—whereas I . . . but at that time I stopped; Rome was far off.

The second day it rained with a steady drab intensity. Mist had rolled in from the sea and the mouth of the valley was obscured. By late afternoon visibility was reduced to less than fifty paces; only the nearest olive trees emerged twisting grotesquely from the thin edge of the mist. In the morning Septimus had said to me, 'What we both need, General, is rest. Sleep, turn about, eh, and keep guard.' I nodded; it seemed natural to abdicate command to the boy.

By evening I was refreshed, but hardly more confident that we could escape. Yet the long sleeps had done something to calm my nerves. Septimus, perhaps sensing my change of mood, talked freely for the first time. His conversation was mostly about his family. His father's holding (he said) was small; it could not possibly support the seven grown sons. Three of his brothers had taken off for Rome; but not him. He had seen something of their life; it wasn't for him. There was no work for them in Rome. They depended on the corn dole, and spent their time hanging about taverns hoping someone would buy them a drink, and their chief interests were lottery tickets and the Games. Two of them were married; 'To foreigners, would you believe it, General; no, the city's no life for a man. I mean, it degrades him,' he said. 'On the other hand, I have to tell you, General, that my father's lot is hardly any happier. It's true he works his fields, and there's some satisfaction in that, and we grow our own grain for bread, and make our own wine from our own grapes, and my mother's brother supplies us with oil and olives in exchange for wine; and we do have a small flock of sheep that my elder brother takes to the summer pastures. All that may sound all right, but it gets more difficult every year. You see, my dad can't compete in the markets with the big landowners and their ranches with slave labour. None of the small farmers can. They undercut our prices all the time. All that's no good. He'll have to sell out if things don't get better. He's more and more in debt every year. So I saw no future, and joined the army. Join the army and see the world, they say. Some world, eh, we're seeing now?'

The next morning the sky cleared and the sun shone in a sparkling world. My spirits lifted with the mist. I began to feel for the first time that we might escape. I even hobbled (being still a little lame) out of the cottage to the corner of the olive grove, from where one could see beyond the mouth of the valley and down to the coast road.

I must set down baldly what followed. As I gazed down to the plain with a new peace in my heart in the brittle beauty of that October morning, I was suddenly chilled. A troop of horse turned off the coast road and up the valley track. It was impossible that they should miss our farm; it was impossible that they should not see us in flight. Our security had proved fool's gold. These were my immediate certainties: I had lost.

I called out to Septimus. He ran towards me. I indicated what it was hardly necessary to indicate.

'Bring my sword,' I said.

'There's no use in fighting,' he said.

'No,' I said, 'there's no use in fighting. Bring my sword.'

He looked at me, but did not obey. I hobbled into the hut, swearing at him, and seized my weapon. I took it by the point and held it out to him. His hand closed round the hilt, but he looked past me. I knelt down before him and pulled my tunic away at the neck...

'Strike,' I said.

Still he looked past me and did not move.

'Strike,' I cried again, near tears. My heart beat fast and I could feel myself beginning to tremble all over. 'Strike in the name of the Gods. Let me at least die a Roman death. Do you not see that I have no wish to fall into Pompey's hands, to be made a fool of and a mockery for all time? Strike, if you love me...'

But he threw down the sword and knelt beside me, and put his arms round me... 'General,' he said, 'you're not yourself. Listen,' he spoke very gently, yet with an urgency that came from the heart, 'I have believed in you. That's why I've done what I've done these last days. When you came to us by the camp-fire and talked of your star and what you would do for Italy, I believed you, and loved you for it. Are you telling me now it was all a lie? That you and your star are cheats too, like everything else? I won't do it, even if you weep and beg me'—(and I was weeping, I was shaking with sobs). 'If you're determined to do so, you must kill yourself, but I'll not promise to follow. I'll leave the job of killing me to others. I'll cling on to life' (and he hugged me tighter as if I was life myself) 'though if they find me by your dead body they'll think I've done it, and either slay me too to give themselves the credit or, who knows, reward me? Only I'd not want that sort of reward. Do you hear me?' he was shouting now. 'Be a man, General. You say you're sent to save Rome, and I believe you, even if you're greeting like a bairn now...'

We knelt there a moment, joined together. Then the gentleness returned to his voice, and he said,

'Come now, General, on your feet. Let's meet whatever fortune brings us, whether it be ill or whether it be good, like men. What happens after death is known to none, but all men I have heard talk on the matter agree that it is better to face the prospect of death with a cheerful countenance.'

His words renewed me. I pulled myself up, and took the cloth he passed me, and wiped my eyes.

'And with your star,' he said, 'we may survive whatever is in store for us.'

'That's all right,' I said, 'I'm myself again. I'll not forget what you have done for me today.'

The horsemen were close enough now for us to hear the horses' hooves and the clatter of harness. The troop halted when they saw us standing there. Then three or four trotted forward and again paused about fifty yards distant. The man in front turned in his saddle and called out, 'It's him, it's the General himself,' and they broke ranks and in a moment surrounded me. I looked up and saw Agrippa's face.

'Where the devil have you sprung from?' I called out. 'How have you happened on me?'

'Soldier's instinct,' he said, looking smug for he had often told me he possessed this, and I didn't. 'Are you all right?'

I glanced at Septimus: 'We're all right,' I said, 'thanks to this man here...'

★   ★   ★

You may wonder, my sons, that I can bring myself to tell this story, and tell it in such detail. It would have been easy to ignore it. The skirmish in which we were defeated was an unimportant episode in the scrambling war with Sextus Pompey. It was a little setback in a contest we could hardly fail to win in the end. There is nothing in the story which redounds to my credit. I lost my nerve; I behaved like a poltroon. I was embarrassed to see Agrippa, and could not meet his eye.

Yet I would be dishonest to omit mention of my failure of nerve and resolution, and I am trying to tell you (and posterity) the truth about myself. This was the one occasion in my life when my certainty of victory evaporated, and I found no defences within myself against fear and despair. I really wanted Septimus to kill me, and I was saved only by this farmboy's confidence in me. His fortitude and the happy chance of Agrippa's discovery of our refuge (and the horsemen might not have been Agrippa's; they might indeed have been Pompey's for he still controlled by far the greater part of the island) together reassured me that the Gods favoured my cause. I had henceforth no doubts.

What could I do with Septimus? I could not keep him by me, for he was a perpetual reminder of my weakness, and I feared lest I should grow to hate him. I sent him first to Livia bearing a letter in which I said simply that he had saved my life—I could not bring myself to reveal to Livia to what straits I had been reduced—and should be suitably rewarded. Eventually we granted him farmlands and olive groves near the spring of Clitumnus. For some years he sent us a gift of oil every winter. Then the gifts ceased. I made enquiries, discovered he had got into debt, had been too proud or too ashamed to seek the help which I should certainly have given. The first reports said he had drifted into the city; but when I gave orders that search should be made for him there, I had no success. Later reports contradicted the first: he had hanged himself from his own lintel rather than see his land pass to his creditors. Strange and disturbing symmetry of life.

★　★　★

The war with Pompey was a bore and a distraction. Gradually, thanks to Agrippa's genius for innovation and the invention of a new device called a harapax—a grapnel shot from a catapult that enabled him to lock Pompey's ships to ours and deny him the advantages of mobility which his pirates' superior seamanship had hitherto given him—we wore him down. Pompey's heart gave way; he fled to the East and threw himself on Antony's mercy: a letter from Antony tells the rest:

> Caesar: Pompey arrived here spluttering with fear and foaming at the mouth with indignation at what he called 'the barbarity of your methods'. I am sorry to say—you'll be heart-broken to hear it yourself, dear boy—that he regards you as a twister. I say 'regards' but I should really use the past tense. I've had enough of Pompey. We've tried everything in the way of co-operation, and it hasn't worked. Now you've beaten him and it really seemed to me that he had cumbered the earth long enough. So I had him dealt with, in the most gentlemanly way, you'll understand. The fact is, though, all Pompeys are losers. And what news of our colleague, the surely now truly superfluous man?
>
> Look after Octavia, and see that the child is safely born. I can trust you for that, brother.

I shall deal with the reference to Octavia in due course. Meanwhile I may as well wrap up this episode.

I could feel no grief at Pompey's execution. We had really indulged him absurdly.

It happened however that, by one of those quirks of military fortune, many of Pompey's legions surrendered to Lepidus who had played a minor part in the last weeks of the campaign. This might have been awkward, if Lepidus had been another man, for he now found himself as he thought in command of twenty-two legions—say a hundred thousand men, an enormous force.

Now over the years of the triumvirate Lepidus had grown resentful; he felt his inferiority and declined to admit its cause. I was breakfasting in Syracuse, after doing sacrifice to the Gods in that city of a thousand cults, when Agrippa stormed into the room, his face the colour of a winter sunset. At first I could make no sense of what he said, for in his fury he gobbled his words. At last however, I compelled him to sit down and relax.

'Now,' I said, 'let's start again.'

'That's just what the bloody hell we'll have to,' he cried. 'That bugger Lepidus.'

'Oh Lepidus,' I said, 'Lepidus is nothing.'

'Nothing is he? He's only setting up to be bloody Pompey.'

'What do you mean?'

'Ah, I've got your interest, have I? Well, that's something. I thought you were so taken up with these Greek cults—or Greek cunts for all I know—that you'd no time left for simple things like war and politics...'

'Come on then,' I said, 'I'm all ears, like a donkey.'

My little joke fell flat. Agrippa looked even blacker than ever. Your father never understood the frivolity of serious moments, I'm afraid. But at last he came to the point: Lepidus had suffered an attack of the delusion of greatness.

'Here's the bugger's letter,' Agrippa shouted. 'He announces, with no end of flowery whatsits, that, Pompey's legions having surrendered to him, he must now regard Sicily as his Province and he therefore commands you to get yourself and your legions out of the island. How's that for brass neck?'

'Whom the Gods wish to destroy, they first make mad,' I said.

'What the hell do you mean? What do we do?'

'Nothing.'

'Nothing? Are you going to take this lying down? Let me, for Jupiter's sake, march on his camp. I'll string him high as the Colossus at Rhodes...'

'Nothing,' I said again. 'We shall sit where we are. However, let Lepidus' communication be generally known. Then let us see its effect.'

Agrippa drew his brows together. I took hold of his arm, and felt it tense beneath my grip.

'There will be no need of war,' I said. 'Wait and see.'

It was fine weather, I remember, though I was little able to enjoy it, for there was a mass of administrative work to see to. We were engaged throughout the civil war, you must remember, in the task of re-animating Rome's government throughout the Empire. True, at this time, I was nominally responsible only for the Western half of that Empire; but that itself entailed a deal of work. Gaul, for example, though conquered by my father, had hardly yet been brought within our administrative sphere. In Rome itself, I had already embarked on my great building programme, restoring damaged temples and public buildings, erecting new ones, and bringing some order to the irregular and haphazard provision of housing for the poor. Much of my work throughout my life has been of this nature. I do not grumble. Indeed, I have always found pleasure in the establishment of order and orderly procedure. My greatest pride has been to serve my fellow-citizens.

But I became aware of an unusual gaiety in our camp, a feeling of irresponsible high humour. Lepidus' command had become known; and all took it as the best of jokes that 'the distinguished donkey' should take it on himself to speak with authority. Then, day by day, the drift from his camp to ours quickened. The army itself was sick of war. It was now eight years since my father's murder, and in that time, none of us had known peace. Now Lepidus would stir us up again, break the fragile balance we had achieved; and he found no takers. He was indeed laughed out of his armour. Within a week of his 'command' his army had begun to desert. I called one distinguished deserter to me. This was Lepidus' own nephew, Paullus. I questioned him closely anent his uncle's state of mind. He was loud in contempt. I resolved the time had come to act and invited him to accompany me.

The next morning, taking with me only a personal guard of a dozen men, I rode out of our camp, flanked by Agrippa and Paullus. We crossed the plain in the cool before the sun rose high. Dew sparkled on the young corn, and the breeze from the south-west gently caressed our faces.

We traversed the five miles that separated the two camps without incident, and were not challenged till we reached

Lepidus' outposts. Even then the challenge was half-hearted. The guard was ill turned out, the centurion a little drunk and unsteady.

'Have you come to see the General?' he called out, and then, recognizing who we were, made a visible effort to assemble his wits.

'Stand easy, man,' I said. 'Your discipline seems to leave something to be desired.'

'Sir.' He tried to come to attention and salute. I have rarely seen anything sloppier. We nodded and rode past into the heart of the camp.

The army's demoralization was evident. You would not have thought they had taken part in a great victory only weeks before. There were soldiers in various states of undress everywhere, and women too. One African girl bared her breasts and cried out to us that we could have her for free, any time we wanted, whoever we were. 'As long as you're not Lepidus himself,' she cried, 'I'd make him pay through his pompous nose.' And the soldiers standing round her laughed, to hear their General insulted.

Keeping together, though I had no fear of any danger, we rode into the parade ground. One troop—defaulters perhaps—was being put through a desultory drill by a bored centurion. They halted—without command—when they saw us, and I mounted the rostrum. Agrippa roared out to the centurion, commanding him to have his fellow-centurions assemble. This they did more quickly than I had expected, and very soon the parade square was full of men—ordinary soldiers as well as centurions—and some officers as well. Agrippa called them to silence, and I stood forward.

'Fellow-Romans,' I called out, 'many of you will know who I am. For those who don't, I am Caesar.' At the mention of the name, a great shout was raised and the crowd surged forward. 'I come to you,' I said, 'disdaining to wear any protection,' and, saying this, I tore off my breastplate and stood with my chest exposed.

'Will any man here strike Caesar?' I cried out. For a moment there was complete stillness in the crowd, and then this was overtaken by a babble of cheering. I raised my right hand. 'Well, you're better than senators then,' and they laughed in agreement. 'But,' I said, 'I'm sorry to tell you your general is of a different mind.' I produced the letter and waved it above my head. 'See here. I've a letter from him. He tells me to get out of Sicily. It's not a friendly letter, though Lepidus has no cause for complaining against me. So I've come here to ask your advice. Should I obey your general?'

Soldiers like irony. It is their own natural mode of expression, and they are pleased when it is employed by men like us at the expense of our social equals. This is not to be wondered at. Irony is after all an invitation to enter a conspiracy with the speaker.

'I confess,' I went on, 'I was in a sad state when I got this letter. Knowing Lepidus as I do, I was really alarmed. So were all my staff. Agrippa here—you won't believe this—was all for packing our bags and baggage and hot-footing it for Rome. But then, we had two thoughts. The first was: what if Lepidus follows us to Rome and tells us to get out of the city also? The second was: I wonder if his soldiers, those brave legions which have won glorious victories even under Lepidus' command, agree with their noble general. (Where is he by the way?) So I came to ask you. . .'

Well, you can imagine the response. I knew I was running no danger. There have never been Roman legionaries who would prefer Lepidus to me (I don't say I could have played the same game with Antony's troops—or even Pompey's). So I was quite safe and I had calculated correctly. They cheered me and roared with laughter, and crowded round the rostrum, stretching up their hands to shake mine or touch me. I let the euphoria develop, then stepped back and held up my hand again. . .

'Thank you, soldiers, thank you, comrades. This is a great day for all of us. We have peace in the Roman world. The Republic is no longer tormented by civil wars that have now lasted since the Senate's threats to his life and liberty compelled Caesar to lead his legions across the Rubicon. I am glad to know that you will not let Lepidus' little ambition disturb that peace. You have done nobly. It is now time to reward you. All those who wish to leave the service in the next months will be rewarded with farms and an end-of-service payment. Those who choose to remain in the colours will receive a cash bounty—as soon as I can get the Treasury clerks to disgorge one. If there is a long delay, and you all know what they can do to tie you up with red tape while they sit pretty themselves, why then, I shall advance the money out of my own pocket, I'll borrow from my own bankers if I have to. And then try to screw it back from the Treasury. And now, let me thank you formally and finally for the courage you have shown and for what you have done for Rome, for peace and for the well-being of the Republic of your fellow-citizens. . .'

Meanwhile there was no sign of Lepidus. I consulted a moment with Agrippa, and left him to bring the camp back to order and discipline. We agreed that there should be a parade in the late afternoon.

'You'll produce Lepidus at that, will you?' Agrippa said; but there was really no question in his voice.

The triumvir had retreated to a villa on the flank of the hill overlooking the camp, and I followed him there. It was a charming spot, a building of pale creamy stone, festooned with roses, wisteria and clematis, a place, I thought, in which to pass an idyllic retirement. It suited itself to my calm mood.

Lepidus had made an effort to compose himself in order to receive me. He was still as handsome as ever, and self regard or self-consequence had not quite fled him. In his first sentences he sought the old tone of patronage; a tremor in the voice betrayed him. I asked that all attendants leave us, and led him out on to the terrace.

The hum of the camp rose to us. Beyond it the great cornfields of the Sicilian plain extended to the mountains. If one made a half-turn, the sea sparkled with a docility I rarely experienced while campaigning. Alone, Lepidus' manner crumbled; he even knelt before me, and pawed the skirt of my tunic. I told him to get up, to remember that he was a Roman noble, a consul and my colleague.

'Though also,' I added, as I sat down, 'a fool.'

There was no pleasure in this meeting. I have never been other than embarrassed by the sight of humiliation. That day at Philippi, when the defeated cursed me as they marched by, killed all delight in victory that I might ever have had. Yet things have to be wound up.

'I could charge you with treason,' I said. 'I could have you named an enemy of the Republic, a public enemy and outlaw. There would be no difficulty in doing so. Antony would support me, and I doubt if you would find any to speak for you. Even your own nephew Paullus urges me to do this.'

He whimpered excuses. He had been ill-advised. I had misunderstood his letter. He had merely been putting in a claim for the governorship of Sicily. It was a long broken speech, and the remnants of that oily ingratiating manner irritated me. I stopped him short and told him what I required in order to display my clemency.

The last act was played out before the army. Agrippa had organized the parade, and they looked unexpectedly smart. A good deal of polishing and burnishing had taken place. They were out to do me and themselves honour, to prove, in the manner of soldiers, that they were worthy of respect, and, at the same time, to express their gratitude and loyalty to me. It may also be that they wished to shame Lepidus.

I inspected the troops, with the usual pauses before individuals whom the centurions had recommended for my attention.

Then we waited for Lepidus. He rode in on a grey horse. That was a mistake for he had never had a good seat, and, now in his agitation, he was bouncing all over the place. However he managed to dismount without too much awkwardness, and only a small stumble. He looked round wildly, having been too occupied in managing the horse (which was, as a matter of fact, absolutely placid) to make sure of his bearings before he was on foot. It disturbed him to see that I was waiting on a dais some ten feet off the ground, so that he had to climb a flight of steps to reach me. Unobtrusively, my guard detained his attendants so that he mounted alone. I remained seated on a golden chair. Courtesy urged me to rise of course, but I had decided that the effect of my superiority would be more effectively marked if I remained seated.

Lepidus was sweating. He halted before me. I looked him

in the eye but said nothing. Silence quivered in the air. I sensed the intensity of the soldiers' gaze. I waited.

Compelled by my silent eye, Lepidus sank to his knees before me. He held out both hands, the wrists together and fingers extended.

'Caesar,' he said.

Behind me, my guards placed their right hands on their sword-hilts. Lepidus gulped.

'Caesar,' he said again, 'I have come to ask for mercy. . .'

'Lepidus,' I said, 'we came together, with Mark Antony, to restore the Republic, to avenge my murdered father and to bring peace to the Empire. But you have tried to steal my glory and my victory; you have planned to make war against me. My grievances are deep, and they are not mine alone. I am ready to forgive your offences against myself, but your offence against the Republic is rank. . .'

I paused, and then raised my voice to make sure that all the soldiers heard.

'Nevertheless,' I said, 'since you have been rejected by the soldiers whom you thought yours, but who have all instead recognized and obeyed their higher loyalty to the Republic, I shall practise that clemency on you which was ever my father's watchword. You will be stripped of your dignities; the triumvirate is dissolved. Yet you shall be left with one office, and that the highest of all. You succeeded my father in the office of Pontifex Maximus. Though you have discharged it unworthily, yet my reverence for the Gods is so great that I shall not presume to dismiss their unworthy priest. Remain therefore what you have been; but, from now on you must discharge your duties by deputy, for you are banished from Rome and sentenced to perpetual exile.'

Believe it or not, the disgusting object crawled forward and embraced my knees. He even licked the dust from my feet in his abject relief. I drew back, and ordered him to be led away. The troops parted and watched him go in silence. I am sorry to say that some of the men spat on his shadow.

'It's the first time he hasn't provoked laughter,' Agrippa said later.

Lepidus' behaviour cast a gloom over us. We would not have thought a Roman noble capable of such degradation.

The soldiers too were ashamed to have accepted him as commander.

My sentence of exile was not strictly legal of course. But it was necessary. Anyway I had it confirmed and ratified by the courts as soon as I returned to Rome.

I was sincere in my decision to leave him as Pontifex Maximus. It was not for me to disturb the formalities of religion.

VIII

There is hardly one moment in a political life when you can relax and enjoy what you have achieved. (In this politics resembles marriage.) I had restored order in the West, planted the seeds of fruitfulness in Italy, commenced the long task of embellishing Rome. Virgil had already sung the promise of a new Age of Gold; a benign sun ripened the cornfields and empurpled the grapes of plenty. But Antony . . .

For three years, while he made Athens his headquarters, he lived agreeably with my sister. She had no more to complain of than drunkenness. Of course, there was also a certain absurdity. It was not seemly for a Roman noble to preface his public announcements with the words: 'Antony the great and inimitable'; and it did make him a figure of some fun to the rest of us. It was impolitic too for him to advertise the favours he enjoyed from Dionysus, when he so often made it clear that he was enslaved to the God; and perhaps it was not in the best taste to claim descent from Heracles—hardly a model husband or father, you will remember. However such excesses could be easily forgiven; after all, everybody knows that Greeks and Orientals like high-flown language, and indeed make a cult of insincerity. (This is why Romans find it so difficult to come to a true measure of Easterners; we do not realize that for them rhetoric is an end and pleasure in itself, frequently quite unrelated to action, never moving beyond a purely verbal significance; I do not think that Antony understood this himself; I believe he was seduced by his own propaganda.)

Nevertheless, in a way, Octavia came to love him (as in a

manner we all did). She said to me, 'He is a great child and so there is a sort of tenderness called forth; it is painful to watch him suffer the consequences of actions which are, I assure you, absolutely spontaneous.' Moreover, their daughter Antonia was a delight to them both, and Octavia, being kind and tactful as she was good and chaste, forebore to raise the matter of the twin children Cleopatra had borne, to whom she had given also the ridiculous names of Alexander Helios and Cleopatra Selene—the sun and moon, I ask you, and even at the time asked myself if Antony had consented to these names; I wouldn't be surprised if he had, for his taste was lamentable.

In Athens too, thanks to Octavia, they contrived to live, despite his habitual excess, with some decorum and restraint. Why, Antony even spent some time studying philosophy in the schools, though, as Maecenas said, he was probably the last Roman capable of benefiting from their subtle disquisitions.

Then, as I have told you, Antony without warning sent Octavia back to Rome; for her health, he said. I questioned my sister closely. She was unable to give any other explanation, or perhaps still too loyal to her husband to advance one. Was he unkind to you? I asked. She denied the charge. Antony, she insisted, was a more complicated being than I imagined. I listened to her with great patience seeking understanding, though in fact none knew better than I the contradictions Antony contained. He was not a simple man of action; I knew that. I knew more than that: I knew that men of action, finding it difficult to articulate or order their thoughts, are indeed far more complicated than intellectuals and poets to whom words come easily. They lack the ability to explain themselves, for they have no power of introspection. (For this reason Pompey the Great was an enigma to all; he had no understanding of himself. For this reason too, your father Agrippa has always been harder to know than Maecenas.)

'Have you quarrelled?' I asked.

She shook her head. For the first time in my life I found myself unable to converse freely with my sister. I resented the influence Antony still exerted.

I asked Livia to talk with Octavia, hoping that she might

speak more openly to another woman. But Livia failed too. There was some barrier between my wife and sister. Perhaps Octavia was jealous of Livia's influence over me, as I was of Antony's. I consulted my mother. She merely reminded me that she had always opposed the marriage. I felt myself disappointed in my womenfolk. It was a relief when Octavia moved into her own house on the Palatine.

Of course I had agents in Antony's household as he had in mine. The elimination of Pompey and Lepidus made things more difficult between us. More important, Antony's long residence in the East corrupted his intellect; he began to forget that he was a Roman nobleman. Seduced by the absurd flattery of the inhabitants of his provinces, he came to see himself as king. And as a god.

He broke his word to me. Within months of Octavia's departure, he was again living with Cleopatra.

I made one more attempt to recall him to his proper path.

Against my advice he embarked on his long-cherished campaign against Parthia. A better soldier than the wretched millionaire Marcus Crassus, whose legions had been cut to pieces in the desert, he took the northern route through Armenia. His marshal, P. Canidius Crassus, a man of the highest ability and most despicable character, had already subdued the tribes as far north as the fabled Caucasus. In the foothills of Erzerum he mustered a great army of sixteen legions, ten thousand Gallic and Spanish cavalry (whom I had sent to my colleague) and a host of Armenian horse under the native prince Artavasdes. No finer Roman force was ever assembled, and I had stripped my own resources to supply my colleague's needs.

The first reports that reached us in Rome spoke of triumph. Antony had advanced unchallenged beyond the frontier towards Phraspa, the capital of Media. The city buzzed with rumours of fabulous treasure and unparalleled achievement. Octavia's house was beset every morning by senators anxious to impress with their devotion to her husband. Agrippa was torn between jealousy and apprehension. He longed to achieve such glory himself; his own recent campaigns on our northern frontier seemed mere police work beside Antony's.

At the same time he said to me, 'You do realize, don't you, that if Antony brings this off, we've lost the game? Once he's conquered Parthia and has annexed the treasures of that Empire, been given the chance to establish his dominance there, he is going to be absolutely invincible. Why, I tell you, Sulla's return from the war with Mithradates, which I've been reading about, will be absolutely nothing in comparison. And you know how Sulla destroyed Marius and the Popular Party then. He's really outsmarted us, and you were fool enough to send him help. You've dug your own grave, and mine too. Oh,' he went on, talking faster and faster as his excitement rose, 'it's no use you putting on that pussy-cat face of yours, or reminding me, as I see you're just about to, that, in your view, Italy is the key to power. Balls! Marius held Italy too, and look where that got him. Asia is the real key. Whoever holds Asia dominates Rome. Pompey did it too, remember. Well, we've got maybe a year to prepare. I tell you, when Antony comes back in triumph, he'll turn on us. Sure as eggs is eggs. Why, already these bastards in the Senate know which way the wind's blowing. Look at how they're crowding round Octavia and swearing they've always been Antony's men.' He went on in this vein, becoming more and more agitated.

At last, I said, 'It's a long way across the desert to Phraspa. And I still say, Italy is the bedrock of power. Meanwhile—understand me well, Marcus—we are all delighted by the success of our colleague's campaign so far. He is winning glory and territory for Rome. I shall praise him in the Senate.'

It was indeed a long way to Phraspa. Moreover, Antony's strategy depended for its success on the trust he had placed in Artavasdes. What a fool! You should no more trust an Oriental than rely on the wind to blow as you wish it to. Naturally, he deserted Antony, and betrayed him. Two legions under Oppius Statianus were cut to pieces. A large part of Antony's supplies was destroyed. Though he struggled on, late in the year, to Phraspa, he lacked the means to reduce the city, and was compelled to withdraw. All through the terrible retreat that followed, the Parthian cavalry snapped like wolves on his flanks. Even Armenia was deemed unsafe; thankfully Antony scrambled back to Syria. Much was later said of his exertions on the march, and I see no reason to disbelieve such accounts, for he was still a brave and resourceful fighting commander. Others however have assured me that the army was in fact only saved by the skill and courage of Canidius. I could not say, for Antony never allowed a full history of the campaign to be published; and it may be that this was indeed impossible, the materials being lost, with the legions I had sent, in the waste of sands.

Of course reports at Rome for some time stressed the positive side of the campaign. We heard much of his achievement in reaching Phraspa. That aroused enormous wonder. It was only gradually that the reality percolated across the sea, and then I was amused to observe the morning crowds diminish at Octavia's residence.

Antony wrote to me urgently begging for reinforcements. 'It only requires one more push,' he wrote, 'for the war to be won.' 'For the Gods' sake, kid (I was briefly, in his need, 'kid' to him again) remember what I did for you against Pompey, remember the love I have borne for you, remember Philippi and our common devotion to your father, remember the bond that our beloved Octavia forms between us, and send me twenty thousand men.'

I replied imploring him to abandon his Parthian plans. 'There is a great desert,' I said, 'lies between the two empires, as you have discovered, my dear colleague and brother, to your cost. The desert ensures that Parthia will never endanger the true interest of Rome. The Republic needs peace. Thank the gods that you did not incur Crassus' fate (which would have grieved me personally, torn the heart of Octavia, and deprived Rome of her greatest general). Take your honourable defeat as a warning from the Gods, that you should not repeat such rashness.'

In return he sent me an incoherent outburst, full of insults and threats. ('He must have been drunk to write this nonsense,' I said to Maecenas.) Again he demanded twenty thousand men.

Agrippa exploded with fury. 'If we had them to spare,' he cried, 'he should not have them. But we need them in Gaul, in Illyricum, on the frontier of the Julian Alps. Caesar, you will not yield to this madness.'

'Peace, Marcus,' I said.

Instead, unwilling to give him the curt refusal that his insane and selfish request merited, I despatched seventy ships, as earnest of my good faith, while sending also two thousand crack troops, veterans of my war with Sextus Pompey. Octavia accompanied these men, and I urged her to persuade her husband to see reason.

Her eyes filled with tears. 'Do you know what you are doing to me?' she asked. 'Do you realize to what you are exposing your sister?'

I affected not to understand, but when I came to kiss her good-bye, the tenderness of my embrace could not but disclose the pity and guilt which I felt.

Her husband received her brutally. He was dressed more as an Oriental potentate than a Roman general, and he refused to see her alone. Instead, speaking from a throne of carved ebony, embellished with amethysts, topaz and rubies, he treated her to a long speech of complaint in which he denounced my ingratitude and faithlessness.

'You were,' he said, 'in our marriage, the mark of my friendship with Caesar. But he himself has torn up that contract. Return to Rome that all the world may see the shameless manner in which he has treated me.'

Was there ever such despicable behaviour?

'Our marriage,' he said, 'must be considered at an end.'

Octavia wept, but tears which would have melted the coldest heart could not unfreeze his demented arrogance.

When I heard the news I wept too: first for Octavia's shame; second, for the import of Antony's actions. I looked over the city and saw war and pestilence again. My heart ached as with the pain of seeing a boat carry a loved one into the wastes of the grey seas.

IX

It is time now to speak of Cleopatra, and I find it hard to do so. It would be as easy to speak of snakes.

When I wrote to Antony, rebuking him for resuming his affair with her in breach of his promise to me at the Treaty of Brindisi, he replied with something of his old jocular insincerity. This is what he wrote:

> What on earth has come over you? What if I am sleeping with the Queen? She's my woman. Besides, it's nothing new. The thing started years ago, as you know, nine or ten I daresay. What about you? You're not really faithful to Livia, are you? I bet you're not. My congratulations—or commiserations—if between the time I write this and the time you get it, you haven't been to bed with Tertullia or Terentia or Rufilla or Salvia Titisenia—or the whole bloody shooting-match. For heaven's sake, I ask you of all people, does it matter a legionary's oath (and we know what that's worth, don't we?) who or what, with, or where, or when, or how often you do it? Sex, dear boy, can be over-rated, take it from me . . .

Such a defence was hardly defence at all. But that he should write in such terms to his wife's brother shows his state of mind. That was the effect Cleopatra had.

She had seduced my father when she was hardly more than a child. He refused to see her when he occupied Egypt because his plans for the kingdom did not include the Ptolemy family. So she had herself delivered to him wrapped up in a carpet. It was unfolded in his presence and all her charms were exposed, because, not unnaturally, though with some art, her scanty costume was agreeably disarranged, and she lay there giggling before him, mischievous as a kitten. (He called her 'kitten'.) Well, you may say—and you would be right—that it was about as difficult to seduce Julius Caesar as it is to eat the first strawberries of the season. Nevertheless, mark the sequel. She not only popped into his bed quicker than boiled asparagus; he popped her on to the throne of Egypt, having her brother (with whom she should have shared the kingdom) disposed of, at her request. What sort of a girl was it who at fourteen would sacrifice her brother for the sake of power? I find that much more remarkable than her ability to fascinate my father.

It wasn't her beauty. Oh, she was pretty, very pretty, as a young girl; small, sinuous, active, with dancing eyes and mobile features, and a voice that always seemed to be choking back a laugh. They talked Greek of course—you do know that the Egyptian royal family are Greeks, and no more Egyptian than, well, your father Marcus Agrippa, don't you? Her Greek was quaint and provincial—Alexandrian Greeks swallow up consonants and run their words together so that their conversation sounds like the chattering of sparrows under the eaves. She made a great many grammatical mistakes. As you know correct Greek prescribes that neuter plural subjects take singular verbs; Cleopatra ignored this. Of course only a pedant concerns himself with grammatical niceties, and it is quite gentlemanly to make the occasional error. Still, our Roman ladies take pride in speaking correct Latin. Cleopatra didn't care; she disregarded the subjunctive whenever she felt like it, for instance. She never troubled herself, by the way, to learn even a little Latin, for there is no doubt that from the start, despite her affairs with my father and Antony, her hatred and resentment of Rome ran deep.

Nothing could have been more deliberate than her assault on Antony. Its blatancy surpassed even her first meeting with Julius, which could be explained as a sort of childish prank and had certainly a childish charm. (As he said himself, 'Well, the last thing you expect from a carpet is to unroll a gorgeous piece of that sort of muslin.') I have already quoted to you one version of that encounter. Whose was it? Salvidienus's, I think. It was, I suppose, accurate enough. The arrival in the barge made an enormous impression and curiously most versions which I have heard agree. Certainly nobody who saw it forgot. Cleopatra was not really beautiful—her legs were too short for one thing (Livia always used to point that out, and add that, according to her information, she had very thick

123

ankles too). But she was quite amazingly made up; her appearance when she set out to captivate Antony represented a superb triumph of art, if not of nature. Everyone agrees on that. What is often ignored is the extraordinary vulgarity of the spectacle. I admire the theatre myself, and I recognize that theatre is an indispensable part of politics too; but private life should eschew theatre, and, anyway, there should be a measure in all things. I really find it impossible to distinguish between Cleopatra's vulgar exhibitionism and the sort of disgusting spectacle put on for tourists in the red light district of Corinth; the only difference I can discern is that her show cost more. Morally, it was just the same sort of whore-display.

Antony succumbed of course, for his own taste was ever deficient. He couldn't see how essentially comical the spectacle was—all the more comical because Cleopatra's very real intelligence allowed for a degree of self-parody. She was playing a part. She knew it. And she enjoyed it. She was the kind of woman who cannot help despising the men she deceives and, from that first meeting, she always retained a certain contempt for Antony. She had not despised Julius because she saw that he approached sex in the same spirit of irony as she did herself. Besides, she was then a child; he was the greatest man in the world; it is possible that even Cleopatra was dazzled by him. She did not love him, for that was not her nature. She was incapable of the dependency without which real love is impossible; she could not lose anything of herself in another.

Antony was a different matter. True, at first he preserved some detachment. When he told me at Brindisi that it was politics—'politics and sex, boy—she's a great lay, the Queen'—I believe he was speaking the truth. He was overwhelmed in the first days, but his intelligence and will reasserted themselves. The proof of that is that he was able for three years to abide by the agreement we made; in that time he never once saw Cleopatra alone.

She didn't resent this. Why should she? She was vain (she would spend three hours a day before her looking-glass) and self-absorbed; but she was without that peculiarly feminine emotional vanity which demands a man's total surrender and is piqued when it is refused. You may find this surprising, but I believe it to be true. Their first affair had achieved her purpose. She had guaranteed her continued control of Egypt; she had placed Antony in her debt. Power was her chief interest, not love.

Yet Antony never quite escaped her. I have talked of this with Octavia. She said, 'Of course I never truly loved Antony. I married him because you asked me to. I could not love him, for I could not respect him. I admired much. Who could fail to? I responded to the grandeur of his gestures. I came close, I confess, to loving the little boy in him; that is something which women find appealing in a man till one day, quite unexpectedly, it revolts us. He was kind to me, and considerate, and gentle; he made love with unexpected gentleness and took pleasure in doing what pleased me. Yet I knew all the time that I never possessed his heart. There was a part in him that always lusted after Cleopatra. Of course, there was another part that was grateful to me for protecting him from the Queen, for I am quite clear that deep down he feared her. What was it he said? "No Roman can stand without Rome." He knew that Cleopatra would lure him to disaster. He knew too that there was something in himself that welcomed that prospect. He feared it. He could never quite deny it. You see, Antony was far more complicated than people realized. They saw the bluff soldier; that was no more than a part of him, perhaps no more than a facade.'

But I never denied Antony's complicated nature. I had after all good reason to know it.

When Antony turned away from Octavia and turned his face back to the East and let his eyes dwell on the Queen, he surrendered to all that was self-destructive in his nature.

They used to drink heavily together. Stories of their drinking bouts are legion. They would tope through the night and then stagger into the morning street where Antony would pick fights with coster-mongers and the keepers of fried-fish stalls, and Cleopatra would hold his coat while he exchanged blows with them. At other times they lay for days downing flask after flask as they sprawled on cushions and rose-petals and slaves wafted branches of palm trees over them. Reports came to us in Rome of Antony's effeminacy: how he had put on women's clothes and tended Cleopatra's toilet. Of course I

125

didn't believe such stories; yet the fact that they were so freely relayed was not only disquieting (and politically dangerous); it showed how Antony had fallen away from the old Roman standards. 'No smoke without fire,' men said.

Cleopatra would emerge from these debauches, bright-eyed and keen-witted. 'If all that's said is truth,' Agrippa grumbled, 'that Queen must have a liver like a senior centurion's.' Antony however was said to be prostrated with nausea after their sessions, sometimes taking as many as four or five days to recover. No doubt it was, as Agrippa said, largely a question of their different livers. Yet I knew there was more to it. Abstemious myself—you have never seen me drink wine without adding water to it; a practice I have adhered to since my late twenties—I have yet made close observation of those addicted to wine. It always represents some degree of self-hate. It is a surrender to the weaker and worse element in a man's nature. Even as he indulges this, and surrenders to Bacchus with every expression of pleasure, he is, in his willed self-debasement, willing his self-killing. Such a man will always suffer worse from wine, for such suffering and punishment is what he unconsciously seeks. In turning to Cleopatra and abjuring Octavia, Antony set himself to kill whatever was good in his own nature; he opened the door to his dark spirits. He beckoned defeat. I have never forgotten hearing a common soldier say, 'Bloody ruler of the world, you call him; a strumpet's fool and nothing else, poor sodding misbegotten bugger.'

I started to talk of Cleopatra and have involuntarily ended by discussing Antony. I have a good grasp of him, but the Queen is like quicksilver. Let me say one thing only: she was depraved, but not evil; my enemy, but, in her own light, justified; an enchantress, but one who, like Circe, turned men to swine.

She was also Rome's most dangerous and implacable foe.

X

I could now look back on a decade of achievement: I had restored order in that part of the Republic under my immediate control; I had avenged my father; none of the self-styled 'Liberators' survived to hold public office, though Antony still indulged the younger Domitius Ahenobarbus whose father had been among them; I had built up a loyal party of friends, dedicated to the service and virtue of Rome; with the able and industrious assistance of Agrippa I had already repaired years of neglect and damage to our public buildings; my policy had ensured the gratitude of my fellow citizens; acting in concert with my friend Maecenas I had encouraged and fostered the arts; under my patronage Virgil, secure in the possession of his ancestral lands, had almost completed his great poem in praise of Italy, the sublime Georgics, and was already brooding, in the deep mysteries of the poetic spirit, his hymn to Rome's destiny ('What, Caesar,' he asked me, 'is Rome's mission?' 'Order and clemency', I replied, a judgement to which he gave lapidary expression in the resounding line: 'to spare the humble and subdue the proud'); in honour of my achievements, my fellow-citizens had of their own will erected a golden statue of me in the Forum.

I had one private grief. Despite a lustrum of profound domestic happiness, Livia and I had no child of our own. Our tenderness continued to be lavished on my daughter Julia and Livia's sons, Drusus and Tiberius, as well as on my nephew Marcellus; the lack of a child born of our loins was nevertheless a sad deprivation; in vain Livia celebrated the mysteries of the Great Mother; in vain visited those shrines, to be found in all the country districts of Italy, to which village maidens resort that the Gods may bless their fertility. Speaking to you, my beloved grandchildren and adopted sons, it would be unseemly to rehearse the private questionings of the reasons for our unfruitfulness which disturbed our night hours. All I shall say here is that your happy presence has long consoled us for whatever might otherwise have been.

Yet in that long summer of my thirty-first year, this private grief nagged me, running like an itch in a muscle alongside a deeper pain. Whenever I lifted my eyes towards the east I seemed to see dark clouds loom over the hills. I could take no abiding pleasure in the lizard basking in the sun; the mimic war of the arena disturbed me. I was weary after ten years of struggle, and oppressed by the knowledge of what was to come.

I sought refuge in Livia and found her adamant. 'Rome cannot have two masters,' she said. When I protested that I was not 'master' of Rome, that, as a true Roman, I found the term 'lord' repellent, she withdrew herself from my embrace, and, resting on her right elbow, looked at me without smiling. 'You can no more hide from the truth,' she said, 'than a man can walk in a thunderstorm and remain dry.'

'The master's in bed,' said the painted slave-boy who guarded Maecenas' chamber.'

'No matter.'

'He's not alone,' the boy smirked.

'No matter. I must see him,' I said and pushed past.

The room was dark. I called for candles. Maecenas lay there, entwined with a blond, pale-skinned boy, a Gaul I suppose, whose face took on a fugitive expression as he woke to my interruption. Maecenas stretched himself.

'Caesar,' he yawned elaborately. 'Dear me. Perfect timing as usual. An hour earlier and I should have been seriously miffed. Run along, ducky,' he said to the boy, who withdrew sullenly now from the bed. He sat a moment on its edge, his hair tousled, eyes bleared with sleep and mouth slack-lipped. Then he rose to his feet, Maecenas patted him affectionately on the buttocks and he left us alone.

'Gorgeous, isn't he?' Maecenas said. 'I don't know why, I've suddenly developed a taste for these manly blonds, such a delicious combination of strength and softness, eagerness and shame. Do you know he . . .'

'Oh stop it,' I said, 'you don't have to put on this act for me.'

'Well, hand me that dressing-gown, there's a love. You look worried.'

'Would I be here at night if I wasn't? I couldn't sleep. My belly's disordered, I have a beastly headache and my nerves are a-jangle.'

'And Livia's no comfort, eh?'

'I didn't say that.'

'No?'

'There are things you can't say to a woman, aspects you can't reveal, doubts you're reluctant to share.'

'Don't I know it. I love my own wife, you know. But she's not for every day. What is it?'

'I don't know what to do,' I said. I sat down on the bed. 'Help me,' I said. Then: 'I'm not telling the truth. I know what must be done. But I'm nervous. I'm apprehensive. There's so much to be done. I don't know if we can bring it off. I don't know if they will stand for it.'

Maecenas put his hand on my shoulder. 'Relax,' he said, 'we have come a long way since the Ides of March.'

'Caesar,' I said, 'travelled far to reach the Ides.'

'Your star shines bright,' he said.

We talked through the night, elaborating the courses open before us. Long talk with Maecenas always calmed me. I saw the subtlety of things, the complicated relations of one event with another; no one I have known could more surely discern the patterns that life traces to form the carpet of history. I always left him more confident of where to go and what to do. And yet this time, though my intellect assented to his argument, I still tasted the sour saliva of doubt and dismay.

Agrippa was brusque. 'Look, mate,' he said, 'it's a damn sight less complicated than you think. Suppose,' he said, 'you're trapped in a defile by the enemy who are blocking both ways out. Well, you can't bloody wait. The only way is to smash your way through. That's how it seems to me. Now, look at the facts. That's what you forget, that you have to look at the facts, not your fears. Antony is Antony. That's bad enough. But now he's Antony and bloody Cleopatra. Rome needs Egypt. We can't feed the city without Egypt. We can't pay the troops without Egypt and the taxes of the Eastern Empire. Everything we've worked for in Italy depends on getting control of Egypt and the East. Conversely, while we hold Rome, Italy and the West, Antony can never feel his power is anything but precarious. I don't know what Antony wants. Maybe he wants to make himself king. Who cares? It doesn't matter a Greek's curse. There are opposing forces that cannot be reconciled. So, my boy, there's only one way out. We've got to biff him before he biffs us.'

'Antony has friends, relations, adherents here in Rome. We are by no means all-powerful here.'

'Well, biff them first. We've done it before.'

I shook my head. Arguing with Agrippa was like being an ox trying to argue with the slaughterer; he held a sledgehammer ready. But this time I shook my head.

'We can have no more proscriptions. The time for that is past.'

I invited Virgil to come to see me in my villa in the Alban Hills. We ate on a terrace overlooking the holy stillness of Lake Albano. Olive trees and vines tumbled down to the lakeside under a sky of the most intense blue. The idle heat of summer lapped around us. We ate perch fresh from the lake and strawberries brought from nearby Nemi, and drank my own straw-coloured wine. Flowers closed in the heat, red, yellow and deep purple slashed with white, and, after we had eaten, the slaves left us alone.

During the meal we had talked of poetry and agriculture and, as ever, Virgil's calm knowledge refreshed me; but when we were alone, he said, in his quiet northern voice, that never sounded without offering a rustic comfort, 'Your spirit is perturbed, Caesar.'

I made a vague fanning gesture over the scene below us, now empty of humanity, as the peasants took their siesta, waiting for the sun to decline before they resumed their labours.

'Yes,' Virgil said, 'you are right. It is good. It is life. Nevertheless...'

'I don't want to fight Antony,' I said. 'It's very simple, isn't it?'

'Oh simple. When we have seen complications we cannot

evade them by a mere return to simplicity. For the peasants who work the fields and groves, life has a rude simplicity. They must listen to the moods and rhythms of nature and the succeeding seasons. But you cannot attain peace, Caesar, as a peasant would. I knew why you asked me here today and I have thought about what I must say.'

He picked up a strawberry and held it up between thumb and forefinger, for a moment against the light, and then replaced it.

'The story of Cincinnatus,' he said, 'is the ideal of every true Roman. To plough harmonious fields, to be summoned from that worthy work, proper to every good man and our rightful heritage, in order to save the State; then to be offered the supreme power of the dictatorship; to put on the toga of State to discharge his duty, defeat the enemies of the Republic and receive the grateful plaudits of his fellow-citizens; then to resign his office, lay aside his toga and resume his place behind the plough, enriching and taming the soil of Italy; is that not the perfect life, as it is the perfect story which every true Roman has imbibed almost with his mother's milk?'

I nodded, but could not speak, for my heart was full.

He picked up the strawberry again.

'The most perfect and delectable fruit of the earth,' he said. 'It comes from Nemi, doesn't it, from benign fields by the water's edge? But in the woods of Nemi lies a grimmer tale. There stands the Temple of Diana, guarded by its sole priest, a man who can never safely sleep, but must, night after night, prowl round the shadowy temple, a drawn sword in his hand. He is, as you know, Caesar, a priest and a murderer, a run-away slave who won the right to guard the holy place of the Goddess by slaying him who was priest before. How men are chosen for this cruel, arduous, and sacred duty we cannot tell. That they are divinely selected we cannot doubt. That his mission is holy, however cruel and fraught with fear, dismay and anguish, is certain. He performs what the Goddess commands in response to some necessity that is beyond human understanding. His life is a symbol perhaps of the decay and corruption of the world which can only be pardoned by the benign action of the Gods and by love. Without Diana there is no fertility; without fertility neither joy nor life. Yet this paradox remains: that Diana's temple, the home of the Great Goddess who brings forth life, is guarded by a murderer's sword, and that the priest himself must die, ingloriously, ignorant perhaps even of the nobility and importance of his achievement. We cannot fathom the mystery, but we can acknowledge its truth.'

He paused, and cast on me a look of the utmost tenderness, in which love, pity and respect, such as I have never seen on another countenance, were mingled. I looked into that sad and noble face, in which the refined delicacy of feature could not hide the strength that derived from his complete honesty, and felt my courage return.

'Caesar,' he said, 'I know little of history and less of politics. But listen. Cincinnatus is legend; he belongs to a young world when everything was straightforward, and right-doing was rewarded by a calm spirit. As legend, it is for children, it is an ideal to present to them that they may grow up seeing and admiring whatever is good, straight and true. But the priest of Diana who guards the Golden Bough and the Temple at Nemi presents no legend but myth, which reveals the truth darkly to grown men. The world has gone beyond Cincinnatus, and you cannot lay aside your toga and return to the plough. You are bound for life to prowl with naked unsheathed sword round the Temple that is Rome. Forgive me.' He smiled sadly and laid his hand on mine in understanding and pity.

Thus, I took my perturbed spirit to the four people whom I loved and to whom I might look for guidance; and though all indicated the same path to me, it was the poet who led me by the hand unscathed through the briars that concealed its entrance and past the wild jaws of the beasts that threatened my passage.

XI

The great wagon-wheels of Mars and Bellona were set in motion. Rome simmered in feverish heat as it had done in the summer after my father's murder. Once again there was taking of sides, jockeying for position (as the chariot-drivers do in the circus), dark eyeing of old acquaintances. Once again true social intercourse was corrupted.

The most terrible stories reached us from the East; Antony, whether because of drink, infatuation, the strange madness of power with which the Gods can afflict great men and render them unmindful of Nemesis, was losing all proportion, all sense of the connection of things. He celebrated a Triumph for his Parthian War, in Alexandria. Do I need to spell out the enormity of this gesture? A Triumph, I surely do not need to tell you, is an honour granted to a Roman general by the Conscript Fathers of the Senate; it may be celebrated only in Rome, for it is not merely a personal honour, it is a proclamation of the greatness and genius of the city. To arrogate to oneself the right to determine one's entitlement to a Triumph is sheer madness, an act of hubris, unforgivable by men, indubitably punished by the Gods of Rome.

He did not stop there. The circumstances of the Triumph were as outrageous as the thing itself. There was no reverence in it; the occasion was made a pretext for the glorification of Cleopatra. She sat on a raised dais on a great carved throne of gold; she there received the gift of captives who should have been offered to Jupiter, the most high and mighty God. The next day, robed as Isis, Goddess of the Nile mud-flats, she shared a throne with Antony; their children, Cleopatra and Alexander, sat at their feet. With them was a lean boy of thirteen or fourteen, also Cleopatra's son—that was not doubted; she had had the impudence to name him Ptolemy Caesar or Caesarion and assert that he was my father's son—a lie notably exposed by the quite un-Roman cast of his features. But now, Antony, his face purple and his eye watery, swayed to his feet, beckoned the boy to him, embraced him, and, showing him to the legions, the eunuchs and slaves of Egypt, proclaimed that this was indeed Caesar's son, 'Kings of kings,' he cried, 'son of the Divine Julius and Cleopatra, mother of kings, and queen of kings.'

'It is a direct insult to you as that man's son,' Livia said.

'He is mad,' Octavia sighed. 'That woman has deranged his senses, and destroyed his judgement. I could almost weep if I weren't so angry.'

'Drink, more like,' said Agrippa.

'Wait,' said Maecenas, 'there is yet more. Carry on, boy,' he said to the messenger.

My agent, a young Greek called Nicias, shrugged his shoulders. 'I warn you,' he said, 'it gets still more bizarre. I only hope, Caesar, you will not treat me as my own countrymen, in their heroic days, used to treat the bearer of bad news. Well, Caesarion—you must allow me to call him that, for at the moment he bears no other name—had some difficulty in getting Antony back on to his throne, and he sat there for a long time in silence, while everyone grew very embarrassed and wondered if he was about to pass out. There could be no doubt by now that he was decidedly drunk, you see, and everyone was speculating nervously as to what would happen if . . . but then Cleopatra gave him a sort of jab with the wand which she was holding as a symbol of something—I'm not very well up in Egyptian symbolism, you'll have to forgive me, it strikes me as a Greek as terribly silly and a bit comical too—and he raised his great head—it's a marvellous head now, in his decline, you know, like a wounded lion's or that of an old bull standing knee deep in a swamp and ready to stand a last charge from an enemy who has already all but destroyed him. Well, he raised his head and for a moment a look crossed his face of invincible self-hatred, and he shot a glance at Cleopatra which was positively venomous—like Perseus holding up the Gorgon's head—and he began speaking again, but this time without any of the swagger of his first speech. And—you'll hardly credit it—he began parcelling out the Empire among the children: Alexander, a little squirt of nine or ten with a wandering eye, typical little Egyptian brat, was given Armenia and all the lands east of the

Euphrates; and the girl Cleopatra, Lybia and Cyrenaica. Can you believe it? And . . .'

'What about Caesarion?'

'Nothing for him; yet. It is said he will, in time, be made lord of Asia.'

'You see what that means,' Agrippa said.

We all did.

'And then,' said Nicias, 'the whole company except for the detachments of legionaries began crying out and hailing Antony as Dionysus and Osiris, consort of the goddess-queen of Egypt and all that exaggerated Eastern nonsense.'

(Greeks are capable of the same sort of nonsense, you know, but Nicias, having identified himself with Rome, had become more Roman than the Romans in his distaste for such emotional and intellectual extravagance.)

'Antony,' he said, 'looked a bit sheepish, but he could hardly deny them.'

*　*　*

There was no need to take special measures to see that reports of this ceremony were disseminated through the city. The news ran fast, and bred fear and dismay. Everyone realized what was implicit in it; Cleopatra had not only seduced Antony; she had suborned his mind. Alexandria would displace Rome. The legions would be commanded by the sorceress of the Nile. The Republic would be destroyed. I have been called a master of propaganda; I had no need of such skills now. The facts spoke for themselves.

*　*　*

Yet Antony retained partisans in the city. I had still to move cautiously. I sent Antony a friendly, yet strongly worded, protest, pointing out that he had no authority to dispose of the provinces of the Roman state as he had reportedly done. He replied insolently, demanding that the Senate approve what he had done in Egypt. His henchmen in the Senate, the consuls Gaius Sosius and Domitius Ahenobarbus, did not dare to present this message, but they conveyed the news that Antony now regarded the triumvirate as having expired, its powers as obsolete. The implication was that henceforth I had no authority, no *imperium*.

I attended the Senate, and in a speech of the utmost moderation, I outlined the course of Antony's actions over the last year. 'Do you wish, conscript fathers,' I asked, 'to deliver Rome into the hands of Cleopatra?' It was a question Antony's friends could not answer; instead Sosius, a man of neither merit nor achievement, tried to shift the argument by attacking me. He even went so far as to propose that I be named a public enemy. A tribune interposed his veto; a kind but unnecessary act, for the motion could not have passed. Nevertheless his veto saved me a momentary embarrassment and I was grateful to him.

That debate however convinced me that the moment had come for a bold stroke. First, I asked Maecenas to call on the consuls.

'Let them know,' I said, 'in your most silky and sinister manner that I am displeased. Let them know that I will not brook such behaviour. Ask them—politely—how many legions they have. Suggest that their friends in the East must be bewailing their absence. Remind them how brief is a consul's authority. Ask them if they imagine the mob will respect Cleopatra's friends. In short, my dear Maecenas, I look to you to put the fear of death into the pair of them.'

'Don't worry, ducky,' Maecenas said, 'when I've finished with them they'll be scared even to shit.'

'I don't want them so scared they can't run.'

They ran; I then announced that all those who regarded themselves as friends or clients of Antony might leave Italy. Perhaps one-third of the Senate departed.

* * *

Traffic however ran both ways. Many Romans who had been attached to Antony could not stomach his exotic and deluded and disgusting debasement. Among these was L. Munatius Plancus.

A word on him whose arrival I greeted with great pleasure. Plancus came from a good bourgeois family of Tibur. He had served on my father's staff in the Gallic wars and at Pharsalus, but he had never before, in all the comings and goings of the last decade, adhered to me. Indeed, he had fought against me in the war of Perusia, for he had been a close friend of Antony's brother Lucius. He had later joined Antony himself, and had recently been proconsul of Asia and of Syria. There was no one more experienced, no one more knowledgeable of how things stood in Antony's party. Curiously, I had only met him once before: at the time of the Proscription when he had proved his zeal for the Republic by assenting to the inclusion of his own brother in the list, and also his eye for personal advantage by seeing to it that the Coponii of Tibur, old rivals of his family, were pricked down.

I would not have recognized the thin grey-haired man who was ushered in. He had a restless, glance-over-the-shoulder, finger-twitching manner which I have often observed as being induced by long immersion in politics. His speech too was nervous and jerky.

I apologized for the search to which he had been subjected before he was allowed in.

'I am ashamed of it,' I said. 'Nevertheless the fact is, that only a couple of months ago, I had a dagger drawn on me . . . so my friends insist that now I should see nobody alone who hasn't first undergone a search, and, my dear Plancus, I very much wanted to see you alone.'

We talked a little about the changes he found in the city, for he had not been there since the year after Caesar's murder. 'Perhaps,' he said, 'this makes it easier for me to applaud what you have done in the way of restoration; perhaps also it has made it possible for me to retain an ideal Rome in my mind; and it was, Caesar, my vision of that ideal Rome which persuaded me to break the old bonds of my friendship with Mark Antony. I could not stomach the perversions he now displays.'

I was sure this was high-flown nonsense. Plancus I had written down as a cunning old time-server, quick to sniff the direction of the prevailing wind and ready to tack—if I have got the right nautical expression—before it. I had welcomed his arrival for just this reason, also of course for the news he could bring . . .

I remained wary though, in case Antony had sent him to deceive me. He soon disembarrassed me of this notion.

'I can't stomach,' he said, 'what's happened and what's

happening over there. I tell you, no Roman could. The last straw was seeing Antony in Egyptian robes walking among that woman's eunuchs. He is about to divorce your sister, you know, and stage a public wedding with that woman. Not that that means much, in my view they've been man and wife for years. He's half-besotted, and half-blind to any other way to restore his fortunes... But, Caesar, I've come, on conditions, to hand you the game...'

'Conditions?' I said.

'Conditions which your natural gratitude and dignity will be happy to satisfy.' He gave a quick forky lick of his lips. 'Caesar, I have served the Republic all my life. I have lived as honourably as a man can these last terrible two decades. I recognize what you have done to shore up the State, but I have done my bit myself even though we have sometimes found our judgements differ. No more of that though. I've attained some honour, I say—do you know, in Mylyssa in Caria where I was proconsul there's a priest consecrated in my honour—awful, these Orientals, aren't they? But honour is one thing and a man can't live on it in his old age.'

'What,' I said, 'do you have to...' I hesitated before the word 'sell'; it hardly chimed with all this talk of honour... 'tell me? I am sure we shall be able to satisfy you.'

'Antony's made a will,' he said. 'I witnessed it and know its provisions... As for me, there's various honours and comforts—a priesthood of Jupiter, an estate on the Bay of Naples—that I have my eye on ... I would like a contract, Caesar ... the provisions of the will are scandalous...'

'Would they be believed?' I said.

'My word ...' he said.

'Words,' I said, 'are discounted these days. The currency of language has been debased. Look at the insults Antony has showered on me. They mean nothing, have no effect.'

Plancus smiled. 'This would be different. Let me tell you what is in the will. He asserts again that Ptolemy Caesar is Caesar's son and leaves huge legacies to him and Cleopatra's other brats. Nothing is left Octavia or her daughter Antonia. He orders that his body be buried in the royal mausoleum at Alexandria. I don't need to spell out the implications of this will, do I, Caesar?'

He did not; I felt my head swim with excitement. Plancus had handed me what I needed to convert a personal struggle (as some persisted in seeing it) into the cause of Rome and all Italy.

'But words,' I said.

'I can prove them ... but first my contract...'

I called for a slave, signed whatever he dictated. (It mattered little.)

'The will,' he said, 'is deposited in the Temple of Vesta.'

Livia was adamant: it could not, must not, be done. It was wrong in itself, sacrilege. Whatever lay in the Temple of Vesta was a sacred trust of the Goddess. No man might enter the shrine; no man might compel the Virgins to surrender what had been entrusted to their keeping. Her eyes flashed as she said this, and love, fear and anger were mingled in my heart. If no man ... could she not herself? 'You have been blinded, Caesar,' she said. 'You are in danger of losing your sense of what is right and what is wrong. I beg you to have nothing to do with this, to forget and lay aside the evil temptation that that man Plancus has sown in your mind. I warn you too, that if you commit this sacrilege, our marriage will be doomed to perpetual unfruitfulness...'

How can a man respond to such a plea from his wife? There are no words. No argument can still a trembling heart such as Livia revealed. I took her in my arms, but she drew her head away, resisting my kiss. There was no answering embrace.

'You will kill,' she said, 'whatever is good and true in you and in us...'

A shadow crossed the face of the sun and the room was cold.

Maecenas, too, hesitated. The news shook him out of his affectations. His hand flew to the carved frog he wore on a chain round his neck. For some time he could not speak.

Then he went and looked out of the window to the hills...

'I'm afraid,' he said, 'I would be afraid to do it myself, and I'm afraid for you, my dear. You can put me down as a dark and superstitious old Etruscan, but... Your star, yes, the

Gods have looked kindly on you and on us. Will they do so after what you propose . . . this violation?'

'We shall fight Antony at sea perhaps. I do not think Neptune cares a rap for the Temple of Vesta.'

'The Gods punish impiety, whatever form it takes. My dear, if you do this, you will suffer, some time, I cannot tell when, but you will . . .'

I remembered what Virgil had said of the Temple of Diana, and knew Maecenas spoke truth.

It frightened me that Livia and Maecenas, who disliked each other, should proffer the same advice, the same warning.

It frightened me; yet I could not turn back. Plancus had handed me a set of loaded dice. When I cast them on the table, they would inevitably roll to my advantage. My hand holding the dice-box felt cold and bony; my mouth filled with nausea, as I hesitated. I turned back, once more, to Livia, and begged her to free me from the guilt. She, being a woman, could act as intermediary. She was permitted to enter the Temple, and wasn't the High Priestess her mother's sister?

Livia said, 'You are asking me to do what I know to be wrong; to ask my aunt to betray the trust vested in her order through all the centuries of Rome's history.'

I felt my face grow obstinate as a small boy's.

'You don't understand,' I said. 'We cannot avoid war, and you refuse me what alone can ensure my victory. Antony has all the riches of the East behind him. I must march against him, for I cannot endure war in Italy. But I dare not leave disaffection behind. That will cook Antony's goose,' I said. 'If you will not help me, I shall ask Octavia.'

'Do,' she said, 'do just that. See if she will commit sacrilege to help her beloved brother.'

And with these words, and a face as full of wifely love as Clytemnestra's, she swept from the room.

As it happened I dared not approach Octavia. I told myself I could not ask her to take this weight on herself. But that was not the true reason. I was afraid of her anger and contempt.

Even Agrippa shrank from the deed. When I talked of the will to him, he at once rattled off a string of military statistics, all claiming to prove that Antony was lost whatever happened in Rome and Italy. Only his refusal to meet my eye told me of his fear, told me he was lying. I couldn't recall that he had ever lied to me before.

So, in the end, I had to take full responsibility. Even Plancus slipped into the shadows, and I wrote to the High Priestess requesting an interview. She declined, politely. No doubt rumour of my intention had reached her; it was unlikely that Plancus had kept his mouth shut. Alternatively . . . but to dwell on the alternative could do nothing for my self-esteem.

Then, one of the tribunes, whose name I now forget, organized a pro-Antonian demonstration in the forum. There was something of a riot, a few houses were burnt, and Agrippa's police had to clear the streets. Men started to talk wildly—as men always will in times of civil unrest. This time word flew round that we would soon be back in the days of Clodius and Milo, those gangsters whose ruffians had made political life impossible for a time some twenty years previously. This talk alarmed Agrippa. Your father was a great man, a great soldier and even finer administrator; at heart however he was a policeman. There was nothing he feared except disorder.

He came to me now like a bewildered bull, to tell me I had been right and he himself wrong. 'It's no longer a question of what to do,' he said, 'but how to do it.'

'I'm glad you see it that way. Have you any ideas?' I said. 'I may say,' I added, 'that we can't look for any co-operation from the Vestals.'

'In that case,' he said, 'it's a choice between force and fraud.'

'That's no choice,' I said. 'Can I leave it to you?'

He bungled it. We were dining late (which was ever Livia's taste, itself a surprise to those who cast her as a conventional Roman lady of the old school, and did not realize that, when Livia abode by conventions, she did so because they pleased her, while remaining always ready to disregard them if they happened to clash with her immediate preferences or inclinations). We were, as I say, dining late, when my stepfather bustled in, full of that simulated consternation with which he was wont to impart the latest news, and, having attracted general attention by his huffing and puffing and hopping from foot to foot, exclaimed, 'You'll never believe the atrocious news I have just heard. There's been an attempted robbery at the Temple of Vesta.'

'Attempted?'

'Robbery?'

Livia's head came up like a startled mare's.

'Who were the thieves? What were they after?'

Philippus, gratified by the attention he had won, seated himself on a couch and clapped his hands for the slave-boy. 'Give me wine,' he said, 'I'm all out of breath with the hurry of coming here. That precisely no one knows. They were slaves of course. Greeks, men say. Whose is not yet clear. Nor what they were after. But I'm told we can expect revelations. They'll be put to the question of course. You look pale, my boy,' he said to me. 'You're overdoing things, I've told you that. What do you make of my news? It's terrible, isn't it, to think of such a thing happening. I don't know what the world's coming to,' and he drank his wine, not, you will understand, as if that could tell him . . .

Livia denied herself to me. I knew she had so determined by the way she refused to look at me, and, when I came to bed, she had turned her face to the wall and was pretending to be asleep.

Before then, however, I had talked to Agrippa, whom I had sent a slave to fetch from wherever he was gambling. The shock having been sprung, I was quite calm.

'They're your men, I take it,' I said.

He nodded. All the colour had been drained away from his face, and his usual composure had vanished.

I said, 'They mustn't be permitted to speak. I don't suppose they can be trusted to keep silence. They're Greeks, aren't they?'

'They're Greeks. Dammit all, they had to be. I couldn't use illiterates.'

'That's all right,' I said, 'but their mouths must be stopped. You know that. You've taken an interest in the city's aqueducts. You know what happens if an aqueduct springs a leak. Exactly. Well, your plumbers have failed in their repair job. They're leaky themselves. They mustn't be allowed to talk. I've had the Praetorian Prefect take over responsibility. But the question is, is there one of them who might sing the right tune to save his skin? Find out will you, before he's killed trying to escape. And if he exists, this is what he should sing . . .'

I looked at Livia in the half-light. I knew she wasn't asleep. The air of our room was heavy and menacing with her resentment and reproach. When I laid my hand on her thigh I felt the muscles stiffen. 'It's going to be all right,' I said. Without shifting her body, she distanced herself from me. I was excluded from all that I most immediately desired, and I dared not move towards her.

The boy was brought before me in the morning. I had taken care to have a dozen senators assembled, at least three of whom I knew to have been friends of Antony. The Greek was very young, about sixteen I suppose, with oiled curls and a smooth oiled body. His mouth was swollen and a bruise was coming up on his cheekbone. He looked frightened, like a puppy expecting to be whipped. I was surprised that he was so young, but Agrippa explained that he had been the look-out boy. 'I suppose Democritus,' (an ex-gladiator who had been the leader of the gang) 'fancied him,' Agrippa said. 'You can see he's a bloody little catamite. Typical Greeks, you know.'

The boy fluttered his long eyelashes over his big doe eyes. I looked at him severely, rejecting the timid smile he was trying to muster. I said to Agrippa, 'What's his name and provenance?'

'Timotheus. Slave-born. Has been a member of a dancing-troupe. Taken up by the gladiator Democritus.'

'Has he been put to the question?'

'Wasn't necessary. He babbled at the sight of the instruments.'

I turned to the group of consulars I had invited to be present at the examination.

'Would one of you like to question him?' I asked. 'You perhaps?' I offered the role to M. Cocceius Nerva, consul three or four years before, who had served under Antony, but who was also, like all his family, a close friend of Plancus. I made the choice carefully. Cocceius Nerva, a leading member of a rising family, was swithering on a tightrope of indecision; he danced in the air unable to decide which side would better promote his career. Now he looked for a moment as if he would rather decline my invitation, considered the consequences of that, and nodded his head in acceptance. He began to question the boy in a harsh guttural accent. The boy stuttered over his first responses (I thought to myself: he has a certain theatrical talent; well chosen, Agrippa). Seeing his fear, Nerva warmed to his work. His voice snarled out his questions, and the boy began to whimper obediently. Then at last, as if giving way to intolerable pressure, he told his story.

He had had no responsibility himself; yet he had to confess he had been in it from the beginning.

'I was drinking,' he said, 'with Democritus—that's my friend, my special friend, you understand, in a wineshop in the Suburra. We were short of money, business has been bad lately with so many patrons out of the city, and we were moaning about it. Democritus was always a moaner, I have to say that. Well, then, as we were drinking, a big hooknosed fellow came up and sat at our table. I didn't like the look of him from the start. He spoke to Democritus as if he knew him, but it soon came out that he'd only been recommended to him. Then he looked at me doubtfully. "You can say anything before the boy," Democritus said. So the man nodded and said there was a job on. "What sort of a job?," says Democritus. "A big one," says the man. "Can you read?" he says. "Not so well," says Democritus. "Bugger that," says the man. "But I've friends as can," says Democritus, not anxious to see the job slip away from us. "That's all right then," says the man, "it's not a one-man job anyway." "So what is it then?" "Well," the man says, "you know the Temple of Vesta?" "Who doesn't? Not that any man's ever been in it," says Democritus, laughing but really intrigued now, because it does sound like it's going to be big. "Well, I don't," says the man. "I'm a Roman citizen, but I

144

was born in a colony and I've never lived in Rome. I'm a soldier," he said, "from the East, and I don't know the city, else I'd do the job myself." "All right, then," Democritus says, "so what is it?" And then the man comes out straight. "The General Mark Antony has deposited his will with the Vestals, and the man wants us to snitch it." "Why?" says Democritus, playing dumb, "why and what's in it for us?" Well, to cut a long story short, what's in it for us sounds pretty good, but I understand you gentlemen want to know the why, and it seems from what I understood that this will was like to prove an embarrassment and so some of the General's friends, maybe the General himself, thought it best that it be got rid of...'

'All right,' Nerva said, 'we understand that. Didn't it occur to you that he had only to ask for its return? Why this elaborate burglary...?'

The boy looked Nerva in the eye for the first time.

'Of course that struck us,' he said. 'We're not stupid, you know, sir. We asked him that very question. And he had an answer. He said that they'd chosen this method because the burglary was sure to be blamed on Caesar here, and that was the reason...'

Oh no, I thought to myself, Agrippa has overdone it. That's one refinement too many. Surely someone will see that if their burglary had been brought off, I would have been able to produce a will of some sort... my stomach twitched ... but of course I was viewing the affair from a different angle; this possibility occurred to nobody else seemingly. Yet it was a possibility that must not be allowed to fester. Someone would spot the weak point in the story.

'This must be nonsense,' I said. 'I apologize, Nerva, for intervening in this cross-examination which you are conducting so ably and which has already elicited such interesting information, but this can't be right. There is a fundamental flaw in the boy's story. Surely, if the burglary had taken place successfully, and the burglary had been blamed on me—which...' I hesitated ... 'is an impious thought profoundly offensive to me—such an attribution could only be convincing if I had had a will to produce. Otherwise the story would not hold water.'

145

The consulars frowned into the muddy pool. The boy turned his huge eyes on me.

'I thought of that too, General,' he said, 'and thinking my friend was being led into trouble, I even raised the point. The agent smiled and answered me in such a way as to leave no doubt that he was indeed your enemy. Then he furnished us with an explanation. You were indeed, after the burglary, to be supplied with the will—by a well-wisher. It was to be such that you could not resist publishing it. But Antony would have the real will, with the Vestals' seal, and the real will would be much more "innocuous"—that was his word—than the one you would have published. Then, you see, he would have sent the real will to the Senate, or invited leading senators to examine it. You see, my lords, the whole purpose of the plot was not to get hold of the will at all, because, according to our information, it really is innocuous; the plot was aimed at Caesar here. Its intention was to discredit him. It would seem he had first committed an act of sacrilege by ordering the burglary, and then discovering that the will he had stolen didn't suit his purposes, had committed a second crime: forgery . . .'

I was amazed by the boy's talent. What's more, he was now evidently enjoying his role, playing the part of a man revelling in the release that comes from the self-abasement of confession. Moreover, I marvelled at the effect of this last speech. It was clear that the consulars were convinced it was true. It was therefore safe to confess myself staggered by the enormity of what had been revealed, and at a loss as to the appropriate action to be taken. I did so, and there was much shaking of heads.

Only one consular, my wife's cousin Appius Claudius Pulcher, seemed doubtful still. He said he would like confirmation from the other members of the gang.

'Killed, resisting arrest,' Agrippa said. 'My police report they were a desperate crew. Only this little rat submitted at once, in tears and without a struggle.'

'We may be thankful that he did,' Nerva said. 'Otherwise who knows what vile conclusions, damaging to the Republic, might have been drawn?'

The upshot was satisfactory. It was resolved that a motion

be put to the Senate requiring the Vestals, in the name of the Senate and the Roman People, to broach convention and deliver to their keeping the Testament deposited there by Marcus Antonius, considering that they had reason to believe that the said Testament contained matter pertaining to the security and sovereignty of the Senate and the Roman People. Even the Vestals felt obliged to heed such a request, which they did, though adding a rider in which they proclaimed the reverence that should be due to testamentary documents lodged in their keeping—a reverence, I need hardly tell you, which I have never ceased to feel.

The publication of the will had the anticipated effect. It aroused fear and anxiety and rumours were soon rife that Antony intended to move the capital of the empire from Rome to Alexandria. There were spontaneous outbursts of popular feeling against Antony who had once been the people's darling. Now his house on the Aventine was fired by the mob. Everywhere one heard stories of his abject subjection to Cleopatra. It was said that he had walked in the train of her eunuchs, himself dressed in Egyptian robes and that he had taken part in the abominable rites with which the corrupt and decadent inhabitants of the Nile valley celebrate their loathsome gods.

No one dared to raise a voice in his defence, not even in the Senate. On the contrary, feeling ran so high against him that, without any necessary prompting on my part, he was divested of his *imperium* and deposed from the consulship for the following year to which he had already been elected. There was even a proposal that he should be named as a public enemy; but here I thought fit to intervene. I had no desire to enflame feeling further against Antony, not because I had developed any tenderness for him—apart from the remnants of the affection which he had always inspired in me, however reluctantly—but for a more politic reason. Four years earlier, after Pompey's defeat, I had formally declared the era of the civil wars concluded. I had no wish to suggest that it was being renewed. On the contrary, the war, now being prepared, was directed against an enemy of Rome, not against a fellow-citizen who wished to subvert the state. Our foe was

Cleopatra. I was calling on all Italy to make a supreme effort in a Great Patriotic War.

Accordingly, I now prepared my master stroke. I called on the whole of Italy, the whole Western world, senators, troops and civilians, to swear an oath of loyalty to me in Rome's struggle against perfidious Egypt. None was compelled to take this oath. Indeed, mindful of Antony's presence in the ranks of the enemy, and mindful too of the solemn nature of personal obligations, I made it clear that those who felt such loyalties to Antony should be under no pressure; I even specifically exempted the city of Bologna, an old cliency of Antony's, and stated that I would not regard its loyalty to its old patron as an expression of disaffection to me or to Rome. It was said that such clemency and benignity exceeded anything displayed by Julius.

Because the oath was voluntary and because my cause was just, being the cause of Rome and Italy, the whole country spontaneously flocked to the special offices established in every municipality to assure me of their trust. Nothing in my life has given me more enduring pride than this. Even those colonies of veterans who had served under Antony took the oath. I may add that this was all done despite the necessity of imposing some of the severest taxation Rome and Italy had ever suffered; denied resources of the East, we found it necessary to impose an income tax of twenty-five per cent to pay for the war. But, since all knew that the war was just, and all hoped that a combined and cheerful effort could bring it to a speedy termination, even this tax was paid, though before its purpose was fully understood and before the oath-taking served to rally the mass of our countrymen to the cause, there were sporadic riots and disturbances in some of the provincial towns. I could understand and forgive these; no sensible man likes to pay taxes. It was soon realized however that this tax was necessary, and it was paid all the more willingly when men remembered the enormous contributions to the public Treasury I had made and was continuing to make from my own resources. Moreover, everyone knew that I lived simply and spent little on myself.

The triumvirate having been abolished, the Senate responded by granting me a right of command without limitation of function or command. The title of dictator had also been abolished, and I had no wish to revive it, for its associations were no longer those of the heroic past of the Republic; but in fact I now possessed all the powers of the dictatorship for an unlimited period. Yet it was important that these had been granted me not solely by the Senate but by the spontaneous confidence of all Italy.

Only one shadow was cast over my serenity. Livia, distressed beyond my understanding by the affair of the Vestal Virgins, still denied me the marriage bed. My love was deep enough to enable me to continue to respect her feeling; but her withdrawal grieved me. My body and senses could find easy comfort, such as a man needs (or thinks he needs) but I felt a cold emptiness in my heart.

I was over thirty, and my youth died in that winter as we prepared for war with Cleopatra.

XII

Had the virtue departed from Antony? I asked myself that question as we lay in our camp at Mikilitsi in the hills on the north side of the Bay of Actium. He had already made so many mistakes that I could not but wonder if his heart was in the war. He should never have permitted us to cross to Greece unmolested. He had then allowed us to take up our strong position on the hills. At first I feared a trap, but, when he crossed the narrows and encamped his army two miles south of mine and despatched his cavalry to the north of us to try to cut our supply of water, his movements, formerly so sure and often surprising, were now so hesitant and lethargic, that I realized there was no such trap. Antony had lost confidence in his own genius.

Agrippa now captured Patrae and Leucas, and as a result was able to place his fleet across Antony's communications. He would have to fight his way back to Egypt and we could meanwhile intercept his supplies.

I had only to wait. We had got ourselves in a position

which we could only lose by making a false stroke. I was determined to sit tight and compel Antony to move.

There were only two clouds. First, my health was poor all that summer, though no doubt I suffered less on the heights than Antony's wretched army beset by flies, fever and on famine rations, in the plain below. Every day we could see fatigue parties sent beyond the lines to dig mass graves for the fever-victims. But I myself suffered from a persistent sore throat. My skin was dry and hot. I slept ill at nights. My digestion was poor and already I was a slave to the kidney-disease which, as you know, has compelled me to follow a strict diet.

And then there was Livia. She had stayed behind in Rome (where I had left Maecenas in charge) to look after the children. I missed her for she had been my companion on my happiest campaigns. Worse, though, were her letters. She could neither forgive nor forget the affair of the will. She wrote coldly and brusquely about the children's health. Here is a specimen:

We leave to-morrow first for your villa at Velletri, then for the house my father left us on the Bay of Naples. I shall be glad to be out of the city which is now disagreeably hot. The children are well and send you respectful greetings. Drusus, I am glad to say, shows sign of developing his athletic abilities. He really rides very well now. Tiberius has been in a silent and withdrawn state. I would pray that he does not fall a victim to the congenital malady of low spirits which so easily affects Claudians. I cannot but remember how his father would sink into supine depression. It is too often the fate of proud and sensitive natures which lack that capacity for self-approbation that enables many much less well-born to achieve more, since their equanimity permits them to do even what they know to be wrong without self-reproach. Tiberius is not like that. When he errs (as all children do) and has to suffer merited reproof, his self-esteem is sorely wounded, and he is then very likely to refrain from any further effort. It is the dark side of that Claudian pride which has on the other hand spurred so many of his family to do great service to the Republic. Julia, of course, has no such inhibitions. She dislikes being reproved (as I am sorry to say she frequently has to be), but it is not pride that is wounded in her case. She has, I am afraid, little natural sense of morality, which is to be regretted even if it hardly surprises me now. Her dislike of reproof is rather an expression of injured vanity—something quite different from pride, as different indeed as the true buffalo-milk cheese of Campania is from the cheap imitations sold in Rome. It offends her that anyone should dare not to think her perfect—I am afraid she is very spoiled—but instead of considering whether the reproof be deserved, and examining her own conscience—which indeed she could hardly do, for Octavia agrees with me that she possesses no such thing—she takes umbrage and is ready to reproach whoever has corrected her; usually, I am sorry to say, myself. Yet, I must say too that she and Tiberius are very close to each other. He is very loving and patient though she teases him endlessly and it may be therefore that his noble character will have some influence over hers, and do something to mitigate the selfishness, waywardness, conceit and capriciousness that are her chief faults. Still I must confess myself doubtful. Julia is so convinced of her own perfections that it is hard to believe her susceptible to any influence. I am sorry to hear that you are in poor health; still, your constitution is such that you cannot expect ever to be free of ailments or infirmities. Moreover, I understand that the Greek climate is too frequently enervating. I am well myself, though as I say, I shall be glad to be out of the city. Your obedient wife, Livia.

Ouch, you might say, what a letter; not a word of love and a sting in every sentence. Everything she said about poor little Julia was clearly intended for me. When I replied I tried to mollify her:

Livia, I know you think you have cause to write to me in the cold and unloving tone of your letters. Believe me when I say that though your voice and words pain me, they only add to the love and respect I feel for you. I know the cause and respect it. Do you wish me to defend my actions?

Perhaps I should do so. Perhaps I can only do so when the sea is between us, and I am poised here on the mountains overlooking Antony's camp and waiting, with a touch of fever in soul as well as body, for the battle that will determine whether my life will be of service to Rome, or will only be remembered as a bitter comedy of trivial ambition. You see, my dear and only girl, the state I find myself in. Do not, pray, be offended that, despite your coldness and your anger that throbs below that coldness and inspires it, I address you in this way. You are the only woman I have ever loved, fully as a man can love a woman, that is to say utterly, and if you withdraw that love from me then there is very little in my private life that could comfort me, that could protect me from the ravages that public life very surely inflicts on a man. You are my strength and my refuge. Do not deny me. You are not only the one woman I have loved in this way, but I know in my bones there will never be another.

I can write these words, though I could not say them to you. And this is perhaps the one flaw in our marriage, and the rock that could break the fragile little raft on which we sail down life's river. In one sense—perhaps more than one, but certainly this one—we are too alike. We are both reticent. We both find difficulty in talking about what we feel. We both retreat when we find ourselves in disagreement into a silence that grows more and more bitter and unforgiving the longer it lasts. And it is this silence which could corrupt and kill our love. Not a single action, but a long brooding in which resentment festers. I do not know if I could survive that. You are in many ways stronger than I am, but, if that happened, if the love we have developed for each other, a love which has matured over the years of our marriage, should be poisoned, something would die in you too. You would, I think, be confined in the bonds of a narrow and unforgiving rectitude. You have, if you will allow me to say so (and try to remember that I speak out of love), a certain timidity which expresses itself in an unwillingness to contemplate the way others live and think. Perhaps this is the form that the Claudian pride takes in you. Indeed I am sure it is. What I can give you is true confidence and gaiety. Do not cut yourself off from what I can provide.

To come to the point at issue, that action of mine of which you so strongly disapprove and which fills you indeed with disgust and even hatred. What can I say? I have a great respect for what is sacrosanct, and would never, in my private life as a citizen, violate a sacred place or sacred obligations. Yet in my capacity as a public man I must sometimes see things differently. A man holding public office must sometimes be conscious of necessity. He must be prepared to do wrong himself if it is in the public interest. Such a recognition informed my actions as Triumvir. Do you think that in my private capacity I could ever have consented to measures so appalling to the moral sense as the Proscriptions? Yet Rome required them. So also with the case of Antony's will. I asked the Vestals to deliver it to me, having carefully explained why I deemed it necessary. They rejected my request. Alas. What could I do? Should I say Rome requires that the will be made public so that Rome and all Italy should understand the peril in which we stand, but, notwithstanding this necessity, I shall refrain from action because I must not do what I know as a private citizen to be wrong? That would indeed have been dereliction of duty.

I cannot put my private conscience above my duty to Rome.

I told you what Virgil said about Cincinnatus and the priest at Nemi. I beg you to brood on his words, and try to understand my position.

Thank you for all you have told me about the children. Julia of course has such charm and beauty that she thinks all should be forgiven her. You are right to reprove her, but she is young and will, I am sure, come to hand. I hope our dear Tiberius, whose intelligence and character have already won my respect, will not fall into melancholy. You are right to be wary of his inheritance. Your ever loving husband, Octavianus.

The last paragraph was perhaps injudicious, but I had to show I had read her letter. Her reply was swift and unrelenting:

That letter was absolutely typical. I don't know why you think I'm afraid or reluctant to say what I feel, but this time I shall play it your way and put it in writing.

What threatens our marriage is whenever you fall below the moral level I have a right to expect of you, for when you do that, I really detest you. There I have said it, and I would wish you to understand clearly that I mean precisely that. I detest you also when you then equivocate and find specious explanations for what you know to be wrong. It is all too easy to console yourself with what Virgil says. I don't know why you should think that likely to impress me. He is only a poet and everyone knows that poets are clever liars, skilful in making good seem bad and vice versa. They are every bit as bad as lawyers, and your arguments are lawyerly.

What you say about my character shows that you have never troubled to try to understand me. I don't recognize myself in your description, but I do see one thing: being in the wrong yourself, as you tacitly confess by your long and sophistical defence, you have tried to put the blame on me, and blame whatever is going wrong between us on me, on my attitudes, my Claudian pride and so on. This is downright dishonest and quite unworthy of any husband, let alone one of your rank, a rank to which, I may add, you have been helped to rise by my family connections.

You had better not write to me again in that fashion. I won't endure it. If you want to divorce me, you will of course do so. But if we are to remain married, well then, I shall have to insist on your abandoning this tone. It really is outrageous, that you should try to make me seem the guilty party.

Julia told me the most shameless lie today. I was obliged to have her whipped.

Please don't write unless you can write in a different manner. By the way, there are unpleasant stories circulating about you and your nephew Marcellus. It is unwise to show such obvious favour to a handsome boy, and it is unfair to him. You know yourself what damage was done to your own reputation by the way you allowed that man Caesar to pet you. I am not saying you were morally at fault then, or even now. But in both cases you have shown a lack of that judicious temper on which you normally pride yourself. Octavia is both perturbed and hurt by the stories that circulate in Rome about you and Marcellus. I don't need to tell you that your friend Maecenas takes pleasure in spreading them.

What could I reply? Only this:

Livia, I love you, and so will accept your reproof without further attempt at justification. I shall even thank you for the warning you convey about Marcellus. It had not occurred to me that my affection for this remarkable and virtuous boy could be so construed. Certainly I love him, but I love him as I love Drusus, Tiberius and Julia. He is one of the family. Maecenas of course has a mischievous tongue (and I think it grows more mischievous the longer he lives). I shall write to tell him to stop it. All the same, do please remember that Maecenas has been more useful to me than any man—even Agrippa... Meanwhile, pray for me ... the reckoning with Cleopatra cannot be long distant.

Antony sent messengers to me. They arrived on the morning that news came from Agrippa of a great victory at sea against Antony's admiral Sosius. I myself broke the news of this triumph for us to Antony's envoys, M. Junius Silvanus and Quintus Dellius.

'You see,' I said, 'your cause is hopeless. You may reply to your general that the only matter to be negotiated is the terms of his surrender.'

Dellius grimaced. 'The Queen,' he said, 'will never permit it. Caesar,' he said. 'We're on the wrong side. It's hardly proper for Romans to take orders from a foreign woman, and that's what it amounts to...'

Not only Romans were now abandoning Antony. The next morning Amyntas, King of Galatia in Asia Minor, rode out with his cavalry on a reconnaissance mission, wheeled his men round the flank of the hills, and presented himself in surrender at our outposts. He was brought to me, a lean leering Oriental, ready to offer treasure to keep his kingdom, self-abasement to win my clemency. Though disgusted by his servility, I prudently enroled him in our ranks.

As I rode through the camp, I saw Dellius sitting outside a tent, guzzling pork, with a wine-flask before him.

'Food and drink, Caesar,' he called out, 'that's more than old Antony can offer.'

I could not but reflect that men like Dellius would have abandoned my cause as happily and with as little compunction; and a thought came to me: I have more in common with Antony than with anyone in either camp.

News was brought that Antony's stoutest general, C. Domitius Ahenobarbus, had also slipped from the camp. Antony, with that self-conscious and theatrical nobility which was an essential part of his strange character, and which so often prompted gestures that caught the imagination of nobles and soldiers alike, ordered that Ahenobarbus' equipment, arms and treasure be sent after him. When Marcellus heard of this, he called out to me, 'Why do we find ourselves at war with such a man?' What could I answer?

Let me pause here and dwell a moment, not on Antony's theatrical gesture, which cost him nothing and may indeed have for a brief moment have restored to him the sense of his own virtue, but rather on Ahenobarbus himself. His career encapsulates the waste of civil war. No man was a more persistent enemy of mine. There was none I would rather have won to my side. But he was deaf to all blandishment, all persuasion, eventually to all reason.

He was an obstinate and virtuous Republican, wedded to a vanished and perhaps always imaginary world. His father, Cato's brother-in-law, as stern and self-righteous as Cato himself, fought and died at Pharsalus. The son adhered to Brutus and Cassius, fought against us at Philippi, and then resisted for years with a fleet based on the west coast of Greece. Pollio persuaded him to join with Antony, which we all understood to mean reconciliation to the new order we were trying to build. I wrote to him, I remember, in welcome. He replied coldly: he had joined Antony, not me, for he could never be reconciled with the heir of the man who had made it his life's work to destroy the Free State. I shrugged my shoulders in despair. What could he understand by that dead term? There had been no freedom from fear, coercion, political dishonesty and corruption, for three generations. But Ahenobarbus belonged to a dead age, when personal and familial loyalty, the clan spirit, was all; when only lip-service was given to the idea of Rome. Cato had been the same. He would have dismembered the Empire for the sake of a purely imaginary politics. How could I have patience with such fools?

And yet I could not but admire Ahenobarbus, even while I recognized that such admiration represented a longing for the infancy of Rome. Again I saw the wisdom of Virgil's words, and I saw too that the story of Cincinnatus was not only a legend but a temptation. The likes of Cato and Ahenobarbus were men who played at living in the past, and assumed an impossible virtue, which enabled them to act with a selfish disregard for the real interests of the State. Beware the idea-list, was all I could tell Marcellus; but Marcellus, with his clear and dark-blue eyes, his high carriage, his neat close-curled head carried proudly, his strong straight legs and his candid smile, and even the proud frown that would disturb his beauty when he encountered what seemed reprehensible, was at the age for impossible Catos. Like any noble youth he lived in a world of moral certainty.

And yet the virtue of a man like Ahenobarbus was never to be disprized. I knew that. Almost alone of those around Antony, he had constantly deplored Cleopatra's power over the general. If only Antony had listened . . . if only Aheno-barbus had trusted me. He refused even to grant Cleopatra the name of Queen. He was with all his faults a true Roman. The last time I saw him, when as consul in 32, he had departed the city for Antony's camp. I had begged him not to. He had looked me in the eye and said, 'Antony is no despot.' No argument could move him and I let him go.

Now Antony too had lost this noble and misguided man . . .

Antony's best general, Canidius, urged him, we later learned, to retreat to Macedonia and seek to settle the issue there where they might hope to find help from barbarian allies. That itself would have been a dangerous and ignoble precedent, but I suppose Canidius argued that it was no more unwise or disgraceful to rely on such northern barbarians than on the Queen of Egypt. Certainly, such a move would have embarrassed us. We would have had to follow, with an ever lengthening supply line, across difficult country, eventually to give battle in a place of Antony's choosing. Anticipating that they might follow this course, I threw the left wing of my army across the passes, but I could not position a strong force there without endangering the main army. However, Dellius reassured me. Cleopatra, he said, would never permit Antony to follow a course which would expose Egypt to our fleet. 'You can be quite certain, Caesar, that the Queen will win any argument. Antony can no more leave her now than a dog can trot off from a bitch in heat. He is bewitched, there's no other word for it. He knows it, and is powerless. It's pitiful to see and to watch him drown his shame in wine.'

Dellius was quite right. We had reduced Antony to the point where he had to fight his way out.

XIII

The storms of late August had died away, and the morning of 2 September dawned bright, fresh and clear. A gentle breeze blew landward and the fleet swayed at anchor, a movement I have always found disagreeable. We had taken up position perhaps a mile beyond the entrance to the Channel where Antony's ships were pinned. I had been roused shortly before first light and called to the deck. My captain, a Greek called Melas, pointed to the land, where the morning grey was pierced with shafts of lurid red.

'What's happening?' I asked, brushing the sleep from my eyes.

'It's beginning,' he said, 'Antony is burning those ships which he does not need. Our information was correct. He is planning a break-out, this day.'

A little rowing-boat approached our ship. A rope ladder

was lowered and Agrippa climbed aboard. His face had the tense eagerness that the moment of decision always called forth from him.

'This is it, Caesar,' he called out. 'This is the hour to which all the campaign has tended. Or rather,' he corrected himself, dropping the rhetorical tone which he had adopted for the benefit of the soldiers who stood around, 'we have a few hours to go.'

'How can you be sure?' I asked. (I have always hated the sea and naval warfare, and found its principles mysterious.)

'Haven't you noticed?' he said. 'Or have you forgotten? The wind is likely to shift in the afternoon, and move round to the north-west. That will enable Antony to run before it. He hopes it will cut us off from our land base, and aid him to break our line . . . but if he fails, then the wind will aid his flight. He will be able to run fast before it . . .'

'It sounds,' I said, 'a desperate gamble.'

'What else is left for him?' Agrippa said.

We had had the conversation before. At staff meetings we had analysed the options open to Antony, and concluded that what would be attempted to-day offered him the only chance of avoiding the slow and humiliating surrender which the crumbling and demoralization of his army, pinned in our blockade, otherwise threatened. I could have wished that his nerve had failed him and he had desisted from this last attempt. For one thing I have always found it uncanny when your adversary does just what you have predicted. I am ever inclined to fear that it will lead to a change of fortune. But Agrippa was buoyed up and excited by the success of his forecast.

A little later, when we had checked all dispositions and wished each other luck (for however well-laid your plans, chance is the arbiter of war), and taken the auspices and sacrificed to the lords of destiny, Agrippa climbed back to his little boat, and was rowed away. I watched till the boat became a speck on the ocean and then disappeared behind the line of galleys on our left.

Towards noon the proud high sails of Antony's fleet could be seen rounding the point and, then, like a dream unfolding, they deployed, and stood off in battle array some half a mile distant. The world held its breath while the soft breeze still rippled landward.

I dunked a piece of bread in the resin-flavoured wine of Greece (which survives better on shipboard than our more delicate Italian wines) and so broke my fast.

For the hundredth time and more I rehearsed the arguments we had held. My own wish had been to avoid this encounter. I would have let Antony clear the straits unchallenged and make a dash for Egypt. I was sure such precipitate flight would dishearten the Romans and Italians in his force. They would, I said, feel that Antony had finally thrown in his lot with Egypt, that he had abandoned all hope of winning the West and resigned himself to being Cleopatra's lapdog. When they felt this, I suggested, many would desert their general; and we would achieve success without a battle. Agrippa heard my argument out, then banged his fist on the table.

'No, no, and again, no,' he cried, and I could see that our officers were impressed by the vehemence of his tone. 'No,' he said again, quietly, to emphasize his sincerity. 'That is no more than conjecture. What is fact is this. Antony's ships are bigger than ours and much faster under full sail. If we shirk the contest and let him run, the chances are he will escape without suffering any damage to his fleet. Then our whole summer campaign will have been wasted. It will all be to begin again. And do you imagine, Caesar, we can tax Italy another year as we have this one? I tell you, on both military and political grounds, we must bring the matter to issue.'

I heard him and assented. I have always been ready to be impressed by solid argument. Indeed, one reason for my success has been that I have never obstinately maintained my own point of view from pride. I have always been willing to concede that in certain areas others know more than I.

So I had assented, and now watched Antony's fleet rock on the water. Sea-gulls screamed overhead. The men shifted their feet and kept their eyes fixed on the enemy, all but a few old sweats who had lain down on deck and were chatting among themselves. They were men who had been in so many battles that they had long ceased to anticipate what might happen. They had seen enough death to know that they might not see the moon rise that night; they would therefore

160

take their ease and conserve their strength. I envied their fatal-
ism.

The sun passed the zenith and still the wind neither rose nor
shifted. The light shimmered in noonday heat. Sweat ran
down the backs of my legs. My mouth felt dry and sour. The
whole world rocked in a pregnant and awful silence.

Then, very gently at first, my nostrils were pricked with
the tang of smoke. The black fumes which had been rising
almost straight from the burning ships before drifting thinly
away over the camp could now be seen shifting towards the
open sea.

Melas shouted orders to his sailors, and my centurions
called their men to stand to. With sails set and oars flailing,
Antony's fleet moved against us in battle order. When
they were still some hundred paces distant, I could hear
the cry of battle from our left where Agrippa was already
engaged.

Literary art such as Caesar's can make sense and order of
battles. All those I have taken part in have left me with a confused welter of impressions: I see a young boy by my side fall
with an arrow in this throat, his hands closing on the shaft
and locking there; he fell, half-turning so that the point was
driven deeper in his neck before the shaft split and he was left
holding the upper part, broken and useless, and his face
turned towards me, as he lay on one cheek, his innocent eye
glazing over, and indignant surprise fading from it . . . I see a
burning brand tossed in a wide arc through the air to land
among the sheets of an enemy ship, and I hear the screams of
terrified and burning sailors. I hear the thud of grappling
irons joining our ships to theirs, the hoarse execrations and
the clash of swords. And, high up on our bridge, I see the
whole ocean turned into a mimic and ghastly theatre, the
water running purple with blood, and hear the splash of
bodies and everywhere the cries of death.

Caesar could have made sense of it, or have pretended to do
so. I cannot, and, while it happened, horror drove out all
thought of triumph.

Then, for a moment, came a lull. Some ships had surrendered, others floundered broadside on. On our wings, ships
manoeuvred to outflank the enemy. There was suddenly one

of those mysterious halts which take place in battles when the first fury and first charge are spent and the Gods weigh fortune in their balance. Someone cried, 'They've had enough, they're going to break,' and in their centre a little galley put out from the great flagship, hurrying with urgent oars to where another ship with purple sails lay off at the head of the Egyptian contingent. How it happened I do not know, but the cry went up, 'Antony flees.' The galley approached the purple-sailed vessel, men were seen to board, and, with a speed that surprised me, it began to run before the wind, with the whole Egyptian fleet streaming behind it. I have a picture in my mind of a grey ravaged face in the stern of the fleeing flagship, a face eloquent of vain ambition, burnt nights and lost powers. I do not think I saw it, except in my mind's eye; but that is Antony, fixed for eternity, the great bull emasculated, his face set against the ruin he had brought upon himself, tears coursing his cheeks, his back to Egypt, the months remaining, and the shame he must endure.

We lay at sea all night, amidst the cries and groans of the wounded and dying. The aftermath of a sea battle is more terrible even than of a land one, for the elements themselves are hostile. The black water laps cruelly against the ships, threatening even the victor lest the wind, which was strong that night, should blow up a storm. All through the hours of the dark, men struggled to rescue others from the burning hulls, to fish men from the hostile water, to comfort the dying and tend the wounded. The cruelty of war can only be fully appreciated by those who have seen the tenderness of soldiers after a battle.

In the morning we returned to land. Antony had left part of his army under Canidius to hold his camp. It was a pointless gesture. They all knew there was nothing to fight for, no hope of breaking out. For some days Canidius obstructed negotiations and declined to answer my emissaries. Then, on the fifth night, he slipped from the camp himself, and rode hard through the hills making for Corinth, from where he too took ship for Egypt. His men were relieved to learn of his departure. They surrendered at once. True to my promise of clemency, I disbanded some of the legions and despatched the men to Italy to await resettlement, while I incorporated others in my own army.

The play was finished. There remained only the epilogue.

XIV

Egypt stank. The Nile, drawn back from its bounds in the dry season, leaves spread over the land a coating of grey mud. The peasants cover it with dung from their cattle, sheep and camels, and from its rich soil produce two crops of wheat a year. Yet it stinks.

And the stink of Egypt is moral too. Alexandria is a noble city, of Greek origin, as was of course the house of Ptolemy to which Cleopatra belonged, descended from one of Alexander's generals. Its harbours, guarded by the Pharos, an astonishing construction four hundred feet high, built in three diminishing tiers of limestone, pink marble and a purple granite from upper Egypt, are truly among the wonders of the world. The city has been laid out, in its public quarter, with elaborate care. Who can fail to be impressed by the great hundred-foot-wide street that runs right across it? Who likewise can fail to wonder at its university and libraries, the tombs of Alexander and the Ptolemies, or at its innumerable workshops where goldsmiths, scent-confectors, ivory-carvers, glass-makers abound, or the factories where papyrus is prepared. The wealth and variety of Egypt's economy must stagger every observer. And yet, as I say, the place stinks.

It is not merely the vulgar reek of humanity, in this city where half a million swelter in the late summer heat, a heterogeneous and excitable mass compounded of Greeks, Jews, and native Egyptians, quick to riot, cowardly and treacherous. Nevertheless their organization is merely a matter of efficient administration, such as we were soon able to provide. What disquiets in Egypt however is the undercurrent of malevolent magic, the strange and repellent cults of animal gods, the underlying assumption that truth is to be found in dark and secret places and not in the light. Beyond the city, in the desert, stand the vast and mysterious tombs of the ancient Pharaohs, monstrous reminders of a vile religion, the cult of the dead. Ancient Egypt is a land of buggery. It is said that the source of power is to be found in the penetration of the anus, achieved to the accompaniment of magical incantations. One Pharaoh reputedly described Egypt as 'looking like the crack between the globes of the buttock'. The fertility of the Nile mud resembles excrement, and one of their most potent Gods, Khepera, is a dung beetle; he is Lord of the Land of the Dead.

How can any Roman fail to be disgusted by this antique superstition; how can he fail to despise the land that bred it?

Had Antony been subdued and subverted by Egypt's ancient magic? In a sense. Of course Cleopatra was not Egyptian but Greek, and since the Ptolemies practised marriage only within the family, she was free of any inherited Egyptian taint; yet, since few doubt that she employed sorcery on Antony, which destroyed his Roman virtue and rendered him her contemptible slave, it is reasonable to believe that Antony fell victim to the greedy and rapacious gods of Egypt.

He had withdrawn his army to the fringe of the desert. One day he resolved to make a last stand, the next to submit and throw himself on my mercy. His plight was indeed desperate. His legions in Cyrene had deserted him and attached themselves to my general Cornelius Gallus. It was reported that Cleopatra tried to rally him; she proposed wild chimerical plans: they would sail to Spain and seize the silver mines; they would turn their backs on Egypt and the Roman World, and head, like Alexander, for India, to carve out a new empire there. Antony heard her in silence. His eye dropped. His hand sought the wine-flask. He looked at Cleopatra with the bitter hatred of a man who gazes on the instrument of his destruction.

He wrote to me:

You have played the game and won. Antony is hardly Antony any more. The God Hercules who loved me now curls his lip in scorn to see how low I have fallen. Yet we have achieved much together, you and I; for the sake of our old love and friendship, for the sake of your sister Octavia, my one true wife, I crave clemency. You will understand how I am humbled to bring myself to ask this. Why, Caesar, should the Roman world still be split by turmoil? I still have legions devoted to my cause. I can still strike a fierce blow, and, rendered desperate by my condition, can promise you that such a blow will hurt. But I am weary of struggle. I am ready to desist. Grant me, Caesar, safe passage to my estates, and I shall drag out my last days in tranquillity, tending my vines and olive groves in the fertile plain and gentle hillsides of my beloved Bononia. Is this too much to ask? Should you grant me my request, I shall deliver the cursed Queen who has bewitched me to your hands.

How could I answer so miserable a letter? It made me quiver with shame to read it, for I could not fail to read the bitter self-hatred and abandonment of virtue that informed it. I could not reply. I could not even show the letter to Agrippa. I publish it now merely for the record, that historians be not deceived.

I knew how low was the morale of Antony's legions, and sent my cavalry against them. Antony's heroes of so many encounters threw down their arms. 'Why die for nothing?' one centurion cried. 'Die for the General,' a staff-officer, bloodshot and distraught, cried out. The centurion looked him in the eye. 'The General is nothing', he said, and planted his sword-point deep in the sand.

Learning of this, Antony's last resolution failed him. He withdrew to his tent. What passed before his eyes at that moment? Did he see that morning when he stood with Caesar's bloodied toga in his hand, and harangued the people? Did he recall that morning on the island shrouded by river-mists when we met to re-order the world? Did he, I wonder, even envy Lepidus, whose insignificance had saved his life? But Antony could not be pictured living in dishonoured retirement. I could not have treated him as I treated Lepidus.

News was brought to him that Cleopatra had killed herself. At once he broke into a wail of lamentation in which mourning and reproach, love and hatred, were strangely mixed.

When he had finished, and wept a little, he called for a cup of wine, drank it and composed himself to sleep. Towards evening he woke. The sun lay low across the desert. Antony stood in the doorway of his tent and looked at the world turning purple in the twilight. He called again for wine, but this time merely touched the rim of the cup with his lips. In the distance he could still hear the cries and moans of wounded men, but his camp, so diminished in size, so silent, with the silence of men waiting for fate, must have seemed a long way from the battlefields of Gaul, Spain or Armenia. The sands stretched out in all directions till they lost themselves in the evening mists.

He threw his head up, they say, called for his sword, told his bearers to hold it steady and launched himself against it.

Perhaps the man shrank from the task, or perhaps a last instinct held Antony back, for the sword did not pierce any vital organ, and, though he fell to the ground bleeding freely, he was not yet dead. He moaned with pain or disappointment, and begged his servant to deliver the final blow. But the man shrank again from doing so, and night closed about the bleeding general. In a little, when he had lost consciousness, they wrapped him in a blanket and carried him into his tent. Meanwhile, hearing the news, his soldiers drifted away, falling from the camp like autumn leaves.

Towards dawn Antony woke; his fearful servants approached and told him that the report received yesterday had been false. Cleopatra was not dead. She had instead taken refuge in the Royal Mausoleum, known sometimes simply as the Monument. He begged them to carry him there, and, very gently, with a devotion it touches me to recall, they lifted him on to a litter, and obeyed his last instructions.

They raised him to the Mausoleum. He was by now very weak and it is not known if he regained consciousness. He probably died in Cleopatra's arms, but it is not certain and the accounts are conflicting. One version has it that Cleopatra reviled him as the author of her ruin, and that the last words Antony heard were full of hatred and reproach; but this I do not believe. In her own way Cleopatra loved him and besides she had too fine a sense of the dramatic to let him die in such a manner.

Of course I mourned Antony when I heard of his death. How could I fail to? I have seen gladiators bedew the arena with their tears as they gazed on the comrade they had slain, and no gladiators have been joined as Antony and I were joined.

So died this most remarkable of men. Agrippa, with his characteristic generosity, observed that a rarer spirit never steered humanity. It is said Cleopatra swooned at the moment of his death, and I myself almost did so, having to seize Agrippa's arm to support myself against a moment of dizziness when the news was broken.

'I am both glad and sorry,' I managed to say. 'Glad for Antony's sake for life could have offered him nothing but sad decline, and glad too for Rome, since Antony's death brings this old barren division of the world to an end. I did not choose this war; he forced it on me, and has paid the price. How did he die?'

'Nobly, on his own sword, a Roman death . . .'

I nodded. 'It ought to make more noise,' I said. 'You would think the death of such a man would shake lions into the streets of Alexandria and send the citizens cowering to their hovels.'

'What did Cleopatra say?'

I do not know, why, after a pause, I had asked the question.

'She said, sir, that there was nothing left remarkable beneath the visiting moon.'

'Do you remember, Agrippa, how he spoke of Brutus? "This was the noblest Roman of them all." Those were his words. They angered me then, for I could not share his opinion of Brutus. But now? Why do I feel like that? Why do I feel like a man who has shot a splendid bird, an eagle, or brought down a noble stag? I had no choice, yet half my heart is torn. He was my brother and my rival, my separated love, my friend and companion in countless fields; and now, a body for crows to pick at. Was it destiny tore us apart, were our stars irreconcilable? Where's the Queen of Egypt?'

'She takes refuge still in the Mausoleum, but has sent to know your will.'

'Agrippa,' I said, 'fetch her to me. You at least will be proof against her charms.'

How would she come?

'Like a right royal bitch,' Agrippa said. 'You never saw the like. I have attended theatres in many cities, but I never saw an actress like the Queen. You'd better be on your guard, lest she seduce you too. It would make a notable haul, wouldn't it? First Himself, then Antony and then you, Octavian. And she's capable of it. Don't fool yourself otherwise.'

She was simply attired, in mourning white, her hair loose; and she wore no jewels. She looked older than her age, with little crevices of lines running from the corners of her eyes and mouth. Only the eyes themselves contradicted this impression. Almond-coloured and rather large, they sparkled with an unquenchable vivacity. When she spoke her voice was deeper and harsher than I remembered it as being. Her manner was composed and confident.

She began with compliments. Her dead lord had spoken much of the nobility of my character. The war between us had been unfortunate, the result of a concatenation of circumstance and misunderstanding. She understood of course that I had been angered by Antony's abandonment of my sister, and his preference for her. But where the God Eros struck, mortals were powerless. Egypt had no quarrel with Rome, and indeed Egypt was sensible that its prosperity depended on the strength and vigour of Rome. She had been taught that early, by none other than my father.

So far, she had spoken as if to persuade me by reason. Though I was of course aware of the depths of her hypocrisy, I still felt the charm of her manner and personality and the strength of her intellect working on my mind and imagination. Now, having introduced Julius' name, she paused.

'Everything I know I learned from your great and most noble father,' she said. 'He was my teacher and master as well as my lover. His presence was intoxicating. He came on me with the freshness of a spring morning, and I blossomed like a summer flower in his Sun's rays. You, Caesar, are, I see now, his most worthy heir, the inheritor of his genius and his vision. He told me he saw Egypt as the garden and granary of Rome, and I as its gardener and farmer. An unromantic role for a young girl, you may say, but he told me that with a laugh, and I found him as convincing as he was irresistible. Caesar, I have erred in opposing you, and my error rested in my willingness to be guided by my dead lord. Antony was a great man, and a noble man, and there is no shame in my memory of him. But there is regret. Regret, because my love for Antony led me to stray from Caesar's precepts, and to follow Antony in his mad ambition which led to war against Caesar's heir. Only now that Antony's splendour can no longer dazzle me, do I see the error of my ways. And so, Caesar, I have come to lay Egypt at your royal and conquering feet, to throw myself on your generous mercy, to remind your father's son of what I meant to your father and to pray that we may together resume the work, the great work of harmony between Rome and Egypt on which we embarked, Caesar and I. For, most noble General, I say this to you: Rome and Egypt are bound together as Egypt is wedded to the Nile and Rome to the Middle Sea; and I am Egypt and you, most puissant General, are Rome'; and, saying this, she threw her head back in proud self-assertion, and sank to her knees before me.

What a performance.

I felt her power, her quite remarkable seductiveness. It was like listening to the deepest most desirable temptation; it held promises of bliss and power. I understood how Antony had found himself caught like a beast in a net. I looked away.

'Great Queen,' I said, 'your words touch me. I too loved Antony and regret the separation of our ways. I too revere the memory of my father, and I recognize that Egypt and Rome are bound together. But this great war has displaced much, and this is not the moment to make any speedy decision on the nature of the future relationship between our countries. I shall ponder all you have said. Rest assured that you will be treated in a manner worthy of your great name and nature, and that your fate will not be less than your deserts.'

Her face grew pale. She quivered a moment, then, very slowly and now unwaveringly, rose to her feet. The audience was over.

I gave orders that she be escorted to the Palace, and kept there with due honour, but under secure guard.

'She shall appear in my Triumph,' I said to Agrippa, 'in

chains, that Rome may be relieved of its long anxiety. And then we shall see what should be done.'

A letter was brought me from Livia:

> Do not forget that the Queen is a woman and you honour yourself in treating her with honour and moderation. But I should be nervous and unhappy my dear, if you expose yourself to her charms. Her reputation frightens me...

Octavia wrote:

> No woman, and no man either, has done me more bitter wrong than Cleopatra. And yet I find I pity her. To have dared so much and to have lost so completely stops my heart. I rejoice in your victory, brother, but I mourn Antony as the father of my children... What do you plan to do with his children by the Queen? I shudder to think of their significance.

Cleopatra's fate was not of course my only concern, hardly even the chief one. The most urgent was the treatment of Egypt itself. I decided it was too rich and too important to be left in its semi-independent state; Julius had surely blundered in deciding so. Egypt must become a Roman province, for the food supply of Rome itself depended on its harvests. Moreover, I thought it best to keep it, for the time being at least, under my direct control. I therefore appointed Cornelius Gallus, a man in whom I reposed infinite trust, as its governor.

Antony's legions had all laid down their arms. Some I incorporated into my own army, but it was obvious that with the triumphal end of the Civil Wars, it would be both possible and desirable to reduce the military establishment, and so I began to plan for the demobilization and settlement in colonies of the greater number of Antony's men. This work of reduction and resettlement was to dominate the next three years, and I may fairly but modestly claim that in its performance I met with a success that none of the great generals of the Republic had equalled, not even Pompey.

Among those who tried to resist and were captured were Antyllus, Antony's son by Fulvia, and the boy called Caesarion, who had been proclaimed Julius' son by Cleopatra.

Antyllus behaved shamefully, having to be dragged from the Temple of the Divine Julius, screaming for mercy. He tried indeed to cling to' my father's image and the soldiers had to prise his fingers off it. Caesarion was captured by a cavalry patrol and accepted his fate with a dignity that did credit to his putative paternity. I ordered both to be put to death; they were too obvious foci for disaffection to make it possible to spare their lives.

Cleopatra cheated my intentions. Fearing the mockery of the Roman crowd, realizing that her plea to be treated as a reigning Queen and confirmed in office had failed, she contrived to have a little snake, called an asp, smuggled to her bedchamber in a basket of figs. She then applied it to her breast. They say she did so lovingly and smiled as the poison worked. I could not be sorry, for, though she would have made a splendid show in my Triumph, I knew that I would have been unable to condemn her to death afterwards (as custom decrees) and that indeed Livia would not permit me to do so. Her continued presence could only be an embarrassment, and, on reflection, I was glad she had removed herself.

I gave orders that she be buried beside Antony, and that their mausoleum be completed. May I be paid like honour by those I have wronged when my time comes!

I was eager to leave Egypt, for its vice and corruption continued to disgust me, and I felt evil in the air. Only the pink delicacy of early mornings before the extreme heat of the day, when the Nile shimmered in awakening light, gave me any pleasure. But there is that in Egypt that can demean a man, and I felt both fear and loathing of the brooding presence of its ancient and obscene gods.

Before leaving however, I fulfilled a last ambition. I ordered the sarcophagus which contains the mummified body of the Great Alexander to be removed from its Mausoleum in Alexandria, and gazed in wonder on the face of the most noble and brilliant of men, whose achievements none has matched, whose glory it is hard even to imagine. Its features were serene and beautiful. I crowned the head with a golden diadem and strewed the trunk with roses, violets and sweet-scented lemon-flowers.

They asked me afterwards if I would now like to view the

Mausoleum of the Ptolemies, and asked it with that syco-phantic relish which the thought of Death brings to Egyptians. I replied, 'I have come to see a King, not a row of corpses'; but it is fitting that the last word of Egypt should lie with Death.

BOOK TWO

Preface

The reader will, I trust, now find himself in full agreement with my judgement that the first Book of these Memoirs, from its happy and impudent denunciation of Caesar's *De Bello Gallico* to its painful Egyptian finale, is written with a brio rare in Ancient, or, at least, Latin literature. He will, I trust, share my pleasure in the delight with which the Emperor so evidently wrote, and it seems to me that it would be but a mean spirit which did not respond joyfully, while hardly managing to restrain a certain envy for the fortunate young princes for whom this record was unrolled.

Alas, the second Book is a different, and grimmer, matter. All is now oppressed with a sad sense of waste and desolation... '*Eheu, eheu, fugaces, Postume...*' Alternatively one may recall those noble lines which Dryden gave to Aurungzebe: 'When I consider life, 'tis all a cheat. Yet fool'd by hope, men favour the deceit.' This is a book made grey by the Emperor's knowledge of whither it was tending. It echoes Virgil's '*lacrimae rerum*', or, as Matthew Arnold put it, with felicitous gloom, 'the sense of tears in mortal things'.

Who shall deny that Augustus had cause for grief? The hopes he had rested in his grandsons were destroyed by their untimely death; he could do no more for them than strew the garlands of his loving praise on their sad tomb! Moreover the book opens at the moment of receiving news of the greatest military disaster of his life, when Quintilius Varus, heedless of Augustus' warnings, rashly led three legions to utter destruction in the German forests.

Here the Book starts and it covers a wide swathe of time as the restless Emperor moves forward and back in memory, forever seeking to account to himself for the afflictions that have befallen his latter years, that withdrawal of the favour of the Gods which brought his 'grey hairs in sorrow to the grave'.

That this Book is harsher reading than the First goes without saying. It is in the first place less compact. It ignores strict sequence of events. Its mood is dark, only occasionally lightened by sunlit passages of domestic happiness or public achievement. There are also passages of an intense yearning which find no equal in the earlier Book or indeed in Latin literature outside Virgil himself. There are fewer vivid descriptions of public conflict, for Augustus had established his superiority, and there are—it must be said—some passages which modern readers may find pedestrian, in which he describes his constitutional settlement or recounts his handling of foreign affairs. Yet without such stuff the book would be incomplete. It is clear that Augustus intended to leave posterity a rounded picture of his work and his achievement; he could not do so if he eschewed the arid pastures of politics. Yet one has only to read these pages, and set them beside those in which he treats of his personal life, and then make a comparison with even the liveliest of modern political memoirs, to see how sparing Augustus has been of the pomposity and verbiage in which such records are generally cloaked; and if one does so, one will appreciate his forbearance and humanity.

That a note of self-justification runs through these memoirs, it were vain to deny. Augustus committed great crimes, and knew it. It was natural that he should seek to explain them to himself and to whomsoever should read his book. There is truth in the old adage, *qui s'excuse, s'accuse*, and yet again one has only to read memoirs of modern political sinners such as ex-President Nixon or ex-Premier Wilson, whose confessions never rise beyond their own justification, to admire the flinty dignity with which Augustus refuses to deny the truth. In this context, one must add that this second Book is indeed more truthful than the first. In particular it affords us an understanding of the relationship between the young Augustus and Mark Antony which he could not bring himself to offer to his grandsons.

It appears that the second Book was written intermittently over a period of five years, the last entries being made on the eve of his death. There are discrepancies: for instance, Chapter I treats with admirable honesty of his *Res Gestae*, that record of his Acts which he caused to be published throughout the Empire, and in this he states that he was then in his seventy-sixth year. Yet, at the beginning of the chapter, he has just received news of Varus' disaster. It would seem either that a preliminary version of the *Res Gestae* was in fact made earlier, and that a contemporary editor then corrected the Emperor's statement of his age to fit the published version, or that the passage relating to the *Res Gestae* was indeed written later than subsequent chapters and inserted here, for dramatic effect, by the same editor. Such questions are not likely however to disturb the common reader.

It must be said that this is an old man's book. The style is sometimes loose, sometimes relapses into a weary formality; it lacks the vivacity of the earlier essay in autobiography. Myself, I find this appealing. Some readers will not agree, and will regret Gaius' and Lucius' deaths all the more for the literary loss it entailed. Clearly this Book was never revised, and sometimes the Emperor's memory is faulty: so, for instance, in Chapter IV he confuses the order of Agrippa's wives. It was not Caecilia Attica whom Agrippa divorced in order to marry Augustus' daughter Julia, but Augustus' own niece Marcella, the daughter of his sister Octavia and C. Claudius Marcellus. One wonders what caused this lapse of memory. Was it perhaps an unwillingness to recall that Marcella then married Iullus Antonius, himself later Julia's most notorious lover, the agent of her disgrace and victim of Augustus' anger, who was executed for treason as recounted in Chapter XI? One cannot tell. There may be no such deep reason. Augustus was clearly distressed while he wrote this fourth chapter for there is interpolated in it, almost at random, a letter from Tiberius written on the Rhine in which he describes the arrival in camp of a miserable remnant of Varus' legionaries—a truly horrible story which brought intense pain, grief and shame to Augustus. Such questions are perhaps for the psychologist rather than the classical scholar to ponder. Let it suffice to say here that the reader must be ever alert to follow the wanderings of the imperial mind through the years transversed in this second Book, and I would urge him (or her) to be ready to forgive the occasional mistakes and self-deception. That the man laboured heroically to be honest I have no doubt!

It is hardly the duty of the editor to play the critic, but there are two beauties in the work to which I should like to draw the reader's attention. The first is the manner in which the Emperor treats of his relationship with Virgil. It is moving (to me at least) to see the humility with which the man of action regards the poet, and the awe in which he holds him. The second is his treatment of his marriage. The distinguished British novelist, Mr Anthony Powell, has remarked on the difficulty, even perhaps impossibility, of treating marriage, particularly a happy marriage, in a work of fiction. Unhampered by fictional demands as he was, it seems to me that the Emperor made a fair attempt! At the very least his sober and loving portrayal of Livia, though never hiding her faults or their disagreements, should rescue that great lady from the vile calumnies fathered on her grandson Claudius by the fecund imagination of the late Robert Graves, itself infected by the most scurrilous rumour-mongers of Ancient Rome.

I may state in my capacity as Chairman of the Editorial Committee that Mr Massie has happily approached the task of translating this second Book with more sobriety than he showed in his version of the first. He shows greater respect for the Latin text (sometimes, it has been objected, even excessive respect), and engages in fewer colloquialisms of the type to which he was attracted by a misplaced desire for liveliness—surely one of the innumerable banes of modern life!

Finally, I cannot resist adding an expression of my gratification at having been associated with this great work, however much I may deplore the commercialism that taints this particular edition, and, on a purely personal note, in which even the indulgent reader may detect a yet pardonable vanity, express my hitherto secret joy at the coincidence of my own first name with that of the hero who was father of the Roman People, the subject of Virgil's Epic, the Emperor's exemplar, and, as one might say, prototype: AENEAS.

Aeneas Fraser-Graham,
Quondam Fellow of Trinity College, Cambridge,
Director of the Institute of Classical Strategies,
Chairman of the International Editorial Committee
established to superintend and guide
THE AUGUSTUS PROJECT.

I

IREVIEWED THESE TROOPS BEFORE THEY
LEFT ARLES FOR THE FRONTIER. THEY
were prime legionaries from the lands north-east of Mantua,
from the Abruzzi, from Calabria and Apulia, and there was
one legion recruited in Transalpine Gaul itself. Many of the
women and children of the Gallic legionaries crowded into
Arles to weep, or wave, farewell to their sons, lovers, husbands and fathers. I looked on all with pride, and a love in
which even then I felt the tender and ready tears of old age
prick my eyes. I warned Varus of the dangers which brood in
the mirk recesses of the German forests. I said to him:
'Advance carefully, behind a fringe of scouts; guard your
flanks and rear; remember always, do not for a moment
forget, that the most valuable and necessary members of your
army in such an expedition are the scouts; it is on the quality
of your intelligence that the safety of our soldiers depends.' I
repeated the warning again and again till he sighed (I am sure)
to be so oppressed by the timid alarms of an old man. This is
the curse of age: to find experience discounted, set at naught. I
took the auspices, which were good, and assured the troops
of my love and confidence.

Tonight there is curfew in the city. I have ordered that the
Praetorians patrol the streets till dawn, that they post guards
by the Senate House to forbid entry and by the Temple of
Capitoline Jupiter, and that the Field of Mars be occupied by
at least a cohort. Guards at the gates have been doubled.

I cannot sleep. I sleep little now, rarely more than two
hours at a stretch, and am accustomed to require slaves to be
on hand to read to me through the black silence of night. But
there is no solace in words now, however well-arranged.

Should I send an order to Tiberius to return to Rome? Or
send him straight to the Rhine? Decisions, which used to be

prompted by instinct, intuition, guided by the counsel of those I trusted, now perturb me. Only Livia remains . . . and she . . . enough of this vein.

I have a cold in the head, and have coughed, sneezed and spluttered my way through the darkness. My legs are leaden and my shoulders ache. I am troubled by the sharp-stabbing pains of gout, and my stomach is disordered. If I close my eyes, I am assailed by nightmare images of slaughter: I hear Roman voices shriek in terror and despair through the limit-less forests; I smell sweat and fear and the reek of horse-flesh, blood, sour marsh vapours and the ordure of panic. I am an old man, nearing my end, trapped in a corner between the walls of achievement and death . . . and what, I ask, does it signify? In some cities of Asia, in defiance of my expressed wishes, they worship me as a God. Who ever heard of a God with gout and a cold in the head?

This disaster, the gravest I have known, leads me to question what I have achieved. There was a little yellow-haired girl, about six or seven, who ran beside the marching legions for some fifty paces, trying to grab hold of her father's hand, and crying 'Daddy, Daddy'; he, not daring to break step, looked down on her with a countenance into which I read love, anguish and embarrassment. But if I were to send for that little girl, what could I do for her that would heal the wound cut open by my policies and by Varus' criminal care-lessness? Deprived by cruel fate of my own children I grow ever more tender towards other people's; old man's tears again.

It was Livia who brought me the news. No one else dared. That thought also distresses me. It makes me feel like a mon-arch, even a tyrant, whereas I call the Gods, in whom my faith tremblingly rests, to bear witness that I have never sought to be more than the First Citizen of Rome, the Father of my Country—that title the Senate was pleased to grant me, in which I had delighted. But now only Livia would approach me with the news that Varus had led the legions into a trap and that they had all been swallowed up and de-stroyed. They were lured into the forest, obstructed by felled trees, swamps and undergrowth, cut down in a rain-storm. Varus, the reports said, killed himself—that Roman death that is no better than an abandonment of faith, the last resort of cold egoists like Brutus; (and I am not forgetting that I was once tempted to it myself). Captured legionaries were crucified, or beheaded and eviscerated as offerings to the savage and unknown gods of these northern forests. I looked into the familiar landscape of Livia's face, and could read nothing there, as, sparing me nothing, she spat out the facts to me in short brutal sentences. Her very laconicism made it impossible for me to find any refuge from the truth. But when I began to lament my legions, she stopped me.

'There may be time for tears later. But now we must be vigilant. Military disaster can be the seedbed of revolution. You can't doubt, my dear, that those who hate your regime will even now be rejoicing at what has befallen Rome. They will be saying that their hour has come. If you take my advice, which I know you are loth to do nowadays, ever since I first gave you advice that tasted like bitter medicine, you will at once round up fellows like Lucius Arruntius, Asinius Gallus and Marcus Lepidus, and clap them under house arrest—at the very least . . .'

I nodded, disregarding the call for illegality. I submitted to what was expedient. Anyway, I could sympathize with her fear; she looked on my old age and weakness and hoped to make the world safe for Tiberius.

So now, I listen to the tramp of the Praetorians and my heart cries, 'Varus, give me back my legions . . .'

* * *

Livia's promptitude prevented any open display of disaffection. We were able to release the detainees in a couple of months. Though I was relieved to be rid of the fear of civil disorder, I was also dismayed by the way in which Roman nobles acquiesced in this disaster. I was indeed the only man in the city who let his beard and hair grow uncut in token of my mourning for the lost legions. When the nobility saw that nothing had changed, they shrugged their shoulders and got on with their hunting and dicing, their love affairs, business matters, theatres and games; 'like so many capons' I found myself muttering. Did Romans no longer care when Rome suffered defeat and disgrace? Was the indifference to be my legacy?

I should have liked to consult Tiberius, who, with all his faults, is a man of the old style, but I had sent him directly to the Rhine to guard against any German incursion. Nobody understands the Germans of course, but Tiberius has a great virtue which renders him the ideal commander against barbarians; he is never impressed by them. Yet, because he is the most prudent and careful of men, he never relaxes his vigilance and would never commit the error of despising any enemy. I have come to rely on Tiberius; it is ironical, and Livia's triumph.

I have been making up my accounts. In the nature of things I am unlikely to live much longer, and my body has become a respository of disease—a doctors' delight, if doctors were less ignorant than they are. I deposited my will with the Vestals some years ago, and have no reason to change it. It will demonstrate my love and high regard for Livia. It is a public tribute to my marriage. Our marriage, I should say, for we have indeed been partners. My mausoleum is in the course of construction. It lies within sight of the Altar of Peace which will for ever be the memorial of what I have done for Rome. Yet I feel the need for something more explicit; not this memoir, which is a personal testament, but a public statement which will spell out my achievement. I am therefore causing to be prepared a record of what I have done and this will be inscribed on two bronze pillars to be set up before my tomb. It will be a statement to challenge the corruption of future historians, for I know only too well how historians can distort a man's life and deprive it of its true significance.

And yet, as I view what I am writing for this record, I find myself conceding that there is justice in the historians' suspicions. Words mislead as much as they inform; after all, I knew Cicero well. What a master of rhetoric he was; every sentence in his letters, essays and speeches cries out for interpretation; he was godly in eloquence and twisted as a corkscrew.

Article I: 'At the age of nineteen and on my own initiative and at my own expense, I raised an army by means of which I liberated the Republic which was oppressed by the tyranny of a faction. For which reason, the Senate, with honorific decrees, made me a member of its order in the consulship of Gaius Pansa and Aulus Hirtius, giving me at the same time consular rank in voting, and granted me the *imperium*. It ordered me a propraetor, together with the consuls, to see to it that the State suffered no harm. Moreover, in the same year, when both consuls has fallen in the war, the people elected me consul and a triumvir for the settlement of the Republic.'

There is no lie here. But anyone who has read the first Book of these memoirs knows that it is less than the whole truth. You will note that I eschew names, save for the consuls used to date the year. Names in this context can only breed dissension. My life has been devoted to stilling this spirit, to the act of reconciliation. Yet here, in the privacy of my secret memoir I may pause. I cannot even yet bring myself to be honest about Antony, the tyrant whose faction oppressed the Republic that year. I told some of the truth in that first volume of memoirs which abruptly halted in the year of my Triumph. Now let me dwell on that word 'faction' which lexicographers define as 'a company of persons associated or acting together, mostly used in a bad sense; a contentious party in a state or society'. Certainly, in the second sense, the word might as well be applied to me and my supporters as to Antony and his. Will historians see in my victory only the success of my own faction? Certainly, again when I recall our landing at Brindisi, three young men—myself, Maecenas and Agrippa—come to claim my inheritance and ready to impose ourselves on the Republic and seize it by the throat, I can't deny that the word 'faction' applies equally to us. Weren't we indeed young and unscrupulous gangsters? 'At my own expense' is disingenuous. Ultimately true of course, but when I think how I crawled before Balbus and Atticus, begging for loans, of how I was granted them with nothing but my name, my ardour and my determination as collateral, well . . . yet I could hardly say 'with bankers' money', could I? Some may also think the claim that the people elected me a triumvir a bit on the rich side. We imposed the triumvirate after all by force of arms. Gangsterism again. Nevertheless the essence of this first Article in my *Res Gestae* is fair: I did liberate the Republic from the domination of faction; ultimately any power I have exercised has derived from the General Will.

Article II: 'Those who assassinated my father I drove into exile, avenging their crimes by due process of law; and afterwards when they waged war against the State, I conquered them twice upon the battlefield.'

I see Cicero in the Senate, his hands flapping like great crow's wings as his eloquence soared, crying out in that seductive voice, from which all the skill of elocution teachers never quite removed the accent of Arpinum, that 'no one but Antony and a few like him regretted Caesar's death'. But I avenged it, and destroyed those who called themselves 'Liberators'. Yet had Caesar lived, what would have become of me? Would I have remained his heir? Suppose he had had his Parthian War, and suppose he had triumphed there—and he might well have done, for only Caesar had military genius enough to make that a possibility (a view I remember expressing to Antony's fury when I was trying to dissuade him from his Parthian War), suppose then he had done so . . . he would have wintered in Alexandria, with Cleopatra. He was already dictator for life. That Parthian victory would have completed the divorce from reality which all remarked in his last months. Would he then have acknowledged Caesarion as his son? I fear he would. He would have accepted the crown he had so reluctantly declined on the Lupercal, and installed Cleopatra as Queen. Besides, Caesar was never comfortable with me. He suspected mockery; he once threatened to deprive me of Maecenas: he 'would despatch that scented dandy to the galleys', he snapped, though who was Caesar to speak against dandies, or scent for that matter? When he died, I was horrified, chilled by fear and the manner of his death; but when I fully realized that he had been removed, my heart expanded, I felt elated, I saw the world open before me. Yes, like Cicero, I rejoiced, though I had the good sense to do so in secret. Caesar dazzled me. I never liked him. I would have feared him if there had not been always something a little absurd, something theatrical in his manner.

My cat, black, long-furred, yellow-eyed, closest friend of

my old age, whose love for me is untainted by thought of possession, who acknowledges obligations for no more than their due, has just leapt on to my lap, digging her claws lightly into my shoulder, thrusting her face into mine, purring with the deep pleasure of intimate contact. My cat, who is my equal as she is the equal of Gods, who neither fears nor resents me, demands no more than I am happy to give. I had such a cat as a child. Then, for all my long middle years of struggle and violence and the search for power, no cat. Now, old, I resume the perfect love one can share with an animal. How delicate and refined her beauty; how noble and independent her spirit; how remarkable her ability to combine liberty with conditional dependence. My perfect companion has four feet and no scolding or complaining tongue.

Article III tells of my wars; *Article IV* of my dusty triumphs and ovations, of how there were led before my chariot nine kings or children of kings. It is both rash and salutary thus to debase greatness.

Article V recounts how I declined the dictatorship offered me by the Senate and the People. That was in the year when Lucius Arruntius and Marcus Marcellus were consuls. I had been in Sicily, settling colonies of retired soldiers, when word was brought of riots in Rome. The Tiber had flooded the low-lying quarters of the Field of Mars. The corn supply had failed. Speculators, a tribe I abominate, were holding on to such corn as there was, to drive the price up. The mob threatened to burn down the Senate House unless I was made dictator. Lucius Arruntius always disliked me; he was one of those aristocrats who felt he should rule the State and sighed for the old days before the Wars. Nor was he appeased by the consulship I had arranged for him. Unlike some of the well-born boobies, he had sense enough to realize the office had become largely honorific. But when he heard the mob cater-wauling round the Curia, and began to feel his limbs loose in his sockets, he squawked loudly enough for my help and endorsed their cry that I should be dictator. He promised them with trembling lips that he would urge it on me, and when I declined broke into degrading sobs. But I wasn't having it. I had seen the effect of Julius' perpetual dictatorship, and I wasn't going to be caught the same way. Instead, I said loftily that it wasn't necessary. I would however take over the supervision of the grain supply. I identified the speculators and gave them a choice which didn't appeal to them: they could relinquish their hoards voluntarily, or they could prepare for confiscation and a long sojourn on a lonely island. They then co-operated in exemplary fashion and the crisis was over.

The nobility several times tried to cajole me into accepting great and open powers. I was too wary for them. I knew that the appearance of power is more deeply resented than its actuality. So *Article VI* informs the People that I three times declined to be named 'sole guardian of laws and morals with supreme authority'. Naturally I wasn't going to fall into that trap. I told them I couldn't accept an office 'contrary to the traditions of our ancestors'. You can always defeat conservatives by an appeal to tradition.

Article VII lists my honours and membership of sacred orders. I allowed Lepidus to retain the office of Pontifex Maximus till his death, when I assumed it myself. It has its uses.

Subsequent *Articles VIII, IX, X, XI* and *XII* tell of the honours paid me by the Senate and the Roman People, of my reforms of the Senate and of the Censuses I took. At the last census there were almost five million Roman citizens. Unlike Julius I have thought it wise not to cheapen this distinction by granting it indiscriminately to provincials. Of these honours I am proudest of the Senate's decree that an altar of the Augustan Peace should be inaugurated.

Let *Article XIII* speak for itself: 'The temple of Janus Quirinus, which our ancestors desired to be closed whenever peace with victory was secured by sea and by land throughout the entire empire of the Roman People, and which before I was born is recorded to have been closed only twice since the founding of the city, was during my principate three times ordered by the Senate to be closed.'

I cannot bring myself to write of *Article XIV*. It tells of my sons Gaius and Lucius, for whom the first volume of these memoirs was written . . .

Article XV records the sums I have given as donations to the Roman plebs. No man has given more money to more people than I.

Article XVI records how I reimbursed municipalities for lands I assigned to colonies of soldiers. No one before me thought to do this, not Sulla, not Pompey, nor Julius. I am surprised that Pompey did not.

Articles XVII and *XVIII* tell how on several occasions I came to the assistance of the Treasury with my own money. I defy historians to impugn this record.

Subsequent *Articles XIX, XX* and *XXI* record my building works. My vaunt is that I found Rome of brick and left it of marble.

I am not however proud of what I record in the next two Articles: the gladiatorial shows I presented. These have become, alas, an inescapable feature of Roman life. The princeps who neglects to provide them will invite disaffection.

Article XXIV records that after the war with Antony, 'I replaced in the temples of all the communities of Asia the ornaments which my opponent in the war had seized for his private use after despoiling the temples.' That was typical of Antony of course; he couldn't see anything pretty or precious without wanting to lay his hands on it. He had no sense of his own dignity, and, what was worse, no sense of what we owe the provincials. That can be put quite simply. We owe them respect. We must respect their traditions and cults as we respect our own. It is right and proper in itself; it is also the only way to reconcile them to our empire. On the other hand, 'eighty silver statues of myself, represented on foot, on horseback, or in a chariot, stood in the city; these I myself removed, and out of the money therefrom I set up golden offerings in the temple of Apollo in my own name and in the name of those who had honoured me with the statues.' This action appeared to me so obviously demanded by common sense that there is really nothing to be proud of in having performed it. Yet, again, I learned from the deplorable example set me by Julius. It pleased his vanity to have Asiatics worship him as a God. What tushery. Men are not Gods; though I have been solemnly religious it has sometimes crossed my mind that Gods may not be Gods either. Yet that is not quite true. It is a matter I discussed often with Virgil, the most profoundly religious man of my acquaintance ... He said to me, I remember, 'Do not let doubts and discrepancies perturb you. No man who has reflected wisely on these matters can doubt that the world is formed, guided, in some mysterious way governed, by potent and immortal spirits. We, in our human ignorance, choose to identify particular elements of these spirits, and give them names, and even human attributes. There may be no Apollo; there is a life-giving and life-enhancing force which our Apollo nevertheless well represents. It is in our nature to endow the Apollonian or Dianic spirit with personality, to make up stories about the Gods we have partly invented, partly perhaps, in dim and shadowy manner, recalled from the past adventures of our immortal souls. When you are in doubt, my friend'—and in memory I dwell lovingly on the tender note which Virgil gave that simple form of address—'turn back to Plato. Read "The Phaedo" and ponder on the great argument for immortality there given to Socrates. Read "The Republic" too, and particularly the myth of the cave. Our knowledge of the Divine can only be shadowy, an imperfect recollection of its reality.' How could I, who heard and believed what my poet told me, have permitted my own statue to be worshipped? It would have been blasphemous. Besides, it was politically inexpedient. A man-God is exposed to the ridicule of both the wise and irreverent.

Article XXV: 'I brought back peace to the sea by suppressing the pirates. In that war I turned over to their masters for punishment nearly 30,000 slaves who had run away from their masters and taken up arms against the State. The whole of Italy voluntarily took an oath of allegiance to me and demanded me as its leader in the war in which I was victorious against Actium. The same oath was taken by the provinces of the Gauls, the Spains, Africa, Sicily and Sardinia. More than 700 senators served at that time under my standards: of that number 83 attained the consulship and about 170 obtained priesthoods either before that date or subsequently, up to the date on which this document was written'.

Not even the most critical historians can impugn the merit of my suppression of piracy. Nothing is more necessary for the well-being of Rome than that merchants should be able to sail the Mediterranean in safety. Some may question my statement that 'the whole of Italy voluntarily took an oath of allegiance to me'; they may point at those senators whom I permitted to join Antony; they may suggest that compulsion was applied to some municipalities and they may find the term of the writs I sent out under my seal peremptory. I admit some pressure was applied; but I stand astonished at my own moderation in that year of crisis. Not only did I excuse the citizens of Bononia from the oath on account of that city's long association with Antony's family, but I punished few of the families who adhered to Antony. Besides the fact is that the response of the great part of Italy and the provinces was indeed spontaneous. After a half-century of civil strife, they longed for peace, and they recognized that I, and I alone, was capable of obtaining it. I also, unlike most Roman nobles, realized that Italy and Rome constituted one polity; that the strength of the Empire must henceforth rest on the full and eager consent of Italy. I was the first politician to be Italian as much as Roman. Even Cicero, though himself an Italian rather than a Roman, never realized this; he identified himself completely with the purely Roman politics of the City-State which we had outgrown.

The following eight Articles spell out my conquests, the colonies I planted, the standards lost by some of my predecessors which I recaptured, the kings I subdued, the embassies from distant lands such as India which I received, the kings I gave to the Parthians and the Medes. I have been in my heart a man of peace. I have never claimed military genius, but one of my qualities has been the ability to select generals, the greatest of whom have been Agrippa and my stepson (now my adopted son), Tiberius. The Gods promised Aeneas and his seed limitless Empire. I have added more to the Empire of Rome than all the generals of the Republic put together; Caesar's achievements pale in comparison with mine, but I have never shown the beastly cruelty he displayed in Gaul, cruelty you may remember which shocked even Cato, and led him to urge the Senate that Caesar be handed over to the Gauls as a war criminal. As for my policy, Virgil once asked me to sum up Rome's mission as I saw it. I thought for some time and answered: 'to spare the subject and subdue the proud.' I am proud myself that he incorporated my reply in 'The Aeneid'.

I shall quote the last two Articles in full: without comment, at this point.

Article XXXIV: 'In my sixth and seventh consulships, after I had put an end to the civil wars, having attained supreme power by universal consent, I transferred the state from my own power to the control of the Roman Senate and People. For this service of mine I received the title of Augustus by decree of the Senate and the doorposts of my house were publicly decked with laurels, the civic crown was affixed over my doorway, and a golden shield was set up in the Julian senate house, which, as the inscription on this shield testifies, the Roman Senate and People gave me in recognition of my valour, clemency, justice, and devotion. After that time I excelled all in authority, but I possessed no more power than the others who were my colleagues in each magistracy.'

Article XXXV: 'When I held my thirteenth consulship, the Senate, the equestrian order, and the entire Roman People gave me the title of "Father of the Country" and decreed that this title should be inscribed in the vestibule of my house, in the Julian senate house, and in the Augustan forum on the pedestal of the chariot which was set up in my honour by the decree of the Senate.' At the time I wrote this document I was in my seventy-sixth year...

No man has been more fortunate than I. I have often thought that. Yet I have never forgotten the proverb: 'Call no man fortunate till he is dead'. And in the years since my day of Triumph on which I ended the first volume of these memoirs, I have known bitter misfortunes, cruel disappointment. I have learned that Fate never smiles with constant benignity on any man. We must pay for our fortune, and often the price is such as to make achievement taste like cold ashes and sour wine.

O Varus, give me back my legions!

II

My happiest memory of my Triumph remains that of Marcellus, my nephew, who rode on the trace-horse on the right of my chariot. Livia was displeased because her son Tiberius was placed on the left. But there were two reasons for this, both good ones. In the first place, Marcellus was the elder, and connected to me by blood. Secondly, the war of Actium and the conquest of Egypt represented for me revenge for the insults which Antony had paid to Marcellus' mother, my dear sister Octavia. The children of Antony and Cleopatra walked chained in the procession, while Marcellus, whom Antony had despoiled, rode a black steed in my triumph. A man would have to be dull to the fitness of things not to take pleasure in this.

But there was another reason. I became middle-aged the year of my Triumph. True, I was no more than thirty-six, but I had suffered seventeen years of war and perpetual crisis since Julius' murder. War and politics had eaten up the youth I had never had leisure to enjoy. It seemed to me, even as my chariot trundled over the paving stones of the Sacred Way, as the crowds cheered and wondered, and the noon sun beat down, and the tramp of the legions raised clouds of dust in the swimming air, it seemed to me, as if a cloud had crossed the sun, that I had thrown away my youth only for this vain show of power. I experienced an awful moment; a sense of waste, futility, of a life as barren and infertile as the desert, swept over me. That hour of glory which soldiers dream of tasted like stale bread. I caught an intimation of the vast and ponderous vanity of war and politics. And then I turned my head, and saw Marcellus, his eyes dancing, his smile wide, accepting, and altogether happy, as he caught the crowd's huzzas and threw them back again; and I felt refreshed.

Tiberius, on my other flank, rode carefully, stern-faced, as indifferent to the mob then at the age of—what?—thirteen, fourteen, I really cannot remember—as he would always be. In time I have come to respect Tiberius' steely indifference to popularity, even his contempt for the mob, I respect and understand it as an expression of his nature, even while I see its danger, and would myself always be incapable of his Claudian superiority; but then, it irritated me that a boy should be so cold, and I delighted all the more in Marcellus' own delight.

And I loved Marcellus. There was nothing shameful in my love, nothing perverse; but it made Livia jealous and it was on account of Marcellus that she remained withdrawn from me. I loved him indeed for his beauty, for his straight limbs (he was an inch taller than I when he was fifteen, but stopped growing that year), for the dancing life in his dark blue eyes, for the curve of his lips, for the way in which his dark-gold hair curled into his nape, for his candid expression. I loved his beauty as it is right to love any beauty given us on earth, but I did so purely, as I would later love the beauty of my grandsons, Gaius and Lucius, whom I adopted as my sons. I relished his conversation too; it was a perpetual fountain of wit and fancy. I loved his speculations which reached beyond his intellect's range. I loved him for his loving lack of respect, for the way he teased me, and called me 'nuncle'. And yes, I saw in him the future of our house. But Livia, jealous of my love for Octavia, as she had always been, was still more jealous of my love for Marcellus. He seemed to her to stand between her sons and the light. She believed the worst, and continued to do so even after I had proved the nature of my love for the boy by giving him in marriage to my daughter Julia.

Throughout my life I have been puzzled by the perversity with which others view love; as if there were only one kind of love. As a matter of fact, sexual love has never been of great importance to me. I can divorce the body from emotions. Naturally, when Livia withdrew herself from me, I took mistresses: slave-girls, professional courtesans, the occasional married woman (but never free-born virgins; that is wrong). They were of little importance save as a means of physical relaxation. None of them touched my heart which was still given first to Livia, and then to other members of my family. Nevertheless these years after Actium were difficult ones in my marriage, as they were in other respects too.

The great question could be simply put: what were we to do with the Republic now that we had saved it? We had eliminated faction. All our enemies were dead. In the mood of relaxed tension, my ardour dull, I sat by Livia as she lay stretched out in the shade of the colonnade, and said to her,

'I can consider my work done.'

She sat up abruptly, but I continued,

'Why shouldn't I imitate Sulla, establish a few constitutional reforms, which will enable power to pass smoothly within the Republic, and retire to one of our country estates? Wouldn't you like, Livia, us to be able to live quietly together, like normal people, without this endless work, this alacrity to crisis, these appalling incessant demands? After all,' I said, 'I have been in politics long enough to know that there are no solutions, solutions don't exist, it isn't a political term, it's just one damned thing after another. I've lost my youth, I realized that the other day, and I'm tired. So tired of it all.'

'You must be mad,' she said.

I took an apple from a bowl of fruit and bit into it; it was sharp and sour.

Livia said, 'Or you are teasing me? Why struggle as you have struggled only to throw all away when the game is won? Do you really believe Rome can return to the old ways? Are you as naïve as that old fool Cicero was? I may have only the body of a weak woman but I should scorn even to make such a suggestion. What's more, I am by reason of my Claudian birth naturally more inclined to the old ways than one of your background is likely to be. I have more consular masks among my forefathers than I care to count. My family has been prominent in the State since the expulsion of the kings, and yet I know that the old ways are finished. Your talk is sheer sentimentalism. It is unworthy of my husband. . .'

It occurs to me that these memoirs may be read by future generations ignorant of the Republic's constitution, ignorant too of the causes of the crisis which had gripped Rome for almost a century. Yet, essentially it was simple. Our institutions were designed for a city state that was guided by a group of aristocratic families, each jealous lest any one family, any single person, should be able to grasp supreme power. They therefore guarded against this by ensuring that no man should hold power for long, and none should do so by himself. A system of annual magistracies was established; the two consuls, who were chief among them, had equal standing. In times of national emergency a dictator might be appointed to exercise supreme power, but, in the great days of the Republic, his appointment was always of brief duration. Julius Caesar had himself made dictator for life; nothing else that he did aroused more animosity, for a perpetual dictator was king in all but name, and we Romans, who love and value our liberty, have always despised and detested the idea of kingship. Only a man of Caesar's profound and infinite conceit could have thought of making himself king. However, as Rome's empire spread, our ancient constitution began to creak, to split at the seams like an old bolster. The first shock was given when, to guard against a barbarian invasion, Gaius Marius (himself barbarous and uncouth) was given five successive consulships. It was then that the citizen army of the early Republic became a professional force; and the new professional soldiers looked to their general for reward rather than to the Republic. They were his troops rather than Rome's. I myself had profited from this, but the Republic suffered. Moreover, the demands of Empire required that these generals held prolonged commands: Caesar's Proconsulship in Gaul was given him for five years in the first instance, then prolonged for five more. The annual magistrates became near ciphers in comparison with the military dynasts, the great proconsuls like Caesar and Pompey; and, let me add, Antony and myself. One magistracy only was not submerged: this was the tribunate. Tribunes, originally appointed to guard the interests of the plebeians, had no executive authority; but they could initiate and veto legislation, and their persons were sacrosanct. All the dynasts found it advisable to ensure that one or more of their adherents were numbered among the ten tribunes; only thus could their interests at Rome be safeguarded. The ostensible reason for Caesar's crossing of the Rubicon and invading Italy was that the sacrosanctity of the tribunate had been violated by his enemies. I early saw the importance of this office, and, though not being a plebeian and so ineligible to be a tribune myself, I arranged that I should be granted the authority, powers and status of a tribune. It was the wisest decision I ever made. It rendered my person safe, and it enabled me to be in touch with the people and so to safeguard their interests against the nobility.

The developments which had taken place were regretted by traditionalists. I could share their regret. I have no doubt that our ancestors' Republic was a fine and honourable thing. But, unlike the myopic Cato, unlike Cicero who was a sentimentalist, I knew it could never be recovered. We had to move on to some new thing, whatever it might be; and, after I had digested Livia's words, and knew she spoke the truth, I realized that my task was now to establish a new structure for Roman political life. It must reflect realities, as Cicero's plan for 'an agreement of the classes' never did; but, if it was to satisfy the old political classes, and, my nature being conservative I had no wish to do otherwise, it must also retain the form and appearance of the old Republic as far as possible.

I make no apology for the dryness of this part of my memoirs. Whoever wishes to understand me, must understand the work I had to do. Those who find constitutional politics boring can always skip this chapter. Only let them remember that their judgement of my life and work will then be flawed, for they will have neglected to examine the heart of the matter. They will be like those who judge a melon by its skin, and do not taste the flesh.

I invited Maecenas and Agrippa to dine with me, that we might explore the courses open to us. We dined sparingly, for there is no deep thinking on a full stomach, just as there is no sound thinking on an empty one.

Agrippa of course was generally as abstemious as I have always been myself, though, like many who are essentially men of action, he was given to occasional bouts of heavy drinking. I avoided him then for it distressed me to see my closest friend give himself over to brutish vulgarity that would end in a stupor so deep that revolution might break out with him unaware. As for Maecenas, he was more and more given to tippling. Sip, sip, sip, all day long, never quite drunk, less and less often wholly sober. That night however he was in full possession of his faculties.

I outlined the position as I saw it.

Agrippa said: 'They killed Caesar because he would not restore the Republic. They killed him in the name of liberty. We fought against the Liberators because it was in our interest to do so. We would have been nothing if we hadn't. And we fought against Antony, partly for that reason too, but also because, with all his Eastern nonsense, he was going the same bloody way as Caesar. He'd even taken up with the same woman, and Jupiter only knows what notions of Oriental tyranny she stuffed his poor head with. That's why Italy rallied to us, supported us, and, with a bit of help from our boys, swore an oath of loyalty to you. But that loyalty was—what's the bloody word?—conditional, that's it, and temporary. People, not only the nobles, but all good Romans, want the Republic back. They respect you, they're grateful to us all even, but they love the old forms of government and won't be happy without them. Don't go getting other ideas into your head, old boy. If you take the same road Julius did, you'll end up where he did, with your body full of dagger-thrusts, lying at the base of Pompey's statue. Don't kid yourself it won't be like that.'

Maecenas said: 'Well, of course, my dears, I'm only a poor Etruscan outsider. But that gives me a certain advantage. I can see things clearly. Now I'm quite sure Marcus Agrippa is right, as he usually is, when he says the Romans love their old institutions and won't be happy without them, but things change, that's the trouble. It's our business to ask, not so much why, as how, and then seek the remedy. I know you've kept me off the wine tonight but give me a small mug while I get this straight. Thanks, lovey. Well, it seems to me that, to put it in the proverbial nutshell, the cause of our troubles—and even Agrippa can't deny we've had troubles—isn't so much the vice and ambition of particular men, as the complexity of our situation. You could say it rests in the multitude of our population and the magnitude of the business of government. The old ways were fine when Rome was a city of farmers and a few merchants, but now ... just consider, the population of the Empire, even of the city itself, embraces men of every kind, both as regards race and endowment. Their tempers and desires are of every imaginable sort, and the business of the State has become so vast, so complicated and demanding that it can be administered only with the greatest difficulty. . .'

He paused. I asked him to continue.

'Let me make a comparison,' he said. 'Our city is like a great merchant-vessel. It's manned by a crew of every race and lacks a pilot. So for many generations now, four, five, I don't know, it's been rolling and plunging, like a ship with neither ballast nor steersman. No wonder it's crashed into the rocks. The miracle is, it hasn't sunk. It's enough indeed to make one believe in the Gods and in a sacred destiny for Rome, that it hasn't sunk. But it can't continue long without the guidance of one directing spirit. Restore the Republic and everything we have achieved in the last seventeen years will be swallowed up. We will have performed a vast waste of effort. Oh yes, and one more thing, when I say a directing spirit, I mean the directing spirit of one man—which, in the circumstances, must be you. Don't even think in terms of a new triumvirate. That's a recipe for civil war. It's happened twice. It would happen again, even if the triumvirate were formed by us three here, who have been good friends for a long time. It's in the nature of things. I tell you, ducky, you have a simple choice. Assume your responsibilities and make the civil wars worthwhile; duck them and make your whole life to now a nonsense. . .'

When I had landed at Naples on my return from Egypt, I found Virgil there. He was living in a villa a few miles out of the city on the Sorrentine peninsula, where, in ancient times, the Sirens dwelled. He invited me to dine with him, but, when I arrived in the mellow glow of the late afternoon, I found the poet pale, listless and unable to eat. It was the first intimation of the illness that would afflict him over the next decade and bring about his death, that came too soon for me, for Rome and for Poetry. He toyed with his food, but brushed aside my concern, and was himself solicitous for my health.

197

'Olives and bread and a little pecorino cheese, and the white wine of those hills suffice me. I am no man of action. But you have aged Caesar, in grief and disillusion,' he said.

'Antony's death,' I said . . . and left my meaning for him to divine. One never had to speak copiously to this master of words who understood silence. 'And Egypt was horrible,' I said. 'I hated it. Flies and corruption and incessant demanding chatter. I caught a fever but the cause was, I'm sure, my loathing for the ancient vice, cruelty, superstition and greed of Egypt.'

He had finally completed his Georgics and I asked him to read me a passage.

He complied, in that soft and gentle voice that nevertheless carried all the authority of knowledge:

Happy—even too happy, if they knew their bliss—
are farmers who receive, far from the clash of war,
an easy livelihood from the just and generous earth.
Although they own no lofty mansion with proud gates,
from every hall disgorging floods of visitors,
nor gape at doorposts bright with tortoise-shell veneer,
tapestry tricked with gold, and rich bronzes of Corinth,
nor yet disguise white wool with vile Assyrian dye
and waste the value of clear oil with frankincense,
still they sleep without care and live without deceit,
rich with various plenty, peaceful in broad expanses,
in grottoes, lakes of living water, cool dark glens,
with the brute music of cattle, soft sleep at noon
beneath the trees: they have forests, the lairs of wild game;
they have sturdy sons, hard-working, content with little,
the sanctity of God, and reverence for the old.
Justice, quitting this earth, left her last footprints there. . .

He gave me his slow smile. 'You envy my farmers, Caesar, who would never envy you. But we are not all called to the same work. Listen to the last line of that passage again.' And he repeated slowly, pausing over each word as if in wonder. 'Justice, in its ideal form,' he said, 'has quit the earth. But we can still discern the footprints. It falls on you, Caesar, to restore the shadow of justice.'

And then he read me another passage, a great hymn of praise to Italy, which I shall not quote since it ends in a compliment to myself—one I value more highly than all the honours that have been paid me. . .

We sat in silence. The air was still warm with the smell of flowers, and the red glow of the dying sun lay like a carpet of roses on the bay. We heard no more than a murmur from the city below. In the distance a dog barked, and though we could not hear it, I sensed the steady munching of cattle knee-deep in meadows, an image of peace and plenitude called forth by the poetry. All at once, I knew that the world was at the same time good and barren; that life had a deep purpose which was not made insignificant (though the actors were all ultimately that themselves) simply because it would never be fulfilled.

Virgil, as if reading my thoughts, said: 'The finished poem is never as good as the poem that was not written; and yet it must be set down as though it were. Every start contains the seed of a new failure, but that is no excuse for not starting.'

'I know what you are telling me,' I said.

Was it that evening that we first talked of 'The Aeneid'? Memory flickers in old age like a dying candle, and I cannot be certain; but I think it was. Perhaps in reality we made a contract, Virgil and I. If I assumed the burden of Empire, he would write Rome's epic: tell all how the Gods promised Aeneas limitless Empire. But it wasn't as simple as that. It never is... All the same, the contract existed. We both knew it. It hung in the soft air between us, and we both knew the cogency of a destiny recognized and accepted.

Once, I said to him: 'What is destiny? Are we not free men?'

Virgil said: 'Leave that question to the philosophers. Act out what you feel and know. And our knowledge is this, Caesar: for both of us: we can only be free when we work out the destiny which we perceive is written for us. I do not know how this can be reconciled. I only know it is how it is.'

The Curia buzzed with the rumour of a great occasion. Even the laziest and most inattentive senators thronged the benches. My stepfather sat with a rose pressed to his nostrils, to ward off the smell of hot flesh. The buzz died away as I began to speak.

The ground had of course been well-prepared. Agrippa, Maecenas and my other friends had taken soundings. We had, for instance, long discussed the question of names and titles. I had rejected the dictatorship, likewise the title of 'imperator', by which the soldiers had so often acclaimed me. It smacked too much of military rule. For a long time we could not come to a decision. Then someone—it may have been myself, it may have been Maecenas—suggested 'princeps'. It symbolized no direct power, merely a recognition of authority; Cicero, I recalled, had used it of both Pericles and Pompey...

Now I began by recounting what I had achieved for Rome. 'For the first time in a generation,' I said, 'civil discord is still. We are at peace.' Sunlight was visible beyond the open door. Philippus pressed his flower against his nose. Agrippa sat, tensed as a fighting bull. I reminded them that I had already rescinded all the acts of the triumvirate: Romans were no more subject to the arbitrary law which our extremity had made necessary. The Free State lived again. 'Accordingly,' I said, 'though speaking as one of this year's consuls, and invested with the tribunician power which I prize as the expression of the love and confidence of the Roman People, and which enables me to do my duty towards the people, I must tell you, Conscript Fathers, that the days of extraordinary powers are over. I shall lead you no longer... Receive back your liberty and the Republic. Take over responsibility for the army and the provinces, and govern yourselves in the manner hallowed by our fathers' example. The ship of the Republic, shaken by storms, almost wrecked on the rocks of ambition, sails free and serene again on the open sea.'

It was a pity I mentioned the sea, because looking over the assembled senators I saw so many mouths hanging open like fish waiting for a hook, that I almost broke out in giggles to see their consternation. However, I gathered up my papers and walked out of the Senate. The silence followed me into the Forum.

★

Livia was alarmed when she heard what I had done, alarmed and angry.

'I'm sorry,' I said, 'that I didn't consult you, but since you have been so unwilling to listen to what I had to say, it was difficult to do so. But don't worry, I haven't flown in the face of what you want me to do. I'm not giving up power. I'm making it legitimate.'

'If it works,' she said. 'I can guess what you're going to say. It seems to me a jolly sight too clever.'

'No,' I said, 'if you had seen their astonishment, you wouldn't say so. What I've done is give them a glimpse of the void. They are appalled. You see, my dear, whatever they say, they have forgotten how to act as free men capable of thinking of the general good. Even in this purged Senate the majority are either beasts or poltroons. Trust me, Livia, please.'

I put my arm round her, drew her to me, and kissed her. I took her chin and turned her face round that our lips might meet. For a moment she resisted, then returned my kiss as she had not done for almost five years. I drew her down to the couch, and, mindless of any possible interruption, we made love, as parched and starving men might fall on bread and wine. Our first intensity slackened and was replaced by that yielding tenderness coming from the knowledge of perfect union, which I had found with Livia and no other woman.

'You were right,' she sighed, 'my damned Claudian pride has kept us apart; but I was right too to revolt. Nothing can ever repair the wound made by your sacrilege. We may be joined together again—oh we are, my love—but it can never be as it was. You can no longer be a favourite of all the Gods, and there is a curse on our marriage.'

'Don't, don't,' and I tried to silence her with kisses.

'No,' she said, when we had kissed long and then drifted into, and beyond, a second and tender love-making, 'it is different now, because I accept it as you have accepted what I feared you might reject or throw away. I love you, I have always loved you even while I hated you.'

'Livia, I shall love you, and no other woman like you, till I die. If I have seemed callous or indifferent, it was because I feared I had killed your love. . .'

'My love,' she murmured, 'is not a slave to die at an angry word.'

'Let us always live mindful of what we are to each other. I know how little I am when your love is withdrawn. . .'

And this time it was Livia who reached her lips towards mine.

Writing that passage I relive its warmth, the sense of relief and comfort which we both felt. I warm myself at the knowledge that in that hour we approached the full flower of human felicity, creating something that the rigours, disappointments, quarrels and, yes, bitterness, of future years could never destroy. We attained then, while the stunned Senate resumed debate, that communion of souls which Plato holds out as the expression of perfect love, and which he considers unattainable in this life. Since that hour, I have known that it can be attained, and, though it is denied to our natures to remain in that condition, once attained is never utterly lost. There is a Greek word, ecstasy, often loosely used; it describes precisely what I knew as I lay with Livia in my arms, and the afternoon died to a winter evening, and I waited for the news I was sure would come.

'They were like sheep deprived of the shepherd and his guard-dogs, and aware of wolves lurking in the woods. You never saw anything so funny, my dear.'

Maecenas drank wine and stretched himself on a couch.

'They positively fell over themselves to do you honour. As arranged, we let them feel the full effect, and then, just as one or two of the bolder spirits—Arruntius for example, seemed about to nerve themselves to accept your donation—old Plancus, that reliable traitor, got up, creaking with rheumatism, his face twisted with congenital dishonesty, and, yet, simply I suppose because he has such a long record of utterly selfish survival, carrying with him an air of authority. He spoke in praise of the Republic, as we had agreed, of the devotion you had shown the Republic, of how unspeakable it would be if anyone suggested that you had ever deviated from the ideals of the Republic—I thought that a bit rich but it got a big hand. You ought to be honoured, he said. Let your house be decked with laurels and let the civic crown be placed on your lintel. Well, no one could object to that. And as for your name—it was customary, he said, to reward those who had deserved well of the Republic with a new name. Pompey had been called "the Great". He proposed that you should be named "Augustus". No other name would so fully express their recognition of your religious veneration for the Republic. Yes, dear, I know you would have preferred "Romulus", but it *is* a king's name, and Plancus agreed with me that it might, just might, be taken amiss. You content yourself with Augustus, it's a lovely name, with all the right associations. Apparently—which I didn't know—it does link you with Romulus, because he was called "the most august of augurs". Well, this proposal too was carried by acclamation. Then he got down to the heavy stuff, and I must say, you can say what you like about his dreadful character, but he really did it very well. The problem was, he said, that the Senate could not accept your resignation. . .'

'Did nobody cry "why not"?'

'Yes, but only Gaius Rufius, who's practically half-witted—I can't think how he escaped your purge by the way . . . Plancus quelled him with a frown. What they had to do, he said, was work out a scheme which would preserve what you had regained for us all. He knew you were eager that the Senate should resume its old authority, and he welcomed that. Nevertheless, everyone knew how the Republic had been imperilled by the Dynasts. He therefore proposed that you should be given proconsular authority in all frontier provinces where there was a military establishment, and that the Senate should exercise its pristine authority in all others.'

'Did he actually mention "military establishment"?'

'He did.'

'And no one objected? No one saw the significance?'

'If anyone did, he kept it to himself. No, my boy, we've done it. I don't know what you call this new republic we've established—dyarchy doesn't sound a bad word to me, even though it is Greek. . .'

So, in this way, I established a framework within which the business of government could be performed. Its success is easily measured. One has only to consider the contrast between the previous four decades, and the four which followed. I had contrived that the nobility should be satisfied by the show of power and the honour of consulships, while only those loyal to me found themselves with military commands. Even then, I early resolved that it was best, as far as possible, to keep these in the family. That was why I had arranged that Agrippa should divorce his first wife, Atticus' daughter (which marriage had made him enviably rich) and marry my niece, Marcella. Agrippa was bound to me in friendship, but I thought it desirable he should also become Marcellus' brother-in-law.

It is one of the curiosities of our nature that we no sooner have established something than anxiety breaks in. What would happen to the State, men wondered, should I die? I wondered myself, and worried, but, before I can explore this question, it is time to talk of family matters.

Our lack of children of our own was a grief to which I had become inured. Julia, however, was growing up to delight me, though Livia still had much to complain of in her behaviour. 'She won't leave Tiberius alone,' she said, 'it's not decent. You spoil her of course, and you don't see that she's becoming the most arrant flirt.' But I could refuse my daughter nothing. Though she was thirteen now, and almost a woman, she would still clamber on to my knee, and kiss me all over my face. I couldn't believe that this imp of delight was the daughter of the frightful Scribonia. Incidentally Scribonia bombarded me with letters asking that Julia should be allowed to come to visit her; naturally that was impossible. For one thing Scribonia was now living openly with a middle-aged Spaniard who had been successively a centurion, tax-collector and (my agents informed me) the keeper of a brothel. I told Scribonia precisely why I could not allow Julia to visit her, and added that she (Scribonia) was lucky not to be prosecuted for public indecency. 'Moreover,' I said, 'my memory of your conversation is such that I would never willingly expose any young girl to it, particularly not my own daughter. You have only yourself, Scribonia, to blame for the sordid mess you have made of your life, but I'm certainly not going to allow you to soil my daughter. What's more, since I am writing to you, I shall take this occasion which is not likely to recur to point out to you that times and manners are changing. I would advise you to be more circumspect in your debauchery.'

'What an appalling woman Scribonia is,' I said to Octavia when I told her about this.

'Yes indeed,' she said, 'I only hope dear Julia hasn't inherited any of her tendencies.'

'Julia,' I said, 'may be a little wild and light-headed, but she is good-hearted.'

That autumn I visited Gaul, taking Marcellus and Tiberius with me, that they might learn something of the business of government. I am too weary to write at length now of the details of my administration and my never-ending task of maintaining order throughout the vast Empire... Like all political work it is never done. 'The business of government,' I told the boys, 'is service. Attend to detail. Forget yourself. The only satisfaction is the work itself. The only reward, the ability to continue the work. It is our task to bring law and civilization to the barbarians. The true heroes of our Empire are the countless administrators whom history will never know. Remember you are only as effective as your subordinates, for in the nature of things, much must be delegated to them. Choose your men carefully therefore.' Whenever we talked of these matters, Tiberius was silent. At first I thought him bored or indifferent. Marcellus on the other hand was full of questions and suggestions.

One night, in Gaul, he said: 'Caesar invaded the island of Britain, didn't he?'

'You know he did. You have read his memoirs, haven't you?'

'Not much of them, to tell the truth, nuncle, he's a plaguey dull writer.'

Tiberius was nibbling at a radish. 'He's very lucid,' he said, 'and the descriptions of battles ring true enough. Except for one thing. He's always got to be the hero himself. Was he really like that, sir?'

'Yes but,' Marcellus interrupted before I could answer, 'I like the sound of this island Britain. There are pearls there, they say, and the warriors paint themselves blue. Why don't we carry on Caesar's work, and conquer it?'

'What do you say, Tiberius?'

Tiberius blushed, and began to stammer, 'I don't know, sir, it sometimes seems to me that we have perhaps a big enough Empire as it is. Wouldn't we be best to consolidate before we bite off any more?'

'You really are an old woman,' Marcellus said.

I respected Tiberius' caution, and agreed with him. Yet my heart went out to Marcellus. Youth should be ardent, as his was. Tiberius, perhaps because I was unable to disguise my preference, withdrew more and more into himself. Yet I also said, 'Caesar was an adventurer. The conquest of Britain would be worthless, for the island is perpetually wreathed in fog, and I have grave doubts about the value of the pearl fisheries. . .'

'But it would be an adventure, nuncle. . .'

Letter from my sister Octavia:

It's curious, brother, that we now seem to find it easier to communicate in writing, when we are at a distance, than when we meet. I think I know why. The shadow of Antony falls between us. You can never meet me without thinking of Antony and the wrong you did me by forcing me to marry him. I don't of course entirely regret it. It is something after all to have been the wife of a man like Antony, vile and pathetic though he was in so many ways, degraded as he became. Moreover, I have my daughters, the two Antonias, and they are the delight and comfort of my life now that my children by my first marriage have left home.

Which brings me to the matter of your letter, and the suggestion you make that Marcellus should marry your daughter Julia. My first reaction, I must tell you, was 'This will never do.' I have to admit that the cause for this response was of course Livia. I said to myself, 'Livia will be furious.' I don't pretend of course, as a mere woman, to understand precisely what sort of constitution you have established, or how you hope it will develop, but it's obvious enough even to me that if Marcellus marries Julia

206

he will become in some measure your heir, and I have no doubt that Livia would like to see Tiberius or her younger son Drusus in that position. I don't want Marcellus to be the cause of a rift in your marriage. Do you understand me?

Then there are other points. For one thing, Marcellus is very young. I don't mean just in years, but in attitude. I'm afraid I blame you partly for that, brother, because there's no doubt you have spoiled and indulged him. He's never had to struggle for anything. You've handed it to him on a silver plate. I'm afraid that's not really good for the character. I know you've done it for the best of reasons, because you love him and also perhaps because you feel that in some way, by moulding my life, you have deprived him of a father. Then of course you've no son of your own, though I do think you should accept that and regard Tiberius and Drusus as your sons. What worries me though is that marriage to Julia might go to his dizzy if beautiful head.

And again, what about my son-in-law Agrippa? (Oh it's ridiculous to have a son-in-law older than myself.) But what will he have to say about this marriage? Won't he see it as being in some way a threat to his position as your right-hand man? I know I'm lost in these matters but I can't help thinking this way.

Aren't you perhaps getting into the way of thinking you can manipulate people's lives? Simply to suit your own purposes?

I hope you are looking after your health. You know how fragile it is. I am well except for a few aches. Give my love to the boys. Don't let Marcellus tease Tiberius as he is inclined to do. You are always likely to be on Marcellus' side because you love him and don't love Tiberius. All the more reason to incline to Tiberius, and try, try not to spoil Marcellus. See that he sometimes has to do things he doesn't want to do. It is good for him.

Even Octavia, I thought then, doesn't understand me.

Letter from Livia:

I don't think I can stand any more. I suggest you divorce me. If women were allowed to initiate divorce I should do so. How would you like that? Not at all, I should say. But only such an action might penetrate your conceit.

Every time we get back on terms you assume that from that moment everything is forgiven and you can do precisely as you please again. Well, this time you have gone too far. Just because I let you make love to me again doesn't mean I have revised my opinion. Not a bit. Understand that.

What you propose is ridiculous and insulting. And you do it without consulting me. You don't even have Julia's interest at heart, or you would realize that Marcellus would be the worst possible husband for her. They are a pair of silly, pretty and irresponsible children, each eaten up—if you want my opinion, which you probably don't but are going to get—with self-love. What sort of a marriage would that make? Disastrous.

But that's not all. They are not—we are none of us—private persons. One would think that in your position you would realize this. Seemingly not. I have known it from birth of course, and naturally you haven't, but still I would have thought you might have learned it. But then you often seem to me to be two people. On the one hand, we have the statesman, and, I admit, you make a good show in that role, especially when you are prepared to listen to good advice. I am still proud of what you have done for Rome. But now you are ready to tear it up, merely to please an empty-headed boy you dote on (I say empty-headed because I've never seen sign of the intelligence you claim for him—a quick wit and pleasant, if rather silly, fancy, yes, but no depth or penetration of intellect) and a spoiled chit of a girl. Don't you understand that any marriage in the family has an inescapable political significance? I suppose you don't. You couldn't, surely, be so besotted as to see Marcellus as princeps? Besides, what do you think Agrippa would have to say to that? Not to mention my Claudian cousins and all the ex-consulars who are only waiting for you to slip to proclaim their great cause of 'Liberty' again. You know my feelings about Agrippa, he's an ill-made, unmannerly parvenu, but at least he's capable. He's a soldier and he's a man, not a silly boy.

You really make me sick. As I say, divorce me if you like. I would rather be divorced than stomach this.

You don't even have Julia's interests at heart, however you fawn and slobber over her. If you did, you would see that she needs a strong husband who can control her and see that she behaves herself, not that peacocking boy. Tiberius might manage her, but I wouldn't wish her on any son of mine.

I suppose you've already written to Octavia about this, and I suppose she's over the moon. Well, she'll learn differently. I won't have it. I swear it.

It is a pity that my original letter and my replies have disappeared. (They were burned in a fire in my tent, I seem to recall.) I wonder if it was the proposal itself, or more my manner of broaching it which aroused such anger. And what could I have said in my reply to Livia to produce such an answer as this?

So: you refuse to divorce me. Typical.

You pay no heed to my advice. You don't even bother to consult me in advance, just write saying what is your intention.

You really have a very odd idea of marriage. Let me tell you, patiently and calmly, how I understand that institution. Since you choose to disregard my wish for a divorce, you would do well to listen. Otherwise I shall in some way contrive to leave you, bring this comedy to an end.

We are Romans, not slimy and loathsome Orientals. A wife and mother has always had an important, respected and recognized influence in the family. Legally, the husband is sovereign, and I cannot compel you to follow my advice. Nevertheless it has been our tradition that the wife has great influence in family affairs. Marriage is a partnership between equals, and, though I am of course better-born than you, I have never claimed to be more than your equal. Understand that. I ask for nothing extraordinary, merely what is my due: that you should seek my advice, ponder it well, and when it is good (as I am bold to say you will usually find it) be not too proud to act upon it. That is how I behave towards you.

I would never act in any important matter without laying it first before you. I have never lied to you or tried to deceive you. And this is how it should be between man and wife. But it is not, I have sadly come to realize, your way. You prefer to keep things close and secret, to fold them to your breast while your plans mature, and then spring them on me as if they were beyond the point of argument or discussion. You are always asking me to accept your proposals as if they were already accomplished facts. Well, your secretiveness and love of deceit disgust me. They pain me too. It is like a thorn-bush growing round my heart or like the poisonous ivy which attaches itself to stone-work and insidiously destroys it. I cannot live without openness and candour, but you seem capable of neither. You talk of loving me, oh very easily, but since you don't trust me, I cannot value the love you profess. Indeed, the more your conduct contradicts your words, the more I dislike and despise you.

There: do you understand what I am saying? I tell you, you make a mockery of marriage.

Now, let me return specifically to this absurd and dangerous marriage you propose. I have told you, you are besotted with Marcellus, and greatly overvalue him. You will find no one who does not agree with me. I know you think I am jealous of the boy, but that is your own guilt trying to excuse yourself. I judge him fairly, as most of those you know him judge also. You are infatuated, and your judgement, which is sound and acute when your emotions are not involved, blinds you to his lightness of character and waywardness of judgement. Moreover, you flatter him the whole time, and in doing so do him no service. I'll go further. Because you love him as a youth, you are making it even more difficult for him to become a man.

There: do you understand that?

Second, your infatuation is making a fool of you. There are all sorts of ugly rumours about your relationship with Marcellus, just as there were about you and Julius Caesar. This time of course your role is reversed, but nobody thinks better of you for being the seducer (as you are thought to be) rather than the seduced. Very few people in these degenerate days think ill of a man for having Greek morals and loving boys, but nobody thinks well of such a man either. You protest that your love for Marcellus is pure. I don't know; I have no reason to believe you, but it may be. Only, it doesn't look like it, and very few people, if any, believe that it is. I am told that stories about your infatuation are staple dinner-party jokes. Can't you see that you are making yourself absurd? Can't you see that, no matter what the truth of the relationship is, it has been too close, and exclusive, to be good for you, for Marcellus, or for your reputation? It is no good saying that, by arranging for the boy to marry your daughter, you will silence the slander. You will only in fact encourage it to break forth more vilely.

There: do you understand that?

Third, by the favouritism you show Marcellus, to put it no worse, you are unjust to Tiberius, and by extension to Drusus too. When you married me, you assumed responsibility for my sons, though you have never adopted them, as you might have done. You are not only unjust to Tiberius in this particular, in that you show your preference so obviously for your nephew over your stepson, but you are generally unjust to him, in that you consistently undervalue him. I am ready to admit that Marcellus has a charm which Tiberius lacks. A man with your experience of the world shouldn't however submit to charm as you do. If you look closely at Marcellus and Tiberius, you will see that my son has all the virtues which really matter in the world and which are absent in your pretty nephew. These virtues are: intelligence, fortitude, industriousness, truthfulness, regularity of conduct, balance and clearsightedness. Marcellus exaggerates, Tiberius does not. Marcellus gives up when things become difficult; Tiberius perseveres; Marcellus is rash, Tiberius cautious; Marcellus is self-centred, Tiberius has a sense of duty which encourages him to put self aside. How can I not believe you are blinded by love when I see you ignore the true character of the boys and value what is meretricious rather than what is solid?

I have one thing to confess. I have done Octavia an injustice. I thought she had connived at what you propose and was certain she would approve it. She doesn't. When she came to see me yesterday, I was at first angry and ready to deploy arguments against the marriage. Imagine my surprise when she said straight out that she hoped I was going to be able to put a stop to it. She said she had written to you telling you so, and I admired her for it. Her reasons are naturally slightly different from mine, or at least they are graded differently, for we found in conversation that we were in very general agreement. Naturally, however, she speaks as a mother; very properly it is her maternal duty which is uppermost in her mind; and she is sure, as she has told you, that Marcellus and Julia are unsuited, precisely because they resemble each other too closely. The marriage would be bad for both of them, because it would encourage whatever is weak in them.

I know you think I am unjust to Julia, and it may be that your own attitude to Tiberius is provoked by this belief. But I am not unjust. I judge her fairly. I admit we are not temperamentally attuned, but I have always tried to do my duty to her. I recognize and am prepared to admire her beauty, charm and wit, but I deplore and have tried to correct her selfishness and levity of character. You have impeded and undermined my efforts, never willing to recognize that I have the girl's best interests at heart.

You always think you know best of course, but even you must surely pause to reconsider when you realize that your sister and your wife are united in opposition.

I trust you have not spoken to Marcellus himself about this, and I ask you not to write to Julia. But probably you won't have. It would be just like you to present them with a gift of marriage out of your hat. I'm not so sure by the way that your precious Julia would be delighted by your scheme. She won't, I rather fancy, welcome a husband as likely to distract attention from her as Marcellus.

But, if you are wise, that won't come to the point of proof!

You say, you could never contemplate divorcing me. Very well, then, I must submit. But I warn you, if you want me to continue to behave like a wife when you return to Rome, you must treat me as a wife, as the partner you profess to love, and not like a rival politician from whom you conceal everything till it's on the point of accomplishment and so hope to outwit. Otherwise I shall deny you my bed again, and you know perfectly well that I shall keep my word. One thing I will say for you; you are not the sort of man to force yourself on me against my will. . .

Of course, that was precisely what Agrippa had recommended me to do. Plancus also had had the impudence to say to me after dinner one night when he was well sunk in a bottle and so beyond gauging his impudence, 'They tell me, Caesar, Livia is putting on airs, in the way women sometimes do. Well, if you want any help, you know I'm willing to supply you with the most desirable of substitute bedmates—I still have Phrygian connections, and you must know how lovely and lubricious Phrygian girls are—but if you take an old campaigner's advice—one who has triumphed in the lists of Venus—you won't stand for that sort of nonsense. Women owe us their bodies in payment for the protection and luxuries we grant them. Everyone knows that, and our ancestors were accustomed to act on the knowledge.' I let it pass of course; the insults of drunk men are not worth bothering about.

My dear Livia, she flew up in anger quicker than boiled asparagus. My first reaction was to write and tell her not to be a beetroot, but I thought better of it. Instead, as far as I can remember, I replied in mollifying tones. It didn't alter my mind; Marcellus should indeed marry Julia.

How, you may ask, did I bring it off? It is hard to give an exact and satisfactory answer. I dropped the matter for a few months without ever telling either Livia or my sister that I had abandoned my intention. Then, from Spain, where we had gone to suppress a troublesome rising of the hill-tribes, I wrote to Livia praising Tiberius' development. 'I have no doubt,' I recall writing, 'that he is going to be a great servant of Rome. He shows a willingness to master detail which is wholly commendable, and I am pleased to tell you that his admirable example is shaming Marcellus into giving more attention to things which are necessary but which do not immediately appeal to him.' Then, a few weeks later, I praised Tiberius again, and into the same letter, slipped a casual reference to the prospects of Marcellus' marrying Julia. 'Of course,' I added, 'in view of the opinions you have expressed, there can be no question of this going forward till it has all been fully discussed. For my sake I hope you can reconcile yourself to the match, but I am not prepared to disrupt the harmony of the family by pushing forward any measure against your wishes.'

I was content. I had planted the seed. It was pertinacious as I am myself, and would grow. Meanwhile, what I had said was true. Marcellus was indeed maturing. The youth who would return to Rome was not the sometimes giddy and careless boy who had left. For reasons of tact I attributed the change to Tiberius' influence, but that was nonsense of course. It was I myself who moulded Marcellus, and taught him that nothing worthwhile in this world can be obtained without application.

That year I spent in Spain had its bitter moments. The health of the Empire depended on its financial stability. (This is the sort of fact which the old Republicans, who bled the provinces, disdained to recognize.) Much of my time in Gaul had been spent in adjusting the system of taxation; in Spain I was engaged in safeguarding the silver mines. My expedition against the Alpine Salassi was aimed at controlling the gold production of their mountain valleys. But the key to the Empire's financial health lay in Egypt, land of endless resources. Conscious of its importance, I had reserved Egypt under my own authority, and appointed an old friend, Cornelius Gallus, as Prefect. I had every reason to trust Gallus, for he was a man of rare intelligence who had fought beside me for many years and whom I had always found resourceful and reliable. He was a friend of Virgil's too and I knew no better recommendation.

Yet one can never be sure how men will respond to changed circumstances. Under my eye, Gallus' prudence curbed his fecund imagination. Given a command which he interpreted as offering more independence than was actually the case, a reversal of nature occurred. Now his imagination got the upper hand of prudence. Perhaps that is a faulty interpretation. It may rather be that nature asserted itself, that the true Gallus emerged freed, as he must have thought, from the trammels of dependence. He began to behave like a proconsul of the old Republic, embarking on a war against the Sabeans. He wrote glowingly to me (after his expedition had started) that he would bring back a great treasure of gems, gold and spices from the remote heart of Arabia. His men suffered agonies of thirst in a long desert march, and he was fortunate to extricate them without disaster; without treasure either. I wrote urging him to be more circumspect. He paid no heed to my letter, for, without even acknowledging it, he marched south into Ethiopia, announcing that he would explore the springs of the Nile. Agrippa wrote assuring me that Gallus had gone off his head, and some senator—I forget which—laid a formal accusation against him. I was alarmed, and dismissed him, forbidding him however, for his own safety which I could not guarantee against the Senate's wrath, to come to Italy... The Senate, in my absence, proclaimed his banishment and confiscated his estates. Gallus, hearing this, did not wait for my response, but killed himself. I had wished no such fate on him. How could I? Whatever he had done, he had not forfeited my affection. I wept when I heard the news; was I the only man whose frown was followed by death? Who could not set a limit to the consequences of my displeasure with my friends?

Gallus had erected statues in his own honour, and had boastful inscriptions carved on the pyramids of Egypt. He had set up a high column recording that he had advanced with his army beyond the cataracts of the Nile where neither the Roman people nor the Kings of Egypt had previously despatched an army. He said nothing of the pointlessness and expense of this expedition. The cursed corruption of Egypt, distorting reality, had perhaps scattered his wits. Thereafter I resolved that that frightful but necessary country must remain under my direct authority.

Perhaps it was my evident grief over Gallus that touched Livia's heart. At any rate, suddenly, to my great joy, she withdrew her opposition to the marriage of Marcellus and Julia. That was how it seemed to me at the time. There were alas darker reasons.

How deceptive is one's progress through life. It is as if we travelled on a footpath cut through a gloomy forest. Because we remain on the path and are able to advance, we feel in control of our destiny. But the surrounding forest remains unknown and hostile, and we are ignorant of what dangers lurk only a few feet from the path.

III

I fell ill in Spain in the spring of 24, a fever that would not leave me. I had to hand over command of the army there to my legates, C. Antistius Vetus and P. Carisius, sound men who, following my plan of campaign, subdued the rebellious tribes. I therefore ordered the door of the temple of Janus to be closed, in order to show to the city what I had achieved for Rome, and to persuade my enemies of the unrivalled blessings of peace. Meanwhile I took the waters of the Pyrenaean mountains, and began to write a fragment of autobiography, dedicated to Agrippa and Maecenas. It did not proceed far but I was to draw on it later for that book which I wrote for the instruction, and, as I hoped, delight of my sons Gaius and Lucius.

To write their names even pains me. How shall I deal with their lives? Better perhaps to abandon these last mutterings this side of the tomb. Yet I have a duty to the Gods, to Livia, to the shade of Virgil, and finally to my own reputation, to persevere.

A letter has just come from Tiberius assuring me that all is quiet on the Rhine. Old age would be insupportable but for him. If he were to die, in whom could I rest my trust?

Trust . . . the word oppresses me. Owls call hunting from the Aventine; the river stench rises to my nostrils. Slaves, seeing my grey countenance and sour look, slink through the palace in whey-faced fear—as if I would vent my misery and displeasure on them. That I have lived to this! Oh, all may be quiet on the Rhine, I am sure it is, Tiberius would not lie for my comfort, though he knows well how little comfort I have now, in anything . . . oh Varus, give me back my legions! I have sent to Gaul to seek out the little girl who ran by her father's side. I shall entrust her, and her mother, if she lives, to Livia.

Is it some kind of judgement that the Gods have deserted me in old age? I spent sixty years the favourite of Fortune, to be deprived of Fortune in my last days.

Trust . . . life is a hollow gourd without it, trust in family, trust in friends, trust in one's own integrity and the integrity of others . . . trust that one's benevolence will be recognized. Such trust is a mockery; it mocks him who trusts and what he trusts in. It denies the sharp appetites of man.

I returned to Rome, weary and still fevered—a frightful journey—in the autumn of that year. I selected Terentius Varro Murena to be my colleague in the consulship. His sister Terentia was Maecenas' wife and he himself had done well as commander of the legions I had sent against the Salassi. Would I however have made him consul if Terentia had not asked me to do so? She had liquid brown eyes and hair the colour of beech-nuts, and when I called to see Maecenas she was desperate. Though we hardly knew each other she told me of her unhappiness. She had not known of her husband's tastes when the marriage was arranged; for the first year she had not believed they could really be exclusive. As she told me this her eyes brimmed with tears. She lay back on the couch and looked at me, her breasts heaving. Her gown was slit up the right side and she let it fall away to reveal the long rounded line of delicious thigh. Everything in her attitude cried out to me, 'Come and rape me, don't you see I shall die of frustration if you don't?' I smiled to her and she crossed the room and sat on my lap and thrust her tongue into my mouth. She was brown and warm and eager and uncomplicated. I felt the cruelty of what we impose on women and was gentle with her. When all was over, and, in her starved condition, our first love-making was as brief as a dog's, she sobbed in relief.

'There's no point,' I said, 'in hoping that Maecenas . . . You have to accept that he is Maecenas.'

'These nasty little Gallic blonds,' she said.

I kissed her pouting mouth and licked the tears from her cheeks. It was the only day that year I felt well, and, though we made love again, it was never the same. Our affair was brief. I felt no guilt towards Maecenas. Later, the poor girl went, as they say, to the bad. She and Maecenas became friends after I had liberated her, and he introduced her to his other friends in the theatre, and she took up with a Greek dancer called Nikolides whose morals were notorious. I'm afraid that, as the years passed, her own behaviour won her the same reputation. Livia and her circle used to talk of her with disgust; they said she had become little better than a common prostitute. She began to drink heavily and died a couple of years before Maecenas himself. She had quite lost her looks by then, poor thing. I used to receive all sorts of frightful reports about her from my agents, and she could certainly have been prosecuted for immorality. I refused to do so, and even Livia did not dare urge me to, because she was afraid that I would regard such a suggestion as being aimed at Maecenas. That wasn't my reason at all of course; Maecenas didn't enter into it. I felt sorry for the poor girl, because I saw that being married to Maecenas would have disturbed any woman. Only once did I have occasion to reprove her. That was when it was reported to me that she had been boasting of the affair she had had with Augustus. I couldn't permit that and I told her so. She wept again and said it wasn't herself she was revenging, but her brother. That was ridiculous, and I told her so, sharply. We were never alone together again. It is a sad story. I have never forgotten her nut-brown laughter.

Once I asked Horace why he wrote poetry: 'There are too many reasons,' he said. 'Because I have to is the simplest. But there is one reason that appeals to me. I write poetry to preserve what would otherwise be lost, or would decay.' When I think of nut-brown Terentia, I understand what he meant.

Her brother betrayed me.

The crisis blew up out of nothing. The proconsul of Macedonia, Marcus Primus, suffered like my poor Gallus from the delusion that can afflict those unaccustomed to authority when it is unwisely granted them. (But it is impossible to know whether a man is fit for authority till he is granted it.) He did not understand that the days of the anarchic Republic, when provincial governors were so little subject to control that they frequently made war without the sanction of the Senate, had gone. He launched an attack on the kingdom of Thrace. I was displeased, both because he had acted on his own account and also because I had no wish to embroil the Republic in a war on that frontier; indeed his act disturbed delicate diplomatic discussions which were then in train. Naturally the dignity of the Senate was likewise affronted. Primus was charged with treason. He had the impudence to allege that he was acting on my instructions. I appeared in the witness box myself to deny this, and the vainglorious fool was condemned to death.

At that point my fellow-consul, Terentia's brother, protested. Primus was a friend of his, he told me, and he was deeply offended that I had allowed the trial to go forward. Moreover, Primus had committed no crime. He was acting for the greater glory of the Roman People.

'We cannot,' I said, 'permit this private initiative. A generation ago it brought the Republic to its knees.'

He flushed, like a man in wine, and banged the table.

'You talk of restoring the Republic, Caesar, but it is no more than cant. I see that now. You invest me in this empty consular office, as if it represented the authority of the Republic, but though the two consuls are of equal status according to all the traditions of Rome, I find I am only a cipher, good for nothing. A Roman general seeks glory and empire, and you declare him a traitor . . .'

'The Senate declared him a traitor . . .'

'More cant. The Senate would not dare declare a mouse a thief without your nod . . .'

'Listen,' I said, but he was deaf to reason.

'What you call authority, I call tyranny,' he cried and turned away and marched out of the room. As he walked he held his head unnaturally stiff and high, like an actor wishing to convey outraged dignity.' I was naturally perturbed. I asked Maecenas what he knew of his brother-in-law.

'Less, my friend, than you know of my wife,' he said.

'Could he be dangerous?'

Maecenas smiled: 'I had thought better of you, my dear, than to think you capable of such naïvety. It's worthy of the comedian you call your father. Think of the gang who murdered him, ducky. I daresay he even disdained to ask that question of them, for he despised men like Casca and Decius Brutus. Yet they were dangerous enough, in concert, to prick him to death. All men are dangerous, and the weak and stupid the most dangerous of all. My brother-in-law is viewy...'

'Viewy?'

'He likes abstract nouns.'

'Like Liberty.'

'His very favourite. Say Liberty and the poor fool enjoys an instant orgasm...'

I summoned Timotheus, the Greek boy whom we had found useful in the affair of Antony's will lodged in the Temple of Vesta. He was a man now, of course, but still the same ringleted and scented epicene, with the same seductive squirm and fluttering eyelashes. I had learned though to respect him, for I had found him uncommonly useful on several occasions. He had indeed come to occupy a trusted position in my personal secretariat, though his duties were hardly secretarial. I am not proud of the use to which I was accustomed to put men like Timotheus (I had perhaps twenty such in my employment); but neither am I ashamed. Of course in the old days of the pristine Republic, spies and undercover agents were unknown, or at least employed only to gather intelligence about Rome's foreign enemies. But for more than a century now, great men had found it necessary to maintain an intelligence service; and in my position as princeps, I could not have done without one. I could hardly fail to be aware that many who appeared satisfied with the Republic I had restored yet nursed grievances. Some did so for family reasons; others because they were ambitious for power; others because they were jealous of what I had achieved. I would have been neglecting my duty towards the Republic if I had not made it my business to keep an eye on subversive elements in the State. I therefore told Timotheus that I wanted a full report on my fellow-consul, together with a list of his associates and notes on them, as soon as possible.

'That will be easy, Caesar,' he said. 'As soon as you announced that he was to be your colleague, I introduced one of my contacts into his household. Frankly, my lord...'

'I have told you, Timotheus, that I will not be addressed by that title...'

'But Caesar, I am only a poor Greek freedman,' he squirmed. 'I think of you as my lord, for I owe my manumission to the noble generosity of your character.'

'Don't, it offends me.'

'Sorry, I'm sure then. As I was saying, I introduced one of my contacts into his household. You don't mind, do you, that I act on my own initiative in such matters? I'll buzz round and get a report from him straightaway...'

'Be careful, Timotheus. There must be no connection between me and this investigation.'

'Trust me for that. I'll be as quiet and circumspect as a mouse.'

I was troubled. My health remained poor, and I had to be bled several times that autumn to draw off fevered blood. In my disordered state I was prey to alarms. It seemed that the stability I had sought for Rome was not yet achieved. Livia said to me, 'Take care. There are whispers, husband, and where there are whispers, daggers glint in the candle-light.' That remark astonished me; it was unlike Livia to use melodramatic language.

I brooded on death, as I awaited the report Timotheus was preparing. Julia came to me with complaints against her husband. 'He's so conceited, and he easily shows he has little time for me.' I begged her to be patient and dutiful. I had passed legislation which would permit Marcellus to be elected aedile that year and to stand for the consulship (to which he would of course be elected) ten years before the statutory age. To appease Livia I arranged that Tiberius and Drusus should also be eligible for office five years before they were of age. Livia was barely appeased, but, since Marcellus was my chosen heir, I could hardly permit them to assume equality. That would have made dissension certain.

Maecenas told me that Agrippa was irked by my promotion of Marcellus. 'He feels that the boy will usurp his place in the State,' he warned me. I put the matter to Agrippa, assuring him that he was my closest companion, and would always remain so. 'But Marcellus is my daughter's husband,' I said. 'You cannot wonder that I wish to advance him. Besides, he's your brother-in-law too.'

'Yes,' he said, 'and your fellow-consul stands in that relation to Maecenas.'

Relations between Agrippa and Maecenas had deteriorated. We had shared the great adventure of our youth, but the memory was not strong enough to enable them to overcome their growing distrust. Each man had hardened in his character, and each found the other antipathetic. It was not the least of the distresses of that difficult year.

Report from Timotheus: agent of the Private Office: to Caesar Augustus: Confidential.

The consul Terentius Varro Murena: The consul is punctilious in the exercise of his official functions. No one has heard him breathe a word of disaffection in public. He has few dealings with his sister Terentia, and has never been known to dine in the house of his brother-in-law Maecenas. The fact that he spent a week last August staying in Maecenas' villa near Cerveteri may be of significance. But Maecenas was not there at the time, though on both the preceding and subsequent weeks he is reported as having sacrificed at his family's ancestral tombs in the vicinity.

Acting on instructions received I inserted an agent into Murena's household in the days following my discussion with the Princeps. I had of course done likewise as soon as Murena's consulship was announced. Unfortunately, my first agent fell foul of the consul's major-domo, and was dismissed for alleged drunkenness and insubordination. (N.B. I have since arranged that this first agent be transferred to the galleys where there is no danger that he will disclose the instructions he received by way of me.) His replacement was a Greek boy, it being reported that Murena's tastes were so inclined. (It is recognized that there is some hazard in employing such an agent, if only because circumstances may arise in which he begins to feel an affection for his subject/nominal master, and thus be himself tempted to disloyalty. In this case

222

however it was judged that the danger was slight. That judgement was based on observation of the character of the agent employed.) The introduction was successful. The agent soon caught his master's eye and was promoted to act as cup-bearer at private supper parties. Despite this, these supper parties seem to have been decorous affairs. There is no reason to doubt the agent's report. Indeed he complained with a visible degree of pique of the tepidity of the subject's interest, the subject doing no more than caress him negligently . . .

'What a sink of iniquity,' Agrippa said. 'How can you bear to employ such people?'

'Come,' I replied, 'it was you yourself who introduced Timotheus to my notice.'

'Doesn't make him stink less.'

'Never mind. Read on. You will find what follows more interesting, more to your taste and to the point.'

'Bloody little catamites. I'd send the whole shooting-match to the Rhine frontier.'

'I doubt if that would secure us against the Germans. Do read on and stop grumbling.'

The agent reports that these supper parties were exclusively male. He found them serious affairs, and was at first puzzled by the tenor of the conversation. He has been regrettably less than completely efficient in obtaining a full list of names of those who attended the parties, of which he attended six in the course of a fortnight. At all of them he and other servants were excluded when the main part of the meal had been concluded. On three occasions he waited at the door for more than three hours between the time of his dismissal and the departure of the guests.

Three men, besides the consul, are reported as having been ever-presents. They have been identified as: Fannius Caepio, Lucius Primus, and G. Aemilius Scaurus.

Notes on the above: Fannius Caepio is the nephew of C. Fannius who served with Sextus Pompey in Sicily, and accompanied him after his defeat there to Asia. It is not recorded how he died, but neither is there any record of him after Pompey's death. Fannius Caepio was brought up by his mother, whose own father was killed fighting alongside C.

Cassius at Philippi. There is therefore on both sides of the family a history of disaffection. The young Fannius Caepio—he is in his early twenties—has expressed disdain of those who accept public office 'in the Republic as now constituted'. Is this in itself not a treasonable offence, or at least an insult to the Senate and magistrates? In character, he is violent, ill-tempered, high-spoken, and given to gaming and wine.

Lucius Primus is the half-brother of M. Primus, recently disgraced proconsul of Macedonia. Though L. Primus is reported as being of timid, even cowardly, disposition, he resents his half-brother's condemnation. He has been heard to say that it is proof that Rome suffers an Oriental despotism.

Q. Aemilius Scaurus is the nephew of the stepbrother of Sextus Pompey, Mam Aemilius Scaurus, whose life was spared and whose estates were restored after the Battle of Actium in which he was taken prisoner. Q. Aemilius Scaurus, who is also a connection of the disgraced former triumvir, M. Aemilius Lepidus, is known to be heavily in debt. He has been heard to say that 'only a real provincial governorship in the old style of the Republic can restore my fortunes...'

Agrippa looked up from his reading, 'What a shoddy gang.'

'They are all obviously traitors. Are they dangerous? That is the question.'

Conclusion: It is clear that these four have been taking soundings among their extensive connections and acquaintances. Though there is no *prima facie* evidence of conspiracy as yet, there is sufficiently strong ground for suspicion to justify intervention. Alternatively it is recommended that some of those who have attended only one supper party at the consul's, some of whom, it is presumed, have rejected overtures made to them, be questioned. A list is appended in appendix one.

'A sorry crew,' Agrippa said, looking over the list. 'Hardly a good man among them. No Marcus Brutus certainly.'

I was always irritated by Agrippa's respect for Brutus, but I let it pass.

'Appendix II is marked "for your eyes only",' Agrippa said.

'Read it if you like,' I said. 'I doubt if we shall have to act upon it. It contains proposals for the manufacture of evidence. Like all agents Timotheus loves to provoke what he thinks is merely dormant. You don't care for him, but he has not only relish for the game. He shows a remarkable aptitude. But, as I say, I don't think it will be necessary. One of these on that list will spill the beans. It's just a matter of whom he tries to implicate.'

'You've no doubt then that there is a conspiracy?'

'Oh none. One can't have, can one?'

'It could be just loose drunken talk. No more. I hate acting on reports from rats like Timotheus.'

'Unfortunately, rats deliver the best reports.'

Agrippa bit his lip.

'Look,' I said, 'it's too much of a coincidence. Nevertheless we have to act carefully. That's why I have asked Gnaeus Calpurnius Piso to call on us. He should be here any minute.'

'Piso? Why him?'

'I'm going to need a new consular colleague, amn't I?'

'That old brute though?'

Agrippa's surprise was not itself surprising. Piso was an old enemy. A heavy dark bushy-eyebrowed man, he had joined Brutus and Cassius before Philippi and fought bravely there. He too had subsequently adhered to Sextus Pompey, but, on Pompey's defeat in Sicily, resigned himself to the extinction of the cause he had supported and retired to his estates in Latium. I had excluded him from my purge of the Senate because I admired his virtue, but he had refused my overtures and declined to return to public life. His self-regard was high; his consciousness of his own superior virtue great. He was in short a prig, and the man I needed.

When he was shown in, I had wine set before him. (All the Pisos are great drinkers, and most of them incapable of rational discourse without the aid of Bacchus.) He quaffed a glass.

'Falernian,' he said. 'On the thin side. My own wine is better.'

He looked at Agrippa.

'What's he doing here? I understood this was to be a private conversation.'

'Vipsanius Agrippa is my closest co-adjutor,' I replied, choosing an old-fashioned word, even one pedantically old-fashioned, to describe him. 'I have no secrets from him, and he is part of my privacy.'

'Hmphm,' he said, 'well, nobody can claim they knew his father.'

Such a remark could still make Agrippa bridle. I placed my hand on his sleeve.

'His deeds supply him with the glory ancestors reflect on others,' I said.

'Hmphm,' he said again. 'I like to know a man's ancestors when I deal with him. Well, you've dragged me here, Caesar, just when the new wine is ready. I hope you have a good reason. Why?'

I motioned to Agrippa to sit down and did so myself.

'Don't like this,' Piso grumbled. 'There's a whiff of a triumvirate in the air.'

'Those days are over,' I said. 'Nothing would distress me more than their return.'

Piso drank wine. It was very quiet, approaching noon, the sun hot for the time of year.

I said, 'Did you ever wonder why you escaped my purge of the Senate?'

'Hmphm,' he said. 'What if I said, "of course not"?'

'I would be disappointed in my judgement of your intelligence.'

'Ha!' he said. I found these grunts and ejaculations irritating, but naturally gave no sign of this. I waited for him to continue, but he remained silent, his eyes fixed on the wine.

I said, 'It was never my purpose to exclude honest men, such as act on principle.'

'Soft soap, Caesar. What do you want of me?'

'Marcus Primus . . .' I said.

'What of him?'

'You have followed his case, I take it. What was your judgement?'

'That he is a man whose own judgement is . . . faulty . . . The kind of man who doesn't know how to adapt to the prevailing wind.'

'Good,' I said. 'You talk as I thought you would, Piso, as a man of sense.'

'Soft soap again.'

'Piso,' I said, 'we are old opponents, but I respect you. I won't ask your opinion of me, because, to do so here and now, would be unfair. Nevertheless, I put a question to you, though it is not one that requires an immediate answer. I ask you to consider whether the state of Rome, the condition of the Republic, are not happier now than they were when we were young, even than when our fathers were young. We have peace, justice, and such liberty as is possible without endangering the stability of the State. I merely ask you to ponder this in your mind.'

Piso said nothing. I might not have spoken. He sat as if deaf to my words. It was possible of course that he was revolving them in his mind, even as he rolled the wine round in his cup.

Agrippa shifted his buttocks.

'There's a simple question,' he said. 'If some of your old . . . allies . . . approached you with a view to overturning the present state of things, even at the risk of a new civil war, what would you say?'

Piso poured more wine.

'Hmphm,' he said, 'what a question in this company.'

'Very well,' said Agrippa, 'has such an approach been made to you?'

'No,' I said, 'no, Agrippa, that question is out of order. Had such an approach been made, we could not expect our guest as an honourable man to answer you, for on the one hand he has a well-merited reputation for honesty, while on the other no gentleman would betray a confidence imparted by former acquaintance.'

Agrippa stood up: 'Piso questioned my birth,' he said. 'Very well, he won't be surprised if I now say that this conversation is being conducted on lines which are too gentlemanly for my taste. We know there is such a conspiracy. . .'

Piso poured himself more wine; his hand was steady as a legion on parade. 'You, Augustus, have a proposition to put to him. Before you do so, it seems to me that we have a right to ask for an answer to my question. To put it another way, in a form you may find more acceptable, Piso, where do you stand politically?'

Piso scowled: then, in a brutal muttering tone that did no justice to the noble rhythm of the lines, he said:

'Happy—even too happy, if they knew their bliss—
are farmers, who receive, far from the clash of war,
an easy livelihood from the just and generous earth...

'When Sextus Pompey turned wolf, he disgusted me. When he fled to Asia, I refused to follow. I returned willingly to my ancestral estates, and have lived quietly there since. I have eschewed public life, since, Caesar, with respect to what you have achieved, I am too deeply steeped in the traditions of my fathers to find a place in your New Order. In my opinion the man who makes two grains of wheat grow where one grew before, "who tends his olives and improves their yield", who makes a better wine—and this Falernian of yours is indeed plaguey thin stuff—deserves better of mankind than lawyers, politicians, rhetoricians, and all the gang of intriguers and spouters of noble-sounding platitudes you find even in your purged Senate. I cultivate my fields and tend my crops and nurse my vines and olive trees. Does that answer satisfy? And I don't know why I'm troubled to give it. Hmphm.'

'It satisfies me,' I said. 'You speak like the man I took you to be. You asked what I want with you. I want you to become my colleague as consul...'

'That's absurd,' he said. 'For one thing, I've told you where I stand. I'm a simple farmer these days, nothing more. If you want more of the truth, I have come to despise the whole game of politics as a selfish ramp. For another thing you've a consul already, and I would suppose others lined up for the next few years, this being the way things are done nowadays as far as I can see...'

'I told you,' Agrippa said, 'we're wasting our time...'

'Wait,' I said. 'You're right of course. I have a colleague. Unfortunately, he has proved disappointing. In fact, he is planning a coup d'état. That is why I turn to you.'

'Is this true? And if so, why me?'

'It's true,' Agrippa said. 'If Terentius has his way, Rome

will be plunged back in the old disorder of assassination, pro-scriptions and civil war.'

'Proscription is not a word that drops well from your lips, Vipsanius,' Piso said.

I beckoned to him to come with me, and led him out of the house on to the terrace from where we could look over the city. 'Look,' I said, 'at the well-ordered, busy and peaceful life of Rome. Listen,' I said, and began to talk at length. I told him what I valued: peace, order, a decent life. I reminded him of how I had restored the Republic. He frowned and I said, 'Yes, Piso, I have indeed restored the Republic. It may not be precisely the Republic our fathers knew. I grant you that. A certain degree of liberty has been curtailed. I do not deny it. No great State can allow absolute liberty, because such liberty in fact threatens to destroy liberty. It breeds fear, dissension, unbridled ambition. Twenty years ago the Republic was sick of a fever that many thought mortal. With the help of the Gods it has been restored to health.'

He continued to scowl over the city. I took him by the elbow.

'Listen again,' I said, 'I appeal to your patriotism. I know you are without ambition. As Agrippa said, a conspiracy is being hatched. To show my trust in you, I shall disclose that its chiefs are old associates or connections of yours. Terentius himself, Scaurus, Lucius Primus and Fannius Caepio. They or their families followed Sextus Pompey, as you did your-self. I turn to you because you offer me the best hope of still-ing old animosities. There are many men to whom I could offer the consulship who would also be worthy of the office. But many of them are Caesareans. My aim has long been reconciliation. These conspirators are giddy-headed and resentful. They are men of poor judgement. Yet, in any state disaffection exists. I would never crush lawful opposition. In the Senate I encourage men to speak their mind, and if you attended the Senate—to which you would do honour and the debates of which would benefit from your counsel—if you attended it, you would see that liberty survives there. Only last week while I was making a speech someone called out, "It's as well for you you spoke that passage fast. Otherwise even the slow of hearing and slow of wit would have realized what nonsense it was." Is that how men speak to a tyrant? I deny no man his say. But, Piso, conspiracy to murder and insurrection cannot be tolerated.'

'Hmphm,' he said.

'I am glad you agree. Now, simply because these conspirators are old Pompeians the best security for Rome is that I should join a noble, respected Pompeian with me in the consulship. Then Rome will see that Terentius and his friends represent no worthy cause, and will judge them to be a resentful faction. You have it, Piso, in your power to safeguard Rome from the renewal of that civil strife which so nearly destroyed the Republic. For ponder this well, when the sword of Mars is drawn from the scabbard, none can predict the outcome.'

I paused.

'What do you say?'

'Hmphm. I should require evidence of this conspiracy.'

'I can provide that of course, but I might first ask you a question. Would I have any reason to make this offer to one I have so long regarded as an honourable enemy, if the state of Rome and the Republic did not demand it . . .?'

He hummed and hawed, swithered and delayed, muttered about old obligations, nodded his head when I observed that obligation to the Republic cancelled out all others, and of course consented. I had been certain he would do so. Piso was rock-hard in his pride. No man of such self-esteem could have resisted me.

Livia applauded my choice of Piso; she has always been pleased when I have associated one of the old nobility with me in my work. Despite all she has seen she still believes that government of the Empire should remain in the hands of a few families, even though she very well knows how degenerate many of the scions of such families are.

Still, this time she was right, and though I try to refrain from self-admiration, I could not help being pleased with my perspicacity. What Piso chose to call my New Order—a phrase that subsequently became popular—was greatly strengthened by his adhesion. Of more immediate moment, the conspiracy was seen, when revealed, to be precisely as I had described it to Piso: the work of a few malcontents. They were arrested, questioned, tried and put to death. The execution of a consul caused me some trepidation; yet it hardly raised a tremor.

Paradoxically this distressed me. My fever returned. The night it came on again, Livia and I supped alone (I could hardly eat). I remember talking wildly. I said to her that I feared my enemies were right, that perhaps I had indeed imposed a despotism under which men feared to speak their mind on important matters. 'It must be so,' I said, 'or the execution of Terentius Murena would have aroused protest.'

'You're talking nonsense,' she said. 'Men knew what had to be done.'

'Catiline was no consul. His crime was even more brazen, for his conspiracy advanced further. Yet look how Cicero suffered from his suppression of Catiline.'

'Cicero suffered because he broke the law. He put Roman citizens to death without a trial, and without the authority of the Senate. You took care to obtain that authority. The two cases are quite different.'

'Oh Livia,' I said, 'how tired of it I am,' and I crossed the room and knelt beside her, laying my head on her breast.

I remember little of the next weeks. My fever raged. My body alternately shivered and was bathed in sweat. Food was repugnant, and my only nourishment was a little wine, cooled in snow and squeezed from a sponge between my cracked lips. Worse however than the pain and discomfort of my body was the disorder of my mind. I lived between sleep and waking and my imagination, as fevered as my blood, summoned up before me horrid and distorted and frightening images. I was unable to distinguish what was memory and what was fantasy. Things I had thrust down into the depths of my spirit, banished from consciousness, rose, more luridly than the original actions they imitated, to oppress me. I saw again Antony as I had first known him in Spain stumble into my tent, mad with wine, as I lay reading. I felt again his reeking body thrust itself against me, felt his teeth dig into my neck, heard his laugh and shout of anger at my resistance, felt again, with a piercing horror that had lurked deep within me ever since and that time will never still, the last degradation as, calling forth all his strength, he hurled me across the room so that I came to rest bent over a table, and suffered, as he held me there (banging my head on the wood), while he had his way with me. Perhaps I fainted from pain and humiliation. I do not know. I woke while it was still dark, and heard the centurions' cries as the guard changed, but could not move being still clasped in his drunken and manacling embrace. Then he woke too, sighed deeply, as with the fullness of pleasure, and moved his sweaty face against mine. I felt the warmth of his pork-and-stale-wine breath, and I heard his muttered endearments and felt his fingers move, and I . . . but even now, sixty years after, cannot bring myself to recall more. It oppressed me in that fever, and I woke screaming, but I have never talked of it, and even now wonder that I can bring myself to write it . . . Yet the reality of that night of horror and degradation has never left me. I have never been clean of the defilement. It was never repeated, for I took good care to remain unavailable for the rest of my time in Spain, and Antony never recalled it, though I knew when he made those gibes that I had been Caesar's catamite (which I was never) what he had in mind, and what he could say if . . . Why was he silent? I have never understood that, for he was a man without shame, I would have thought.

That question rose in my mind when I gazed down on his body in the decorated gloom of Egypt.

How, with this memory, could I have had Octavia marry Antony? Curiously that did not perturb me at the time of their marriage. Was my tenderness to Marcellus an act of atonement? I do not think so.

In this illness I was assailed too by images of the horror of war. I recalled a battle in Sicily when some of our auxiliary troops were repulsed and panicked. They tried to flee through the ranks of the legions, whose commander, aware how easily panic might spread and lead to rout, ordered the legions not to let them pass. The wretched men—Balearic slingers for the most part—thus found themselves caught between two resolute enemies. All at once, one of them began to scream, in a high uncanny pitch. The others, infected, joined in, and the air was full of the clash of swords and this unearthly screaming. Not one of the auxiliaries survived; only their screams rang down the years.

In my memory now they mingle with the cries of Varus' legions, caught in the vile miasma of the German forest, the Teutoburger wood.

One afternoon, the fever left me for a few hours, though my hands shook, my body shivered and I still saw strange shapes form and re-form themselves before my eyes; but my mind was clear: I knew them for fantasy. Yet my clarity was the clarity of despair. I felt a sense of being beyond everything, which I recognized as an intimation of death. I sipped a cup of Sabine wine, and sent for Livia. She could not be found. They said she was at the Temple of Vesta offering prayers and sacrifice for my life. I despatched slaves to fetch her, and also sent for my fellow-consul Piso, and Agrippa. These two came first, and I was perturbed at Livia's continued absence.

I raised myself on one elbow, but could not maintain the posture, finding myself weak as a new-born kitten.

'Piso,' I said, and heard my voice thin, as if it came from a great distance. 'You see me, as I think, in extremity. I have prepared, with Agrippa's help, a detailed statement of the military and financial state of the Republic. I entrust it to you as my colleague and I pray you to deliver it to the Senate. That is the last duty I can carry out for Rome.'

Piso said nothing in reply, held out his hand for the document which my secretary had ready, and seating himself on a bench in an alcove began to peruse it. Flies buzzed in the afternoon silence; I may have drifted into sleep.

'Comprehensive,' Piso said at last. 'Well, Caesar, I shall do as you ask, but I observe you make no recommendation to the Senate as to the future governance of the Empire.'

I could hardly fix my eyes on him; he seemed to sway before me, in half-shadow.

'How can I?' I said. 'What would it serve? I am no king to hand down the succession.'

'Very well,' he said, 'in this you have deserved well of Rome. Farewell, Caesar, I fear you will find but a cold welcome in the Shades...'

When I was sure he had gone, I beckoned to Agrippa, and held out my left hand to him.

'Take my ring,' I said, and felt him draw it from my finger.

'With that ring,' I sighed...

'I know, he said, 'don't trouble to speak. I can command the legions and provincial governors. Letters patent, under the seal.'

He held my hand...

'You won't die,' he said, 'your work's but half-done. Nevertheless...'

Livia entered. Even with my vision misty I could see that she immediately grasped what was happening. I knew her gaze had fixed itself on my ring. I heard a sharp intake of breath.

'Take care of it, Agrippa,' she said. 'My husband despairs too easily. He's not going to die. I've found a new physician...'

She was though relieved to find Agrippa there and not Marcellus, for though she never fully appreciated Agrippa, being prejudiced against him by her birth and manner, she trusted him. 'A loyal old dog,' was her description, and having said that, she thought she had him satisfactorily placed. Such confidence in her judgement was Livia's strength and her weakness. On the one hand, it meant that both decision and action came easily to her; being never doubtful she was rarely prey to that indecision which can afflict those who realize the subtleties and duality of the world. On the other hand, this speed of judgement and complete self-confidence made it impossible for her to have anything more than a rough-and-ready appreciation of character. She was no politician for she saw everything (and everybody) in black and white. So, for instance, she thought that because Agrippa had always seemed content to serve me, he had reached the summit of his ambition. She did not discern Agrippa's certainty of his own merit, which, in the years since Actium, had smouldered jealously. I knew it even before, without a moment's hesitation or a word of demur, he slipped the ring from my finger and eased it on to his, even while he told me that I wasn't going to die.

The new physician was a Greek freedman called Antonius Musa, and it was indeed Timotheus who had sought him out and recommended him to Livia. Had Timotheus, I have always wondered, affection for me, or was he merely protecting his position? Probably the latter, for a man such as Timotheus makes powerful enemies who can render transfer from a dead patron to a living one rather difficult.

'Your fever,' the man said, 'has been wrongly treated. They have wrapped you in rugs and bled you. Both these weaken the body rather than fortifying it.'

He prescribed a regime of cold baths (four a day) and beef and olives. I have never cared for beef, but very soon, I was eating two sizeable steaks a day.

'The blood needs fortifying,' he said, and made me drink red wine instead of the white I have always preferred.

'You have taken no care of your diet and digestion for years, Augustus,' he said. 'No wonder when you catch an infection you catch it more severely than another man might. Not only are you over-worked. You are under-nourished. I can't think what your wife's been doing to let you get in this state. A regular diet and a cold bath form the basis of health.'

'I have always hated and suffered from the cold,' I said in protest.

'Precisely. That is why a cold bath is so good for you. It gets your blood moving. You should eat fish too.'

'Good,' I said, 'at least I like fish.'

His treatment may have been eccentric, but it worked. My health, poor in my youth, improved enormously when he took charge of it. I have been faithful to his regime of cold baths, always starting the day with one, but I have found more difficulty in following his diet. My work has simply not permitted me—as I often assured him—to take regular meals. Many a day I have kept myself going with little snacks. 'If you can't eat a proper meal, at least eat something,' Musa would say. Bread, pecorino cheese, dried figs or dates, and a sour apple have kept me going. 'That's all right,' he would say, nodding his head. 'Most Roman nobles eat far too much. All this gourmandizing is as bad for the health as the long periods of starvation you used to inflict on yourself. Regularity is the thing, Caesar. Do you clear your bowels every morning? You should, you know; it not only promotes health, but improves the judgement . . .'

I owe a lot—long life and health—to Antonius Musa, and I rewarded him with a small estate in the Sabine hills. When Timotheus sought leave to retire from my service, on account of failing eyesight, he went to live with Antonius there. Their conduct gave rise to some scandal, since those who live in the Sabine hills are mostly conservative and respectable folk with little experience of Syrian dancing-boys and no time for them. But, as I say, I owed much to both Antonius and Timotheus, and so ignored all protests. Their amusements harmed no one, for their catamites were already corrupted beyond redemption.

On my recovery I not only resumed my ring (which Agrippa of course returned without waiting to be asked) but I resolved to make some adjustments in my constitutional practice. I would no longer hold one of the consulships. There were three reasons for this decision. First, the experience of sharing a consulship with Terentius Murena had convinced me of the potential embarrassment of the office. Both consuls were nominally equal, and, had Murena been more intelligent and circumspect in his opposition, he might well have been able to summon up specious constitutional justification for his obduracy. I could see no value in putting myself in a position where I might appear at loggerheads with a nominal equal, and indeed there was nothing to be said for having anyone in such a position. Second, I found the official and ceremonial duties of the post irksome and time-consuming. Third, realizing how many of the nobility valued the honour of the office, even though it was shorn of its power, I saw that there were advantages in having more consulships to offer. Moreover, it was useful to increase the numbers of men of consular rank. Accordingly since then I have only held the consulship when I have wished to grant the honour to a member of my own family, with whom it has pleased me to associate myself in the office.

Giving up the consulship deprived me of legal authority in Rome and in those provinces whose government I had allotted to the Senate. Such a position was unacceptable. However, Plancus' fertile brain suggested a solution, and he proposed in the senate that I be granted a *maius imperium*, that is to say, a legally constituted authority over-riding all other authority in the Republic. Consequently I now possessed paramount authority. I was supreme military commander, enlisting troops, commissioning officers, controlling promotions; all soldiers took an oath of loyalty to me. I alone was responsible for the distribution of public lands and the settlement of veterans in colonies. Responsibility for the declaration of war and conclusion of peace and treaties was mine too. Moreover, I could intervene even in the Senatorial provinces in any cases of misgovernment or incompetence, and the Senate graciously restored to me those privileges belonging to the consuls which I had abdicated by my resignation of the office: that is to say, I was permitted to introduce business into the Senate, to convene that august body, to settle the agenda for each session and to issue senatorial decrees.

At the same time, the People chose to grant me the tribunician power for life, though, for dating purposes, I requested that this be formally renewed every year. I have spoken before of the importance I attached to this office. As a tribune, I spoke directly to, and on behalf of, the People. And my person was sacrosanct.

These reforms worked admirably, and I have found no occasion since to augment my power, or in any way to reconstitute the structure of the Republic. Be it noted however: all my powers rested firmly on regular laws passed in the Senate. They in no way offended the principles of the Republic, and, as I have already observed, on several subsequent occasions, I declined the dictatorship.

IV

Call no man happy till he is dead. Yet it seemed that year, as in the last sun of September we holidayed as a family in an old villa I had bought on the Bay of Naples, as if twenty years of struggle had at last been stilled. I was happy with the reforms I had effected. With the recovery of my health the doubts and depressions which had afflicted me ever since Actium seemed to have dissipated as the morning sun scattered the sea-mists in the bay. Livia and I were reconciled. My new vigour made our love-making warm and eager; a man's heart rests most truly in his marriage bed. No other love affairs can equal the felicity to be found there, and Livia, now in her thirty-eighth year, was in the full summer bloom of her beauty. Her reticence in public had never failed to enflame me. The knowledge I had developed over the years of her vulnerability, the self-doubt that she concealed behind a manner that seemed to everyone else brisk and decisive, gave my love a tenderness it had lacked before. I saw her indeed as a rose, a rose that would never cease to bloom; but each summer's flower was easily bruised by cold wind or rotted by untimely rain. Yet that year, whether my illness had frightened her or whether my new health, making me franker and more open in my happiness, removed constraints between us, and in particular that resentment she had sometimes expressed, I can't tell, but our communion seemed perfect and absolute. I recall long afternoons of love-making while the world slept drugged in the most bountiful of Septembers; and as I picture her nakedness approach our couch, her high carriage, small breasts (which I have always preferred) and strong, well muscled, but ever shapely thighs, desire pricks me even now, and my heart aches at the shipwreck of old age. Of the poets, only my beloved Virgil has even hinted at the joys of married love, which he never experienced himself but could nonetheless discern. It is my knowledge of the reality of married love which makes me so despise pernicious and trivializing twaddlers like Ovid. His 'Art of Loving' is a disgusting, meretricious and vulgar book. He reduces love merely to artifice, subterfuge and manipulation; a matter of conquest and a degrading search for novelty. Of course we all experience such desires from time to time, and most of us yield to them, and in yielding do not damage our character if we realize how little such love-making matters, and do not confuse excitement of the flesh, even the lift of the heart, with the reality of love. The love that matters, that enriches and comforts the heart, is of a different order. It depends always on time and shared experience. Time changes its expression; we even pass beyond love's ripeness when we attain its culminating joy. But even in its decline, which comes with the infirmities of age and the dulling of the heart, a long-lasting love takes on a tenderness, an unwillingness to pain, which has its own beauty. Married love, whatever empty fools like Ovid may think, is never unchanging. It has its own mystery; it endures, like a landscape that is always with one, always familiar, always the same and yet always different. It is new and familiar at the same time.

The children, Livia's boys, were with us that September. How different they were: Tiberius, cold, haughty, yet diffident, withdrawn, taking little part in our games and picnics, burying himself in his books and mathematical studies, unsociable to the point of rudeness, yet saved from rudeness by a natural dignity of manner; Drusus warm, friendly, handsome with the glow of youth and laughter, kind and generous, never selfish. I found it as easy to respond to Drusus, whose affection I never doubted, as I found it hard to be just to Tiberius in those days. Was it for that reason that Livia preferred her elder son? Or is it always a mother's instinct to love better the child who will have the most difficult passage through life? Or was it simply because he was the elder and she remembered him as the consolation of her unhappy first marriage, while her joy in Drusus' infancy, though real enough as I remembered, had yet been swallowed up in the delight and excitement of our first year together?

For all my reservations about Tiberius in those days, and the preference for Drusus which I found hard to conceal, I nevertheless recognized the older boy's qualities. I recall saying to Livia that she was rearing two boys who would be heroes of the Republic; how I remember too her grave smile of pride and how she touched wood when she heard my words.

Julia and Marcellus joined us towards the end of the month, coming from the Capri villa I had given them as a wedding present. I was a little nervous before they arrived, not only in case the difficulties between them persisted but because I knew how Livia was unsettled by them, and I feared lest the perfect happiness of September would be disturbed. But Livia, secure in my love and praise for her sons, smiled to see them. They too glowed with health and pride and happiness and seemed at one together; and on the second morning Julia made my joy complete by telling me that she was with child. I was nervous too of course, as one must be in such a case. Any child may prove difficult to bear, a first one most of all. But Julia shone with health, and assured me that she had suffered no ill-effects in the first weeks of pregnancy.

Then, 'You remember,' she said, 'how I told you we weren't getting on. What a fool I was. Marcellus is a perfect dear, he couldn't be sweeter. Really, Daddy, I'm as happy as ... oh, I don't know what, I can't imagine anyone or anything as happy as I am, I'm happy as the flowers would be if they knew what happiness is. Poor flowers, not to know...'

Flowers ... I hardly noticed them when I was a young man, and even that day, took Julia's words as being merely conventional. After all, the brevity of a flower's life has long been a commonplace of poets, though few have expressed the idea as felicitously as Horace. But I could not understand Livia's enthusiasm for gardening and flowers, could not see that a garden is to be valued because at one and the same time it denies whatever is discordant in life, and affirms mortality. Now it is with melancholy irony that I recall Julia's words.

October brought wind and rain, a sudden drop in temperature, and squalls throwing up sea-foam on the rocks below the villa. Marcellus caught a chill. I found him shivering over a game of dice and, irritated by his carelessness, snapped him to bed. His condition worsened during the night. Julia sent to wake me, and I found her crouching by his bedside, her face swollen with fearful weeping. I sent urgently for Antonius Musa, but even as I waited for him, despair stabbed me. Marcellus choked and struggled for breath, sweated, tossed and babbled. I ordered Julia to be led from the chamber, for her grief added only to her husband's distress. I knew he was going to die, and yet could not believe it. His eyes opened in momentary lucidity and I read terror in his gaze. I pressed his hand, but I do not know that he recognized me, or drew any comfort from it. In the hour before nightfall I saw him weaken, and with the dark, he crossed the Styx.

Later, I could hear Julia howl among her maids. I begged Livia to comfort her, but she was unable to do so.

Between waking and sleeping our world was torn apart.

The next day Julia miscarried.

There are many who say I over-valued Marcellus. Tiberius, I know, is certain he would have disappointed me. Perhaps it is true. Perhaps his charm would have died as he lost the ardour of youth and he would have seemed less remarkable. Perhaps Livia is right, and he was never indeed remarkable. I cannot tell, and it is so long ago. But I was not alone in what I thought. In Book VI of 'The Aeneid' Virgil honoured my nephew by having Aeneas meet him in the Shades: I cannot recall his lines, even now, without tears and an aching heart.

Whom the Gods love die young, and I am old. Fortune and misfortune rattle against each other throughout my life like dice in a box, they fall to the table as capriciously. Marcellus died but the work of the Republic was unceasing. I had sent Agrippa to the East. Now stories were put about that he had gone there in pique, resenting Marcellus. What nonsense! I needed him to report on the administration and morale of the Eastern provinces, especially Syria and Judaea. Both were troublesome for different reasons, Syria because it had been mismanaged, Judaea because it was unmanageable. Its inhabitants, the Jews, are a nation of narrow cantankerous monotheists, as reluctant to pay Roman taxes as to honour Roman Gods. They needed a few cuts from Agrippa's swagger-stick. How best to govern the Jews is difficult to know. I have tried direct rule, and also governing through a client-king, Herod. They like neither one nor the other. Revolt always simmers below the surface, for they are religious fanatics who believe, absurdly, that they are the chosen people of the one true God. I say, absurdly, for two reasons. First, we have no cause to believe there is only one God, and indeed all rational enquiry and observation of human history suggest that it is nonsensical to believe there is. Why should the Jews alone march in step? Secondly, if they were indeed the Chosen People, one would have thought they might have made more of God's favour. As it is, they live, squabbling like monkeys among themselves, pinned between the sea and the desert. One cannot avoid the conclusion that their assumption of God's favour is the most ridiculous evidence of man's infinite vanity and ability to deceive himself.

What was to be done with Julia? I was not surprised to find her grief for Marcellus shorter-lasting than my own. She was young, still at an age when six months can seem an eternity.

But I was displeased when Timotheus, tremblingly, warned me that she was frequenting disreputable late-night parties at the houses of dissolute young aristocrats. Such conduct was both unseemly and dangerous. I upbraided her.

'So you're spying on me,' she said. 'Well, that's delightful.'

'I don't have to spy on you, your behaviour is apparently common knowledge even though I am one of the last to hear of it.'

'Then it's Livia.'

The blood flooded to her cheeks and her eyes sparkled. She had never looked lovelier.

'Really, Daddy, your wife's an old cat,' she said, and giggled. One of her most charming features was her inability to maintain a sour or angry mood.

'Livia knows nothing of the matter.'

'Don't be naïve, Daddy. Your wife knows everything that's going on in the Palace, and especially anything concerning me. She's never approved of me, and she's always on the look-out to see if I slip up.'

'You mustn't talk like that,' I said, though I knew of course that I couldn't stop her. 'Marcellus has been dead less than half a year. Don't you ever think of that?'

'Oh Daddy, just because I go to parties doesn't mean I don't miss Marcellus. But I would miss him more if I didn't go and lay around at home. Don't you see that?'

'It's a matter though of decent behaviour.'

'Oh really, decent behaviour! All my friends think that old-fashioned mourning awfully stuffy. It's just not done nowadays. I bet if it was me that was dead, Marcellus wouldn't be glooming at home. No, and I don't suppose you'd be ticking him off for gadding about either. So there.'

I would have to provide her with a new husband. It was, as I said to Livia (who sniffed on hearing it) unnatural to expect a girl as full of life as Julia to deny herself; besides we had to consider the effect on her of losing a child; and finally, if she didn't marry again soon, I was afraid she might get into trouble. A scandal was the last thing we wanted.

'Well,' Livia said, 'you are right there anyway. Have you anyone in mind?'

'It can't,' I said, 'be any of the young men she is frequenting now. They're none of them politically reliable ... I had thought, perhaps ...'

I paused. Livia was sewing. Her needle moved to and fro, quick, certain, exact. She didn't look up to question my silence, but waited for me to continue. It was cold outside, and the slaves had let the furnaces which served our heating system die down. I shivered, despite the thick under-vest I was wearing—I have always hated extremes of climate, and the north wind, scudding across the mountains, was bringing snow to the fringe of the city. I had noticed that afternoon that the Alban Hills were white.

'Tiberius,' I said.

Livia made no reply.

'You have often observed,' I said, 'that Julia is fond of him, and you have said too that his stability is what she needs.'

'You're misquoting me.' Livia looked up from her sewing. 'I have never said she is fond of him. I have said she runs after the boy. That is not quite the same thing. It wouldn't do ...'

She must have been tempted. I have always been certain of that. What was I offering after all? My only daughter, and hence, for Tiberius, the position in the Republic which she knew I had been reserving for Marcellus; surely she must have been tempted? Yet, not only then, but a few days later too, after 'many hours of consideration' she turned my proposal down, flat. 'It wouldn't do,' was all she would vouchsafe me, no explanation. I didn't understand it. I had thought to please her. It has taken me years, much pain and perplexity, to come to an understanding. She knew of course, and valued, what she was declining. Once, a few years later, she half-suggested that she had been unwilling to expose Tiberius to the envy of his contemporaries, but that wasn't the true reason. It was rather that she didn't trust my daughter, was sure she would make Tiberius unhappy, would bruise that Claudian pride of his, and would retard the development of his character. She feared he would withdraw into his secret world of brooding, drawing those heavy eyebrows down, fixing that long mouth in a sullen and recalcitrant line. If that happened, his career would suffer. Livia had no desire to see Tiberius a recluse. She was ambitious for her sons. I had counted on her ambition to secure agreement, but I had given insufficient value to her intelligence. I had failed to realize how well she knew Tiberius, and how she feared his nature. I could hardly blame myself for that, not knowing him well enough; so I blamed his mother. She had failed me. She had done nothing to solve my problem. More exasperatingly, I had thought to please her by this suggestion, and had not done so. I resented her refusal to be pleased.

It was Maecenas who turned my mind to the solution for Julia. Over the last couple of years I had seen less of him, partly because Murena's conspiracy and his brother-in-law's execution had caused a coolness, but more because Maecenas found politics interesting only in times of crisis. He took no interest in administration, and had been drifting into a different world. His pleasure now lay in being a patron of the arts rather than in politics, and he was carrying on a new and far too blatant love affair with the actor Bathyllus. I disapproved of his public displays of affection for him, and had told him so. I suppose he resented my reproof. For Maecenas had in fact fallen in love, as comprehensively as a middle-aged man who has only flirted with his emotions all his life can do. If I had given him the choice (which crossed my mind) between life in Rome without Bathyllus and exile in his company, he would have chosen the latter. There was accordingly some constraint between us. I believe too that he was jealous of the regard Virgil felt for me, for he considered the poet his protégé.

Nevertheless enough of the old affection persisted to allow him to speak frankly to me, and enough of mine remained to make it improbable that I would ever offer that choice to him, for to do so would be to deprive myself of the one man who had never given me bad advice, and who, though he had often bored me, could still make me laugh. The one man too who still spoke as an unchanging friend of my youth . . .

'It is difficult,' he said now, 'disposing of people, isn't it?'

I said, 'Fathers have a duty to provide for their daughters . . .'

'Don't be so stuffy, dear. Between you and me and a deaf slave, we can surely speak without flummery. I know precisely what your problem is, and you're quite right. You see, my dear, I know these ... types ... that Julia's, shall we say, frequenting. They're riff-raff, old Republican riff-raff, spouters of rhetoric with the morals of an alley-cat. And I speak as one who knows.'

'I can't let Julia marry one of them, certainly. The consequences ...'

'You can't even let her be laid by one of them ...' Maecenas waved his ringed hand before me, and played with his jewels. 'There's only one man who will do,' he said. 'Agrippa.'

'Agrippa? I hadn't even thought of him. It had never occurred ...'

'Of course not. You still think of Agrippa as your bosom chum, the utterly reliable lieutenant. It's very odd, my dear, how you keep your innocence and still fail to understand power. You really believe in affection, don't you? Oh yes, I'm sure Agrippa's fond of you, but haven't you ever wondered what really goes on in the block of wood he calls a head? Have you asked yourself what it feels like to know that you are the greatest soldier in the world, and the greatest administrator, loved, feared and trusted by the legions, but still, always and forever, compelled to stand a half-pace behind your oldest friend whose every weakness you know, and to whom you feel yourself superior in so many important respects ...'

'You have always told me the truth, Maecenas ... why do you say this now?'

He smiled and did not answer.

'Of course you hate Agrippa,' I said.

'Of course I do. He has never forgiven me for being more intelligent than he is. Agrippa is a lion. Can you keep a lion as a pet? Can you ever really trust a lion? My dear, power imposes its own imperatives, and you have a choice. You can kill Agrippa and so check his power, or you can bind him still more closely to you. Let him marry your daughter. Feed him with honour, trust and glory, and the lion may consent to purr, docile as a domestic cat ...'

Julia was dismayed. Her lips pouted and her eyes filled with tears and narrowed or contracted at the same time. I could see what she would look like in middle-age: piggy, her looks lost. I felt tenderly towards her, but I could not of course relent, so tried instead to persuade her. I pointed out that I could not live for ever, that indeed I had nearly died last year, and that, when I did so, Agrippa would be the most powerful man in the world.

'What do I care?' she said. 'I want fun, not power...'

Inadequate desire! Poor Julia, who understood so little about life! I tried to explain, but without success. Livia however assured me that she would make her see sense. There would be no trouble at any rate. I had been doubtful of her own response to the proposed marriage. Rather to my surprise, she approved. Did she feel, I wondered, that Agrippa would never be acceptable to the Roman nobility, and that this marriage would leave the way clear for Tiberius? But then she puzzled me further by coming forward with the suggestion that Tiberius should himself marry Agrippa's daughter Vipsania. I had no objection, but she observed my surprise.

'Of course,' she said, 'it is no great match in terms of birth, but a Claudian can elevate any connection. Besides, she's a sweet well-behaved girl. Very affectionate and sensible. I've quite taken to her.'

On reflection, I understood that she thought the marriage would secure Tiberius' position if Agrippa survived me. He would feel obliged to promote his daughter's husband. At the time Livia believed too that Julia could have no children.

A long letter to-day from Tiberius on the banks of the Rhine:

All is quiet, Father. The Germans attempted a raid last week. We gave them a bloody nose, and drove them back in confusion. Some of our young officers were eager to pursue them, and two were quite insubordinate when I ordered them on no account to do so. I have no doubt they think ill of me, and probably even consider me an old woman. (Few have much experience of how tough old women can be.) I have however made orders absolutely unequivocal. I will permit no forces to advance more than five miles beyond our lines.

I have been pondering deeply on the talks we had when I was last in Rome. I am glad that we are in complete agreement that the Empire is large enough and that we have entered on a period of consolidation which may well last two generations. There is nothing to be gained from annexing the gloomy and unproductive forests of Germany, and I must say that my observations gathered after many years of campaigning on our frontiers have convinced me that the Germans, unlike the inhabitants of Illyria or Thrace, are fundamentally unsuited to civilized life. There is therefore nothing to be gained from trying to incorporate them in the Empire. They are by nature savage. They worship gods as vile as can be imagined, and they have neither gift for urban life nor interest in it. Moreover, they barely cultivate the earth.

If it were feasible, I would lay waste a wide swathe of southern Germany, burning the forests for a hundred miles beyond the frontier, and so creating a depopulated zone, which would act as a sanitary cordon between the Empire and barbarism . . .

I repeat: it is my considered judgement that nothing is to be gained from adventurism on the northern frontier. Those who advocate an expansionist policy are fired by the ardour of ignorant and ill-judging youth . . .

(He means his nephew, Germanicus, of course. The young boy has charm and I love him, but this time I am on the same side as Tiberius. Even if I had doubts, his last paragraph would still them . . .)

Yesterday something remarkable happened. A cry went up that a body of men had been spied debouching from the forest. Naturally the alarm was raised, but it soon became evident that it was only a small band. Stragglers, we assumed, or perhaps a fragment of a tribe which had suffered in one of the petty wars that are always breaking out between the various Germanic tribes, and who were now approaching our defences in search of sanctuary. I at once resolved that they should not be admitted, since past experience has shown that Germans invariably become bored with civilized living very quickly, and are then a disruptive nuisance. I therefore despatched a cohort with orders to drive them back into the forest. Imagine my surprise when I learned that they were in fact bringing them in. I went into the camp to upbraid those responsible for disobeying my orders, only to be met with a sight that aroused pity and horror, for these refugees were not Germans but a score of survivors from Varus' legions. They had in fact been prisoners who had escaped, and you never saw such a miserable crowd, or heard such horrors. Their account of their treatment chilled the blood. I say treatment, but mal-treatment would be the right word. A dozen of them had had their tongues torn out, simply for sport the others said, though one legionary, an Italian from Calabria, told a hor-rible story of how some of their barbarian captors had announced that they wished to learn to speak Latin, and be-lieved that they could do so by cutting out and eating the tongues of our soldiers. Have you ever heard anything so disgusting? They actually did so. And yet some people say you can civilize the Germans. I ask you.

You will be glad to know that these poor men have been treated honourably by us, and given every comfort. I have however ordered that they be escorted from the army as soon as they are fit to travel. They should be settled in a colony of veterans. It is undesirable to keep them near the frontier, because, though on the one hand one wants our men to have a dislike of the Germans and even to feel slightly apprehensive of them, sufficiently so to deter adventurism, one doesn't on the other hand want them to develop an unhealthy fear of the enemy. It occurs to me however that you may wish to receive them in Rome, that you may honour their sufferings endured on behalf of the Republic. I should be grateful if you could let me know as soon as possible whether this is so.

I trust, sir, that you enjoy good health. Please convey my dutiful sentiments to my mother. Tiberius.

I recoiled from his suggestion. I have always hated dwarfs and physical freaks, and the thought of meeting these unfortunate mutilated men made me feel sick. I wrote at once telling Tiberius they should be settled in a colony near Mantua, and assuring him that I would supply money from my private treasury to defray all expenses and establish them in a new life with ample pensions. I concluded my letter with these words:

> Your campaigns of last summer, dear Tiberius, deserve all the praise I can muster. No other man alive could have conducted them as capably, in the face of so many difficulties and the war-weariness and low morale of the troops under your command. Everyone praises you, and what Ennius said of Quintus Fabius Cunctator, who saved Rome from Hannibal, may be applied to you: 'Alone he saved us by his watchful eye...' Do not neglect your health, my son. If you were to fall ill, I can't answer for the effect of such news on your mother and myself, and, what is of supreme public importance, the whole Fatherland would be endangered by uncertainty about its leadership. You kindly ask for my health. It matters little now compared to yours. I pray daily that the Gods keep you safe, if they have not taken an utter aversion to our dear Rome...

What more could I write to convince Tiberius that I need him, that Rome needs him? Yet how little I once thought to write such words to Livia's son...

I have been unsettled though by his news of the survivors. I sent therefore to ask if there was any news of the little girl who had danced by the line of march. Do they think my request that she be found but a senile whim? I have been unable to concentrate on work since I dictated my letter to Tiberius and scrawled the last words in my own hand.

Agrippa was still in the East when I decided he should marry Julia. I wrote to him telling him of what I intended. It would of course be necessary for him to divorce Attica, but her father was long dead, and Agrippa had secured his millions. He could easily afford to make a substantial settlement, and it might well be that Attica, like many middle-aged ladies, would be happy to be freed from the marriage bond. I have observed often how easily they can adapt to single status, provided the financial arrangements are satisfactory. And why not? Who would not prefer to have only self to please? Moreover, I was certain that Attica would be appeased by the honour proposed for her daughter Vipsania. After all, it is still something for the granddaughter of a mere banker (however many times over he may be a millionaire) to marry a Claudian. There are those obscurantists who sneer at such social elevation; nothing is more necessary than that it take place, and that there should be a certain fluidity in the social order.

I am told that Agrippa was flabbergasted by my invitation, and even went so far as to ask his staff whether they thought it was some sort of plot. He even had my letter scrutinized by his secretaries in case it was a forgery, though I had written to him in my own hand which he had known for years. Of course when he was finally convinced that the offer was genuine, he was delighted. Julia was after all intensely desirable as well as being my daughter.

She was intelligent enough too to realize that her objections to the marriage could be of no avail, and so to put a good face on her acceptance. And of course though Agrippa was hardly the sort of young man in whom she delighted, he was a hero. He was commanding, brave, dignified and surprisingly epigamic, as Livia pointed out. We agreed that Julia would benefit from being deprived of the company of the epicene young men who thronged her apartments; and certainly, for a time, they were scared off by Agrippa.

As for me, I basked in the achievement of the marriage. I owed much to Agrippa and was delighted to pay my debt in this way. The knowledge that he was one of the family added to my security, and I was pleased to see how his influence brought stability to my beloved daughter's character and conduct. Best of all, she soon proved that the fear that she could bear no children was unfounded. Four were born in the years of their marriage, and a fifth, the unfortunate Agrippa Postumus, six months after his father died. The two eldest, Gaius and Lucius, were to be the joys of my life.

It was pleasant too to see how Vipsania made Tiberius more conversable, and eased his stiff and withdrawn manner.

V

The security of the Empire depends on two things: ordered liberty at home and the inviolability of the frontiers. It has been my life's work to establish both, and maintain them. Only two frontiers are in fact insecure: the northern and the eastern, which latter marches with the Parthian Empire. In central Europe my generals, especially Tiberius, have at last made the Danube a line of safe defence. We have met with less success in Germany, and as that exchange of letters with Tiberius, which I quoted in the last chapter, shows, I have concluded that there is little to be gained from pushing forward to the River Elbe as I once intended. I confess that to have been a failure of judgement, and, though I do not entirely share Tiberius' gloomy scorn for the Germans (being of the opinion that even these ferocious tribes are not altogether insusceptible to the ordered charms of civilized life), yet I bequeath this advice to those who will have authority in the Republic: Rome is a Mediterranean power, and further expansion to the north is dangerous, unprofitable and immaterial to our true interests.

The East however is a different matter. We are there confronted, not with hordes of barbarians, loosely organized in tribal confederations that are inconstant as water, but with a great Empire. If we are to believe the historians the valleys of the Tigris and Euphrates are the very seed-bed of civilized life, older even than Egypt. Cities were known there before Troy was founded. Even the Jews trace their descent from one Abraham who came, they say, from Ur in the Chaldees. A succession of Empires has held sway in these river valleys, rich in crops. Every schoolboy knows of the Empire of the Persians which tried to conquer Greece and which it required the genius of Alexander to subdue.

That Empire has been replaced by the Parthians, and their politics are a complicated business. I cannot do better here than to reproduce, with tears in my eyes, a memorandum which I wrote for my beloved Gaius when I appointed him to an Eastern Command:

My dear boy, it is a great task I have set you, for I have asked you to deal with peoples whose way of life is very different from ours, the like of which you have never encountered. I am therefore going to supply you with as much background information as possible. Always remember: knowledge is power. It is necessary to study closely whatever and whomever you have to deal with.

You have read of course of the old Persian Empire. The Parthians, who conquered it, were originally savage nomads, horsemen who swooped down on the rich cities from the wind-swept plains of remotest Asia. They found there a great bureaucracy, which they hardly understood, but which they were wise enough not to destroy. Though they remain in their manner of warfare what their ancestors were, yet they have added oriental refinement to their barbaric splendour; and the combination is formidable. They have even assimilated something of Greek civilization— that potent brew which corrupts and poisons even while it enlightens and invigorates. Do not underestimate them therefore.

Their Empire has never approached what we Romans understand by a Civil State, for liberty is unknown there, and the will of the ruler is all-powerful. The only check on it is his need to conciliate the nobility, lest they become so disaffected that they resort to assassination or rebellion. It is therefore a tyranny, for one means by which you can identify a tyranny is by asking whether a ruler is fettered by law or immemorial custom, or whether there exists any legal authority independent of his. We of course have such authority in Rome, for our Government depends on the will of the Senate and the Roman People. As you know, my authority derives thence. When I restored the Republic, I was entrusted with its care and management by my fellow-senators. They have no such independent authority in the Parthian Empire and therefore we are right to consider it a mere tyranny. Remember this distinction, and ponder the implications, dear boy.

Don't forget however that this Empire is formidable. It represents a great military force. Fortunately, for much of its frontier, it is divided from us by the torrid wastes of a great desert, that desert across which the vainglorious millionaire, Marcus Crassus, who was so eager to emulate his fellow-triumvirs, Pompey and Caesar, marched his legions, leaden-footed and faint from thirst, to the carnage of Carrhae. Crassus should be a warning to all Roman generals. 'What a fool!' you will say, and you will be right... Did he think his fortune proved that the Gods loved him? Yet all legend and history teach us of the Gods' jealousy. Hubris and Nemesis—all men of power should dwell on these words—but the wretched Crassus was too busy with his Account Books to read the Poets.

The existence of the desert means that the Parthians (who are wiser than Crassus) hardly constitute a threat on the southern marches of our Empire; the desert lies between us, horrid, life-denying, trackless sands, godless waste—it makes me shudder to think of it. The northern fringe is a different matter. There, Armenia juts into the Parthian Empire, like a peninsula, and invites attack. Such invasion, if successful, would open the road to the Asiatic heartland so vital to us: Cappadocia, Bithynia, Lycia would all be exposed, and the Parthians would be established on the shores of the Black Sea, even threatening the Mediterranean.

Rome must therefore control Armenia. That is the first rule of our eastern policy. Easier said than done however! Armenians are difficult, unruly, treacherous and xenophobic. They are mostly Highlanders given to quarrels among themselves which are only momentarily stilled in the face of foreign invasion. The land is mountainous, bitterly cold in winter (be sure to wear sheepskins), swept by snow-laden winds; harsh and unrewarding too in their dry summers. Few Romans are happy there, for it is utterly alien. Yet nowhere is of greater strategic importance, and great trade routes cross it too.

I have thought it best to leave it more or less independent, while making sure that its king is friendly. Antony chose it as his base for his Parthian War, and though he thereby avoided the disaster which befell Crassus, his retreat was ignominious enough. His men suffered terribly in the passage of the Tabriz mountains. The Armenians gleefully snapped at his flanks and rearguard, battles had to be fought daily, horrid scrambling affairs, and stragglers were nipped off, killed and mutilated. As you know he had the gall to celebrate a Triumph for his Armenian campaign (quite illegally) in Alexandria, but the truth was his war achieved nothing and did great harm to our prestige.

From the start, I was convinced of the folly of imitating either Crassus or Antony; yet I knew we had to resume our old influence in Armenia, and wipe out the disgrace these two rash idiots had brought on our arms. The question was: how to do it? And you can imagine, it perplexed me for some time. I resolved to be patient. Then I saw my chance.

Artaxes, King of Armenia, was a fox, an acrobatic fox, I may say, for his policy was to play off the two Empires that threatened to dominate him. However, I got information that his own authority was precarious, and realizing this himself he chose to try to bolster it by making a formal alliance with the Parthians. Now the strength of our position is simply this: many Armenians fear and hate Parthia far more than they do us. The reason is simple: Parthia is near and familiar, Rome itself distant and strange to them.

I was wintering on Samos—you have been there and know its delights—when I learned of his plans. I at once sent agents into Armenia to ascertain the strength of the opposition to Artaxes and offer them our help.

Events then began to move quickly. Artaxes called on the Parthians for aid. They sent in an army commanded by the son of the Emperor Phraates (likewise called Phraates), and a tribe of Armenian rebels took the young Phraates prisoner. Their instinct was to blind and mutilate the boy, according to their charming custom, but fortunately one of my agents, a Greek called Philip, learned of his capture and took it upon himself to offer the Highlanders a great sum of gold if they would hand the boy over to him. In doing this of course he exceeded his authority, but I would urge on you the importance of having agents prepared to use their initiative. Naturally, the Highlanders, demanded to see the gold first, but when it was produced were delighted with the bargain. (Philip told me that one of them pleaded to be allowed 'to mutilate him just a little. One ear at least.') The poor boy, brave enough in battle, but absolutely overcome by the unusual nature of his experience, fell into our arms with relief.

While these negotiations were going on, another Parthian prince arrived in Samos. This was Tiridates, a half-brother of the Emperor, with in his opinion a good claim to the throne. I have never understood the Parthian laws of succession, and know no Roman who does. Tiridates was younger than Phraates (the Emperor) but based his claim on the fact that he had been born while his father was a reigning monarch and Phraates hadn't. 'I was born in the purple, you see, in the purple,' he repeated over and over again in a whining, canting voice that irritated me extremely. Apparently however this claim carried some weight with Parthians, and perhaps this sort of nonsense is endemic to hereditary kingdoms where ability is valued less than birth. It seems of course quite remarkably foolish to us Romans.

What's more I disliked Tiridates, a lean squinting fellow, given to lewd conversation in appalling Greek. Still he could obviously be useful, one mustn't let personal animosity cloud one's judgement, and I ordered that he be treated with whatever honours were thought suitable for royalty. I rather liked young Phraates on the other hand. Once he had recovered from his nervous crisis, brought on by his capture, he was a pleasant youth, with something, it occurs to me, of dear Lucius' charm, though without his good sense. I couldn't imagine either Phraates or Tiridates making a satisfactory ruler, but that was no business of mine, except in so far as I intended to impose my will on Parthian foreign policy.

Meanwhile I waited to hear from Philip. You may be surprised that I should have chosen to employ a freedman in so delicate a diplomatic affair, even though you have been brought up to be free of many of the prejudices of our class, but I have found that Greeks are adept at any under-

hand or undercover business, and he had been recommended to me by another trusted agent. I had though
another reason for choosing him. The situation in Armenia
was so fluid and so fertile in opportunities for mischief that
there were few Roman nobles I would have cared to trust.
They might have found occasion to proclaim inconvenient
Republican notions—from a position of strength. As I
have often told you, I have ever been on my guard against
the seductive cry of Liberty—which generally means
demanding a licence to feather the crier's nest. A freedman,
owing everything to me, and being nothing without my
support, was a more suitable intermediary. I commend this
policy to you. Besides, a Greek can undertake action such
as a Roman nobleman should disdain.

I didn't plan the subsequent murder of Artaxes. It was no
business of mine what the Armenians did with their King.
Indeed, in some ways, it would have suited me to receive
him in exile—there is much to be said, when dealing with
client-states, for having an alternative king in baulk. However, Philip made me aware that Artaxes was very deeply
committed to Parthia, and had even made plans to retire
there (for like all prudent tyrants he had made provision for
a change of fortune). He told me too that feeling against the
King ran high. His rule had been bloody and treacherous
and all through the Tardiz mountains were to be found
men sworn to avenge the murder of their friends or kins-
men. It seemed best therefore to leave him to the mercies of
his countrymen. Armenians are not given to tenderness
and his death agony was prolonged and painful. It was also
highly popular; when the King's body was displayed to the
people of Erzerum, they fell on it with glee and tore it
apart.

Some clans remained loyal to the memory of the dead
King and proclaimed his son. Our allies asked me to send
troops to maintain order. I thought it best to entrust command to your stepfather, Tiberius, then a young man (if
you can believe it), for I was still cautious lest the heady
wine of Armenia go to a general's head; but I was careful to
give him an experienced council of advisers such as I have
now provided for you. We secured the situation and set

Tigranes, the late King's brother, on the throne. He had long resided in Rome and seemed a man of decent mediocrity, though, as you know, we have had trouble with him since. Kingship does go to a man's head.

You have asked why I didn't make Armenia a Roman province. I thought of doing so, but desisted for two reasons. First, I had no wish to perturb the other client-kings in the East (though I thought all might benefit from a contemplation of Artaxes' fate). Second, I had observed the character of Armenia and couldn't believe the Armenians would submit tranquilly to direct rule. They would be blind to its benefits and alert to their loss of liberty. They are proud, resentful, untrustworthy and clever. They would make awkward subjects. Better, I thought, to leave them in a state of grateful and conditional self-government. They should be free to be ruled by a native king so long as they did not abuse that freedom and remained loyal to Rome. Artaxes' fate would be a warning to subsequent kings. This is still my opinion.

Having established a friendly government in Armenia I was able to turn my attention to Parthia. I assured Phraates that I had no desire for anything but good relations with his great Empire. I told him I was honoured by his son's presence in my household and hoped that the boy would enjoy a glorious future. I added that his half-brother Tiridates was urging a course of action which didn't, at the moment, seem to hold out advantages for either Rome or Parthia; though of course things could change. I informed him that I proposed to despatch an embassy led by my stepson Tiberius Claudius Nero to discuss matters of disagreement between the two greatest Empires in the world.

'There is however,' I added, 'one cause of grievance which makes it difficult for Rome to resume friendly relations with Parthia. You retain standards and trophies taken from the armies led by Crassus and Antony. Their loss was a disgrace which Rome burns to avenge. I believe you may also still hold Roman soldiers taken captive in these campaigns. Rome cannot rest easy while Roman citizens languish in foreign lands.'

I ended with a flourish of the peacocking compliments

which delight Orientals, and which I should advise you always to employ.

Phraates was alarmed by the shift in the balance of power and by my veiled threats concerning Tiridates. He welcomed the embassy, more especially because his brother proved to command more support in the Empire than we had believed. So Phraates was eager to conclude a Treaty and agreed to my demands after less than the usual long-drawn-out argument. The standards were handed over to Tiberius who made a dignified speech (though I was told that he used so many old-fashioned expressions that his translator was baffled; that won't surprise you, we have always had fun with your stepfather's archaic pedantry, haven't we . . . ?)

The recovery of the standards was a great achievement. Not a drop of Roman blood was spilled. But the standards were themselves soaked in the blood of Crassus' and Antony's folly.

I hope this account will be valuable to you, darling boy. It will furnish you with much necessary background information. You must combine strength, subtlety, caution and imagination in dealing with Orientals, and you must try to conceal the natural distaste we feel for them. I have no doubt you will succeed . . .

Reading that letter now plunges me into renewed grief for Gaius, so cruelly torn from me in his full flower. And I recall too the return of the prisoners. There were even a dozen survivors of Crassus' army, old men who had suffered almost forty years as slaves and lost all hope of seeing Italian skies again. Three whom I talked to had almost forgotten the use of Latin . . .

Their faces rise to haunt me as I brood on Tiberius' letter from Germany. Then I was sturdy enough to overcome my natural reluctance and welcome them. I could not do so now. Is it guilt, for after all it was I who despatched Varus, or merely the softer sentiments of age? These soldiers of Crassus and Antony had been robbed of life even more completely than if they had been killed in battle, for they had been forced through their long years of slavery to contemplate what they had lost. How, I wondered even then, would they greet their generals in the Shades? And what will Varus' soldiers have to say to me?

Nobody questions the morality of war, or almost nobody. I have never doubted Rome's mission. Even if I had, Virgil's words would have allayed my doubts. Yet I have seen too much of war not to feel its cruelty, or to retain any belief in military glory. Accursed term! I have come to detest generals who delight in war. I prefer Tiberius, my dear dour Tiberius, to Julius Caesar who delighted in battle because it gave him opportunity to win glory and exhibit his genius. I owe something to Caesar, but my life's work has been to repair the destruction wrought by that genius.

VI

I remained on Samos till the spring, for I have always loved islands. The Parthian settlement brought me peace of mind and there were now matters of interest and pleasure to divert me. I received there an embassy from India. They brought me as a gift a striped cat which they called 'tiger', about the size of a lion, but more graceful and, they said, more dangerous. It was the first ever seen in Europe and I delighted in its beauty. The forests of their land, the ambassadors told me, are rich in tigers; villagers fear them, for they kill their cattle and goats, and sometimes turn maneaters. Some of those with me were eager that my tiger be displayed in battle in the arena, but I refused to entertain the suggestion. Its caged beauty disturbed me, as well as delighting, but I would not have it made the sport of the mob.

In spring I crossed to Athens. The weather was benign, flowers bloomed, wisteria and jasmine tumbled from the walls, mingling with roses, and, best of all, Virgil was waiting for me. He was drawn and ill, his face lined with the experience of pain, but we ate young lamb and kid and drank the resin-flavoured wine of Greece, and it seemed as if, with returning warmth, his health improved. It was a relief for me to be able to discard the cares of State for a short while, and talk of poetry and philosophy.

I asked if 'The Aeneid' was finished.

'One never knows enough,' he said.

It was in pursuit of knowledge—the quest which alone distinguishes man from brutes—that we travelled to Eleusis to be admitted to the Mysteries. I hesitated to do this. All good Romans are nervous of foreign gods and goddesses, and though one does not like to compare the deities of Greece with the disgusting cults of Egypt and Syria, everything I had heard of the service of the Great Goddess disquieted me. Our Roman Gods are either familiar, with local habitations, and a long heritage, or they appeal to the lucid light of Reason. We do of course retain some aspects of our ancient religion, the origins of which are unknown and the exact purpose often too, but these are hallowed for us by their long association with our ancestors, even wild ceremonies, like the Feast of the Luparcal when men dress in skins of wolf and goat, and run round the Palatine Hill whipping every woman they meet to cure her of barrenness; this Feast is of course time-honoured. It would disgust us if we did not know that our ancestors had practised it so long. Even so, we no longer believed in its efficacy. It has become in a strange way a sort of sport. Our lack of belief can be demonstrated by the fact that Livia and I, even when we still hoped for a child of our own, never considered whether she take part in the ceremony and expose herself to the test. We continue it because it is good for men to act as their fathers did.

Our religion is a matter of duty and reciprocal obligation. It is informed with light. So are the Olympian Gods of Greece, who are mostly our own Gods under a different name. Thus our Jupiter becomes their Zeus, our Juno their Hera, our Diana their Artemis, and our Mars their Ares. But Greek religion is also rich in the mystery cults, which are not masculine and reasonable like our Roman ones, but feminine and emotional. They speak with a strange music to parts of our nature that we do not, and cannot, know. All Romans fear them in their hearts, and, without Virgil, I do not think I would have gone to Eleusis.

We approached the valley in the late afternoon. It was surprisingly small and green, and large pines glowed with a deep greenness in the golden light of the westering Apollo. Soon he would decline below the mountains and leave Earth to the Goddess. The beauty of the scene caught at my heart, and I was impressed by the silent reverence of the troops of worshippers. My doubts were allayed: there was no fearful frenzy here.

'What do you seek?' a priest asked at the gate of the chapter-house to which we had been led.

'We seek truth,' Virgil answered.

'Enter.'

Our clothes were taken from us and we bathed, and were anointed with sweet-smelling unguents, and were given saffron-coloured robes. All this was performed in silence, and, though the rooms were crowded, there was no noise but the shuffling of feet and the rustle of vestments.

'You must clear your mind of the past if you wish a vision of the future,' the priest said when we were ready.

For two days we prayed and fasted, and drank only the pure water of the Springs, obeying the silence still enjoined on us. I watched Virgil carefully, and in doing so began to understand something of the mystery of the poetic spirit. He was emptying himself of all but the desire to imbibe knowledge.

On the third night we were led out after dark. We proceeded between lines of torches, held by chanting initiates. The moon was up and the temple of the Goddess of Mysteries shone candid in its pure light. Shadows dappled the earth which was still warm under our bare feet. The chanting grew more resonant as we advanced: stranger, wilder, as if it came from a great distance, recalling what we had never known and yet seemed always to have known.

A priestess stood at the portico of the temple, a flamen raised in her right hand.

She spoke in a soft and sibilant voice.

'Are you prepared?'

A cry of assent rose.

'Here,' she whispered, 'is neither life nor death, past nor future, but the eternal present. Here is neither rich nor poor, bond nor free, but the immortal soul. Here, for a passage of time that belongs to all time, we offer you escape from the thralldom of the body and union with the Goddess who is the primal source of life, from whom all things grow, without whom is dearth and death.'

Then the torches were extinguished. Lit only by the moon we mounted the steps, entered the temple and were escorted to the sanctuary.

It is forbidden to relate what happened there, to what rites we assented and what promises were given. And yet, though I cannot reveal what we experienced, I cannot leave the matter, for, to do so, would be to deny those for whom I write, my ... children, Rome's children (though not alas, the children of my body) of such illumination as I have received. There are those of course who say that wisdom which is partaken at second hand, is no true wisdom. I do not know. I write what I feel I must.

It was the next day, for we were both weary and I slept long, that I spoke of the Mysteries to Virgil. Fatigue showed in his face; his eyes were dark and remote pools. I did not know how best to approach the matter, and so did so clumsily. But he took no notice of this, and smiled ...

'It confirmed,' he said, 'what I needed to be reassured of ... I have not slept, but have been working, for I know now that little life is left to me, but I must soon go down into the underworld. I fear I may do so before I have revised my poem, and, if that is indeed so, I must ask you to destroy it as an imperfect thing. Will you do so?'

I was silent, knowing myself. But he urged me, and at last, to calm him, I promised I would carry out his will.

'But,' he said, 'I may be spared. I must believe I shall be spared, and I have been working all morning on a passage in the Sixth Book, which I knew did not express what I meant it to express, and yet, before I came to Greece it told all that I knew. Now, I think I have broken through. Caesar,' he said, 'we do not die for ever. Listen, everything, sky, land, sea, sun, stars and moon, is strengthened by Spirit and enlivened by Mind.'

'But what is the distinction?' I said.

'Spirit is the life-force, mind the conscious intelligence. All created things—men, beasts, fish—all derive their life from

Spirit and Mind. What strength they have is the strength of fire and comes like fire from heaven. Their weakness resides in the body's evil and those earthly parts which are corruptible by death. The body itself is not evil, but it contains evil. It is the cause of fear and desire and of sorrow and joy. Because we are chained to the body, we cannot look open-eyed on free air, as the Gods can. Even when we pass from this earth, dying as we call it, all the evil and ills of the body do not pass from the soul, for long habit has engrafted them on it. So souls must endure retribution and be punished for their old offences. The punishments are numerous and diverse—they must be, as sins are. Each of us finds a world of death suited to ourselves. Fire, wind, or water cleanses us in the Shades. We are at last set free to wander in the Elysian Fields till the last corruption has been removed, and our eyes are clear, and we become a spark of elemental fire. Then, finally, the Divine Spirit calls us in long procession to the river Lethe, that we may visit the sky's vault purged of memory and then in time may feel a desire to enter bodily life again. For that we do so, I cannot doubt. All this I felt before, and now know...'

It was at that moment that I saw what I must next do for Rome. Virgil told me how Anchises (to whom he allotted this revelation of the meaning of Life) then displayed to Aeneas his whole destiny, how he showed him 'what manner of men will be your descendants of Italian birth, souls of renown now awaiting life who shall succeed to our name...' It is this noble passage which tells how I myself, 'Augustus Caesar, son of a God, will bring back a Golden Age to Italy, in lands where Saturn reigned'; this passage too which concludes with the invocation of my beloved and too soon departed Marcellus. And, as I say, listening to him, I conceived the purpose of holding once again the Secular Games, instituted in the year of the foundation of the Republic and repeated every century. The fifth celebration should have been held in that ill-starred year when Julius Caesar led his troops, to the tune played by the Piper at the gates of a cold dawn, across the Rubicon, and exposed our dear Italy to the horror of civil war. There would be difficulties in holding them soon, I could see that, but had no doubt that we would find means to overcome them, for, listening to Virgil, I knew that we required to consecrate our restored Republic, the New Order of Rome, by a ceremony which would join its future to our past. (And in fact it did prove easy to correct the date, for my lawyer Ateius Capito recalled that an Etruscan century lasted one hundred and ten years and that the Games were therefore due to be held in two years' time; he raked up a Sybilline prophecy to support his opinion.)

The time was ripe. The Sibyl had announced the coming reign of Apollo. Virgil himself, divinely inspired, promised an Age of Gold, established by me. Some philosophers of the school of Pythagoras teach that after four hundred and forty years body and soul live in their former state and society returns to its former condition. The ceremony would proclaim and prove the regeneration of the world, even as the mysteries of Eleusis promised the regeneration of the soul.

The next weeks were occupied with the details of provincial administration, and I saw little of Virgil, who was working with a like intensity on revising the Sixth Book of 'The Aeneid' . . . Letters from Livia were loving and contented— she asked several times if I had fixed the date of my return. Julia was with her husband in Spain and I was overjoyed, though at the same time worried, to hear that she was with child. Tiberius had pleased me by his conduct in Armenia; it was clear that both he and his brother Drusus would be of great service to Rome. 1 felt, more than ever, that my long years of toil were bearing fruit.

Towards the end of the first week in September, I was ready to sail back to Italy. Virgil would accompany me. The night before our departure, he was looking dreadfully ill. He had lost flesh even from his lean frame, his face was lined with pain, and his eyes were great black hollows. He asked me if we might postpone our departure for a day.

'I shall not see Athens again,' he said. 'It would please me if we could pass a day on the slopes of Hymettus.'

The air was full of honey and the mingled scent of thyme, myrtle and origano. Bees hummed around us and a lark soared high in the sky, trilling its song of praise. The meadow slope where we lay was richly flowered, and our companions rested in the warmth of the sun some way apart from us. I told Virgil he had been working too hard, too long indoors. He needed the sun.

He smiled and shook his head, but with his perfect manners declined to talk about his health. We looked down on the city. The Parthenon shone with a brilliance such as I had never seen.

He said, 'I have valued this last time in Athens. Nowhere in the world has truth been sought with such diligence; nowhere has beauty been better apprehended and created; nowhere has the human spirit flourished so finely.'

'And yet,' I said, 'for all their speculations about the art and end of politics, how slight was their achievement. Why did the Greeks, with all their genius, fail to establish a polity that would endure?'

'The Greek spirit,' he said, 'was ever one of enquiry. Asking the questions was more important than answering them. We are their heirs, and Rome would be a lesser place and a lesser thing without the achievement of Athens. Those who doubt a divine purpose must consider how Rome and Greece have been entangled since the Achaeans burned the topless towers of Troy and sent our father Aeneas on his travels. So many generations ago, and now Rome, the child of Greece as well as of Aeneas, rules an unimagined Empire and Mycenae is a little village where pigs run to and fro through the Lion Gate.'

Our crossing was foul. The equinoctial gales came early and buffeted our ship. We lay a week anchored off Corfu not daring to trust ourselves windward of the island. Then the wind changed and we scudded across the Tyrrhenian, but still sometimes plunging and heaving. It was the worst weather for a sick man, and Virgil lay strapped to a bunk, the miserable prisoner of Neptune's wrath and his own weakness. I did the little I could to alleviate his sufferings, but he could not retain even the spoonfuls of chicken broth which I fed him. He was delirious when we reached Brindisi.

He rallied briefly in the villa outside the town to which I had him carried, but his brow was still damp, his throat charged and he was miserably feeble. I knew the end could not be long delayed. On the last night he babbled again of failure and reproached the Gods that they had not granted him time to refine his poem. He reiterated the request that I would destroy it, as unworthy of his genius and of Rome's, and he would not rest till I consented.

He died just before dawn as the cock threw its vulgar message to the world. He died in my arms, and his last words were 'peace, longing, destiny, the shades glimmer before me . . .'

So died the best and rarest man I have known. I cannot pretend that I could enter that secret world of poetic magic where he communed with the spirits that gave birth to the world and shape its course. There were half-lights in his soul and in his work, which I can only dimly understand. No poet has equalled him in range and none could play on so many instruments to touch the heart. None so truthfully and nobly admired whatever is good and noble in man. He moved from the exquisite artifice of the Eclogues through the self-denying honesty of the Georgics to the sublimity of this epic of Rome. He drew for us our Italy in a form that made the familiar strange and magical; he made us conscious of the duties of Empire, as of our greatness. I am but an indifferent literary critic, and I leave it to those with more skill in letters to indicate the beauties of his work and to try to account for his genius. All I can say now is to repeat the thought that repeated itself in my mind as I knelt by his bier, my eyes full of tears: of all men I have known, Virgil most completely exemplified what we mean by virtue; he was everything that may become a man.

The executors of his will were terrified when they came on his instruction to destroy the manuscript of his epic, and, knowing my long interest in the work, approached me to ask whether they should obey. It is of course wrong to tamper with testamentary depositions or to set them aside, but despite my own promise to Virgil twice-given, I had no hesitation in doing so. The instruction was partly due to his final delirium, partly an expression of his innate perfectionism. No doubt the poem was in detail unfinished. No doubt he would have added further felicities. I respected his request, but I could not accede to it. 'The Aeneid' had passed out of Virgil's possession and belonged to Rome, to the city and the world. I gave instructions that it should be published, and, if it was wrong to ignore the poet's wishes, I took that responsibility on myself. The wonder with which it was received justified my action.

I was sure I was right. I am still sure. Yet I did wrong too, and that wrong has not gone unpunished. So Aeneas himself was driven from Carthage and the loving arms of Dido by the divine imperative which set him to sail to Italy to be the father of our People. In executing that divine command, he destroyed the unhappy Dido and when he encountered her in the Underworld she withdrew from him, no more moved by his words 'than if she had been hard flint or a block of Parian marble'. Aeneas, who loved Dido and obeyed the Gods, destroyed the queen to fulfil his destiny. I, who loved Virgil and am also obedient to the divine word, broke my promise to him that I might keep my promise to Rome, and let all Romans see how their destiny had unfolded. I was wrong to break my oath, but I would have been wrong to destroy the poem. Should I then have denied my friend my word, and denied him comfort at the hour of death? And do not think Aeneas did not suffer. Will Virgil withdraw himself from me when we meet in the Shades?

I have suffered for Rome. Cruel fate tore my sons Gaius and Lucius from me. Was that the awful prize I paid for foreswearing Virgil? Can there be worse to come? Oh Varus . . .

Enough. I travelled by slow sad stages from Brindisi to Naples, where the poet was laid in his simple tomb:

> Mantua gave me life, Calabria death. I lie
> In Naples—poet of herdsmen, farms and heroes.

I arrived in Rome in October. There had been trouble in the city over the consular elections. In my view the trouble arose from maladministration of the food supplies, but it alarmed some senators. A deputation met me in Campania to urge me to make a public entrance to the city in order to impress the people. I declined to do so, and refused to celebrate the Triumph they also urged on me. I was not a monarch returning, merely the first citizen, and anyway I was hardly in the frame of mind for pomp and ceremony. Public adulation grows more irksome with the years, for all but the vainest of men.

Agrippa and Julia returned from Spain, and my first grand-child, Gaius, delighted me. Since Agrippa was now my son-in-law and the father of a child of my blood, I thought it proper to associate him even more closely in the government of the Republic. He therefore was now also granted the tribu-nician power and a supreme imperium. My personal author-ity ensured that I still held the chief place, but I had no more power than Agrippa. If I died, his imperium and authority would ensure that Rome did not revert to the selfish struggle for power which had disfigured the years before the Civil Wars. Moreover, Agrippa would in time in like manner as-sociate Gaius with himself.

Business was unremitting, but business makes no story. The details of administration can hardly delight the reader. What does he care that I assumed the powers of a censor again, and removed unsatisfactory members from the Senate?

About this time too however I embarked on my campaign to reform the manners and morals of the age. Livia was an en-thusiastic supporter of this necessary but unpopular venture. We both agreed that dissolute and immoral behaviour could corrupt public life as well as private. Measures were taken to punish adultery and fornication, to control speech, to protect minors, to make divorce more difficult, to give wives more power over their own estates and so elevate their condition. I recognized that marriage is an institution which must be healthy if society is to be stable, and so I taxed unmarried men more heavily than married ones, and granted sub-stantial privileges to the parents of large families.

Many opposed these measures; others were sceptical. The aged and wicked Plancus, whose services had won him a measure of tolerance from me which his general conduct hardly deserved, openly laughed at me, and said that you can't legislate people into morality. I asked if it might not be possible to legislate them out of immorality. No, he said, all you do is drive it into dark corners. Better than the Forum itself, I said.

Though I was anxious to elevate the condition of women, I still thought that they were properly subject to their husbands' control, and I told the Senate that it was their duty to reprove their wives and correct their misbehaviour. 'Come off it, Augustus,' someone called out 'when did you last reprove Livia?' 'I'd like to see you try,' shouted another humorist. 'Fortunately,' I said, 'my wife doesn't merit reproof. I wish you were all as fortunate.'

Meanwhile preparations advanced for the Secular Games. The Senate sanctioned the Festival and entrusted arrangements to the priestly order of the College of Fifteen, who chose Agrippa and myself as their representatives. In previous celebrations the principal deities had been (we discovered) the Gods of the Underworld, Dis and Proserpina. I acknowledged their power, but could not believe that gloomy Dis was the deity Rome should most reverence on this occasion. Virgil had agreed with me. The great ceremonies should be held under the auspices of the Gods of the Upper World, Apollo and Diana, for we were celebrating light and reason as well as the antiquity and historic mission of Rome.

I have discovered a note I made during those distant ceremonies. It gives my mood then better than anything I could now write:

It will not be dark tonight. Already, if I step out of my house and look towards the east, I might see the Alban Hills fringed with rose-touches of a new day. It is but three hours since we returned from the Field of Mars, and I cannot sleep. I sent the boy a moment ago to fetch me bread and dunked a piece in the jar of wine from my own municipality of Velletri, and held it to my lips. The wine, poured a little early in anticipation that the ceremony would be over at the appointed hour, is already sharp with a faint musty tang of vinegar; it is always thin and yellow; yet I suck it from the bread gratefully.

Down in the plain tonight, before the altar in the Field of Mars, with Agrippa by my side, I slit, with one sweep of the curved blade, the throat of a pregnant sow. The pig's blood spurted out—the sleeve of my toga stank of it so that I was glad when we came home to exchange the garment for this dressing-gown; then it trickled down the steps of the altar, and seeped through cracks in the marble to the imbibing earth. But there was one pool formed from an errant spurt, that escaped the marble and formed on the bare earth, which parched by our long hot May refused at first to receive it. It lay on the earth in a viscous pool. I do not believe anyone noticed it but myself, and I am glad of that; they would be sure to see it as an evil omen when it is only the slow working of nature.

I am tired, and yet cannot sleep. I know the mood. It has come on me before, on the eve of great occasions, and I have learned to recognize it as an expression of divine intimations. Tomorrow is consecrated to Apollo and Diana—her chariot sails high now above Tiber, I can see her glint on the marble of the Forum that is sleeping almost below me, and very soon the Sun-God's rosy fingers will touch the Palatine and her own temple here on my Palatine hill; touch them with the new light I have been instrumental in giving Rome. I say tomorrow, but it is already by some hours today, first of tomorrows. And there will be no blood in our sacrifices to sun and moon. The children will sing the new Carmen Saeculare to bring these Games to full conclusion: I have instructed that every purpose of our four days' ritual be woven into the song: the first night's ancient ceremonies with prayers in an antique Latin none now understands; then the recognition of our dependence on the bounty of Mother Earth; our prayers by day to the old tutelary Gods of Rome, and our welcome to the Gods of Light. How I wish Virgil had lived to write the piece, for his spirit broods over these ceremonies which are designed and, I trust, also destined, to fulfil what he promised: 'Caesar Augustus, son of a God, who shall establish the age of gold in Latium, over fields that once were Saturn's realm.' But Horace has done a commendable job; he has taste if not vision . . .

I look to the east, as once, under the mountains of Illyria in a cold dawn of March, I gazed westwards . . .

Strange reflective note, written in high emotion. I did right to associate these Games and ceremonies with that sleepless night when I brooded over what Caesar's murder meant for me and for Rome. The Secular Games represented—I see still more clearly now—the completion of the task I had set myself; they were the apogee of my life. Of course I must admit that the young student who found himself Caesar's heir hardly thought of what he could do for Rome. The city was for him merely a field of opportunity. That young man now seems impossibly remote to me. Trying to remember his feelings is like trying to understand an historical character. I am amazed by his nerve. When I consider the arguments that his stepfather Philippus advanced, I wonder at his temerity in rejecting them. I am staggered to consider how he set himself to outwit Cicero, and even more so by his success in doing so. Yet one thing still rankles: Cicero's gibe: 'The young man must be praised, decorated and disposed of...' He should not have said that.

Always, in my dreaming memories of those days (and my sleep now is ever shallow, disturbed by dreams) the figure of Antony rises before me, in its beauty, panache and vulgarity. How I envied him ... How I wished that I had his power to arouse devotion with a careless word, a smile breaking from his frowning face like the sun emerging from behind clouds. Yet how little judgement he had. 'You, boy, who owe everything to a name.' Had he been generous to me, had he even refrained from swindling me, how willingly I would have thrown myself at his feet. Even the horror he had inspired in me in Spain had changed to a sort of glamour.

When I met him that first time after the murder, on a late May morning in a house that had been Pompey's, he was insolent and unsmiling, and I sat in silence. Why did he disdain to employ his charm on me? I was still so young, and afraid in my heart. I yearned for him to take me in his arms, and promise ... what? That he would see me right? That he would avenge Caesar? I do not know. I recall the flickering mood, as the light flashed on his jewelled hand. I see him lying back, tawny and full-throated, the wide generous mouth drawn down at sneering corners. My flesh crawled when I remembered that night in Spain; yet, if he had approached me ... The truth is, I was at least half in love with him. Remember, I was only eighteen, still a boy, and for six months schooled in love by Maecenas. Was he deterred by my Spanish negative?

These are the maunderings of senility. Love could no more have held us together, than it was love that made Antony turn to Cleopatra. Nor was it merely ambition caused my break with Antony. We were divided by our different visions of Rome. For Antony the State existed to be plundered. I trust I have shown what my view has always been. Yet now, looking back, how full of regrets my memories of Antony are. What we regret most in life are not the crimes we have committed, but the opportunities which we let slip to be someone other than the person one has become. In a small secret tucked-away part of my nature, I have always desired to be Antony's lover and to have lived as such without responsibility.

Of course, when we came together again, it was too late. I had grown up, pushed Maecenas to the hinterland of my affection, formed other tastes. Moreover, Antony and I then did in concert that which made any intimacy impossible. The Proscriptions were a crime. My name is stained with the blood of those we pricked. They were necessary, an imperative imposed by the fact of civil war. I have never doubted that. Yet I have never been able to forget the children we made fatherless, the sons we slew who should have been the joy and stay of their fathers. Antony and I were divided by the deed that joined us together. On the one hand we were partners against a revengeful world. On the other I could not look him in the eye.

And the Fates, which give so much, drawing out a long thread of promise and fulfilment, never fail to act without savage irony. The scissors cut the thread, promise is buried, fulfilment turns to smoky ash in the mouth. The crimes I committed on other unknown fathers have not gone unpunished. The mocking Fates have destroyed my own hopes and joy in living.

How little of that I foresaw as I gazed to the Alban Hills and dawn brought roses to the sky that would overlook our bloodless sacrifices to the deities of Light.

VII

Yet the next years were the happiest of my life. I look back on them now as a man shivering in January wind may pine for the beneficent skies of June, hardly able to believe their reality. Well is it said, whom the Gods wish to destroy they first make mad. My euphoria these years now seems to have been an idiot's joy. It was as if I trusted that the laws of the world, the inexorable working of action and consequence, had been suspended for me. It was as if I was being rewarded for my struggles with happiness, and it did not occur to me that you are never allowed to pay for happiness in advance.

The Republic was calm and orderly. True, the Germans threatened on the Rhine, and even defeated Marcus Lollius, capturing an eagle of the Vth legion; but this defeat was more humiliating than serious. The following year I arrived in the province myself, with my stepsons Tiberius and Drusus, and taught the barbarians a sharp lesson. That brief campaign pleased me, for it showed that both the boys were ready to take their full part in the government of the Empire. Both revealed military talent. Tiberius was a stern disciplinarian, but unlike many such was admired and trusted by the soldiers; they knew he would never be prodigal of their lives, and he never has been. Every advance was meticulously planned. However, though prudent to the point of caution, he was never indecisive; he took time to brood over a decision. Once taken, he saw to it that execution was brisk and efficient. There has been no general of Rome, not even Agrippa, to whom I have more happily and confidently entrusted my soldiers. Drusus had more dashing qualities, and a charm of manner his brother lacked (though it is one of Tiberius' qualities that he has never felt this lack; he has been aware of it of course, but it has never perturbed him, and he was never jealous of his younger brother).

I was so impressed by their conduct in Gaul that I gave them joint command of the north-eastern part of our European frontier. Unrest was seemingly endemic there, especially among the mountain tribes of the Tyrol and Bavaria. The territory was of strategic importance, for only by commanding it could we obtain a satisfactory land route to Illyria and Macedonia. My stepsons conceived and carried out a brilliant pincer movement, defeating the Rhaeti and Vindelicae and pursuing them through the Alps. They drove forward to the Danube, and won territory for Rome and glory for themselves. I asked Horace to celebrate their achievement, which he did in noble lines. This was a supreme example of the ancient virtue of Rome. Livia burned with justified pride at what her sons had done, and was grateful to me for the confidence I had shown in the boys.

I myself passed two years in Gaul. I inaugurated the building of more than twenty towns, transferring the rude inhabitants of the old hill fortresses of Bibracte and Gergovia (both of which had offered stiff resistance to Julius Caesar) to new cities which they were proud to name in my honour, Augustodonum [Autun] and Augustonemetum [Clermont]. I made Lugdonum [Lyon] the centre of financial administration for the whole of Gaul and established a mint there. I encouraged the use of Latin, built roads and bridges and let it be known that I was always ready to act myself as a judge of appeal. I admired the noble bravery of the Gauls, and found them honest and frank in speech. No provincials appealed more to me. It gave me deep pleasure to foster the spread of civilization there. I had another reason for my tender care for the province. No one can read Julius Caesar's account of his Gallic wars without having his pride in Roman achievement corrupted by the shame he must experience at reading of Caesar's cruelty. I know nothing in the annals of warfare so horrible as his lapidary account of massacres, and I could never forget that Cato had proposed Caesar be handed over to the Gauls to be tried as a war criminal. As Caesar's heir, it was my duty to expunge the memory of these atrocities, to make the sufferings of the Gauls in some way worthwhile. I succeeded. I did not try to suppress local customs or even the Druid religion, of which all civilized men stand in awe, but I held out to them all the riches of Greece and Rome, and, because I did so in a generous and admiring spirit, the Gauls welcomed my gifts. My treatment of Gaul stands second in my estimation to my ending of the civil wars and restoration of the Republic in the catalogue of what I have done for Rome and mankind.

Meanwhile Agrippa was in the East. He established colonies for veterans in Syria. I may say in passing that this sort of colonization is the best means of stabilizing lands of uncertain loyalty. It provides a focus for what, to coin a word, I may call Romanization. He then visited Judaea and wrote to me from there:

You are quite right about the oddity of the Jews. It seems to be true that they worship only one God. I could hardly believe this was possible, and made enquiries, but no, it seems to be the case. It is flying in the face of everyone's experience as well as common sense. What's more, it doesn't seem to do the one thing you might think useful. I mean of course, that there might be something to be said for asserting that there is only one God—monotheism is, Julia reminds me, the Greek word for this, and it's typical of the Greeks to have a word for a foreign concept—if it achieved some sort of tribal unity. I mean, we have our national Gods, don't we, and I could see some point in having a single deity for Rome. But it doesn't work out like that. No fear, not with the Jews. They squabble among themselves the whole time, just as if they were all adherents of different and hostile gods. They are divided into sects, and one thing I have understood quickly is that it is better for us to keep them in that condition, 'divide and rule' as Julia puts it.

I think however I have gained some credit by offering sacrifices to their 'one true god'. They wouldn't allow me in their Temple to do so. It seems they keep some sacred relic there which they call the Ark of the Covenant, and non-Jews may not set eyes on it. Sacrifice doesn't play an important part in their religion, which is odd too. However, they were pleased by my actions, though I am told that some extremists called Zealots thought it an act of what they call blasphemy. These zealots are a wild bunch who totally reject everything Rome has to offer. Fortu-

nately the dominant sect, who are called Pharisees—
sounds Egyptian, doesn't it? And we both know where
you can put the Gyppos—fear the Zealots themselves, and
are very happy to see us smack them down.

We were invited here by King Herod. I can't remember
how well you know him. I met him first years ago. He has
an abundance of charm, of a rather slimy sort, but he
doesn't improve with age or acquaintance. I don't like the
way he keeps sniffing around Julia. Fortunately, his wife
(who is his second wife and a cousin too) is what the
soldiers call 'a tough cookie or ratbag' and your Jewish
Majesty doesn't dare do more than sniff. Needless to say,
Julia finds his attentions repulsive, but it would be undiplo-
matic to choke them off too abruptly.

Julia is in marvellous form and wins hearts wherever she
goes. For all that, she is a loving and faithful wife to her
middle-aged husband. For we are, alas, middle-aged, you
and I. (I suppose Maecenas is still painting his face so as he
can look young?) The boys are splendid. Little Lucius had a
slight fever last week, but is better again. He keeps asking
when is he going to see Grandpa. We would all like to do
that, old friend. As for me, my gout is hellish painful. I
sometimes wake up screaming with pain. I tried to read
Virgil's poem—too deep for me—there was a bit though
in the Sixth Book which Julia picked out about the horrors
of the Underworld: They sounded a bit like gout. Not bad
stuff that bit.

Finally, the good news. Julia is pregnant. The child is
due in six months, and now that she is over the morning
sickness, we have decided she should sail back to Rome
with the boys.

Maybe you can meet them somewhere in the summer.
She proposes spending the hot weather at one of my villas
on the Bay of Naples...

Take care of yourself. Rome could spare me, but not
you, old friend. M. Agrippa.

I replied as follows:

My dear Agrippa, I am of course delighted by your news,
though as usual my joy is overlaid by worry that Julia will

come through all right. How pleased it makes me when you write so lovingly of my child, and how glad I am that this marriage (of which, it amuses me to recall, you were so nervous) should have cemented our old friendship so firmly that nothing but death can break the bonds. I would worry about her fitness to travel in her condition if I were not quite certain that you would never have permitted it without taking the best advice and every precaution. I shall indeed be in Italy this summer, and long to see her and the boys. They must of course come to stay with us.

As for your gout, I feel for you, and have consulted my physician Antonius Musa. He tells me that there is no certain cure, but that you can alleviate the condition by abstaining from red wine and red meat. White wine and cheese is what he recommends. He really is a flibbertigibbet and jack-in-the-box. He takes me off white wine and puts me on red, though I have always preferred white (and actually still drink it on the sly) and now he would have you do the reverse. It seems that our natural preferences are always wrong where doctors are concerned.

Of course I know Herod well, very well indeed. He was in Rome the year before the Secular Games and I saw a lot of him then. Where were you that year? I would have thought he would have boasted to you of his intimacy with me, but of course you wouldn't believe him. You would be right not to. I dislike him extremely. He is a twister and a hypocrite and was originally, as you may have forgotten, a client of Gaius Cassius. Then he made a play at Antony and won his favour by pandering to his vices. He is, I think, unbalanced, the sort of man who shrinks away from a straight path and can't see a belt without hitting below it. He is no true Jew of course—his mother was a sort of degenerate Greek—but he is alas the sort of instrument we need, and you do right to flatter and conciliate him. They say he sacrifices daily in my honour, which is somewhat disgusting, and makes his subjects swear by my name. He doesn't actually give a fig for me. But, with all his faults, and they are legion, he and Rome are linked together. No good Jew would promote our Empire or try to pull his co-religionists into our civilization. Herod is a Hellenist and sympathetic to the wider culture of the Mediterranean world. He has no sympathy with the extremes of Judaism like the Zealots you mention. I have had agents among them for some time. You are quite right. They reject us utterly, and wait for a leader whom they call The Messiah. Their god has promised he will be a new king for the Jews. He is even expected to throw us out. Naturally, the Zealots who hate and despise Herod could never cast him as their Messiah, though he is so twisted that he would play the part if given half a chance. However he is sufficiently intelligent to realize this will never happen, though characteristically he resents the Jews' rejection of his claims for he is quite eaten up with vanity, and only his natural prudence prevents him from letting it destroy his judgement. He therefore knows that he depends on Rome to keep him in power, and so we are, as I say, and as I am sure you know, bound together. Still, in view of Herod's unpopularity, you are quite right to make every effort to please the Jews. They are so cantankerous however that I doubt even your ability to please them for long.

It would distress me if you felt more warmly towards Herod, for, when everything is said and done, he is really a disgusting fellow. I tell you, my dear friend, I would rather be his pig than his son. That's a pun by the way if you translate it into Greek.

Do look after yourself. Rome depends on its greatest general and I on my dearest and oldest friend...

The sun shone on the deep blue water and set blood-red behind the islands, leaving the sky a streak of glorious colour that faded like a man's life. That summer was a time of languour and picnic excursions. Livia was as serene and bountiful as the weather. Nothing could quench her good humour: one day she encountered a band of nudists not two miles from the gates of our villa. Her shocked attendants would have cut them down or had them carried off to prison. My wife however, without the hint of a smile, asked them to do nothing. 'To a woman such as myself,' she said, 'a naked man is no different from a statue.' She maintained her gravity then, but giggled as she told me the story. 'Poor things,' she said, 'their eyes nearly popped out of their heads, when they realized who I was. It was certainly a close shave for them. All the same, you should send someone to tell them to put some clothes on. Not everyone can take the same detached view as I. I suppose they are a bit deranged, and though I know it's the done thing either to mock the mad, or regard them as some sort of portent, for my part I find them insignificant but to be pitied. Do get someone to dress them, my dear. It would distress me if anything happened to them.'

It was an odd family party though, if only because, except for myself, the husbands were all missing, and except for Livia, the women were all with child. Agrippa was of course still in the East, Tiberius on the Danube and Drusus now on the Rhine... Of their wives Julia was naturally the resplendent figure. She was in the zenith of her loveliness; her pregnancy gave her the air of a ripe and luscious peach. She reflected the sun, and, with her boys, Gaius and Lucius, by her side, and her baby daughter, little Julia, in her arms, might have posed for a statue representing the fertile bounty of Mother Earth. Her happiness did not dull her quick tongue or teasing manner, and she was especially ready to make a butt of Tiberius' wife Vipsania. The fact that Vipsania was also Julia's stepdaughter amused her greatly, and she delighted in posing as the guardian of her chaste morals. The other wife was my niece Antonia, the daughter of my dear sister Octavia and Mark Antony, whom Livia had selected, to the great joy of my sister, as a suitable bride for her beloved and dashing Drusus. No choice could have been wiser. Antonia inherited nothing but beauty and charm from her father. She was altogether free from the moral aberrations which disfigured his character; in her seemly virtue and modesty she took after her mother. Livia and I both loved and revered her, and indeed continue to do so. I regard Antonia as one of the props of old age, and she has proved as admirable a mother as she was a wife and daughter.

But the chief delight of that summer for me was to be found in my two little grandsons... I write these words and know that I can never grow resigned to their loss. Every time I try to describe them, my heart fails. All I can say now is that that summer seemed then to lay open before me a garden of perfect felicity. The boys were so lively, loving and natural as flowers. 'Grandpa,' they would say, pulling at my hands, or climbing on to my knee, 'come and play ball, come and play dice, tell us a story ...' 'Grandpa,' Gaius would say, 'have you heard the joke about the elephant and the mouse...' It was to me that little Lucius would run in tears when he had fallen and cut his knee...

I felt a patriarch that summer, and put the cares of state aside. We picnicked in the uplands above Sorrento, and lay in meadows abundant in flowers that only Livia could name. The sea sparkled below, meadow birds called happily about us, and we ate simply, disdaining the elaborate dishes of Roman tables, rough country food: wind-cured hams, red mullet and sardines rushed from the coast that morning in baskets of snow, sprinkled with origano or fennel or thyme picked in the meadow, and grilled over charcoal, rough bread and salami, the white tangy cheese the shepherds make from their sheep-milk and the dewy and dripping mozzarella brought from the girls who tend the buffalo in the marshlands. Livia always brought a basket of dried figs and apricots for which we both had a passion, and there were strawberries to be picked in the woods that fringed the meadows. How clear and vivid is my picture—as if time was arrested at that moment—of the three girls, all great with child, strolling back from the woods, ankle-deep in the meadow grass, dangling baskets overflowing with the sweet berries from those woods that always had a lingering aftertaste that was fresh and tart. I see too little Lucius, naked as a baby Cupid and his face pink and white with the crushed strawberries and mozzarella.

If only time could indeed have stopped.

VIII

Agrippa came home ill to his Campanian villa. His face was streaked with grey and there were deep lines of pain running down from his mouth. I besought Julia, who was about to have her fifth child, to take the greatest care of the hero who was her husband. 'I depend more on Agrippa than on all other Romans,' I said, and my exaggeration was pardonable. I sat long hours by his bedside, and watched his light flicker. Livia, who had learned to love him too, who had rejoiced by reason of her own incorruptible virtue, in his fidelity, moral worth and good sense, herself nursed him tenderly. She was angry because Julia seemed less caring, and refused to accept either her pregnancy or her youth as an excuse. 'She is no longer a girl, but a woman of twenty-eight,' she snapped.

I assured Agrippa I would care tenderly for his children, even though I knew he had no need of reassurance. I would adopt my grandsons. 'They shall rule the Empire we have won together,' I promised.

'Take care, Caesar,' he murmured through his cracked lips, in a voice that had lost any echo of the parade ground, 'take care not to breed them as princes. Remember we are all only citizens of the Republic.'

That was Agrippa's strength. The doubts which afflicted me that we had corrupted the Republic by the manner of our restoration never disturbed him. No historian, he believed that the great Scipio Africanus would have lived happily in our Rome, content with its forms, and did not realize that he could have done so only as Agrippa or Augustus. No great man has ever had so modest a sense of his own merit as Agrippa, and yet I have known none prouder. Perhaps in the end every character remains an enigma. The better you know a man, the less clear your picture of him. Perhaps again that is as it should be. Who would care for the world to know him as he knows himself? Looking back over this autobiography, I shudder at what it reveals to the world. I should kill the slaves to whom I dictate it. (No, if you have taken that down, cross it out; it's a joke for your own benefit. You find it a sour one? The best jokes so often are.)

Agrippa died peacefully in the hour before dawn when Death is most greedy. I decreed him the posthumous honour of burial in our family mausoleum. Having assumed the office of Pontifex Maximus the previous year on the long-delayed death of the wretched Lepidus, I conducted the funeral service, and delivered the laudatory oration myself. Because of this I had had to absent myself from the moment of death, for it is written that a Pontifex Maximus may not look on the dead. Of course, in the nature of things, this is a prohibition impossible to enforce, since it is usual for the High Priest also to be a military commander. (Remember that Julius was Pontifex Maximus as he slaughtered Gauls and citizens.) But I was determined to do all in correct form, lest careless neglect of what was right might offend the Gods, and sour Agrippa's reception in the Shades.

My peroration summed up the significance of Agrippa's life, after I had recounted the many feats he had performed:

'His birth, as I have said, was insignificant; yet no man has done more for Rome. Moreover, unlike many men of comparatively humble birth, he did not allow this accident of fortune to make him envious of those who were nobly born. Rather, he set himself to demonstrate that, if some men acquire merit from their ancestors, a single man of virtue and great qualities can confer honour and nobility on his descendants. Whatever has been achieved for Rome in the last three decades owes much to Agrippa. He has been a great general, a great proconsul, a great administrator and a great builder. He was never corrupted by ambition or riches. He refused many honours and triumphs. He worked selflessly for the public good, and found his reward in the work he accomplished. He himself used to say: "From concord, small seeds grow to great trees, from discord stem great disasters."

'My right hand is burned in the pyre. I have lost my noblest friend, my daughter has lost the truest and tenderest of husbands, Rome has lost her greatest son. His work only remains to sweeten our grief. His monument may be found in the happy condition of the Republic . . .'

★

What more could I have said? At such moments words are inadequate. Agrippa himself was no man of words. The memoirs he left behind are plaguey dull and do him no justice. Indeed, they might be read as the work of a quite unremarkable man. My grief was intense. With Agrippa departed my sense that I might still build. My youth slipped into the shadows, and I felt myself old. I would never leave Italy again, as it happened, for without the security of his support, my disinclination to travel intensified.

Agrippa made me his principal heir. I am always of course proud and pleased to receive legacies, for nothing else so surely lets one know the esteem in which one is held by one's friends; in this case, of course, I regarded the inheritance as being held in trust for the boys.

Julia gave birth a month after her husband's death. Whether this cast some malign influence on the child's fate, I do not know, but this boy, known as Agrippa Postumus, was very different from his brothers and sisters. He grew up dull and even brutish, and has been a sore trial to us all. To my great grief he has proved unable to take the place in the State that should have been his. Yet he has, more than Gaius and Lucius, a look of his father (they took after Julia and myself); but it is an Agrippa without insight or fortitude, an Agrippa, as it were, who had never left the family fields, one who plodded behind oxen and cursed the weather.

My heart went out to Julia, widowed a second time, and left with five children, though of course I made myself responsible for the older boys. I was also disturbed by thoughts of my own mortality, for in our youth Agrippa's robust health had seemed to mock my own illnesses. I was fifty-one, and Gaius was only eight. What would happen if I died? I knew there were many rancorous nobles who would be happy to avenge on the beautiful and innocent children the slights they imagined they had suffered at my hands. It was essential their safety should be secured. It was essential Julia should marry again, and marry someone who could be trusted to protect the boys' interests if I died.

Livia agreed with me.

She said, 'I respect your love and care for Gaius and Lucius, and of course I share it. You may rely on me to do all I can to safeguard them, but I am of course only a woman, and so cannot have any constitutional status. I am enough of a realist to know that any influence I now have is only what you choose to allow me, and has been earned only by the trust that has grown between us in the long years of our marriage. But I am sensible, my dear, that this influence will wane, should I be so unhappy as to survive you. In any case, I don't know that I would wish to take any part in political life if that happened. I imagine my mourning would be too profound and prolonged. So you are right: it is essential that Julia marry again.'

I pressed her hand and touched it with my lips.

She continued: 'There's another argument which I feel bound to advance even though you won't like it. Even if there were no children, Julia would need a husband. Otherwise, I'm sorry, but she is likely to disgrace us. Sex isn't a subject I have ever felt comfortable talking about. Nevertheless I've got to. Julia has appetites. That's all I can bring myself to say, except this. I've always tried to behave as if I was indeed her mother, but I'm not of course. And you've always regarded her as your child entirely. Well, that's understandable, but she is in fact Scribonia's daughter, and we all know what she's like. It's nonsense to suppose that children don't inherit qualities from both their parents, even though I'm happy to say that I don't see anything of their wretched father in Tiberius and Drusus. So we're agreed Julia must have a husband. The question is: who should it be?'

We argued that matter for some time. Julia had a good many friends of her own age among the nobility, and as far as birth went, there was a fair choice of suitable candidates. Some of them, though by no means all, had character and achievement to recommend them too. But they all suffered from one irremediable defect: there was none I could trust to act as a guardian for Gaius and Lucius.

Livia herself failed to suggest a solution. I therefore decided to consult Julia. I pointed out how important it was that she should marry for the boys' sake. I spoke more openly to her about this than I have ever done to anyone else.

'Listen, darling,' I said, 'you are my only child and your happiness is of the first importance to me. Never forget that... My dearest wish is that you and your children should enjoy enduring good fortune... Now I am already old, and in the nature of things may die at any moment. I have had two passions in life: Rome and my family. They are inextricably interwoven in my love and my ambition. I have, as you know, restored the Republic...'

'I know those,' she said, 'who consider that a fraud. They say it's only a façade. That behind it you're a king in all but name...'

'I'm the First Citizen, that's all,' I said. 'Your friends are mischievous talkers, my dear. At another time I'd ask you for their names.' (I hardly needed to of course; I could put names to them without difficulty.) 'What I've done,' I said, 'is restore order and stability. You can hardly, thank goodness, recall the Civil Wars. They were horrible, and I've made it my mission to see that we don't have any more. That's meant, I admit, a curtailment of some liberty. Well, liberty is only good when it is obedient to the law. I don't want to give you a lecture on political philosophy, you'd soon be yawning your pretty head off if I did, but what I say is true. No state can exist without an organizing intelligence. I hope that that will be supplied by Gaius and Lucius, in time.'

'They're charming,' she said, 'and I dote on them, but we can't really measure their ability. Poor Gaius isn't even nine yet. Besides, they might be happier as private citizens. None of my friends has to work as hard as you—you won't allow them to of course, but then it's true too that they mostly delight in leisure. The art of life is seen among those with leisure, not among the worker bees. All I'm saying is that you're wrong to assume everyone wants to work as hard as you. Or that it's necessarily a good thing. You may be trying to force the boys into a mould that doesn't suit them.'

She was wrong, absolutely wrong. I knew it then, and it angered me. The boys' lives were to prove how wrong she was. I caught a glimpse of Julia and her idle friends, laughing away everything I valued. I heard the tinkle of mockery that ran through the Smart Younger Set. What had I done? I had outlived my time and emasculated Rome. I felt that in a moment of horror like the emptiness that comes when you awake from sleep in the black of night and hear only silence.

'Besides,' she said, and laughed, 'I seem to have been always married. I rather fancy a freedom from husbands.'

She kissed me on the top of the head and flitted away, not even conscious of my anger. Or was she conscious, and did not care? It might be that it pleased her to have made me angry.

Of course I turned to Maecenas for advice, as I had always done. Though our relations had grown more distant Maecenas enjoyed poor health (with some stress on the enjoyment) and declared himself frankly bored with public affairs nowadays, a residual loyalty which we felt for each other could be relied on. But, whereas I would once have strolled to his house on the Esquiline, I now sent a message in advance. That would allow him to get Bathyllus, whom I found repellent even in his stage performances, out of the way.

Maecenas kept me waiting in a room over-furnished and cluttered with bibelots. The wall-paintings depicted a variety of acts of congress. It was a tease asking me to wait there; there had always been a sharp streak of malice in my friend.

'Of course you're out of place here,' he said, 'these decorations aren't your taste now, are they? You've gone all stuffy. But it's just as well to remind you, old dear, that there are other sides of life.'

He was a frightful colour and mere skin and bone. That took my anger away. Even his mockery was now interrupted by a hacking cough.

He grimaced, and said, 'Not that there's much life left in me, ducky. Still, always smiling, always smiling, as the Greeks say. You want something. It can't be a boy, which I could perhaps provide, so it must be advice. Julia?'

'That's clever of you.'

'Obvious, my dear. Poor Julia. I saw her at a dinner-party last week. She looked stunning, and so eager and yet wasted. I said to myself, poor dear, you haven't really got a lot out of life, have you? Not for a fun-loving chap, which you are. Of course, I have a certain empathy with Julia. She's my sort of girl, old dear.'

It was far too hot in the room and a sickly scent wafted through it.

'You're just the same as always though, when I speak in a way you don't like.' Maecenas poured wine and passed me a glass; too sweet as usual. 'You just sit there like a demure little cat and wash your face with your paws. But I'm not going to let you get away with it. You don't understand Julia and I'm going to tell you a few unwelcome truths. She loathed being married to Agrippa. She had to close her eyes and grit her teeth when he made love to her. Don't ask me how I know, I just know. And don't put my words down to spite. I know just what Agrippa was worth, but I know Julia too. She's a big strong girl and she likes men (or boys) who are softer than herself. She's androgynous enough not to feel happy with anyone but a fellow androgyne. You've forgotten your own youth, that's the trouble with you, old dear. The first marriage to Marcellus might have worked if it hadn't been that she knew that you and Marcellus and she made a triangle. She was besotted with you then, old dear, and you were besotted with Marcellus who was alas, alas—a charming girl but one who couldn't look away from the mirror. So really that was no good. Have some more wine. You can't think how I've been dying to tell you this.'

He stretched out on the couch ('I can't stand for long these days, in any sense of the word,' he giggled), and dangled his jewelled hand.

'So what did you do then? You married her off to old Agrippa who was quite the wrong sort of father-figure, and who bored the poor girl silly with his boasting, as well as disgusting her physically. She turned against you then. It was one thing being married off to Marcellus, whom she was jealous of, but fancied, quite another being handed over to that old bruiser. But she's game, your daughter, and she did her best. She toed the line. And now at last she's free.'

Maecenas could never tell the truth about people. The disability had grown more acute with the years. He was a slave of gossip and innuendo. You could discount most of what he said. You could never discount the core. I sat there, neglecting the too sweet wine, oppressed by the cloying perfumes blown through the room, and waited for what I had after all invited.

'Love,' he said, and let it hang in the air. 'You know, old dear, till Bathyllus came along I fought shy of love. Oh yes, I have never been without my loves, none knows that better than yourself. But I avoided, except in one case, love's degradation. You know the case of course. What do I mean by degradation? Enslavement, what else? Knowing you can never please, knowing you can never possess, longing to possess fully, utterly, and yet at the same time longing for your beloved to trample on you. Isn't it strange, after all these years, to be saying this to you, and you still can't understand. You still have to be in control. You find my association— that's the word you use, isn't it?—my association with Bathyllus degrading. It's abject, isn't it, my surrender to him? You've never surrendered to anyone, not even Livia. I'll go further. You chose a wife who would be embarrassed by surrender. Oh yes, you're subject to her in little things and everyone laughs at it because it makes you seem human. But not in big things, eh? All your life everyone's had to yield to your monstrous will. Monstrous.'

He broke off in a fit of coughing. His skin shone yellow. I couldn't move, in fact I waited for him to continue. I felt nothing but impatience. There was absolute silence when he finished coughing. Nothing moved in the house. Whatever fan had been blowing the perfume through the room must have been stopped. We were held there, like prisoners, in the room's cloying stillness.

'What is this world, O soldiers? It is I. That's what you've come to, Augustus. Poor lovely lost Julia, victim of your will. You couldn't allow yourself to do what you wanted with Marcellus, bugger and be buggered, so poor Julia was your surrogate. Then she fell victim to Reason of State, to keep Agrippa in line. Oh yes, I advised it myself, you're going to say. I told you what you wanted to hear. I've always known how to do that, haven't I? Now I'm pleading with you. Let the girl be. Let her marry if she wants to. If she does it will be a pretty boy like Iullus Antonius. Oh I admit that, and he's the grandson of Antony and Fulvia, but he's not dangerous, he's a pretty playboy. She'll have fun with him. Don't sacrifice her again to Reasons of State.' He paused and held up his hand. 'I know what you're going to say. You're going to talk of Gaius and Lucius. You want a husband who'll ensure their succession. Oh yes, I know you don't like the word, succession, but be honest, old dear, that's what it is, disguised monarchy. Do you remember that conversation we had with old Agrippa, when he wanted a return to the old Republic—really, you know, he was no brighter than Pompey—and I said what we needed was a ruler. Well, that's what you are, dress it up how you like. And you want to ensure the succession for your grandsons... So to get it, you'll sacrifice Julia again. And you won't feel a thing, certainly not guilt. Still nothing to say...?'

I shrugged my shoulder. 'It's easy to talk,' I said, 'I've done my duty as I see it. And of course I'm trying to provide for the future...'

'I'm sorry for you, you know,' he said. 'My hands are free of the responsibility of crime, even moral crime. Virgil knew what was happening to you, and pitied you. Yes, you've achieved great things, and in a way we're all in your debt, but what has it done to you? It's killed your imagination, your sympathy. All that's left is the will. Virgil loved you, as I have done, and yet you filled him, as you do me, with a sort of horror...'

'If I were what you say, you would not speak to me in this way. You would not dare.'

'Dare? See the words you choose.'

'Oh,' I said, 'Maecenas, there's truth in what you say. Of course. I recognize that. Parts of me are dead. They don't feel a thing. A moral numbness. Yes, sometimes, I've had to cultivate that. But we all kill part of ourselves. Don't pretend, old friend, you haven't done that yourself. You have deliberately excised a sense of decency, for one thing. And in not falling in love...'

'But I have,' he said.

'And in rejecting family ties, you have denied and smothered much that was good in you. But I haven't rejected love. I want what's best for those I love...'

'You want what you choose is best...'

'Every man must use his own judgement...'

'If you loved Julia, you would let her be, let her marry her pretty playboy...'

'Loving Julia, I cannot encourage a match that will diminish her...'

'Diminish? Am I diminished?'

'You are diminished, Maecenas, by your infatuation with that actor. I'm sorry to say this, but who respects you now?'

'And yet you come to me for advice...'

'I always have. But I'm told you can't now appear in the theatre without suffering mockery and cat-calls...'

He smiled.

'Let us not quarrel,' he said. 'Perhaps we are both diminished. Perhaps on the other hand one can put it differently. Perhaps life consists of a stripping away of whatever are the inessentials of each soul. The shy and pretty boy I loved has been eaten up by the man of will; and I, yes, you are right, I am now a slave to the emotions, to beauty and to pleasure. My dignity has been ripped from me. I am a laughing-stock, an old queen, quite absurd. In becoming what we have become, in shedding much that was good, we are revealed in our true selves. So, my dear, you can't follow my advice, can you? You can't set Julia free, without betraying your will, and that's impossible. What we have done, I suppose, is work out our destiny, and we end as prisoners of our own character. Is that too metaphysical for you, too fanciful? Put it down to the ramblings of a degenerate Etruscan if you like. But one who still loves you. Besides, I know what you'll do. You'll compel Tiberius to divorce Vipsania—she's no value, has she, now that her father is dead? and it doesn't matter that they have been happy together—and marry him off to Julia. He's a strong man after all, and a man of honour (if you'll allow me to use the word, since you know I don't have the thing—by your standards anyway), and so will do the right thing by the boys. Isn't that what you came here to hear?'

'Tiberius?' I said. 'Of course. Julia had a passion for him when they were younger. Livia used to complain that she would never leave him alone.'

'Of course not,' he said. 'He represented a challenge, a strong silent challenge. But ... anyway, that's not my advice. It's a forecast. You see how I know you. Well,' he picked up his wine, 'I'm glad we've had this talk. I doubt if there will be many more, will there? Not now we've said all this we've been waiting to say so long. There won't after all be much left to talk about. One final thing: you know you asked Horace to be your secretary—of course I know, he consulted me as to how to refuse—what I was going to say is do you know why he refused?'

'He didn't want to leave his Sabine farm. . .'

'Oh yes, he's fond of the place. Still, that wouldn't have been enough in itself. No, he said, "I admire the princeps from a distance, and am proud of my admiration. But to assist him would corrupt me and disgust my Muse . . ."'

I made no reply. Horace was obviously right. The Philosopher-King, the Poet-Prince, could not long survive the exercise of power. Authority's servants are stained with the responsibility of action . . .

'Now,' Maecenas said, 'do run along, there's a dear. Bathyllus will be back soon. He won't be pleased to hear that you have been here, but he would be furious to find us still together. And he's a bore when he sulks.'

'Ah, yes . . .'

'Don't try to look wise and knowing. Of course the slave will tell him you've been here.'

'Of course they will. Slaves always do,' I said.

IX

As usual Maecenas had exercised his great gift: he had told me what I wanted to hear, even though I didn't realize that in advance. A counsellor resembles an orator who reveals to the crowd he addresses their unconscious desires and passions. I had shied away from the Tiberius solution to my problem without even examining it, because, I suppose, Livia had rejected it after Marcellus' death. But things were different now, I told myself. Tiberius was no longer a gauche youth, but a great general and a man of wide experience who had met with nothing but success in his career. His public spirit was unquestioned; likewise his sturdy morality and devotion to duty. Who better to protect the boys when I was gone?

Of course, even apart from any objections that Livia might raise, there were other matters to be dealt with. Julia herself might not be delighted; there had been little sign of her old childish passion for Tiberius in recent years. He wasn't exactly the sort of young man with whom she happily consorted. Then again there was the problem of Vipsania. Tiberius was admittedly a man of tepid emotions, but it was clear he felt a considerable affection for his wife. He would not willingly consent to divorce her. (On the other hand it might amuse Julia to supplant her late husband's daughter). Moreover, Tiberius and Vipsania had a son, called Drusus after his uncle. Could I be certain that Tiberius would not prefer his own-born son to Gaius and Lucius? Yes, I could, I thought; not only was Gaius the oldest of the next generation—and I must assume that Julia would protect his interests—but Tiberius' inflexible sense of duty would not permit him to over-ride my wishes. That left only one reservation. Tiberius was averse to the theoretical discussion of politics; he liked to concentrate on what must be done. Yet I knew that in his heart Tiberius was a rigid aristocratic conservative. His father—that shifty fellow for whose memory Tiberius nevertheless maintained a stubborn reverence—had adhered to Brutus and Cassius. I suspected that the cause they proclaimed still attracted his approval. He knew in his heart that the days of Republican licence were over, never to return without dire consequences for Rome. Yet his adherence to the New Order was never more than intellectual. It did not appeal to his heart. He despised the Senate and its members— 'oh generation fit for slavery', I had heard him murmur; but he yet retained an ideal conception of senatorial government. He knew it was impossible and longed for it not to be so.

All the same it was Livia I had to convince. If she decided Tiberius should marry Julia, he would obey, however reluctantly. I could not be sure however of my ability to persuade her.

I said to her, 'I am afraid you are right. Julia is going to disgrace us. It hurt me when you reminded me she was Scribonia's daughter but you were right. I have talked to her about a possible marriage, and she says she rather fancies being free. What's to be done? That surely can't be permitted.'

'I have already explained to you that it can't. For one thing her behaviour in such circumstances would be likely to make a mockery of your laws on morality.'

I felt myself flushing; it was disagreeable to have to listen to such an observation on my daughter, and to know that I could not contradict it.

I said, 'It is clear she must be married, as you yourself have insisted. It is clear that all members of the group she frequents are unsuitable. She requires a husband who will command her respect as Agrippa did'—Maecenas' words flitted across my mind, but I ploughed on—'he must therefore be like Agrippa a great public servant, a great general too.'

Livia smiled. 'Are you so sure she respected Agrippa? Are you so sure she did not deceive him?'

'Have you any reason to think that?'

She smiled again but did not answer.

I paused, hoping she might herself bring forward her son's name, but she continued to sew, the very image of a demure and submissive Roman matron except for that enigmatic smile which played at the corner of her lips.

'Come, Livia,' I said, 'it's not right for us to play cat and mouse.' The smile was unwavering. 'You know what I have in mind and you know that I have been hoping you would introduce the possibility yourself.'

'Tiberius loves Vipsania,' she said.

'I don't deny it.'

'He's always been a difficult withdrawn boy. You could call him secretive, a dutiful son but never one who has confided in me as Drusus does.'

'Oh yes, Drusus is different.'

'And Vipsania has been good for him. I believe he may talk to her as to no one else.'

'And that doesn't make you jealous?'

'Of course it does. Show me the mother who isn't jealous of her son's wife. But I subdue that emotion. I repeat, Vipsania is good for Tiberius.'

'I don't deny it, but let me put forward another argument,

or rather shift the argument to different ground. We are not private persons.'

'Are you saying we are a royal family? I could never approve of that.'

'Of course not. Why will you put words in my mouth? No such thing. But we are a great family. We have obligations to something beyond our private happiness. We have obligations to Rome. Tiberius as a Claudian, a double Claudian, as you have often reminded us, must realize this...'

'And Rome's need is that he marry your daughter?'

'You are laughing at me, Livia. Very well, it's true. Rome does require that, because Rome requires stability when I am dead, and only a marriage between Julia and Tiberius can ensure that. There. What do you say?'

'What can I say? You accuse me of mockery, but I'm a good Roman wife. I'm not going to dispute your words, especially as I've reached the same conclusion myself. It's true I don't fully share your certainty that Gaius and Lucius will continue your work—you always forget how differently and indulgently you have had them raised—but I fully realize that dynastic marriages are necessary. I can see that, Agrippa being dead, Vipsania is of no account, and I can see that a marriage between Tiberius and Julia is the best way of securing the future for the family and for Rome. But don't expect me to be delighted. On the contrary. I feel like Volumnia, and I fully expect Tiberius to greet me with Coriolanus' words, "Mother, you have saved Rome, but you have destroyed your son..."'

Livia had again put me in the wrong. She made it seem as if I was demanding a sacrifice from her son. Yet, once he had recovered from the unease which the ending of his marriage to Vipsania would cause him, surely he would appreciate the glittering prospect I was holding out. He was, after all, being invited to succeed Agrippa as the second man in the Republic, and to demonstrate this, I arranged, even before his marriage to Julia, that he be invested with the tribunician power for a period of ten years. Furthermore, he could not fail to be gratified by the confidence shown in him, not only by me, but also by the Senate and the Roman People. Finally, was not Julia the most desirable match in Rome, not only beautiful but brilliant, the mother of children to whom it was an honour to be asked to serve as guardian?

Yet Tiberius sulked. He tried at first to refuse the honour, saying he was unworthy of it. That irritated me, as false humility always does, and I snapped that there should be an end to it. When he still protested, I told him that he was insulting my daughter, myself and Rome. Not so, he said, he respected all, but Vipsania was his wife and he loved her. I told him that was fustian, and when he received this rebuke in silence, I quite lost my temper (a rare happening of which I was subsequently ashamed) and told him he was so much dung stuffed into a toga. Eventually, I had to get his mother to speak to him. 'Tell him,' I said, 'that he can either do my will, or I will see to it that he is stripped of his-offices and responsibilities, and banished to a remote island in the Mediterranean.'

'I wouldn't say that,' she said, 'Tiberius has always had a taste for islands. He has often said he can imagine nothing more agreeable than an island retreat.'

'Has he indeed? You can assure him there would be nothing agreeable about the one I would send him to.'

The fact is, Tiberius, for all his virtues, has always been stubborn as a mule. There are times when he behaves with as much intelligence as a beetroot, and I knew very well that he was taking a perverse pleasure in defying me. Fortunately, Livia saw that my mind was set, and talked persuasively to her son. I don't know what she said, for I thought it wiser not to enquire, but it was effective. Tiberius returned much chastened, prepared, though sullenly, to do my will.

Yet that wasn't the end of the matter. Incredible though it is to relate, Julia now dug her heels in and refused point-blank. She wouldn't marry Tiberius if he was the last man on earth, she told me. By now my patience was, understandably, near breaking-point. I told her I had loved no one as much as she, that I had always been proud of her, and asked her if this was my reward. 'A fine return for my devotion,' I cried. 'Well, young woman, if you are determined to prove yourself an undutiful daughter, I can only conclude that you are an equally unloving mother. I propose to you a marriage which will safeguard your sons' future after I am dead—and that may happen any day now. I wonder indeed that it hasn't in the face of this obstinate defiance—and you refuse it. Why? Because you want to be free to whore with every loose-living young spark in Rome? Is that why? Very well, the boys are not going to be contaminated and corrupted like that— you have a clear choice, young woman. Marry Tiberius, as I tell you to, or prepare to be separated from your children and exiled to some remote spot. And be sure I'll choose a climate that will cool your ardour.' Whereupon she screamed that I had never loved her, that I only pretended to, that I had made her the victim of my insane ambition, that I had chosen her husbands to please myself, and that she wished she was dead. There was a good deal of nonsense in the same vein, but I could see that my ultimatum had fazed her. Even so, I cannot be certain that she would have complied if she had not learned of Tiberius' own reluctance. She took that as a challenge of course. How dare he not wish to marry her?

So, in the end, both consented. The necessary marriage took place. It was not altogether a happy occasion, for I was dismayed by the selfishness and unreasonableness both had displayed. I had only had their best interests at heart, and I regretted having been compelled to employ such means of persuasion. I knew they were unworthy, and accordingly I felt the resentment one always experiences towards those who have forced one to behave in a shabby fashion. Nevertheless, the marriage accomplished, I knew I had done what was right for Rome and the boys.

Yet even this was not the end of the matter. A few months after the wedding it was reported to me that Tiberius and Vipsania had encountered each other at a reception. The General, I was told, couldn't take his eyes off his former wife; his gaze followed her round the room with a pathetic ardour. That night, and for two days afterwards, Rome's greatest general surrendered himself completely to Bacchus. Eventually, Livia had to order all wine to be removed from his rooms, and herself took over the supervision of his recovery. He was pale and shaking when I next saw him, declined to meet my eyes (his own were bloodshot), shuffled his feet, and muttered sullen replies to my questions.

Clearly such an encounter could not be permitted to recur. I went to see Vipsania myself, and was pleased to find that she received me with a very proper sense of her own dignity. She made no complaint. I assured her of my continued respect, but indicated that, for reasons which it was unnecessary to elaborate, I had decided that she could no longer live in Rome. I asked her which of her father's many estates pleased her most. She named one in the Sabine Hills some fifty miles from Rome. It was perhaps too close to the city to be ideal, but at least Tiberius had no property there. Agrippa had of course left the estate to me and I was happy to make it over to his daughter, along with another in Greece. I told her it would please me if she would retire to one or other of these properties and divide her life between them. I promised that I would supply her with a handsome income, and I even made over to her part of Agrippa's capital. She was a sensible woman—I had always admired her good sense—and set herself to create a pleasing life within these confines.

It had been a difficult business to negotiate. I was pleased when it was over and settled. It never occurred to me that I had made a mistake. Certainly I had acted in a manner that disturbed and even pained the three people involved, but I was confident that, when things had settled down, they would realize that I had been acting for their best interests as well as Rome's. They could see after all that I had derived no personal advantage from what I had arranged. And they were all sensible people, capable of coming to terms with the changed situation. Moreover, it was a comfort to know that Livia and I had acted in concert. It was she who had finally persuaded Tiberius that he should fall in with my plans.

Apart from that one occasion when he caught sight of Vipsania and lost control of himself, he gave no indication that he had reservations or regrets. He resumed his duties with his former efficiency. His brother Drusus was doing great things in the far north, and in the year of Agrippa's death reached the River Weser, having cut a canal between the Rhine and Zuyder Zee to facilitate the supply of his troops. Tiberius' task still lay in Dalmatia and on the Danube frontier. It was demanding work, hard slogging, requiring close attention to detail, nothing glamorous about it, well-suited to his temper. No man could have done it better. Let me say this clearly, for I am well aware that I have been accused of injustice to Tiberius, and that events have been so misconstrued as to suggest that there was ill-feeling between us. That was nonsense. The proof is that I gave him my daughter in marriage. Anyone who doubts that as evidence of my high regard for Tiberius should consider how I esteemed her first two husbands.

Julia accompanied him to Dalmatia. It was good for her to get away from the frivolities of the city and to be reminded of the real unremitting work of Empire. To wake in camp, to the rattle of harness and the champing of horses, to feel the cold nip one's fingers and see the rime-encrusted flaps of the tent glitter in the morning sunshine, or feel the chill of river-mists penetrate one's bones, to see the flies swarm round the horses in July heat, and to be jolted miles in cumbersome baggage-wagons—these are the experiences, unremarkable in themselves, yet real and demanding, that the city fops Julia had made her friends have never known. I am a man who has seen enough war to prize the blessings of peace, but I can never forget that Rome's greatness depends on the army. The meaning of Empire is certainly to be tasted in the simplicity and order of rural Italy, but it is something which cannot be grasped by one ignorant of the harsh realities of the frontier camps.

A child was born to them after eighteen months of marriage, but lived little more than a week. It was the Gods' will that the little boy be taken from us, but I wept, for the death of a child is a frightful thing and I feared its effect on Julia and her husband.

Death began to absorb too great a part of my thoughts. I was in my middle fifties, and, though my own health remained good, and was indeed, thanks to the Gods and Antonius Musa, better than it had been in my youth, I could hardly fail to be aware that I was now old. The unveiling of the Altar of Peace seemed to me my apotheosis. It represented the sum of my accomplishment and a statement of my vision of Rome. The frieze round the altar shows me and my family on our way to sacrifice in the Field of Mars. I look on the figures now with sadness as well as pride: so many memories, so many regrets. Another carving displays Italy as Mother Earth, the source, provider, guarantor and witness of the prosperity I had enabled our people to recover. Aeneas too is there, sacrificing a pregnant sow on the site of Alba Longa, Rome's mother city.

I summoned all the family to the unveiling. Only Drusus was absent, still campaigning in Germany. The sky was cerulean, the sun intense.

We proceeded on foot down from the Palatine, along the Sacred Way, round the base of the Capitol, all the time through throngs of the happy and sweaty crowd. The loudest cheers were reserved for my boys, Gaius and Lucius, who, having no known foibles, were free from the affectionate ribaldry directed at Tiberius and myself by veterans who had served under us. But there was another reason for the cheers which greeted the boys: Gaius and Lucius were recognized by all as the hope for the future; they would themselves provide and guarantee Rome's continued victory and the lasting peace. Their eyes shone as brightly as the sun as they delighted in their reception; it was in that day and hour that they first tasted glory.

Celebrations continued for several days in the city, but our own were cut abruptly short. News was brought from the north that, in returning from his campaigning, Drusus had suffered a severe fall in a river crossing. He had caught a fever and was gravely ill. Livia's grief and alarm were terrible to see; she snatched Drusus' wife Antonia to her bosom, and I saw what I had never seen in our thirty years of marriage, tears spring into her eyes, and run unrestrained by pride down her cheeks, which were themselves pale. Horrified at this sight, I knew there was nothing I could do to comfort her, but called Tiberius to me. I told him to ride at once, with no ceremony or delay, to his brother's bedside.

'As soon as you are there, write to us, that we may have some reliable knowledge. I have never seen your mother so afflicted.'

The letter from Tiberius was brief indeed:

I arrived here to find my poor brother barely conscious. He

recognized me, commended his children to me, expressed his love and gratitude to his mother and yourself, and died before nightfall. It was as if he had been waiting my arrival in order to die. It seems that his horse slipped in the river, and fell on top of him, crushing his ribs and breaking a thigh. Men have survived worse injuries, but it is the will of the Gods. I shall accompany the body to Rome.

I pictured Tiberius tramping by the side of the bier, down the dusty roads of Gaul, into the high Alpine passes, cool even in September noon, descending to the rich plain of the Po valley, skirting the Apennines, and at last coming in sight of the city. The stamp and shuffle of the march, the creak of the wagons and the long silence in his heart. 'We are the Gods' sport,' I had heard Tiberius say. Would he not believe that even more thoroughly now?

As for me, I wept for Drusus, but no tears of mine could assuage his mother's grief. A mother's love for her son is something more profound than any other love between man and woman. There is no pride of conquest in it. And Drusus had been a warm and loving son.

His ashes were laid in the family mausoleum, and I could not escape the reflection that the two most brilliant men of the younger generation, Drusus and Marcellus, would never fulfil their promise. My heart ached to think of the sad waste.

Fortunately Drusus and Antonia had had three children, and so Antonia was not left without consolation. I assured her that I would do whatever was in my power to care for them.

Many drown in the sea that surges round the shipwreck of old age. Maecenas died the following year. Our ways had drifted apart, for I had found it hard to forget what he had said to me on that occasion when we had talked of Julia's marriage, and, though I offered to go to see him on his deathbed, my olive branch (as I thought it) was rejected. Yet there was something of his old wit and panache in the terms of his reply: 'Maecenas, weak with fever, wasted with disease, and now incontinent, has no wish to meet Caesar on even more unequal terms than usual. Let us delay our next encounter till we both find ourselves in Pluto's realm, whither I hasten to prepare your couch.' It was like Maecenas not to be able to maintain his third-person formality to the end of the sentence.

With his departure went the last companion of my great adventure, for even Livia did not know me till I was established. It was perhaps memory of these salad days that persuaded Maecenas to name me as his heir.

The poet Horace did not survive his patron by more than a few weeks. I never felt for Horace as I did for Virgil, for there was little sense of the uncanny in him, little sense that he brought us mere mortals intimations of the divine purpose. But I liked him; he was a man with whom one could be easy, content with little, a strange contrast to Maecenas, and yet the affection between them ran deep.

Virgil had promised the inauguration of a golden age.

The air was chill with death.

X

I myself supervised the boys' education. I saw to it that they studied mathematics, philosophy, rhetoric, literature; that they grew adept in martial exercise and equitation. I took direct charge myself of their political education, devising a number of Socratic dialogues for their instruction. I had come to admit to myself precisely what I was doing: I was training the rulers of the Republic. Some may see in this a primarily dynastic pre-occupation. There were, I knew, those who grumbled that I was treating my grandsons as princes. I ignored the slander. Those who uttered it were ignorant of the nature of Republican government. Precisely because a Republic permits more liberty than a monarchy may, so for that very reason it is the more essential that its leaders be thoroughly educated and taught the principles of political ratiocination: for a Republic is more easily swayed by sentiment than by reason.

Among the doubters was Tiberius. He wrote me several carefully-worded letters from his lonely frontier outpost (to which Julia, distressed by the death of their child, had no longer the heart to accompany him, the place being, as she told me, full of wretched memories). He acknowledged my care for his stepsons, but protested that I should remember they were as yet untried.

I knew that of course. It was my intention that they should receive trial soon, for I was aware how debilitating the life of Roman society could be even for ardent youth, and I was determined that they should not frequent the society that circled round their mother.

There were many eager to flatter them, and the Senate even passed a resolution permitting Gaius to hold the consulship when he was fifteen. That was too early, and I quashed the proposal though it pleased me to see the esteem in which the boys were held.

That year Tiberius was accorded a Triumph for his work on the northern frontiers and his tribunician powers were renewed for five years. Though I was distressed by the apparent coolness between him and Julia—it was reported to me that they never addressed one another in private—I could not avoid satisfaction at the unfolding of my plans.

'I am worried about Tiberius,' Livia said.

'But why? I don't understand. He is surely a notable success. Our greatest general, consul for the second time, my trusted partner . . .'

Livia sighed and looked away from me.

'You will never understand him,' she said, 'your natures are so different.'

'Perhaps that is so. Nevertheless Tiberius and I are in constant correspondence, as you know, when he is away from Rome, and I have had several long discussions with him. He is always lucid and level-headed, eminently sensible. I don't understand why you should be worried.'

'You have always seen just what you want to see, and the habit has been growing on you. As for Tiberius, when you talk to him, what does he reveal of his sentiments, of what he feels in his heart? He denies entry even to me. I love Tiberius, husband, second only to you, and indeed more deeply in that different way, with that intense responsibility which mothers feel towards their sons. And he withdraws from me. I see only what flickers on the surface of the waters, nothing of the dark swirling currents below. But I know three things: first, he has never recovered from Drusus' death . . .'

'Ah, which of us has?'

'For Drusus was his only confidant. Much I have known of Tiberius throughout his life, I have learned by way of Drusus. Second, Tiberius' pride is a fearful and secret thing such as we can never measure, for you have no pride of that sort and no understanding of it. Third, allied to this pride, runs a deep resentment . . .'

'Resentment?' I cried. 'What has Tiberius to resent . . .?'

Livia smiled, 'Resentment,' she said, 'is an inborn quality.'

Was she warning me, or merely expressing her own doubts and fears?

It mattered little, I reflected. There was work for Tiberius to do. Whatever the difference between us, we had this in common: that neither had ever shirked a job. A renewal of unrest in Armenia demanded the presence of a strong man in the East. Tiberius' prestige was high there. The legions would be reassured by his arrival. I therefore summoned him before me, and invited him to take up this command, with a grant of full imperium.

'I am offering you,' I said, 'exactly what Agrippa had. And the job is even more urgent and demanding now.'

He stood before me long, lanky and balding, his eyes a little bloodshot, as if he had drunk deeply the night before. (It was his only vice: fortunately one the troops admired; they used to call him *Biberius Caldius Mero*).* He seemed to sway, and it occurred to me that he might even be still a little drunk. When he spoke I was sure he was.

'No,' he said.

Nothing else; just the blank negative.

I was taken aback.

'You can't have understood me,' I said. 'What I am offering you confirms your position as my partner in the Government of the Republic. Is that nothing? Oh, you may feel that your place is still on the German Frontier and I am indeed loth to take you away from there, but this matter is really urgent. It is

---

* 'Drinker of hot wine without water'

303

a task of the utmost importance and one in which you will win great honour.'

'No,' he said again. 'I've had enough. I want out.'

'What do you mean?'

What sort of trick was this, I wondered. He fixed his gaze on a fly buzzing round the rim of a wine-jar, and stood there, like a great bull in sullen silence.

'I don't understand you,' I said again.

'That's too bad, but it's plain enough,' he muttered, turned on his heel and shambled out.

I was mystified, then I was furious.

'What,' I cried to his mother, 'does your son think he is doing? How dare he refuse to serve the Republic? How dare he throw my offer back in my face? Is he mad? Was he drunk?'

'Listen,' she said, 'and stop shouting at me. I have told you of my concern for Tiberius. I told you I was worried about him. This is precisely what I feared. Something in him has been rotted by the gnawing worm of resentment.'

I threw my hands up: 'He has cause to feel resentment! What about me?'

'I shall discuss the matter with him, and see if I can persuade him to see sense.'

Her discussion bore no fruit. Instead I received a letter from Tiberius:

> Augustus: I esteem the offer you have made me and express my gratitude for the confidence you have always shown in my abilities. Nevertheless I must decline. I have served Rome now for more than twenty years...

(On reading that line, I crumpled the letter up and hurled it into the corner of the room; what right had he to boast of his mere twenty years? While I ... then I told a slave to retrieve the document and read on ...)

> It is my desire to retire to an island and study philosophy and science. The Republic will manage very well without me, for it is not desirable that one man monopolize honours and commands as you have been kind enough to

permit me to do. Moreover, I feel that Gaius and Lucius, my stepsons, should be able to embark on their careers without being in the shadow of my achievement . . . I have fixed on Rhodes as my place of retirement. I have always been fond of islands, and the climate is said to be pleasant.

I have never read a more insolent letter.

Livia said, 'I can get no other sense from him. He gives me a half-smile and shakes his head, and says it is time for the boys to take up the torch.'

'Lucius is eleven. Eleven. Does your dolt of a son expect him to command the army of Armenia?'

'I know, I know. And then he talks in a faraway voice about the pleasures of astronomical studies.'

'It doesn't make sense.'

'Something broke in him when Drusus died.'

'Haven't we all suffered losses?'

Reluctantly, at Livia's insistence, I consulted Julia.

'You would have me marry him,' she pouted. 'But I can do nothing with him. If he's barely civil to you, he's as rude as an angry bear to me. I think he's a bit mad, if you must know. And of course he's as jealous of the boys as a bear with a pot of honey.'

'But they're still children.'

'The Senate proposed Gaius should share your next consulship.'

Tiberius retired to a villa he owned in the hills, and gave out that he had embarked on a hunger strike. Naturally the news aroused great excitement among the gossips of the Senate where Tiberius, because of his long and frequent absences on campaign, was largely an unknown quantity and an enigmatic figure.

My agents reported that some senators saw his expressed wish for retirement as being in some way a challenge to my authority; it was said that he was warning me not to advance the careers of my grandsons. Tiberius knew he was indispensable and was using his threat of retirement merely for bargaining purposes; he wanted his open elevation to a position of equality with me. Those who viewed my restored Republic as a disguised monarchy said he was making a bid for the succession.

Others however accepted his wish as genuine. Tiberius was weary of virtue, they said. All his life he had been a hypocrite, nursing secret vices which he was ashamed to practise publicly. Desire had however now overcome him, and the purpose of his retreat was to enable him to indulge his lusts.

Nobody dared bring me the one rumour that had any base of truth, and so I continued to think harshly of Tiberius.

I took care that he should be made acquaint with what was being said. I hoped that he would be either alarmed or shamed into changing his mind. He replied in quite unequivocal terms:

Augustus, how could I wish to challenge an authority which I have served willingly to the best of my poor abilities these twenty years? I am well aware that your authority which I respect is founded in the decrees of the Conscript Fathers, which no good Roman could wish to challenge.

The sincerity of my wish for retirement acquits me of the charge of ambition. It would be a stupid manoeuvre to put myself in this position if I was truly ambitious, for you have only to grant my wish for retirement, to bring my public career to an end.

The charge of vice is absurd. I repeat that I wish to devote the rest of my life to study. My chosen companions in my retreat will be Thrasyllus the astronomer, and other mathematicians. They are hardly the company I should select for an orgy.

I am worn out, disturbed, have never recovered from my brother's death, and there is now a new generation ready to serve Rome. My continued presence at the head of the armies would be likely to cause them embarrassment.

I am ashamed now to say that this letter, which was so dignified, truthful and yet reticent, in no way calmed my anger. I was indeed furious with him, and remained so a long time. I replied asking him what sort of example he thought this selfish abnegation of duty would be for the new generation of which he spoke. 'I have worked longer than you for Rome, and every bit as hard,' I said, 'but I have never thought to indulge in the luxury of retirement. It would be a fine state of affairs if we could all slip off our responsibilities as you are doing. Do you realize how you are hurting your mother and me?'

He did not reply to this letter and I asked Livia to go to plead with him. She returned in tears:

'I humbled myself,' she said, 'I went on my knees to him, and begged him not to forsake his duty. He is very weak from hunger, and could scarcely reply, but he shook his head. Husband, we must give way. I think he is demented, I have already told you that; it wounds my pride now to beg you to let my son desert his post, for I think as badly of his behaviour as you do. But he is my only surviving son, and I can't consent to his death. And he will die. His Claudian pride will not permit him to give way, and then he will for ever be lost to Rome and to me. But if we give way, he may recover. Surely astronomical studies on a little island will not content him long? Perhaps we should think of this as an illness from which he will recover.'

I put my arm round her and kissed her.

'Livia,' I said, 'you know in your heart that I can't pursue a course which will give you such pain as you will suffer if Tiberius dies. Therefore, I have to give way. Let him go to Rhodes. But—and I shall make this clear to him—if he goes there, he can stay. He can stay and rot there, for I shall never forgive him, nor trust him again. Let him go and study the stars with his Thrasyllus. He will read a bleak destiny for himself written there.'

And still not even Livia would tell me why Tiberius ran away from Rome.

His departure left me curiously isolated. I missed him, for his achievement had been such that I had come to think of him as my partner in government, an awkward partner certainly, one whom I could never talk to with the frankness and ease that I had always experienced with Agrippa and Maecenas, but a true one nonetheless. Now I felt deprived of an equal. It was a new position and I did not like it.

I became, for perhaps the first time in my life, introspective, and began to keep an intermittent journal. Some entries reveal more than I can recall, more perhaps than I care to remember:

'What a strange life mine has been and what a strange character I find I have. Now that I can see Death glowering at me, though he has left me so long after he has taken so many of my friends and loved ones, I ask myself whether any man has achieved so much with so few talents. Consider: my education was broken by civil war and, for all the generosity with which Virgil and Horace treated me, I have never been able to regard myself as being more than half-educated. I am only a poor orator and have never been able to rely on my powers to sway an assembly, and indeed many of my speeches have been disastrous failures. I am at best an indifferent general. Inasmuch as military ability can be separated from the quality of an army, I would have to place myself in the second rank. Agrippa, Antony, Sextus Pompey, even Cassius, Tiberius and Drusus have all had talents superior to mine—to say nothing of Julius Caesar. It may be that as a general I am no more distinguished than the wretched Lepidus. And yet consider my achievement. I have brought the Civil War to an end, which was something denied great commanders like Caesar and Sulla, and I have added more to the Empire than Caesar, Pompey and Sulla put together. If you judged by my achievement you would rank me with Alexander . . .

'As for my character I detest cruelty as I loathe deformity. I take no pleasure in the Arena, neither in the animal fights nor the gladiatorial contests, and would, if I thought it feasible, abolish them. Yet historians will, I am quite certain, judge me pitiless and cruel, and when I descend into the Shades I shall meet not only Agrippa and Virgil, but Cicero and those others who died at my command.

'I sometimes think the justification of my life has been my marriage, but yet I have never been certain that Livia so much as likes me. She disapproves of many of my actions and most of my opinions, and, though I am thought by many to be domineering, yet Livia can reduce me to hopelessness by her implacable silences.

'I revere the institution of marriage, and yet I have been cavalier in my making and breaking of the marriages of others. Why do I always know I know best?'

'I have days when I envy Tiberius, when I would fain stretch out the afternoon in a vine-wreathed arbour, while in the bay below the sea flicks its white foam against ancient rocks. This makes me still more bitter towards him. I envy his ability to detach himself from the business of government.'

'There are days when Livia and I do not speak to each other. People talk of the tranquillity of silence. No such thing. The menace of silence.'

'"You know", Maecenas said to me once "people say Livia poisoned Marcellus."'

(That entry appears on its own, without comment. How, I asked myself when I read it just now, could I have thought to record it starkly, and have added nothing? Yet now, what can I find to say but that it is patently absurd? You might as well say ... oh there is no end of people's willingness to repeat noxious scandal.)

'Perhaps my anger with Tiberius rests not in his defiance of my will, but in his happiness.'

'Have I made a fool of myself, as many hint, with my laws against immorality? Some say that this matter is no business of government, others that governments are powerless against what they call the spirit of the age. I don't give a radish for the spirit of the age which is a meaningless phrase. Nor do I see how any paternal government can avoid trying to correct social vices. Yet, when I speak of these matters in the Senate, the younger members titter.'

'The other day I took a strange whim on myself. I had been thinking, as I often do, of Virgil, and I recalled a conversation in which he spoke of Cincinnatus on the one hand and the priest of Diana at Nemi on the other. It occurred to me that, though I was born so near, I have never seen that temple of Diana, nor that priest who guards the Shrine and is known as

309

the King of the Wood; and then I read again the sixth Book of "The Aeneid", and that noble passage where the Sibyl says to Aeneas:

"Seed of the Blood Divine and Man of Troy, Anchises' son.

The Way down to Avernus is not hard. Black Pluto's gate Gapes wide, both night and day . . ."

and proceeds to tell him, that in order to enter the Underworld he must first pluck the Golden Bough from the tree which is sacred to the Juno of the Lower Depths, since Proserpina has decreed that this must be presented to her as a votive offering. Now Avernus is identified by the priestly scholars as being on the shores of the Lake of Aricia or Nemi, and the sacred tree is to be found within the sanctuary of Diana there.

'And so, prompted by piety and curiosity, I made an expedition thither, being carried over the hill from Aricia.

'It was a pale autumn day, being that succeeding the October Ides and so some two months past Diana's Festival, when her groves are brilliant with a multitude of torches, and from the brow of the hill the lake gloomed stagnant-black, swallowing up the light of the sky. Our early passage was beset and disturbed by hordes of deformed beggars who infest the Arician slopes importuning pilgrims for alms. These are those Manii notorious in these parts. Their misery and the degeneracy of their features pained and disgusted me. Then we moved beyond them into the shade of the trees which had not yet parted with their leaves, and the lake was out of sight. We descended the hillside by a winding track in an intense silence. There was no bird-song and no wind rustled the branches. Even the panting and straining of my bearers seemed an offence. Oaks and chestnuts enfolded us. Once a milk-white hart bounded across the path and once the bronze-grey back of a boar crashed through the undergrowth; but there was no other sign of life in the deep forest.

'As we approached the level of the lake a wailing rose to our ears and we found ourselves in a little clearing before a rude temple. I ordered the bearers to halt and sent Maco* to summon those within the temple. The wailing gave way to a

---

* My personal bodyguard, the grandson of that Maco who had joined me at Brindisi.

snarl and a yelp and he emerged driving three women before him. Two were very old, the third a girl who had not yet attained the age of puberty. All wore black garments torn in several places, as with knife slashes. I questioned them as to which deity they served, but they replied in a babble and a dialect or antique tongue which I could not understand. I called forth the countryman who acted as our guide and he advanced with the reluctance he had shown all day.

'"Come my man," I said, "you can hardly be frightened of two crones and a little girl."

'My mockery failed to brace him. After muttering to the women, he told me that in his view they were witches.

'"But what do they say themselves?"

'"That they worship the spirits of the dead."

'And the old women gave vent to wild laughter.

'"They say this lake is the gateway to the abode of the dead and that therefore Diana the huntress is served by a dead priest."

'"But the priest is a living man, a runaway slave and murderer, but no corpse or ghost."

'"Whoever has murdered has entered the realm of the dead and given himself in the service of the Gods of the nether world," was the reply.

'At this moment the little girl tore her rags apart and threw herself to the ground, arching her back over a fallen tree and offering herself. I told the bearers to cover her with a cloak, and give money to the old women because it seemed prudent to do so.

'The path twisted round the fringes of the lake from which emanated a foul and putrid odour. The bearers stumbled and swore and rocked my litter horribly, and I knew that they were eager to turn back, being infected with the fear of the place. But I felt a pricking of excitement which I knew betokened some revelation.

'Then the track widened, and a meadow stretched before us, covered with little white flowers that had a pungent smell. Though the afternoon sun still shone there was no joy in that place, but an uncanny stillness.

'We crossed the meadow, followed an avenue of trees and saw the grove open before us. It nestled by the lakeside under precipitous cliffs. In one corner stood a round temple, where a holy fire is maintained in honour of Diana in her vestal capacity. The sun had now dropped in the sky and gleamed redly through the trees, so that the leaves, already changing colour, were lit up as if by many thousands of fires. We halted. I disembarked from the litter, stiffly, feeling my rheumatism. The rustic directed my attention with quivering finger to the far corner of the grove where the sacred tree stood alone ... Its branches shone with a deep red-gold, but I could not tell whether this was caused by the setting sun.

'Then a figure emerged from the shadows; grim, with lank grey hair, lean but big-boned, wearing a yellow shift. He carried a naked sword in his left hand. When he saw us he halted, and then backed against the tree. I advanced towards him, and he barked out a challenge. I held out my hands, spread wide, to show I was unarmed.

'I told him I came in peace.

'"Who are you?" His voice creaked as if with disuse, and he spoke in a way that suggested both fear and anger.

'"They call me Augustus. I am no runaway slave, but one come to do honour to Diana, and talk to her priest."

'"Stand away," he said. "This tree is sacred, and must not be approached. Who bears its bough commands entry to the world of Death."

'"Are you a Gaul?" I said, for his accent suggested he came from that province.

'He shook his head, as if uncomprehending.

'"How long have you served the Goddess?"

'"Many years. Look," he pulled at his shift, "three times I have been challenged, three times wounded, three times sent my challengers to prepare the way for me below."

'"Do you accept gifts?" I asked.

'He shook his head.

'"How do you live?"

'He gestured towards the temple and I concluded that the priestesses there prepared food for him and laid it out for him to snatch in the few easy moments of his restless vigil.

'When I asked him how he slept a cunning look crossed his

face and again he shook his head, as if I was seeking information which could destroy him.

'I asked him why he had undertaken so cruel and dangerous a post, where every instant he must fear for his life, and in which he could find no comfort.

'"I serve the Goddess and do as she commands. She is a jealous Goddess and would punish me had I declined her call."

'"But what do you hope for?" I said.

'He gestured towards the black waters across which lay a single deep-red streak. Then the moon rose behind me and lay on the lake, and it seemed as if the waters opened to disclose a staircase of rough wet stone leading into what was no longer and could never perhaps be visible. The moment passed. The sun sank out of sight and the moon surged higher. The priest rested against the tree and his hand which had been raised to fondle the Golden Bough sank to his side...'

And that is all. The account breaks off there, as if my emotion was too great to allow me to continue, or perhaps as if my understanding was so dimmed that I simply did not know what to say further. I cannot now, fifteen—no nearer twenty—years later, even be certain that I did see what I then recorded and that it was not some sort of dream. Dream, vision, revelation, illusion, shadowy representation of some ultimate reality—who is to say? Why, I ask myself in my puzzled decrepitude, was I so enchanted by the cult of Diana in that sacred wood? Was it just because of that use of myth by Virgil, of those few lines in 'The Aeneid'? Was it because, sensing as I have always done, that Virgil saw realities hidden from me, I felt a compulsion to seek evidence to which my senses could afford credence of the mysteries of the Divine? Was I seeking assurance of some future life, or hoping to find its denial?

I do not know. I have been an eminently practical man. My temperament is genial and social. I have put my trust in the visible world and the working of my reason. I have achieved more than I dreamed possible. And yet, something has been lacking.

I made it my business to investigate what happened at Nemi. The worship of Diana there was instituted by that

Orestes, who slew Thoas, King of the Tauric Chersonese and then fled with his sister to Italy, carrying with him the image of the Tauric Diana hidden in a bundle of sticks. Now that Tauric Goddess is known to have been a savage and demanding deity; every stranger who landed on these harsh northern shores was sacrificed on her altars. In stealing her image, Orestes no doubt committed a great crime, and perhaps the ritual is intended to expiate this. After his death, his bones were brought from Aricia to Rome and buried in the gateway of the Temple of Saturn on the Capitol. It is said that the flight of the slave represents the flight of Orestes and that the rule of succession by the sword recalls the human sacrifices offered on the Tauric shore.

But for my part I find this unsatisfactory and believe the truth runs deeper. This explanation takes no account of the presence of the Golden Bough at Nemi; nor does it disclose why the priest also guards the descent to Avernus. I am no scholar, but it seems to me that the cruel ritual enacted at Nemi speaks of the responsibility of man's actions and the implacable justice of the Gods, from which there is neither escape nor mitigation. We are what our actions have made us. I am aware that this flies in the face of what most people believe about our character: that is, that it is immutable; that we are born the persons we become; and that life merely reveals what was already there but hidden. I hesitate, being neither philosopher, scholar nor sage, but only a soldier and administrator, from contradicting wiser men than I, but yet I cannot bring myself to believe this. I am what I feel, and I know in my bones that I have been formed by experience and my own deeds. True, I have been driven on by my native genius; but I have made myself by what I have done, and stand responsible for it.

Considering the matter now, it seems that it was Tiberius who in a strange way led me to Nemi. My anger with him had not abated, but my puzzlement had grown. I could not believe the reason he had given for his retirement to Rhodes, and I could not continue to believe he had done it to spite me. Nor did I believe that he acted—as some suggested—out of Republican leanings. Oh, I have never had any doubt that in many ways Tiberius disliked the form of my restored Repub-

314

lic. As an old-fashioned aristocrat he longed for Rome to be able to return to the days of the Scipios, as did Agrippa, different though his background was. Both, especially Tiberius, suffered from a nostalgia for a lost world. But both were also practical men. Tiberius was, and is, distinguished by a hard sense of political reality. He knew very well there was no other way but mine to manage the Roman Empire. He knew that, given more liberty, it would return to the frightful internecine strife of my youth. He despised his own generation too completely to believe otherwise for he saw how little of civic pride or antique virtue was there.

No, his withdrawal to Rhodes must, I thought, have deeper roots. (I know now of course that my explanation was too metaphysical.) It seemed to represent a profound dissatisfaction with the way things were, a hunger for some assurance of significance. Consider how he occupied himself on Rhodes, with his astronomical studies.

When he gazed into the heavens, and I into the mouth of Avernus, were we not both seeking the same thing?

XI

For the last three weeks I have been sleepless and irresolute. My nerves jangle. Every now and then, two or three times a day in fact, a mist has swum across my eyes. I have a pain in my left side, and my appetite cannot be tempted even by anchovies, cheese or peaches. I have caught Livia observing me with a measuring scrutiny, and I cannot work. Even my correspondence has fallen behind.

I have told myself all this is the unavoidable working of old age, that I can feel Death's dusty breathing. I know this is no more than a half-truth, and all my life I have tried to go beyond half-truths; not for any moral reason, but because, whatever one says in public, a politician cannot rest content with the knowledge of half-truths. Ability to see things as they are is the pre-condition of judgement.

And I cannot escape the conclusion that it is this autobiography that has made me ill.

Oh, I have troubles enough. As ever the family worries me. The next generation, how remote from me. Drusus' son Germanicus is a fine boy, with the coltish confidence of youth, but he irritates Tiberius who sees him only as a poor version of his father. There is enough of Drusus in the boy to remind Tiberius of the brother with whom alone of men he was easy; and yet the differences—Germanicus' callow optimism which renders him inferior to his father—are such that Tiberius views him with suspicious resentment, not unmixed with contempt. I see rough water ahead in that relationship.

Then Drusus' other boy, Claudius, is a sad problem. He stammers and slobbers. (It is disgusting to be near him at mealtimes.) His own mother, Antonia, though the best and noblest of women, describes him as 'a monster'. 'Nature began to make a man, but gave up on the job,' she once said to me. Livia can hardly bear to look at him. She has often said that she can't understand how Drusus and Antonia, both splendid creatures, could have produced such a . . . and then she snaps her finger and seems lost for a word that will adequately describe the unfortunate boy.

Naturally his presence has been embarrassing and we have had all sorts of family discussions about it. Can he be permitted for instance to appear in public? 'The question is,' Tiberius once said to me, 'whether he has full command of his five senses.' 'Until we can decide on that,' I replied, 'he had better be kept in the background. The public mustn't be given the chance to laugh at him, and I'm afraid they would.' Yet the boy is not altogether a fool; he has brains of a sort; but he looks the sort of freak they display at fairs. I'm afraid he will have no sort of future at all, for he is clearly unsuited to public life.

And then there is my own grandson Agrippa Postumus, given to fits of uncontrollable violence . . .

Still, it is a May morning, and the sun is shining. The sea sparkles as if the world was young . . .

I must bring myself to it. I have this absurd notion—no, I don't think it is really absurd—that I won't be well again till I have done so. And what is the point of autobiography if it doesn't tell the truth? (A question I remember Horace asking, with a smile so self-consciously impudent as to be in fact apologetic, when he told me he had been perusing Caesar's memoirs again, and found them disingenuous; I was so pleased that I sent him some Rhaetian wine, telling him it was much better than the Falernian he was in the habit of praising, though I didn't actually say why I was sending him the present. I wonder if he guessed.)

But I digress. I digress because I want to. There is always truth in digression—it reveals the speaker's mind. And mine is uneasy.

It was just such a morning as this. I remember that bird-like lightness of morning spirit when sunlight dances on the young leaves, and the day is not yet hot. Finches flitted, pink, gold and green with a flash of white among the fruit trees, and a blackbird was singing in an ilex at the bottom of the garden. I had not yet retired to the loggia but was dictating a letter to Lucius, who was then in Spain. As I spoke, I could see him clearly, and it was as if I heard his affectionate chatter.

And then Livia emerged from the house. It was going to be a hot day but she wore a dark gown. I remember thinking: how worn her face is.

She sat down beside me, and told the slaves to go away. She was holding a document, perhaps a letter, in her hand, which shook slightly, and, perhaps to disguise this, she raised it before her face and began to fan herself with it . . .

I don't suppose the birds really stopped singing . . .

She said, 'I don't know how to tell you what I have to tell you.'

'Which of them is it?'

'No,' she said, 'it's not the boys.'

It was as if a crab released its claws from my heart.

'It's worse, because it's not only sad but disgraceful too.'

From the farm across the lake a cock crew, loudly, several times while we sat frozen in the climbing sun.

At last she said: 'I had decided as I came down the garden just to let you read this. It's a police report. But now I find I can't—just lay it before you. I can't be so cowardly.'

And then she told me. Her words have died away, though the cock still crows its derisive challenge to the morning, and I cannot piece them together in my broken and disordered memory. She spoke as gently and, as it were, lovingly, as she knew how. I am sure of that.

The police report concerned my daughter Julia. Agents had watched her for a long time, for she had been suspected of contravention of the laws against immorality. At last her behaviour had become blatant—Livia pressed the document into my hands, and the fingers that touched mine were icy-cold—'Subject, after a dinner-party, where much wine had been consumed, staggered with her companions into the forum, and there mounted the Rostra from which position she solicited the custom of chance passers-by, to the pleasure of her associates, who called out, "Roll up, roll up, for the best-born f—— in Rome..."'

'Have you read this?'

Livia nodded.

I had to order a thorough investigation. In Sicily there is an expression: 'to swallow a toad'. It is employed when one has to accept an unacceptable fact. My own daughter was the monstrous and slimy toad I was compelled to swallow. The catalogue of her lovers and debauchery was long, detailed, and nauseating. As I read, I felt her loving and deceitful arms pressed round my neck, her soft lips proclaiming love against my cheek. But where else had those ruby lips been? What noisome work had that tongue done?

The pictures in my mind ... I forced the toad down.

The catalogue of lovers ranged from members of the old nobility to lusty slaves and freedmen.

'Augustus,' said my chief of police, 'we have evidence of worse than immorality. There is criminal conspiracy here too. Look at these names, Iullu Antonius, grandson of the triumvir, Sempronius Gracchus, Cornelius Scipio, Appius Claudius Pulcher, it's a roll-call of the disaffected old nobility. We have evidence which suggests that there was a plan to poison Tiberius so that Antonius might marry the widow and be in a position, in the event of your death, to supplant her sons the Princes. We have a letter too which suggests that the poison that would be employed on Tiberius should then be used on you. I am sorry to tell you this, but you have been kept ignorant too long. I urged your wife to tell you some months ago...'

Maecenas had called Iullus Antonius 'a pretty boy'.

'We have evidence that the affair with Gracchus goes back even to the days of her marriage to Marcus Agrippa...'

So Agrippa wore horns?

'We have evidence...'

'We have evidence...'

'We have evidence...'

She asked to see me. I saw her eyes swimming with tears and her body slack with apprehension, and I heard soft lies, and declined.

'We have evidence...'

Screeds and screeds of eye-witness accounts, too horrid to brood on, depositions taken from slaves, some tortured to extract the truth, some spouting evidence like fountains to escape torture. (But tortured all the same, to test their story.)

'We have evidence ...' crowing vice and defiance to the morning air.

'We have evidence ...' secret meetings, plots laid, seditious talk, laughter and resentment, the mockery of soft men who had never ventured to the frontier camps, the anger of empty men who resented government...

'We have evidence...'

'Prepare a digest for Gaius and Lucius, the Princes of the Youth Movement'; but when the digest, which recorded their mother's vice in the barest terms, had been made, I could not bring myself to send it.

How could I tell them what I had feared to know myself?

'We have evidence...' The cock crew, the documents piled up unfolding, in the May sunshine, the record of love-less coupling, debauchery and treason. Julia wrote again, a long epistle, now grovelling, now whining, now defiant, now abject in self-justification: my love had always been self-ish and domineering; I had never asked her what she wanted; I had made her my instrument; I had forced her into loveless marriages; I had sought to steal the love of her first husband

319

and I had stolen the love of her sons. She was repentant, she promised she would amend her life; her disgrace was my disgrace; any pain she suffered would be compensated by the pain she was inflicting on me, for I deserved it, I had brought it on myself by my callous manipulation of her life, and it was my fault. And in the next sentence she promised me enduring love and swore she would be dutiful.

'We have evidence...' Livia never once, by any flicker of a cold and satisfied eye, reminded me of her thirty years of warnings.

'We have evidence...' Julia's handmaiden, a Greek called Phoebe, alarmed by its weight piling against her own reputation, rose before dawn and hanged herself from the lintel of my daughter's house. 'I would I were Phoebe's father!' I cried out; but Julia, my agents reported, wept to hear of the girl's death. Were they lovers too? 'We have evidence that...'

Tiberius wrote to me from Rhodes. His letter was calm, dignified and laconic...

My wife, suffering perhaps from a species of desperation that can, my doctors tell me, afflict women as they approach middle-life, has behaved in a manner that is worse than foolish. The peculiarly public nature of her conduct must touch the bounds of forgiveness, for, as princeps, you can hardly fail to interpret it as a public challenge to the admirable legislation you have caused to be passed. Yet I appeal to you, in your public and private capacity, to show clemency. Clemency would become you both as Father of our Country, and as father of your unfortunate daughter. I would beg you to consider that my own absence, the result of my intense weariness of spirit and body, and of my desire to allow Gaius and Lucius to flourish, may have contributed to my wife's aberrations. Clemency is good in itself. The harsh letter of justice will be like a knife you yourself drive into your own heart...

When news of Tiberius' plea became known—as these things always do—there were many quick to say that he was anxious primarily to safeguard his own position as my son-in-law; but I am now convinced that his plea on his wife's behalf was an illustration of his true nobility of character.

At the time I felt differently. It seemed impertinent. Perhaps in my heart I agreed with the reproach he directed at himself. If he had done his duty as Julia's husband we would have been spared this. I would have been spared. I did not then comprehend the part played by Julia's conduct in his decision to withdraw to Rhodes.

As it was, I immediately commanded a bill of divorce to be drawn up in his name. I wrote informing him of this. As if to reprove me, he allowed Julia to keep the presents which he had given her. This is not of course normal custom, and it could only be interpreted as a protest.

The evidence overwhelmed me. I wrote in guarded terms to the boys, merely telling them that their mother had disgraced herself, imperilled the whole family's future, willingly associated herself with a group of dissidents, and must suffer the appropriate penalties. They were horrified, but saw reason, welcome and reassuring proof of their civic virtue, which I had never doubted. But then, till the cock crew evidence to the open air, I had never doubted Julia's love for me.

I was left no choice. Had I been a private citizen, I would still have had to punish my daughter's crimes. Their nature and their full extent could not be hidden. I therefore forwarded the evidence to the Senate, asking them to take the appropriate action against her lovers, who had offended against both the laws of morality and the statutes of treason. Their sedition was manifest. The court had no hesitation in condemning Antonius, Gracchus, Appius Claudius Pulcher, Cornelius Scipio and the vile T. Quinctius Crispinus, whose presence in the list had made me choke and spew, to the death they merited. All five were consigned to the Mamertine prison, historic execution-chamber of Rome. The sentence relieved the public mind of the fear of Revolution; yet deepened my depression. It was forty-two years since Julius' murder, forty since Philippi, twenty-nine since Actium, and it was now revealed that numerous members of the old political class had not reconciled themselves to the New Order, but still craved the savage excitements of disorderly faction. After long study of the evidence, I recommended that only Iullus Antonius should be put to death, and that the others should be sent into perpetual exile. That fate would, I hoped, be sufficient warning to other dissidents. I could not bring myself however to ask for mercy to be extended to Iullus Antonius, for I regarded him as the engineer of my daughter's fate. This son of Antony and Fulvia inherited the beauty of both parents (though his was of a more effeminate stamp than either his mother's or his father's) and the selfish and vicious temperament of Fulvia; there was nothing in him of that generosity of spirit which shone among Antony's vices like a jewel in a dunghill; I shuddered to think how he would have disposed of Gaius and Lucius had he achieved his ambition of marrying Julia.

I could not bring myself to see my daughter, though Livia reported her to be penitent. She had hurt me too deeply. Livia suggested that she be required to live on one of my country estates, but I knew that she would soon resume her former way of life in such circumstances. When a woman has once become a whore, no reform is possible; she is like a dog which has turned to killing sheep. I therefore determined that her exile should be more complete, and banished her to the island of Pandataria. I ordered that she should not be permitted to drink wine, but this command was not intended primarily as a punishment. Julia was in danger of becoming an habitual drunkard, and I believed that compelled to abstain from wine she might come in time to review her conduct and arrive at a correct judgement of her behaviour. For obvious reasons I also ordered that she be denied male company.

I have never seen her since, though some years ago, learning that her quiet and narrow life had indeed had some of the consequences for which I hoped, I permitted her to live on the mainland of Italy, at Reggio Calabria.

Julia's beauty and charm had always made her popular with the Roman people. When they received the news of her sentence, a deputation approached me begging that I rescind it and permit her to return to Rome. I read in their faces a condemnation of what they judged to be my harshness; they pitied Julia, careless of how she had wounded me.

I put an angry stop to their nonsense.

'If you ever bring up this matter again,' I said, 'may the Gods curse you with daughters as lecherous as mine, and with wives as adulterous as Julia.'

XII

It was painful writing that chapter about Julia's disgrace, and when I had at last brought myself to do so, I sickened of this memoir. It felt as if the bile deposited by that episode had collected itself in a ball, and made it impossible for me to continue. I laid the task aside, and only resume it now, in this the seventy-seventh year of my life because I hate things to be incomplete, and because death now stares me in the face. It is necessary to make some kind of summing-up, and to ask myself to judge how I have played my part in this comedy of life.

A painful comedy, where promise is so often dulled, and where the Gods work with a keen and cruel irony.

I could not help myself blaming Tiberius for his part in Julia's disgrace, even though in my heart I knew that he had fled to Rhodes because he was as disgusted by her behaviour as I was to be, and because he knew that he was impotent to control her. Nevertheless, it seemed to me in my misery that he had abdicated his domestic responsibility as completely as his responsibility as a servant of the Empire, and, so, when the term of his tribunician power expired, I saw no reason to renew it. Let him crumble in Rhodes, I said to myself, let him taste leisure.

He was himself alarmed by this lapse in his nominal authority, or perhaps he had become bored with his narrow life on the island. At any rate he now wrote to me requesting permission to return to Rome:

'Now that my stepsons, Gaius and Lucius, are full-grown and taking their places with distinction in the government of the Empire,' he wrote, 'I may say clearly that my principal reason for retiring from public life, apart from weariness, and the long fatigue of service on the harsh frontiers of Empire, was to avoid the suspicion of any rivalry with them. But, since they are now acknowledged as the heirs to the Principate, that reason is no longer valid, and I am anxious to return to the city if only to visit my family, whom I sorely miss, and in particular to be whatever comfort I may be to my beloved mother and you, my gracious stepfather, in your old age.'

Tiberius has no gift for correspondence. This letter seemed to me as insolent as that in which he had announced his desire to settle on Rhodes.

My reply was brief:

'It was of your own choice that you settled on Rhodes, against my will, denying me your help. You had better remain there and abandon all hope of visiting your family, whom you were so eager to desert. Your mother is in excellent health . . .'

In fact, Livia was also keen that Tiberius should return.

'Now that his tribunician power has lapsed,' she said, 'it looks as if he is in disgrace. That's an unfair reflection on my son. No one has served you and the Republic better. What's more, it's a slur on me.'

But I was moved neither by her arguments nor by her tears. Tiberius had made his bed and should lie in it. The most I would consent to was to accord him the status of an ambassador, so that it should not look as if he had been utterly discarded.

'When I needed him,' I said to Livia, 'he ran away.'

'And didn't your daughter have some part to play in that decision?' she said.

There was no answer to that, beyond repeating my request that I should be spared mention of Julia.

I spend much of my time now on Capri, enchanted island which some say was Circe's where Ulysses' men were turned to pigs. I doubt that; it is more likely to have been the island of the lotos-eaters, judging by the behaviour of my staff. The atmosphere of the island owes much to my friend Masgaba, a Greek who settled here to plant vines and olives and beautify his estate. It was Masgaba who, more years ago than I care to think, first drew my attention to Capri, and so I called him 'The Founder'. He died last year. When I noticed that a crowd of torch-bearers were honouring his tomb, I improvised a line of Greek verse: 'I see the Founder's tomb ablaze with fire', and asked Thrasyllus, Tiberius' admired astrologer, who had written this appropriate line? He hesitated, afraid in the manner of intellectuals to display his ignorance, so I capped it with another, 'With torches, look, they honour Masgaba'. He suspected a joke and made the diplomatic reply: 'Both lines are excellent, whoever the poet was.'

Capri is a place of such relaxation, a place for jokes as well as beauty. There are many Greeks here, and in this holiday atmosphere, their good looks and gaiety are refreshing. The other day I had all Romans dress as Greeks and vice versa; that caused hilarity, though I suppose my own pleasure in my whim was what really pleased the islanders. They delight in my presence and happy mood.

One cause of my pleasures in recent years has been the little Gallic girl, Moragh, whom I have unofficially adopted. It was she whom I had seen run by her father's side as Varus' ill-fated legions left for Germany. It took a long time to find her, and I never understood my determination to do so. I gave her to Livia as a maidservant, but in fact she spends more time attending to my needs, or chiefly amusing me. We play dice together, and her naïvety is a delight. Old age being in some way a second childhood, its best companion is a child.

Death is close. Two months ago, before I left Rome, I attended a purificatory ceremony in the Field of Mars. While I was doing so an eagle circled round my head several times; it then flew off and perched on the nearby temple, settling itself on the first A of Agrippa's name. 'That must be an omen,' I said to myself, 'my time is almost up.' Accordingly I asked Tiberius to take the vows for the next *Lustrum*, since I was unwilling to make myself responsible for vows which would be payable after my death.

The next day there was a thunder-storm and lightning melted the initial letter of my name on an inscription below one of my statues; that caused some public disquiet for all took it as a sign that I was near death. The removal of C from Caesar left the name reading AESAR, which is the Etruscan word for God; will I then live only a hundred (C) days?

How Maecenas would have laughed! But the laughter would hardly have concealed his profound faith in portents.

That was, as I say, some sixty days ago.

*

After Julia's disgrace, my only pleasure lay in the achievements of the boys, who showed every sign of justifying the confidence I had placed in them. Their gaiety, beauty, courage and intelligence were equal; I looked forward with serenity to leaving the Empire in their tender and capable care. 'Light of my eyes,' I wrote to Gaius once, 'I miss you desperately when you are away from me, especially on such a day as this. Wherever you are, I hope you have kept my sixty-fourth birthday in health and happiness, for, as you say I have passed the grand climacteric, which is the sixty-third year. I am now an old man and I have prayed to the Gods who keep Rome that I may spend the time remaining to me in prosperity, while you are playing the man and learning to take up my work...'

The Gods denied me that...

I had appointed Gaius to that command in the East which his natural father Agrippa has held with such distinction. I gave him Marcus Lollius as chief-of-staff. On departure I wished the dear boy 'the integrity of Pompey, the courage of Alexander and his own good luck'. He might indeed have been an Alexander.

Livia was still begging that Tiberius be permitted to return to Rome and I felt that this decision was one that should properly be taken by Gaius. Gaius replied with sagacity:

'You know I have never been on easy terms with my former stepfather, but I am disquieted by the animosity he arouses. The other day at my own table somebody cried out, "Just give the word, Gaius, and I'll sail off to Rhodes and bring back the Exile's head". I think there is danger in such sentiments and of course reproved the man. Lollius believes that Tiberius should stay where he is, but I must tell you, sir, that I have been disappointed in Lollius and suspect him of taking bribes; nor has his advice always been good. On the other hand there are rumours that Tiberius himself has been nursing treasonable projects. The matter is therefore difficult. He came, at his own request, to see me on Samos. You would think having done so he would make an effort to be agreeable, but he was as chilly, sardonic and difficult as ever. He told me I should insist that my staff-officers addressed me with more respect. In fact of course he simply doesn't understand modern manners. It always amazes me that he should be so much more out of touch with my generation than you are, considering that he is at least twenty years younger...'

I at once acquainted Tiberius with the rumours that attached themselves to his name. He replied requesting me to attach 'some reputable and responsible person' to his household that I might receive detailed reports of his words and actions. There was a disagreeable note of false humility in the tone of this letter, but it was certainly a request calculated to disarm suspicion. Not that I held any myself. I knew my Tiberius too well. He would never demean himself by conspiracy. However, having decided that Gaius should properly determine his former stepfather's fate, I relayed this request to him. He at once concluded that Tiberius should be permitted to return to Rome 'before he chokes on his own dignity', but he asked that he be excluded from any political activity. In the circumstances, no decision could have been wiser; I marvelled at the boy's acumen and maturity of judgement, for no decision could have been better calculated either to serve Tiberius' own interest. Tiberius himself acknowledged the wisdom of Gaius' judgement by the speed with which he acted on it, and by the circumspection he showed on his return. In fact, it was not difficult for him to abstain from politics. They had never been to his taste, and he despised politicians too much. Livia was warmed by his return; it was touching to see mother and son together, both too reticent fully to display their feelings, yet giving off a glow of contentment. Yet here was pain for me too; they sharpened my own sense of what Julia's conduct had deprived me.

Deprivation ... Julia, and her own daughter Julia who turned whore too and had likewise to be consigned to an island. (The immoral poet Ovid was involved in her escapade. I sent him to Tomi on the Black Sea, from where he wearies me with self-pitying epistles.) But these were mere personal pains; the daggers touched only me.

Lucius died suddenly, without warning, of a fever at Marseilles on his way to Spain. He had never had the chance to justify his life or display his merits. Only I knew what Rome lost when this flower was cut in its May morning. Gentler than Gaius, more loving than Marcellus, as honourable as Agrippa, he was a boy of infinite capacity.

His death devolved as great a weight on Gaius, as that of Drusus had on Tiberius. Greater indeed, for Gaius was destined to an authority I had never envisaged for my stepsons, and he was also younger and therefore less able to bear the weight imposed on him.

At the time of Lucius' death, he was embroiled in the endlessly recurrent ferment of Armenian politics. Phraates of Parthia had been murdered as a result of a conspiracy encouraged by his son Phraataces; the parricide had succeeded to the throne and promptly instigated a revolution in Armenia, where the slimy, and, as it had turned out, utterly untrustworthy Tigranes was installed as King. It looked as if Armenia would slip out of the Roman sphere of influence, but my dear Gaius acted with exemplary decision and celerity. First, he came to an agreement with Phraataces. It was not ideal but it served the immediate purpose, for the threat of Roman might which Gaius displayed persuaded the Oriental King to abandon his Armenian puppet. Gaius then marched against Tigranes who was killed fleeing from a lost battle, and established Artabazanes of Media on the throne. In a few weeks he had restored the situation and salvaged our interests. No one could have done better, and fired by his success he proposed an expedition into Arabia. Alas, in a frontier skirmish he received a wound. I begged him to return to Italy and rest. He died at Limrya in Lycia.

There is nothing to say, nothing to add to the stark fact. I have only wept once since that day, when I heard of Varus' folly.

Only Livia brought me any comfort in my grief. But what comfort could there be? In the East they worship me as a God; it is folly. But what have my prayers to Apollo or Jupiter been but like folly, that they should requite me in this manner?

I have lost interest in religious speculation since Gaius' death. The other day I even thought: perhaps Virgil is merely the poet of our vain and noble dreams? Perhaps it is the trivial and meretricious Ovid who really tells the truth about life?

In such moods I approach despair. Why struggle, as I have always struggled, if the end is stale bread and foetid water?

I have caught myself saying, time and again, 'I found Rome of sun-baked bricks, and leave it of marble.' No doubt the marble will endure; it is something to boast of. I have heard that Antony facing defeat cried out for 'one other gaudy night', called 'all his sad captains ... to mock the midnight bell'. I envy him; I cannot swagger in like manner to the Shades ...

I was sixty-six when they brought me news of Gaius' death. Ten years ago. Ten years of labour that has seemed ever more necessary, ever more meaningless. But of course that is only one mood. I cannot in the end deny my life's work, the restoration of Rome to stability. When I look round the Empire ... well, for example, last week when I was sailing through the gulf of Puteoli, we came on a corn-ship from Alexandria. On learning of my presence, its crew decked themselves in white with garlands, and burned incense, explaining that they did so, and wished me enduring fortune, because they owed me their lives and their freedom to sail the seas. Without my efforts, they said, they would certainly have fallen prey to pirates. I was so touched by their gratitude that I gave each member of my own crew and all my attendants forty gold pieces to spend on Alexandrian ware.

The moment recalled the proudest of my life, sixteen years ago, when the Senate hailed me as 'Father of our Country', the motion to do so being proposed by an old enemy Messella Corvinus, who had fought against me at Philippi. His speech ran as follows:

'Good fortune and the favour of the Gods attend thee and thy house, Caesar Augustus; for thus we feel that we are praying for a lasting prosperity for our country and happiness for our beloved City. The Senate and the people of Rome hail thee Father of thy Country ...'

To which I replied:

'Conscript Fathers, I have attained my highest hopes. What more have I to ask of the immortal Gods than that I may retain this, your unanimous approval, till the last day of my life ...?'

I have done so, even in the dark days when news came of Varus' folly, but the mocking Gods took me at my word and withdrew their favour from me.

I could not abstain from public business in mourning Gaius. It was necessary to make new plans for the succession, for the transmission of power and authority in orderly fashion, that my life's work be not destroyed in a renewal of civil strife. I therefore announced my intention of adopting Tiberius and also my surviving grandson Agrippa Postumus, whose unsuitability was not yet manifest.

Tiberius hesitated. His disinclination for an official role had hardly, he said, abated. Moreover, in accepting adoption, he would have to surrender his position as head of the Claudian family and all the privileges that went with this position.

'And for what?' he said. 'Will I be cast aside again in a few years, when you have determined to promote the interest of your grandson?'

'Tiberius,' I said, and then paused. At that moment I felt his wounded pride for the first time, not as an expression of a jealous and self-regarding nature, but rather as something honest. It came to me that in my treatment of Tiberius I had been less than just. Perhaps it was because I had never been easy with him; only now did I see his fundamental goodness and realize that his resentment was not unreasonable. On the other hand—and this is the last harsh criticism of Tiberius that these memoirs will contain—I had been right in thinking him less than ideal as the master of the Empire. He lacks the geniality and conversability that the role of princeps demands, for he cannot speak to the senators as if they were equals. Only a few months ago, I found myself muttering, 'Poor Rome, to be chewed between those slow jaws...'

But now, I met his objections head-on. I did what was necessary and turned his mind to practical matters. I spread out before him a map of the northern frontier.

'Look,' I said, 'your brother Drusus advanced here. His glory is imperishable'—this was the sort of noble language Tiberius warmed to, and I knew anyway that he had always found praise of his brother irresistible—'but his achievement is less secure. Our armies are being pressed by your old enemy Marboduus, chief of the Marcomanni, and though last year our general, L. Domitius Ahenobarbus, advanced as far as the fabled Elbe, this summer he is embroiled with the Cherusci, and our line is shaken. I want you, as Rome's greatest general, refreshed by your period of rest, to take command of all our northern armies. There is no one else I can ask to do so, first because we have no general of your ability, second because there is no other general whose success, if great, might not persuade him to undermine the stability of the Empire. In short there is no one but you that I can trust, Tiberius.'

Faced with this appeal, what could he do but accept?

The adoption went through. I am told that Tiberius resented my form of words: 'Cruel fate,' I said, 'having robbed me of my sons Gaius and Lucius, for the sake of the Republic I now proclaim the adoption of my stepson Tiberius Claudius Nero and my surviving grandson, Agrippa Postumus...' But what else could I say? I would have insulted Tiberius had I not lamented the occasion of his adoption. And he knew how the boys' death had pained me. To my surprise it had hurt him too, for he had composed an elegy on Lucius himself. (The verse was stilted and old-fashioned, but redeemed by sincerity.)

Tiberius proceeded north and his long absence on campaign cemented our relationship. I have never found him conversable; indeed I don't mind confessing that I have found his company inhibiting. Livia once asked me why I always broke off my conversation when Tiberius came into the room. I hadn't been aware of it and said so. She said,

'Well you do, and Tiberius of course thinks you have been criticizing him...'

'Nothing of the sort,' I said. 'As I say, I wasn't aware of it, but since you tell me so, it must be true, and the only explanation I can offer is that I always expect Tiberius to find my conversation frivolous and so feel it necessary to change the subject when he comes in. The truth is, my dear, that your son is a bit forbidding.'

But at a distance our friendship and the trust between us have grown stronger. And, though his letters often make me laugh with their pedantic phraseology, I have grown to value his advice. Indeed I wrote to him saying, 'If any business comes up that demands unusually careful consideration, or that is irritating, then I swear by the Mouth of Truth that I miss you, my dear Tiberius, more than I can say. And then Homer's lines run in my mind:

'If he came with me, such is his wisdom
That we should escape the fury of the fire.'

I might also quote two other letters because I wish once and for all to disprove the suggestion that I have not valued Tiberius:

'When people tell me, or I read, that this constant campaigning is wearing you out, I tell you I get gooseflesh in sympathy. Do please take things more easily. If you were to fall ill the news would kill your mother and me, and the whole country would shiver from doubts about the succession. Bear this in mind, my most valued Tiberius...

'My state of health is now of little importance compared to yours. May the Gods keep you safe and in good health, for if they do not, I shall fear that they have taken an utter aversion to our beloved city...'

I can't, in an odd phrase I have picked up from Moragh, say fairer than that...

I have revised my will again. The bulk of my estate is divided between Tiberius and Livia in the proportion of two to one. I have directed that he take the name Augustus, and she Augusta. My estate is not large. Indeed it amounts to no more than 1,500,000 gold pieces. From this I ask them to pay 400,000 to the Roman commons and ten pieces to each member of the Praetorian Guard and three to each legionary. Of course my properties are considerable. The shortage of ready cash may surprise some, for it is known that I have received some 14,000,000 gold pieces in legacies over the last twenty years. But nearly all this sum, as well as what I inherited from my father, my adoptive father and others, has been used to support the national economy. As I have recorded in my statement of my deeds, the Res Gestae, no man has given more of his personal fortune to Rome than I...

★

The value of Tiberius' return was soon shown when a revolt broke out among the Pannonians on the Danube frontier. This is now known as the Batonian War, because the two leaders of the revolt were both called Bato. One of them shamed me, for he said to Tiberius: 'It is no wonder that we rebel, for you Romans send wolves, not shepherds or sheep-dogs, to guard your sheep.' This complaint impressed Tiberius, and, as I say, pained me myself. I ordered him to investigate it and see whether it had a basis in fact, for on one thing especially I have prided myself: that my regime has out-lawed the spoliation of provincials which was such a deplor-able feature of the old Republic; remember the virtuous Marcus Brutus and his forty-eight per cent rate of interest.

Nevertheless this Batonian War was a grim affair, so grim that I even took the field again myself and led an army to the north-eastern frontier of Italy lest the enemy break through on that front or reinforcements be urgently needed. Fortu-nately Tiberius was equal to the situation. With the help of young Germanicus and the consular M. Aemilius Lepidus he bore down resistance. One of the Batos was killed by the other who himself yielded to Tiberius the following year. He was imprisoned in Ravenna, but we agreed to spare his life.

Nothing could have been more worthy of praise than Tiberius' conduct of this arduous campaign. He showed him-self a fit successor to Pompey and Agrippa. Eventually the whole of Illyricum, that vast country bounded by Northern Italy, the Danube, Thrace, Macedonia and the Adriatic, was brought under perfect control. It was proposed in the Senate that Tiberius be granted the name of Pannonicus, but I vetoed the suggestion, saying that he would be satisfied with the title of 'Augustus' which I intended to bequeath him.

I did this not of course to deprive him of the honour of his victory, but to make it clear that he would be my successor. I had also had to acknowledge that talk of the succession was inevitable. The Empire requires a princeps and in these last years I have continually found myself lured into discussion about the succession. Only a few months ago, someone approached me and asked my opinion of various candidates. I replied that while Marcus Aemilius Lepidus might be suitable in some respects, he was surely too proud; that Gaius Asinius

Gallus was of course eager, but rash in judgement and therefore unsuitable; and that Lucius Arruntius, though doubtless capable of making the venture if the chance arose, was yet, in my opinion disqualified by... Do you know, I can't recall what disqualification I found for him. At any rate, whenever the matter is raised, I make it my business to praise all the candidates mentioned, and then discover some quality which makes them unsuitable; at the very least, I damn them by the faintness of my approbation. I am determined of course that the job must go to Tiberius, and I wish him to be succeeded by Germanicus. Germanicus is a most capable youth with something of the audacity of his father Drusus. He lacks the charm and sweet nature of Lucius and the intellectual capacity of Gaius, but he has quality. Moreover, he is married to my granddaughter Agrippina, who appears to have escaped the taint that infected her mother and sister. Accordingly my blood will in time inherit through the children of this marriage. I have discussed this with Tiberius and he acquiesces; Germanicus is after all the son of his beloved brother Drusus. Only in one respect do I have doubts about him. Tiberius and I are agreed that no further expansion of the Empire is desirable. The horror of the Teutoberger Wood has convinced us of this, and Tiberius himself has stabilized the Danube frontier; but Germanicus is an ardent youth. Tiberius may have a hard task to control his ambition.

I had hoped that my surviving grandson Agrippa Postumus might be able to share the labour of Empire. Alas, it was not to be. As I have said, he grew up dull and stupid, caring for nothing but field sports and the spectacle of the arena. Watching him one day lick his blubbery lips with eager tongue as he watched death being meted out there, I recoiled from him. The disgusting spectacles in the arena are necessary to keep the People happy, but it is intolerable that a gentleman should enjoy them. Then the boy has a nasty temper which he makes no effort to control. One day he even struck his grandmother. That decided me; he wasn't fit for civilized life.

It is the brief hour of twilight. The sea has taken on a deep purple and the olive trees stand out black against the fading light. The summer moon rises behind the temple to Minerva. I have just heard the first cries of Minerva's bird, the hunting owl. What a long way I have travelled. Now, in my secret musings, about to die, I salute whatever Gods rule the world and mankind in it, and I can confess to myself that I indeed sought that Empire which I attained. But in following what one wishes, one never understands the meaning of that wish. In possessing Empire what have I found? Certainly there are pleasures, there is the consciousness of duty performed which must always give some satisfaction, but they are always accompanied, shaded and soured, by endless and frightful anxieties, unending alarms, thousands of secret enemies; since Agrippa and Maecenas died I have held no equal conversation with any man. For more than twenty years! Twenty years of chilling isolation. Virgil foresaw it and hence the look of deep pity he used to direct upon me. Only Livia has survived to remind me that I am only a man . . . Only Livia, and me. There has been no pleasure free of an accompanying pain, and there has been no rest. For almost sixty years now I have not known a single moment of true repose.

The other night I did what I have not done for twenty years, visited Livia's bedchamber. She looked up in alarm when I entered, fearing that I was ill or about to bring her some evil news. But I smiled and put my finger first to my lips and then to hers, and crawled into bed beside her. For a long time we lay in silence pressing together; the last reality.

Towards dawn we woke and talked tranquilly for two hours, but it is not suitable to reveal even to posterity what we said. Let me repeat merely that I have known nothing in life so deep and so mysterious as my marriage. It has sustained and fortified me in all my endeavours, and I would truly wish such a marriage for all I love.

As I left her room I said, 'Live, my dear, mindful of our marriage and what it has signified for both of us.'

Without Livia I could not have survived.

Antony appeared to me in a dream last night. He lay against me and spoke words of praise, and when he vanished, as figures may in dreams, it was like the extinction of a flaming

335

torch, and I awoke empty, afraid, and with a hollow sense of loss.

One regrets what one has not done, rather than any action one has performed.

Will Virgil guide me through the Shades, will Cicero make speeches there, will I be confronted with bloody and accusing eyes?

We travelled by slow stages to Benevento to greet Tiberius who was on his way to Brindisi from where he would take ship to our armies in Illyria. Thinking I would not see him again, I first thanked him for the support he had been.

'I could not,' I said, 'have sustained these last years without you. In particular Varus's folly would have destroyed me. Now listen, I have had reports from my agents about the state of opinion in the city. Briefly, some welcome the prospect of my death and are, I am told, already chattering of the blessings of freedom—ah, the crimes that have been committed in the name of liberty! Others however are apprehensive and mutter fears of civil war. I know you well, Tiberius, and I know that your tendencies incline you to be sympathetic to those who babble of liberty. But I know also that you have too much good sense to give way to them. You cannot remember what they used to call the Free State—how long ago, in what unimaginable springtime it seems, since I heard Cicero roll that expression round his mouth like a ripe and luscious plum. The Free State—it cannot return without the destruction of the Empire. It took me a long time, my son, to admit my achievement, though Maecenas told me just what I was doing forty years ago. In a word, I have saved Rome and its Empire at the expense of the privileges of the class into which you were born. They hate me for it, and are blind to the benefits secured at the same time. They will hate you too, but like me you will care little for it.

'Now, as to the danger of a renewed civil war, I have taken such precautions as I can. You have direct command of the armies; pay them a donative when my death is announced.

Try to achieve a partnership with the Senate, but remember that it must always take the second place...

'I have done one other thing for you. Two months ago I visited the island where my surviving grandson, Agrippa Postumus, is confined. I hoped I might find him improved. I hoped that it might be possible to suggest to you that his case is not hopeless and that he might even be able to help you in the management of the Empire, as you have helped me. Alas, the visit was useless and painful. I found the young man as brutish and violent and stupid as ever. Worse even. In placid moments he fishes happily, but the captain of the guard told me that these moments are becoming fewer. He spends much of the time in a violent rage. I have therefore concluded that he is incurable, and so I left the captain of the guard with sealed orders to be opened on the occasion of my death. They instruct him to put my grandson to death. You will find a copy in that travelling bureau there...

'What else? They will call me a God. What fools! Are you and I the last two sane men in a demented world? Don't you ask yourself about the deterioration in our race? They would never have thought to name Cincinnatus or Scipio a God.

'I am tired. Do you see how withered those laurel wreaths above my statue are...?

'Remember Bato, sheepdogs not wolves ... revere your mother, love her and protect her ... and the children, Agrippina's children who carry my seed ... don't let them mock the poor crippled Claudius, he's not altogether a fool.'

We started back to Rome the next day, yesterday. I felt dizzy from the motion of the litter, and we have halted here at Nola, still eighteen miles short of Naples. It's an old family villa. Indeed my father died here, perhaps in this very room. I must send for someone to find out...

They brought me news: my cat died yesterday. Herodotus says the Ancient Egyptians went into mourning when their cats died: only good thing I ever heard of them.

That museum I established at Capri, with the giants' bones, how strange...

I have arranged that little Moragh should marry my freedman Pithias. That should secure her future. He's very sharp.

So many memories, so many regrets ... it was not my fault that Cicero was killed, I take responsibility but not blame ... responsibility ...

'νὺξ δ' ἤδη τελέθει ἀγαθὸν και νυκτὶ πιθέσθαι' ('The night is at hand and it is good to yield to the night'—Homer, *Iliad* vii, 282)

I dreamed last night that forty young men were carrying me off, and woke with a start of terror. Silly; I suppose they were the Praetorians and I caught a glimpse of my funeral rites ...

It is fifty-seven years ago, to this day, that I entered on my first consulship ... I shall see Gaius and Lucius in the Shades, Marcellus smiling to me, Agrippa and Maecenas, Virgil and Horace ... and ... I don't wish to talk with Julius ... Antony will be there ... August, my month, ripe with harvest ... I always wanted an easy death ... they tell me my granddaughter Livilla has been ill, but is recovering, Tiberius is hurrying back from Brindisi ... Livia, remember whose wife you have been ... remember. The horses by the olive groves and Marcus Agrippa forcing me to eat bread and cheese ... red-hot walnut shells are ... so few gaudy nights ... so much work ... Varus, give me ... they spat on the ground as they ... Comedy, comedy ... Livia.

★　★　★

338

These last words were taken down by attendant slaves and added to the manuscript by an unknown editor. Augustus died on 19 August at about three in the afternoon in the year when Sextus Pompey and Sextus Apuleius were consuls. He died in the same room in which his father had died. His body was brought by slow stages to Rome, travelling by night, owing to the hot weather. His funeral procession followed the triumphal route along the Sacred Way, and he was buried in the mausoleum he had himself built which already contained the bodies of his adopted sons, Gaius and Lucius. A few days later, Numerius Atticus, a senator of praetorian rank, saw the late princeps ascending to the heavens, and the Senate decreed that he had become a God.

Thirladean House,
Selkirk
October 1984–March 1986.